THE TALISMAN TRILOGY
BOOK ONE

The GYPSY THIEF

KELLIE BELLAMY TAYER

ISBN: 0615667740
ISBN-13: 9780615667744
Library of Congress Control Number: 2012944143
Vagabond Press
Shaker Heights, OH

Dedication

For Jessica Megan Davis Quittenton

ACKNOWLEDGEMENTS

Writing a book is a solitary endeavor, but a writer is truly never alone (not with all those voices in her head!). A special thanks to Jessica for being my first reader and to Kathryn for being my second reader (and both such great friends and awesome lunch companions). Thanks to David, my editor at FirstEditing, for helping shape The Gypsy Thief into the book I intended it to be. Thanks to CreateSpace for the stunning cover. It is truly gorgeous. Thank you to my oldest and dearest friends (and I mean that in terms of how long we've known each other, not how old you are!): Dana in Rhode Island (special thanks for living in paradise and for having a beautiful daughter named Michelle who was the physical inspiration for Laura as well as the provider of Laura's middle name); Melissa in Iowa (and your two beautiful daughters, Lindsey and Jessica); Fiona in Australia (and your beautiful daughters, Chantelle, Georgia and grand-daughter Annabelle (whom I've never met but hope to one day)); my local buddies, Gretchen (I borrowed your name and your husband's too!); Laura (I'd already named my main character Laura before you and I really knew each other, but it is a nice coincidence); my Zumba buddies (a writer needs an outlet for all that pent-up energy!). And, of course, thanks to my family: Kraig (I lucked out having you for an ex-husband!), my handsome sons, Jordan and Thomas, and my own beautiful daughter, Kayla, and a special shout out to her beautiful buddy, Ali, and my grandson Maximus. A special thank you to Marley for the massages (you are one weird dude, but you're cute so that makes up for the weirdness). And finally, thank you M, A and L for being such amazing companions and for being real, if only to me. P.S. Thank you to my readers (I can't forget you). I'd love to hear from you. Write me at kelliebtayer@aol.com.

The
GYPSY
THIEF

TABLE OF CONTENTS

PROLOGUE

LAURA

If you had the chance to go back into your life and change one thing, would you do it, even if it meant that every single thing that came after would be changed as a result? What if I had ignored that boy who'd told me I'd dropped something on the ground when I knew I hadn't? What if I'd picked up that gold disk and tossed it to the boy and then gone on my merry way? What if I'd given it away to a stranger? What if someone else had found the gold disk before I had? *What if?* They say life can turn on a dime, but my life turned on a gold disk about the size of a fifty-cent piece. I knew it wasn't mine, but I chose to keep it anyway and in so doing, I set the course of my life. If I could go back in time and choose not to keep that gold disk, would I? Knowing everything that came after? Knowing I could escape all the pain, suffering, tears and heartache that came as a result of keeping that gold disk? Knowing I would never taste the sweetness of a prince's kiss or feel the heat of a gypsy's passion? Even though it seemed to bring me more heartache than not, without it, I never would have known how far I was willing to go—how much I was willing to sacrifice—for love. But I know what my choice would be. Yes, I would have to say—I would keep the disk every time.

ANDREW

Early summer 2011, in a royal estate in
Buckinghamshire, England

To say I was shocked was a bit of an understatement. And I could tell that my mother wasn't expecting to hear this news either. My brother, Tristan, however, wasn't surprised at all. He wasn't happy about it, but he seemed to be expecting this announcement. We were in the family dining room of our estate in Buckinghamshire having what I thought was going to be a normal family dinner. My father, Prince Ernst, was seated at his usual place at the head of the table with my mother, Duchess Beatrice, to his left and my brother, Prince Tristan, to the right. I sat next to my mother. Father had just announced that we were moving to America.

"Now I know this is unexpected, but I think it will be a good thing for our family. An educational opportunity like this doesn't come along every day and I think it will be good for all of us to expand our cultural horizons. Andrew, you especially should enjoy this, considering your fascination with all things American. And, as for you, Tristan, there are horses in Portsmouth, Rhode Island, so you can play your beloved polo all you want. You should all be happy." My father's booming voice resonated around the room. I was quite sure Queen Elizabeth could hear him all the way over in London.

My mother didn't say much. She seemed resigned to my father's decision. Oh, well, it was only for a year—maybe less, so I guess she figured she could deal with the disruption in her life for that short a period of time.

The servants entered the room and removed the first course dishes and another round of servants brought in the second course. I was rather too excited to eat anymore now that I knew we were moving to America. I'd decided that as soon as dinner was finished, I would go to my chambers and Google Portsmouth, Rhode Island, U.S.A., and see what I could learn about my soon-to-be new home.

When the last course of coffee and biscuits had been cleared away, my father turned to Tristan and spoke in a serious tone. "Tristan, please join me in my study. I'd like to have a talk with you." He turned to me and hesitated—as if unsure of what he wanted to say. "Andrew...I'd like you to join us, also."

I shrugged and nodded.

My mother pushed her chair back in a rush and glared at my father. "Really, Ernst? Andrew, too? It isn't enough that Tristan has to be involved in this trav..."

"*Hush, Beatrice!*" my father yelled, cutting her off. "That is more than enough out of you. Please find something to do to occupy yourself elsewhere and do not disturb me and...my sons."

"They're my sons, too!" she cried. My mother looked at us with a mixture of pain and anger in her eyes and stormed out of the room. I was astounded. What the hell had just happened here? I was afraid to open my mouth, but Tristan wasn't.

"Do we have to do this today, Father?" He slid his chair back and made to get up but Father put his hand on Tristan's arm and stopped him.

"Do what?" I asked. "What's going on?" I felt a knot forming in the pit of my stomach. The roast duck and deviled quail eggs we'd just eaten suddenly weren't sitting well.

"Yes. Both of you take a few minutes and then meet me in my study at...," he looked at his watch. "Nine o'clock." And with that, he scooted back his chair and left the room abruptly.

Upon his departure from the dining room, the servants came in and began to clear away the remaining dishes. It was normal procedure for the servants to keep their eyes down and not make eye contact with us—not that I minded, but my father certainly didn't like it. But one of the servants, Sarah, who'd been working for my family since I was a baby, glanced at me and then at Tristan. It was the quickest of looks but her eyes were...frightened. And sad...resigned. It was as if she knew what my father was going to say to us. It didn't bode well.

In the main hall I asked Tristan what Father was going to talk to us about. At first he acted like he didn't know, but I could tell he just didn't want to get into it. Finally, he answered. "My dear brother... brace yourself. You're about to hear about our royal destiny or some such nonsense. I've talked to Father about this before—back on my seventeenth birthday. He didn't tell me everything, but I suppose we're going to hear it all tonight. See you at nine." With that, he retreated down the hall.

I looked at the grandfather clock standing silently in the great hall. With only fifteen minutes before the big talk, I ran to my room on the third floor and paced around, wondering if I should be worried or not. Then I figured, what's the point? What could be so bad? Royal destiny? Shouldn't that be a good thing? Something to look forward to? Or was it something to dread? I would soon find out.

At nine o'clock, I approached my father's study in the west wing of the house. The door was ajar and I could hear that Tristan was already in there with him. I could hear them talking quietly but Tristan's voice was a bit louder. It sounded like he was arguing with Father—something I never dared to do. I knocked lightly on the door and stepped into the room. Tristan moved back from Father's desk where he had been standing and took a seat by the window. He looked unhappy—angry even.

"Andrew, please have a seat," Father said, pointing to a chair near Tristan.

I felt like I was in the headmaster's office at school more than in my own father's presence. His formality annoyed me. I vowed to myself that one day when I became a father, my children would never fear me and they could always come to me freely…any time…always. I sat down in the chair and waited. And I hoped this would be quick and painless.

And then the ax fell.

"When I told you we were moving to America for…cultural reasons…or for diplomatic reasons if you will…I was not lying. But…I was also not telling you the whole truth. We are moving to Rhode Island for another very important reason that is crucial to our family's royal legacy. We are going there to right a wrong—a wrong that was committed hundreds of years ago." He stopped for a moment to gauge our demeanors.

I felt nauseous. I had a really bad feeling about this but I didn't dare say a word. I knew in time all would be revealed—whether I wanted to hear it or not. I glanced at Tristan, who looked annoyed and bored. He obviously knew where this story was going and he didn't look like he wanted to hear any more of it.

Father got up from his desk and walked over to a safe that had been standing in the corner of this room for as long as I could remember. Never once had I seen anyone open it to put anything in it or take anything out of it. I guess I had always assumed it was just for decoration. But now Father was spinning a dial back and forth on the door of the safe. He swung the door open and reached inside. Very carefully he lifted out an ancient, silver metal box. But if I thought the box looked old, it didn't compare to what he took out of it. He laid the box on his desk and removed a key from the top drawer. He opened it and removed three items: an ancient scroll, a more modern-looking document and some sort of golden talisman.

I looked at these items and again wondered what in the hell was going on. This seemed like madness. Like something out of a movie. And I had the feeling that my father was enjoying the theatrics of this—whatever it was.

He gently picked up the ancient scroll and laid it on the front of the desk where we could see it. It was very old and yellowed with age, the paper so thin you could see though it in places. It was frayed around the edges and one side even had old burn marks.

I wanted to ask what it was. I wanted to say something to break the ominous silence but I knew my father would not approve so I kept my mouth shut and waited. I sneaked a look at Tristan and I noticed that he was looking uncomfortable now. Like he knew what was coming. I suddenly felt afraid.

Father cleared his throat and began. "This ancient document is a decree that dates back to the early 1700s. It is an edict from our forefathers. This document has been in our family for more than three hundred years just waiting for this moment. How our descendants even knew that the world would still be standing is a wonder. But they had their reasons for choosing now—for choosing 2012. Reasons we may never know and probably don't need to know, though there is speculation. The only thing that matters is that the edict must be obeyed. And it falls on you." He looked directly into my brother's eyes as he said this. I could see that Tristan was not thrilled or even impressed—but I was. This was kind of exciting and I couldn't wait to hear the rest.

"But it's 2011," I pointed out. Father shushed me.

"I am aware of the date, son. But I couldn't spring this on you at the last minute. Preparations need to be made. Things don't happen overnight." He stopped talking for a moment to pour himself a brandy. Then he continued.

"Andrew, this is something that Tristan, as the oldest son, must do. But I am telling you as well, in case, God forbid, anything were to happen to Tristan—then it would fall on you. And now I'm going to tell you a story."

Tristan sighed. I could tell he did not want to hear this. I wondered just how much he already knew. I waited, barely breathing, with no idea where this was going. Father began the story.

"It has always been known in our family history, as direct descendants of King George the First, that King George had two children and three illegitimate children. You have learned this as you've grown and studied our family history. But there is something you didn't know—something that has been kept secret for some three hundred years. There was one other child born to King George. It has been rumored that he had many mistresses—we know this because he had bastard children—that is a documented fact. But there was one mistress that was never spoken of. I am going to tell you about her now as it has been decreed."

Father stopped talking for a moment and sipped from his glass of brandy. He set the glass back down and continued.

"Her name was Gabriela. She was young—just twenty when she first met the king. She was tall and olive-skinned with dark eyes and long black hair. And George fell deeply, madly, hopelessly in love with her. She lived on the outskirts of the kingdom in the gypsy village and George happened upon her one day, bathing in the river when he was out riding one of his many horses. Soon, a pattern developed. He would ride his horse alone every day to the river and watch Gabriela bathe. And he wanted her. In every way. Finally one day he approached her. She was frightened and grabbed for her dress to cover herself. The king spoke to her but she did not talk back. Finally it occurred to him that she could not understand him. He remembered that most of the gypsies were Portuguese and did not know English. Any other time it would have angered him that she could not speak English but acknowledging that his own grip on the language wasn't all that tight—German was his mother tongue, he was born in Hanover, Germany, as you know from your family history—he did not hold it against her. He was kind to her and he came to see her at the river nearly every day. He would bring her food and clothes and gifts of jewels. And finally one day, he got what he really wanted—*her* in every way."

Father paused to let us take this in. I fidgeted and stole another look at Tristan but he was unmoving and stoic. *What is it with him anyway?* I wondered. Father continued.

"As you can guess, she became pregnant. When she told George about the baby—and by this time they had found a way to communicate—he was happy at first. But he knew that his family would not be if they ever found out. It was one thing to have illegitimate children with other women—but *never* a gypsy. He knew there was no way she could keep this baby. A shame like no other would fall upon the House of Hanover if the baby's paternity was revealed. He told her that when the baby was born he would make sure it was taken care of and she would never have to worry about it. Of course, like most mothers, she was protective and begged the king to be allowed to keep her baby and raise him or her in the village among the other gypsy children. The fact that she was an unwed pregnant woman didn't seem to be a concern to her—it must have been a normal occurrence in the gypsy village. But King George would have no part of it. And he told her that if she ever told anyone he was the father, his justice would be swift. She was frightened into remaining silent."

"Finally on a cold December afternoon the baby was born. When Gabriela failed to meet him at the river he suspected that she must have given birth. And he had prepared for this day. He told one of his guardsmen to sneak into the village and find the baby and destroy it. And he was told to kill Gabriela, too, to guarantee her silence forever and keep his royal reputation intact. He felt badly about taking her life but concluded there was no other way."

Father picked up his glass and swished the dark liquid around in it, then cleared his throat. I stole another glance at Tristan. He sat still, his arms folded across his chest, his face expressionless. Father sipped from his glass and continued.

"The guardsman went to the gypsy village in disguise and found a way to enter Gabriela's small, makeshift tent of a home. She was sleeping with a small bundle tucked inside her arm. The guardsman placed his hand over her mouth and pressed down so she could not scream."

"'Give me the baby,' he demanded. Under his hand she shook her head back and forth in a silent 'no.' While still holding her down, he grabbed for the small bundle and snatched it from her arms. He gasped in surprise and for a moment his hand let up from her mouth. She started to scream but he instantly clamped his hand back down, stifling the sound. He held up the white bundle and shook it out but there was nothing in it—no baby. He saw the look of relief in her eyes. It made him angry. 'Where is the baby?' he asked her. He loosened his hand just enough for her to whisper, 'he's gone and you will never find him. A curse on you and the king!' She spat out the words in a harsh whisper—in perfect English. 'A curse from the royal House of Braganza on the House of Hanover. I put this curse on your king—a curse that will bring an end to the House of Hanover. May it last forever.'"

"But the guardsman was not daunted by her words. 'You silly gypsy female. You know that I am going to kill you now. You cannot put a curse on the royal family. *And you are not royal*!' He pressed harder on her mouth. She managed to push his hands away and spoke her last words before he broke her neck."

"'A curse on your king! Even if the world lasts forever—until…2012…this curse will follow you. May it come down upon your head with the first flowers of spring. My child is not *only* the son of a king, he is also the son of Princess Gabriela of the House of Braganza. You will never find him. I curse you!' And with that, he ended her life."

I gasped. Wow. This was quite a story. And up until the word 2012 came out of my father's mouth, it was just that to me—a really interesting story. But I had a feeling something was coming and I guessed I wasn't going to like it. Tristan shifted uncomfortably in his seat. I waited for more.

"The guardsman returned to the king and told him what Gabriela had said. The king was angry. He sent the guardsman away and told him to find out the true identity of Gabriela and report back to him. Eventually the truth was revealed. Gabriela was indeed a princess from the Portuguese royal family—the House of Braganza. She had run away from her home in Sintra, Portugal, to be with her lover, a soldier in the Portuguese Royal Army. But he was killed in combat. She was broken-hearted and couldn't or wouldn't go back to the palace so she joined a band of gypsies and never returned to her kingdom. She travelled with these gypsies throughout Europe and eventually settled in England and, well, you know the rest."

Father finished his brandy and poured himself another. I took this as a sign that there was a lot more to this story coming our way. I sensed the relevance was about to be revealed. I wasn't entirely sure I wanted to hear anymore but, in for a penny, in for a pound, as they say.

"When Gabriela issued her curse on King George, no one had any reason to know or understand why she said the year 2012. We think it was because she was 20 years old and it was December. That's the only thing that ever made sense. Perhaps the child was born on December 20—who knows? In any case, after thinking it over, the king, in his agitation, wrote out a decree. This decree stated how his wishes concerning the child were to be carried out."

I stole a look at the old scroll on the desk and had a feeling we were about to hear the decree, whether we wanted to or not. I thought Father would pick it up and read it to us and I fervently hoped that wouldn't be the case because it looked quite lengthy, not to mention fragile.

Father did not pick up the scroll. Instead he picked up the newer document and held it up.

"This document has been taken directly from the scrolls and updated into the English language that we know today. It has the meat of the matter in it, so to speak. And now, my sons, this is when we get serious about the decree and our part in it. Because the time is nearly upon us to settle the score—to carry out the vendetta that has been passed down for more than three hundred years. To put an end to the lineage born of George the First and Princess Gabriela."

I swallowed a lump in my throat and felt my stomach twist into a knot. Tristan sighed and leaned forward in his chair. He seemed to be thinking things through. Then his head snapped up and he yelled at Father. "No!" he hissed. "I won't do it. You can't make me."

"Son." A single, ominous word. "Tristan. Listen. Listen carefully." Father looked at Tristan and then at me. He looked…fierce and unmoving.

"The decree says that the oldest son of King George's lineage in the year of 2012 will carry out the vendetta. It has been written and signed into law by the king himself. And it has also been signed by the ten kings and queens who have succeeded him. It is a royal law and it must be obeyed. As the oldest son, it is your duty to carry out the order. It is your duty to put an end to the lineage of the House of Braganza."

"No!" Tristan yelled again. "I won't do it. I refuse to kill an innocent human being over some document that dates back to the damned Dark Ages. I won't! I am not a killer!" He jumped from his seat and was about to run out of the room but Father was up and blocking the door so fast I barely had time to register that he had even moved from his desk.

"Tristan, sit down! Now!" Father's voice boomed.

I half expected Tristan to tell Father where to stick it, but he surprised me and sat back down. But I couldn't hold my tongue. I had to know.

"Father! What is this talk of killing? What does Tristan mean? I can't believe you would allow your son to commit murder. What the hell is going on?" With each word I felt myself getting more and more worked up.

"Andrew, listen to me. You both must hear the decree. You need to hear the legacy. You need to know about the vendetta." He stopped a moment and walked back to lean against his desk, staying close to Tristan, perhaps to prevent him from trying to make a run for it again. I kind of wanted to make a run for it myself, but I felt compelled to see this nightmare through to the end.

Father continued. "King George was distraught at the knowledge that not only did he have a son out in the world that he would never see, but that he had not known that Gabriela was a member of a royal family in her own right. He was angry knowing what could have been. If he had known, he could have divorced his wife—or had her killed to make it easier—and married Gabriela, thereby joining two powerful European royal families. When he thought of the money and the land and titles that were lost, he was distraught. And he wanted that child gone. He wanted that child dead. And if the child could not be found before he grew up to have his own child, then he wanted *that* child killed. But he knew he didn't have the patience or the manpower to take care of this matter. There were other battles to be fought and domestic dramas to be dealt with. So he made it easy on himself. And he used the dying Gabriela's own words against her. He decreed that the eldest son of his successive generation of the House of Hanover in the year 2012 would carry out the vendetta—that the eldest son would end the life of the eldest son in the successive generation of the House of Braganza. That lineage must be stopped. The king's law must be carried out once and for all, so that this *matter* can be laid to rest. And now that time is upon us."

I was stunned—but also a little relieved. There was no way anyone could have tracked down this person—this royal son in the House of Braganza. I was sure this was all a big misunderstanding that we could put back in that damned vault and throw away the key and call it a day. I looked at my father and expected to see him smile and say, 'ha ha, gotcha.' But that didn't happen. I could tell by looking at him that he was deadly serious and he was really going to make Tristan take a human life. And I got the feeling that Father knew who that life belonged to. I had to do something. I had to put a stop to this madness.

"Wait! Father, you can't be serious. This is wrong. We aren't Barbarians. We don't kill people. How can you do this? What would Queen Elizabeth say?" I hoped the mention of his queen would have an impact.

"Andrew, every king and queen since George the First has signed off on the decree—even Queen Elizabeth. She signed her name to this document years ago." He held up a page from the document and waved it in the air. "This is the latest decree. With each successive monarch, a signature has been added. Some of these documents are so old that we had to copy them on to sturdier paper—but the originals are all here in these pages. And all of the monarchs' signatures are here—eleven of them in all."

"Wait!" Tristan finally spoke. "If the damned queen is OK with this travesty, why doesn't *her* firstborn son do it? Why not bloody Prince Charles?"

Father slammed his fist down hard on the desk, causing brandy to splash all over the polished surface. "Prince Charles is not a direct descendant of the House of Hanover. You know that, son. Yes, we're all related one way or another but he is from a different branch of the family tree. This falls on us."

"Falls on me, you mean," said Tristan, almost resignedly. Was he agreeing to this? There was no way he would do this. Not Tristan. My brother was a lot of things—but he was not a murderer.

"Father! Tristan would go to jail—forever…if he got caught. You would never forgive yourself if that happened." I knew my father would listen to reason. We just had to wear him down. It was the twenty-first century, for crying out loud. Things like this just didn't happen anymore. I wouldn't let it.

"Son, it has been decreed and so it shall be. We are moving to Portsmouth, Rhode Island, and the vendetta will be carried out. Tristan will not be caught. In any case, we will have diplomatic immunity. If he were to get caught—*and he won't*—the worst that could happen is he would get deported."

"But why Rhode Island? And why do you call it a vendetta? That makes it sound like someone wants revenge on us, too." I was getting confused and tired of this crap. And why was Tristan suddenly not putting up a fight?

"The members of the House of Braganza are not stupid. They are most certainly aware of the decree. There are no secrets in royal circles. They know and they will be expecting us. But this won't be a battle between armies. It will be between Tristan and the Prince of Braganza. And Tristan will win. And why Rhode Island? Because the prince and his family are moving there very soon. Relocating to the United States affords us the diplomatic immunity that I spoke of before. We will move to Portsmouth under the guise of fostering relations between our sister cities and enjoying a cultural exchange, something I had planned to do eventually anyway. It will be the perfect cover. We will settle into the community and they will accept us. And not only will Tristan emerge the victor in this 'showdown,' he will also be a hero—a true hero. Now, Andrew, you may go...Tristan and I need to talk alone."

And with that I was dismissed. I looked at my brother but he would not meet my gaze. I walked out of the room without saying a word. I was angry and shocked. Did my mother know about this? I went in search of her. She would never allow this to happen. But when I found her in her salon she wouldn't talk about it, except to say that the queen had spoken and so had Father and the decree must be honored. I was flabbergasted. My sweet and loving mother was in on this? She was just giving up and willing to let her son fight—possibly to the death? Now I totally understood what history meant about the 'madness of King George'—so what if it was a different King George. This was madness of the highest caliber.

I ran to my room and slammed the door. This could not—would not—happen. I loved my parents and I loved my queen, but this was wrong. There had to be something I could do. I paced around in my room for what seemed like hours in a state of extreme agitation. I knew I would never be able to get to sleep tonight. So I sat and stared at the walls.

Sometime well after midnight, there was a knock on my door. Tristan opened it and stepped inside. He looked gray and worn out. He walked over to the big bay window and sat down wearily on the edge of the window seat.

"Tristan, tell me you're not going to do this," I whispered. "We can work this out some other way. I've been thinking about this and I have an idea. It could work." I had to make Tristan understand that there was an alternative to violence and murder. Because I knew he didn't want to be branded a murderer for the rest of his life—if he even survived this madness. I was quite certain that his 'victim' would not go down without a fight.

"I have to, Andrew. Father made me see reason. But don't worry, it will be alright. And it will be fair. I will challenge him to a duel or something. I'm not afraid."

"Well, I sure as hell am!" I nearly yelled the words. "This isn't right and you know it." I paced around my room in frustration. "Tristan— listen to me. We could fake this, you know. We could find this…person…and warn him. We could give him a chance to escape or…if it came down to it, we could help him fake his own death. We could make it look real."

Tristan sighed. "But Father made me see that this isn't wrong either—well, it isn't illegal, according to the decree. Besides, is this Portuguese son willing to lose a hand to prove he's dead? Because that's what it would take."

"What!?! What are you talking about—lose a hand? What bollocks are you uttering now?" I couldn't take any more of this. It was beyond absurd.

"Father says the decree states that the reigning sovereign must be shown proof that the deed has been done. We have to give the queen the left hand of the prince—*ooh, how I hate to call him a prince*—of the House of Braganza. How would we ever fake that?" He sighed wearily.

"No…no…no," I whispered. "No, Tristan. I will go to the authorities. I will stop this from happening. I won't allow it." I was pacing around the room now, wearing a path in the ancient carpet.

"No, Andrew! You will not interfere. Don't think for one minute that Father doesn't have a contingency plan. You will be punished harshly if you interfere. Trust me. And don't think I didn't ask that if this deed absolutely has to be done, then why couldn't someone else do it. Because I tried everything to talk Father out of this. He read me parts of the decree. It is very clear. The first-born son of the current House of Braganza must be killed by the first-born son of the current House of Hanover. It has to be me and no one else or a curse will fall on our family that could destroy us—that would end our pure lineage. I won't be the cause of that. And I won't let our family down. I will do this. And when it's over, I'm leaving. I don't know where I'll go, but I'm leaving for good."

I sank down onto the edge of my bed and buried my face in my hands. This was impossible. A chill ran through me as I thought about what my father could and would do to me if I interfered with the plan. Was it worth it? I would have to think long and hard about this. I could always make myself disappear, too, if it came down to it. But I doubted that there was any place in the world I could hide that my Father would not find me with all of the money and resources he had at his disposal.

"Andrew…just stay calm and try not to worry. Maybe we'll meet this guy and end up hating him. Then it will be easier." Tristan tried to force a smile. He pulled something out of his pocket and handed it to me. "Father gave me this thing for good luck, but I don't want it. I don't deserve good luck. I'm disgusted enough with this nonsense that I don't want another burden to hold." He thrust a gold disk at me. I turned it over and over in my hand. It was a talisman of apparently great value—the one Father had taken out of the safe earlier.

"What is this thing?" I asked him.

"It was in that damned vault with the papers. It may have been a gift that King George had given to that Portuguese princess and when the guard killed her, he ripped it from her neck and returned it to the king. It's been kept with the scroll all these years. Father says it doesn't look like anything King George would have had—maybe it was from her family—I guess no one really knows for sure. Father thought I might like to have it for luck but to me it's nothing but bad news. So you keep it and do with it what you will. I don't give a damn." And with that, he stalked out of my room and left me alone with the talisman. It was beautiful but ominous. I studied it carefully under my bedside lamp, taking note of the crossed swords on one side and some sort of coat of arms and a strange configuration of numbers on the other. I had no idea what it meant but decided that in the morning I would study it more closely and try to figure out the significance of the numbers. I slipped it into my pocket, also determined that I would give it a good home one day, for I didn't feel it was really mine to keep. And then I laid down on my bed and did not sleep.

We spent the next several weeks preparing for our move to Rhode Island in America. I was excited beyond belief in spite of the horrible reason we were really going there. Because I had nearly convinced myself that Tristan and I would be able to reason with Father and talk him out of this nightmare. Even though Father had a reputation for being a bully and a taskmaster, I still felt that even he had a conscience and wouldn't stoop so low as to allow his own son to commit a heinous crime in the name of a family legacy. So I allowed myself to feel some degree of excitement about our upcoming sojourn in America. And the numbers on the talisman continued to bother me, so I let them ruminate in my subconscious in the hope that something would trigger an answer.

My mother insisted that we were to attend regular, non-exclusive schools albeit against my father's wishes. But because of the real reason we were going there in the first place, Father apparently decided that letting her have her way in this one instance might be for the best. But he insisted that a security detail would accompany us everywhere we went and on this he would not bend. So to educate myself on what to expect, I spent my days on the Internet researching America and New England and Rhode Island and the town that was to be my new home–Portsmouth.

A week or so before departing for America, I decided to go online and check out my new school—Portsmouth High School. On the home page, I saw a link to an online yearbook. I clicked on it and it took me to a selection of graduation dates. I chose 2012, the year of my graduation, and proceeded to peruse the photos and short bios of the class of 2012. It seemed to be a fairly large school—it would take an awfully long time to look at all of my fellow classmates so I decided to use the filter I'd noticed at the top of the screen. It allowed me to filter out the boys and look only at the girls. Now this was more like it. I already knew that Father would never approve of my having an American girl-friend, but I didn't let that stop me from looking at the prospects. I knew I would need a diversion if I were to get through the nightmare that awaited us there in Portsmouth.

I scanned the faces of the girls and read some of their bios. It looked like Portsmouth was swimming in a sea of pretty girls. I stopped on one that captivated me. She had long blonde hair, blue eyes, full pink lips and an angelic face. Her bio stated that she loved classical music and books and hoped to have a career in publishing one day so that she could have some small say in what people would be reading in the future. I liked that. It stated that she was active in field hockey and track and it gave her birth date as December 12, 1993. I was exactly one month older than she was. So that made her a Sagittarius. Interesting. And then suddenly her date of birth screamed at me: December 12, 1993. 12121993! I yanked the talisman from my pocket and studied it in amazement. What a coincidence. It was almost a number-for-num-ber match. Of course there was another row of numbers underneath that didn't seem to mean anything. This seemed so strange. There couldn't possibly be a correlation—the world didn't work that way. Ha. And then I remembered the decree. Maybe it did. I looked at the name beneath the photo of the girl with the angel's face. Her name was Laura Calder and I decided that she would become my friend.

MIGUEL

Late spring 2011, in a country house in Sintra, Portugal

My father, Alfonso Dos Santos de Braganza, was a man of great honor. He was a man of intense passion as well, and he believed strongly in family legacy. As his firstborn son, I knew that it would fall on me to carry out that legacy as it had been handed down to him and my mother. My mother was descended from royalty—from the House of Braganza and upon their marriage, my father had taken my mother's royal name. My father was also a blue-blood, having descended from a lesser royal family, the House of Dos Santos, but because my mother's house was considered greater, he took her name, thereby joining houses and forming a new branch of the family tree. Upon his death-bed one month ago, he told me the story of my ancestor, Princess Gabriela. And today I would be telling it to my younger brothers. Part of me didn't want them to know. It was bad enough that my mother knew and was refusing to be involved. She was so frail and so deep in mourning over my father's death that it didn't seem fair to further burden her with details of the upcoming disruption in our lives. So I left her in the care of my sister, Catarina. They would remain in our home in Sintra and I and my brothers would go to America to fulfill the legacy. But in order to make it look like we were a normal family we needed a parental figure. So I asked my mother's younger brother, Antonio, to accompany us to Portsmouth, Rhode Island, as our guardian. Uncle Antonio, a skilled boat builder, had received a commission from a wealthy man in Newport who wanted a special sailboat built for a race he wished to enter. I didn't particularly care about the details of this arrangement but the timing was perfect. My brothers and I could settle into our new lives among the residents of Portsmouth, Rhode Island, and with luck, settle the vendetta against us peacefully.

I had not wanted my brothers to be a part of this. But my father had made me promise that I would take them with me to America to support me in my endeavor—to have my back, as he'd said. And now I was waiting for them to return from a soccer match in Lisbon so I could break the news that we were going to America. Uncle Antonio had already left for Rhode Island to find us a house and cars. We would be joining him there in less than a month's time.

I heard Mateo and Tomas arriving. They were noisy and excited and on a victory high—Lisbon had crushed Barcelona 3-0. I had been watching the match on TV so I already knew the results. Lisbon's triumph almost made it harder for me, considering what I was about to do—I hated to crush their buzz, but it had to be done.

I walked out of the kitchen into the front hall to greet them. We spoke about the game for a few minutes and then they both started up the stairs.

"Mateo! Tomas!" I stopped them. "When you've had a moment to catch your breath and come down from your victory highs, please join me in the study for a chat—say…about twenty minutes, OK?"

They both shrugged, nodded, and continued up the stairs. I smiled to myself as I went back into the kitchen to make myself some food. I would need the energy to get through the next hours. I loved my brothers—they were so innocent and they were good boys—even though they scared people. They were both so tall and big, not unlike me, that I understood people's first impressions. But once someone got to know them, they realized what a couple of pussycats Mateo and Tomas were—especially Tomas. I grabbed a Coke from the refrigerator and went into the study to wait.

I waited at my father's desk for my brothers to join me. I opened a drawer and removed the ancient document, now so old that it was encased in a plastic sheath for protection. I read it again for what seemed like the millionth time. It was so strange to find myself in this position—at the age of seventeen I was now the head of my father's household. I would not be eighteen until October 12, the age considered to be an adult in America—the same as Portugal.

I heard my brothers coming down the stairs so I drained the last of my Coke and prepared myself.

"What's up?" asked Mateo coming in first, Tomas trailing along behind him. They were fraternal twins but, ironically, they looked exactly alike—very few people could tell them apart—sometimes they even fooled me. They were sixteen and athletic. My father had been very proud of them, and they were the apples of our mother's eye. That is not to diminish my parents' love for me. They adored me as well and also my sister. Actually, Catarina was not really my sister. She was my first cousin—the daughter my parents never had. Her parents—my mother's youngest brother and sister-in-law—were killed in a private plane crash when Catarina was little. She was the only survivor of the crash that killed twelve passengers. And now she was twenty-four and a recent graduate of a university in England. For the next few months she would be tending to my mother while my brothers and I were away. She had no idea why we were really going to America and as long as my mother kept the secret to herself, Catarina would remain in the dark.

Mateo and Tomas sat down on the sofa across from my father's desk. Their smiles faded when they saw the serious expression on my face. "Hey, guys. We need to talk."

"This doesn't sound good," Mateo frowned. "Is something wrong?"

Tomas gave a nervous laugh. "Seriously, Miguel. I don't think I can take any bad news right now." He crossed his arms over his chest and leaned back on the sofa.

I swallowed visibly and let out a deep breath. "I called you in here to tell you something. I don't want you to panic or freak out and get angry." Mateo started to speak but I cut him off with a wave of my hand. "Please, Mateo, let me finish." He sighed and remained silent.

"Per our father's wishes, we are going to move to America for a few months to carry out a...," I hesitated over the right word, "...mission. This is something that comes from our family's history—a sort of legacy that must be fulfilled. Did Papa ever talk to either of you about our ancestor, Princess Gabriela?"

"I've heard stories but I don't remember much," said Tomas.

"Same for me," Mateo said. "No offense to Papa but I never really cared about the past."

I sighed. "Well, I'm going to tell you about her now because she is at the root of the legacy that we have been ordained to fulfill."

"Is this going to be bad?" whispered Mateo. His complexion paled.

I forced a smile. "I will let you be the judge of that." I cleared my throat and began.

"Princess Gabriela lived during the time of the reign of England's King George the First. Remember that because it will be significant to the story. Gabriela was the daughter of the king of Portugal—our many times removed great grandfather. When she was eighteen she fell in love with a member of the royal guard, Pedro Silva. But, as he was not a blue blood, their romance was forbidden. Her father threatened him with death if he did not stay away from Gabriela. But their love was too great for them to be separated so they decided to run away together. They were planning to pass themselves off as gypsies and move elsewhere in Europe. Just before they were to run away, the king ordered the soldiers to the palace. A group of insurgents was rumored to be coming to attack and everyone had to be ready. Pedro decided to do this one last mission while Gabriela settled herself into the gypsy camp northeast of Lisbon. She took two people into her confidence regarding her true identity—a young married couple, Jose and Marta Coelho, who welcomed her into their gypsy family. She waited and waited for Pedro to join her but he never came. Sick with worry, she asked Jose to try to find out what was taking so long for Pedro to return to her." I stopped here to make sure the boys were still with me. They nodded and I continued.

"Jose found out that Pedro had been killed in the battle. Needless to say Gabriela was distraught. And she feared that her father would try to find her. She hated her father and wanted to get as far away from Portugal as possible. The gypsies were vagabonds anyway, so when Jose suggested that perhaps it was time to move on, none of the others questioned it. They decamped and left the country. For the next two years they moved from place to place, eventually ending up in England. This is where George the First comes into play."

"King George met Gabriela by a river and over a short period of time he fell in love with her. Their relationship resulted in a pregnancy." I saw Tomas wince at this and I had to suppress a chuckle.

"Naturally, news of this sort would derail a monarchy and he wanted it kept a secret. Gabriela kept the secret for most of her pregnancy but as the birth neared she became fearful for her unborn child. She worried that if she died in childbirth someone from the palace would take the baby and she couldn't bear the thought of not knowing if he or she would be safe. She wanted him or her to be raised by Jose and Marta if anything were to happen to her. And something did happen to her."

I stopped a moment to catch my breath and again make sure my brothers were still with me. I was impressed with their rapt attention and the fact that they were not interrupting me. I just needed to get these words out so we could move on.

"In fact, Gabriela did die. But not in childbirth. She was brutally killed by a soldier from the king's army. A couple of days after the birth of her son, Felipe, the king, worried about his reputation, sent the soldier to kill her and kidnap the baby. He grabbed the bundle of blankets from her arms and was shocked to find the blankets empty. When she refused to tell him where the baby boy was, he snapped her neck. But before she died she uttered a curse on the House of Hanover—a curse that had been known only by the reigning British monarchs and some of their descendants over the years. But we learned of it, too. By way of a letter that Gabriela had the presence of mind to leave with Jose and Marta."

I picked up the ancient paper in its plastic sleeve and looked down at it. "I will read it to you both now:"

The Last Will and Testament of Her Royal Highness, Princess Gabriela, House of Braganza, Sintra, Portugal:

In the event of my premature demise, I bequeath my few possessions to Jose and Marta Coelho. I grant them parental rights over my son, Felipe. Please raise him as you would your own—raise him to be a man of honor. I know you will love him almost as much as I do. If my death is a result of the king's hand or the hand of someone who works for the king, take Felipe and run. Do not let King George ever near my precious son for I am certain he would have him killed.

If the talisman I wear everyday is still around my neck at the time of my death, please take it with you and give it to Felipe when he becomes a man. If the talisman is not around my neck at the time of my death, know that it is in the possession of the king. Do not try to steal it back. It is not worth risking your lives for. It will work its own special black magic over the king in its proper time. For in the right hands, the talisman is a symbol of love and legacy. But in the wrong hands, it is a symbol of hatred and death. She who wears the golden talisman is the future of the House of Braganza. Protect her as I have not been protected and right the wrong I set in motion when I left my kingdom—when I chose true love over my royal legacy.

I fear that someday the king or future kings will try to destroy my family. It could be soon or in hundreds of years. If you are able, and feel it is safe, when Felipe reaches adulthood, take him to the reigning king of Portugal with my last will and testament as proof that I have lived and died. Help him regain the birthright that I forfeited when I ran away with Pedro—an act for which I have no regret. And tell the king that if I were able, prior to my death, I will have placed a gypsy curse on King George and his descendants, a curse that will bring an end to the House of Hanover, to be fulfilled in 2012, when the earth gives birth to the first flowers of spring, should this insane world still stand at that time.

This is my last will and testament signed in my own hand on this date: 20 December, 1700.

I laid the document on the table and looked into my brothers eyes, fairly certain I knew what they were going to say.

"Well, that was a really fun story, Miguel. Thanks for that," grinned Mateo. "Of course, I didn't hear a single thing in it that explains why we have to up and move to America."

"Seriously," agreed Tomas. "And I didn't hear anything in the story that sounds like a legacy needing to be fulfilled…so why all the drama?"

I reached into the drawer and pulled out another document and a small velvet box. They looked with great interest at these things and I could tell they were intrigued.

"This document is one that came many years later. One of the British monarchs decided that the Portuguese royal family needed to know about a certain vendetta that King George had placed on the House of Braganza. Father believed it may have been George the Fifth though I'm not sure why George the Fifth would have cared. But I'm glad *someone* cared enough to reveal the knowledge of this vendetta against our family. It may be that King George the First's vendetta was made to counteract the gypsy curse Gabriela had placed over his head. In any case, here's the situation: There is a contract on my head."

My brothers gasped in shock. Tomas jumped up from the sofa and began to pace. Mateo appeared to be in shock.

"What do you mean a *contract*? Who would want to kill you? This makes no sense!" cried Tomas, his voice rising in anger.

Mateo looked up then and asked, "And why America?"

I looked into my brothers' eyes. Tomas was livid and Mateo looked frightened.

"Do you remember a few months ago, before Papa became ill, he took a trip to Paris?" I asked them. They both nodded. I continued.

"While he was in Paris, he had a meeting with Prince Ernst of Hanover who is also known as the Duke of Easton. They chose Paris for the meeting place as a neutral middle-ground. Father had known about the vendetta and with 2012 fast approaching, he felt like he couldn't assume that this story was all a bunch of legends and folklore. He couldn't take a chance with my life. So he met with the duke to discuss the possibility of ignoring the silliness of something that had happened hundreds of years ago. He argued the point that we were all civilized people and there was no need for blood to be shed over a silly gypsy curse. He was certain Prince Ernst would listen to reason and agree with him. After all, there was danger ahead for his own son, too, and he surely would not risk his own child's life."

"Why do I have the feeling that this duke or prince or whatever the hell he calls himself didn't see it that way?" Tomas spat out the words in a huff.

"You're right. Not only did the duke refuse to call off the vendetta, he was downright bloodthirsty, according to Papa. Papa couldn't believe the hatred coming from this man. They argued and eventually came to a mutual conclusion. Papa did not want me watching over my shoulder for the rest of my life wondering when the ax was going to fall. I wouldn't have been safe anywhere. And neither of them wanted bloodshed in their own countries. So they agreed on Rhode Island in America. Apparently the duke had been considering going there on some sort of cultural mission and Papa and Uncle Antonio had potential boat-building clients in the same area so it made sense to go there. Of course, the British royal family has a distinct advantage in America—diplomatic immunity. They can't be arrested for crimes committed—only deported. We have no such immunity as our royal house is not a seated one. We are inactive and, technically, Portugal no longer recognizes our status in the world—which, by the way, is fine by me."

"So what do you plan to do?" asked Tomas, a hint of suspicion in his voice.

I walked over to the window and looked out at the night sky. "I plan to honor Papa's dying wish or avenge his death, whichever comes first." I turned back and saw the fright on my brothers' faces.

"Avenge Papa's death? And what dying wish?" Mateo asked.

"Papa was a healthy man. He should never have had a heart attack. I'm convinced that the stress he felt about my safety and the duke's unwillingness to cancel the vendetta caused his heart attack. I cannot let that go unpunished. As for Papa's dying wish, he asked that I find a way to convince the duke's son not to carry out the plan to kill me. At the very least I want to ask for a fair fight."

"How do you plan to get revenge for Papa?" asked Tomas.

"I hope I don't have to. But if Tristan—that is the name of the one who has been tasked with killing me—intends to honor his father's barbaric wish, then I will have no choice but to…" But I couldn't say the words—words that would make me sound no better than the monster that was Prince Ernst of Hanover.

"*What*?!" they cried together.

I hesitated. I did not want to disappoint my brothers. They had always looked up to me and if I saw disgust in their eyes it would cut like a knife through my heart.

"If I have to…I will kill the Duke of Easton."

Mateo walked over to me and grabbed my shoulders. "Miguel, whatever you choose to do, I will stand with you. And I will protect you. There's no way we will let this Tristan hurt you."

Tomas also came to me. He pulled me into a hug and whispered, "I second that."

Mateo stepped back, a look of fear crossing his face. "But Miguel, they have the element of surprise on their side. You will never know when this Tristan is going to come at you or how he will do it."

I walked over to the desk and sat down, picking up the small velvet box that lay there. "According to Princess Gabriela's curse, the vendetta is to end when the earth gives birth to the first flowers of spring—in the year 2012. That gives me time to get to know the duke's son. If I can befriend him and get him to agree that this is wrong in so *many* ways, maybe this whole thing can be labeled a misunderstanding and we can all go back to our lives and try to forget it ever happened.

As for how he would do it…I think I know." I turned the velvet box over and lifted the clasp to open it. I reached in with two fingers and lifted out the item inside.

"Wow!" said Tomas. "What's with this?"

In the palm of my hand, I laid an ancient ring: a silver band with a blue sapphire at its center. On one side of the ring was a tiny crest with a flag on each side. On the other side was an engraving of a pair of crossed swords. Inside the ring was an inscription written in an ancient language which I translated into our language:

Royal Birth—Gypsy Death—In Darkness, Light.

"What does this mean?" Tomas asked. He leaned in for a closer look. "Is it going to be a sword?"

"I'm guessing so. But there are two swords on this ring so, to me, that indicates a chance for a fair fight."

"Where did this ring come from?" asked Mateo.

"We believe this ring was meant for Princess Gabriela. We think it goes with a necklace that has been missing from our family since her death. She mentioned the necklace in her will, you remember. The soldier who killed her must have taken the necklace from her after killing her and possibly he gave it to the king. It is assumed that the necklace has been passing through the hands of the many generations of British royalty. I wouldn't be surprised if the Duke of Easton or his son Tristan has it now." I turned the ring over and over in my hand, watching the sapphire sparkle in the light of the lamp on the desk.

"But where did this ring come from?" asked Mateo. "How did we get it?"

"This ring was found in the pocket of Pedro Silva—the soldier Gabriela loved. No one knows how it came to be in his possession— if he bought it, stole it or found it. But when it was found, it was given to Gabriela's father, the king. He put it away for safekeeping. Many years later when Felipe was grown, he returned to the family and was given this ring. He wanted it kept with the original copy of his mother's last will and testament and to remain there until the year 2012 at which time it was to be given to the eldest child in the line of succession to the Portuguese throne—you know—the one that is inactive now thanks to Portuguese Parliament. And that child is… me."

"But it isn't 2012," Mateo pointed out.

"True, but Papa gave it to me early when he knew he was dying." I remembered with great sadness the evening of my father's death. He had lasted less than two weeks from the day of his heart attack. He had had so much to tell me in that short time.

I then lifted out the velvet cloth into which the ring had been nestled and pulled out a small piece of paper. I unfolded it and looked at my brothers' faces.

"What does it say?" breathed Tomas.

I read it slowly: "*She who wears the sapphire ring is the future of the House of Braganza.*"

Mateo gasped. "What does that mean? Who is *she*?"

"I have no idea." I folded the note and placed it back in the velvet box with the ring and slipped it into my shirt pocket.

"Miguel," Mateo said quietly. "Are you afraid?"

"No," I said without hesitation. "I am confident that this situation will come to a peaceful resolution."

"Good," he said. "That makes me feel better." Tomas agreed.

I spent the next half hour explaining to my brothers that their safety was of the utmost importance to me and I would not let anything happen to them. I explained about Rhode Island—the place chosen by the duke—and Uncle Antonio's involvement. I told them everything they needed to know and they both promised me their unwavering support as I knew they would. Finally we finished talking and the boys left me alone in the study.

I removed the ring from my shirt pocket and again turned it over and over under the light. I watched it flash and sparkle and I wondered, *where is the golden talisman...and who's wearing it now*? I knew my father wanted me to find it and return it to my family so that one day it would be worn by the one who was destined to carry on our family name—the woman who would one day become my wife. And I also acknowledged to myself that, yes, I was a little bit afraid.

C h a p t e r   O n e

PSYCHIC

LAURA

August 2011, Portsmouth, Rhode Island

As soon as Lily and Gretchen saw the sign, I knew they would drag me into their nonsense. Lily didn't let a day go by without reading me my horoscope and Gretchen, who I would've thought was too smart for psychic crap, was even beginning to believe the stuff. Just because her horoscope had once said she would meet the love of her life and the next day she'd met Colin Cowan, the apparent love of her life, she'd become a believer of astrology and palmistry and, well, psychic nonsense. I sighed audibly and stopped dead still in my tracks.

"Don't tell me...let me guess. We're about to pay Madame Jeanette a visit," I said, reading the name on the sign. "I bet she already knows we're coming, too." I cast a smirk at Gretchen as Lily grabbed my hand excitedly.

"Aw, come on, Laura. You know you want to. You know you're curious about what Madame Jeanette has to say. Look what happened with Gretchen and her horoscope. I'm telling you…I believe in this stuff and you should, too." Lily pulled me toward the psychic booth, her long, dark pony tail bobbing up and down around her shoulders.

We were at the end-of-summer carnival in Watch Hill, Rhode Island. We came here every August the weekend before school started to enjoy the last days of summer and eat sweet potato ice cream at North's Creamery. They had olive oil ice cream and sweet corn ice cream and garlic ice cream and just about any weird flavor you could imagine along with the traditional chocolate and vanilla. I loved the sweet potato best—with crunchy toasted pecans swirled inside and cinnamon dusted across the top. I wanted my ice cream, but I supposed it could wait until after we'd paid a visit to Madame Jeanette. Reluctantly, I let them drag me along the street, past food vendors and the flying-horse carousel and a very scary-looking clown making weird animal shapes out of balloons for googley-eyed kids.

The psychic booth was new this year. I certainly didn't remember ever seeing it before. It resembled a little A-frame hut with a red curtain for a door. A man sat at a card table just outside the curtained door. He had white hair though he didn't look that old. I could see that he held a metal box on his lap under the table. He smiled at Lily and said hello. He pointed to a sign on a stand in big red letters with Madame Jeanette's name at the top and a listing of her 'services' below:

Psychic Reading: $12
Palm Reading: $15
Tarot Card Reading: $20
Crystal Ball Reading: $25
Chakra Cleanse: $35
Aura Cleanse: $38
Bad Energy Removal: $40
Pick any two and save $5

"Ladies," the man said. "How can Madame Jeanette serve you today?" He looked first at Lily, then Gretchen, and finally at me. He smiled sweetly enough at them but his smile seemed to freeze when his eyes met mine. I stared at him a moment but then looked away quickly. I glanced back longingly toward the Creamery and wished I were eating sweet potato ice cream or maybe riding on one of those flying horses. When I looked back at him, he was still staring intently. I shivered in spite of the summer heat and turned to the 'menu.'

"So many choices!" Lily shrieked in excitement. She looked at me and Gretchen with anticipation in her eyes. "Oh, this is gonna be great," she said. "What do you guys think? The crystal ball reading sounds cool." She studied the board like she was about to order off a McDonald's menu. I half-expected her to order a number four, super-sized—to go.

Gretchen pointed at the board and said, "I'll go for the palm reading." She dug around in her purse for her wallet and pulled out fifteen dollars. "I already know what my future holds so I may as well go first," she grinned. She sounded like she was getting into this as much as Lily. She handed her money to the white-haired man and he put the cash into the metal box. He reached over and pulled back the edge of the red curtain and said, "You may enter."

Lily started to follow her into the hut but the man put his arm out and blocked her entry. "Madame Jeanette doesn't work at her best when she has an audience. You will have to wait outside." He looked at Lily and indicated the chairs at the table where he sat.

"Hmph," breathed Lily in exasperation. "I've been to these before and they never minded someone coming in to listen. What's the big deal?" She pulled out one of the metal chairs and plopped herself into it with a huff.

"She doesn't want any witnesses to hear the mound of bull-crap that's about to pour forth in there," I said, a little surly. The man's frozen smile in my direction earlier had me a little miffed. What? Didn't he like blondes?

"I can assure you Madame Jeanette does not speak bull-crap as you call it. You, of all people, will see for yourself soon enough." He gave me a look of hostility that was totally undeserved, considering he'd never seen me before in his life. And *me*? *Of all people*? What the hell was that supposed to mean?

I walked a few steps away and turned my back on the man. I looked toward the ocean, where dozens of white sails were billowing in the breeze. I wondered if my dad was out there somewhere. *Nah, probably not*, I thought. He would've stayed closer to Aquidneck Island, closer to where we lived. I looked at my watch and wondered how long these 'sessions' were supposed to last. I was getting bored and anxious to get home and we still had a long drive back to Portsmouth.

Lily interrupted my thoughts. "Which one are you getting, Laura? I'm splurging for the crystal ball reading and the bad energy removal."

I stared at the board again. "I'm not sure if I'm gonna get a reading. Can't really see the point. It's not like Madame Jeanette really knows anything about me, you know."

"*What?*" Lily freaked. "You *have* to get a reading. I mean, it's not every day we meet a real psychic, you know. Don't you want to know what the future holds?" She was quite adamant in her little rant.

I shrugged. "I mean…I guess it wouldn't kill me. I'll get a psychic reading then, if it'll make you happy. But, seriously, Lily, a *real psychic*? Isn't that an oxymoron?"

She was just about to respond when Gretchen walked out of the hut looking all dreamy-eyed and wistful. *Oh, man*, I thought. *I bet Madame Jeanette just told her she was going to marry Colin and have lots of babies and live in a mansion on Bellevue Avenue in Newport.*

"Wow!" she gushed as she walked over to where Lily was just getting up from her seat. "That was eye-opening." She sat down in Lily's seat, a half-grin slowly forming on her face.

Lily handed her money to the man and he directed her inside. "Wish me luck." She tossed the words over her shoulder as she disappeared inside. I wanted to ask Gretchen about her session but I didn't want to talk in front of the man. Something about him wasn't sitting well with me. Every so often I caught him staring at me very intently and it was starting to creep me out. I left Gretchen to her reverie and stared back out toward the ocean and the sailboats gliding by on the summer breeze. A boat with a rainbow sail glided past, heading west at a nice clip, until it disappeared from view behind a stand of trees near the water's edge.

It seemed like Lily's session was lasting forever. While we waited, several people walked by the table and read the board's offerings. I heard a lady tell her daughter that she couldn't have a tarot card reading because it was against their religion. For some reason, that made me want to get my own reading a little more. But I was getting impatient…and hungry. I was just about to complain when the red curtain parted and Lily came bounding out of the hut, a glowing smile on her pretty face.

"Well, that was interesting," she said. "Your turn, Laura. Hope yours is as good as mine."

I shot her a look of doubt and walked toward the red curtain. I handed the man my money and when he took the bills, his hand brushed against mine. He snatched his hand away from me and leaned back like I had leprosy or something. I scowled at him, made a tsk-ing sound, and reluctantly entered the hut.

Inside, the room was dark and surprisingly larger than it appeared from the outside. Hanging from the makeshift ceiling were rope beads and strings of crystals and other stones. In the center of the room sat a woman with blondish-gray hair and large, round, plastic-framed glasses perched on the end of her long nose. She sat at a round table covered with a dark cloth. The only light in the room came from a lantern on a side table and a three-wick candle on the table where the woman sat waiting for me. A meowing sound came from somewhere in the room but I didn't see a cat. It must be in one of the corners where it was too dark to see. The woman, Madame Jeanette I presumed, motioned to the seat across from her and I sat down in it somewhat reluctantly. My instincts were telling me to turn tail and run but I ignored them as I settled myself into the chair and awaited my reading.

Madame Jeanette looked to be about in her mid-fifties and when she spoke, her voice did not match her physical appearance. She sounded manly to be exact—deep-voiced and raspy, as if she had spent many years with a cigarette in her mouth. I sighed deeply and waited for her to say something, but for at least a full minute or more she just stared at me in silence. Just when it was starting to get really awkward, she spoke.

"I wondered when you were going to show up. I've been expecting you for some time now, Laura." She continued to stare at me intently and I felt my stomach tighten.

"How did you know my…oh…never mind. One of my friends told you," I said. *Good one, lady, you almost got me there*, I thought. I tucked my hands under my thighs and crossed my feet at the ankles, hoping this would be over soon.

Madame Jeanette closed her eyes for a moment and inhaled deeply through her nose. After a while she exhaled audibly through her lips which I noticed were painted with bright red lipstick. She then slowly opened her eyes and stared me down. At least that's what it felt like she was doing. "I see change is coming," she said.

Imagine that, I thought.

"Your home life is unstable. Are your parents divorced?" she asked.

I swallowed a lump and replied hesitantly. "It's headed that way," I whispered the words—words that could make my head spin if I thought about them for too long.

"Don't worry about the divorce, my dear. It's not likely to happen. You and your brother will help your parents through the tough times and everyone should be just fine." Madame Jeanette continued to stare at me, her eyes seeming to lose focus. I did not respond to her comment—not even to ask her how she knew I had a brother. I decided to chalk it up to a lucky guess.

"Laura...there is a blackness around you. And yet, there is also light. Two opposing forces circling around you, confusing your aura. Have you experienced dizziness lately?"

I looked at a dark shadow over her right shoulder. "Not that I've noticed." I decided that any commentary from me would have to be minimal so as not to give Madame Jeanette any material to mine for crazy predictions. I stole a glance at my watch and wondered how much longer this nonsense would last.

Suddenly Madame Jeanette jumped. Her seat tipped backward a few degrees but it did not fall. She gasped and then leaned forward, grasping the edge of the table. "May I see your left hand?" she asked in a low voice.

I grabbed the edge of my chair under my thigh where my hand was still wedged. "I'm not paying for a palm reading," I said vehemently. These psychics and their tricks—I wasn't falling for it.

"I don't want to read your palm," the woman said. "I would just like to see your hand."

When I didn't offer my hand right away she reached across the table toward me. Her right hand had a ring on every finger—even the thumb. A ruby on the index finger, a sapphire on the pinky and opals on the other digits. Some were quite large—and all probably fake, I'd bet. She could do some serious damage on someone's face, though, if she ever decided to throw a punch. When I continued to hesitate, she whispered one word to me—a word that caused one of the wicks on the three-wick candle to flicker and flame out.

"Please."

Whoa. She seemed to go all intense on me—even more than she already was. I decided it might be a good idea to give her my hand, let her say her piece and then get the heck out of here. I pulled my left hand out from under the table and laid it palm down in front of her. Then I waited…and waited…and waited. For the longest time she didn't even look at my hand. She stared penetratingly at me until I began to fidget in my seat. Just when I was about to snatch back my hand and make a run for the red curtain, she took my hand and looked down at it. Hers was icy and rough. It felt weird and dry—almost scaly. After a moment of intense staring, she ran her finger along the bones and blue veins and tendons of my hand. This was beginning to freak me out and I'd had enough. I was just about to pull my hand back to safety under the table when she suddenly tightened her grip on my hand and began to whisper—words I couldn't understand and couldn't really make out either. After a couple of minutes of this, she let my hand go and leaned back in her chair, her eyes closed once again. Finally she broke the silence.

"Laura." She said my name as a statement—not a question. I waited.

"Your fate is sealed. Already I can see that it cannot be undone. It is what it shall be. That being said, you do have the power of choice. Always choose wisely but still knowing that your destiny has already been determined. The outcome will be the same but you have the power to make the pathway to your providence easy or difficult… short or long…happy or sad. Choose wisely."

I thought about this for a minute and then decided—like I already knew—that she was just talking a load of crap. But I also thought I'd ask for an elaboration—may as well try to get my money's worth. Because up to now, I'd heard nothing even remotely interesting about my future. That crap about my destiny was generic nonsense that she probably told everybody stupid enough to pay her to tell it.

"Could you maybe be a little more specific? Like maybe give me something to work with here? Because quite frankly, all that mumbo jumbo isn't good enough—I mean, just not interesting or even unusual. You could literally say that to anyone." I crossed my arms over my chest and waited to see if Madame Jeanette could offer me something worth twelve dollars.

Madame Jeanette smiled at me and shook her head in a sort of resigned manner. She sighed again and removed her glasses, laying them on the table beside the candle, the two wicks flickering in the dimness of the room.

"I can tell you three things of the utmost importance. Three things, Laura." She appeared lost in thought for a moment—probably trying to figure out three random things to throw at me that would make me feel like I got something for my twelve bucks. Finally she spoke in a hushed voice.

"Number one: As I said before, there is darkness and light all around you. But do not assume that the darkness is bad and the light is good. This is not always the case. Your subconscious will become aware of this darkness and light long before you will consciously sense it. Always listen to your instincts and trust your gut feelings."

"Number two: Your heart. It is in danger—of becoming shattered. But always know that a crushed heart does not have to kill you—metaphorically speaking, of course. You always have control…you just have to take that control. You will be pulled in two directions. But do not assume that one way is the right way and the other is wrong. When you find yourself in a situation where you have to follow your heart or your head—always, *always*, follow your heart. Your head can talk you into and out of something over and over again. But your heart knows the true path to follow. Do not ignore it. Ever."

"Number three: The darkness and the light that I mentioned earlier? They have names. But I cannot tell you those names. But you will meet them soon. And only you will know which one is darkness and which one is light. There will be pain. There will be suffering. But there will also be great love. But it is impossible for the darkness and the light to co-exist in peace. You and you alone will have to make the choice to live in darkness or to live in the light. As I said before…do not assume that darkness is bad and light is good. Nothing is ever as it seems."

Finally, she stopped talking. I sat quietly and took into consideration what she'd said. And I came to one conclusion: she hadn't said a damned thing.

"So…you're not going to tell me what I should do with my life, how long I'm going to live, if I'll ever be rich or get married or have babies or if I'll get accepted to college?" *Really? Nothing concrete that I can take away from this little chat we've had?* I thought. I was clearly exasperated. I'd sat through this so-called reading and didn't get anything good to brag about. It was all just mumbo-jumbo nonsense, just as I'd figured it would be.

"Laura, I want to tell you more but I cannot. This is all I can offer you. Please go in peace." Madame Jeanette pushed her chair back from the table and stood up. Her movement caused the other two wicks in the candle to extinguish. The hut was now lit only by the light of the lantern on the side table. I heard the cat meow again somewhere in the back of the room.

"Well, thanks for…whatever that was," I said. I stood up and walked toward the curtain. Just as I was about to open it, her voice stopped me.

"Laura? she whispered.

"Yes?" I replied, looking back toward her over my shoulder.

"Do you have a passport?" she asked.

"Yes…somewhere…why?" *How could this be relevant to anything she'd said so far*? I wondered.

"Find it. And make sure it's current." Her voice was almost inaudible now. She sounded weird—sad even.

"O…K…," I said slowly. "Uh…," I hesitated. "Where am I going?"

Madame Jeanette walked over to the corner and scooped up a gray cat into her arms. She then went to the side table and turned off the lantern. I barely heard the words that escaped from her mouth in a whisper into the darkness.

"To the land of the gypsies."

And with that she seemed to disappear into the back of the hut. I swallowed hard and stepped out into the bright sunlight where Lily and Gretchen were waiting. As I walked past the white-haired man, he pushed something forcefully into my hand. I looked down and saw that it was my twelve dollars. I looked at him in surprise but he immediately disappeared into the hut. I noticed that Lily and Gretchen were eating ice cream cones. Funny…I didn't even mind that they couldn't wait for me to get ice cream…I'd suddenly lost my appetite. All I wanted to do now was just go home.

C h a p t e r   T w o

FiRSt ·DAY

I swallowed two Tylenols with a drink from my glass of lemonade that had turned warm from neglect. It was on my nightstand along with my cell phone, which I'd turned off—uncharacteristically for me. I glanced at the book I'd been about to start reading—*The Prince and the Pauper*—ugh. I hadn't chosen it for pleasure, that's for sure. For some ungodly reason, the English department at Portsmouth High School had decided that we seniors should spend some quality time with Mark Twain. I had been trying to start the damned thing all day but every time I read the first page, I'd feel a headache coming on. I'd finally given up and decided to take some Tylenol before making another attempt at the book. It was kind of a moot point anyway since tomorrow was the first day of school and I should've read it weeks ago.

I lay back on my bed and rested my head against the pillow. I closed my eyes, thinking I would allow the Tylenol thirty minutes to kick in and then give Mark Twain another go-round. As soon as I closed my eyes, my mind went back to yesterday and the visit to the psychic. It had been an interesting ride home, that's for sure.

Lily and Gretchen had babbled on and on about their readings. And every time they'd asked me about mine, I'd just kind of shrugged it off as a bunch of crap—which it totally was.

Apparently Gretchen was going to marry the man of her dreams (who supposedly worked at some job that required him to wear a uniform—hello Mickey D's!), have three kids and a house with a picket fence near the beach. Please…could it get any more clichéd than that? And Lily was going to be massively successful in her career, which would involve inventing something ground-breaking, and she would live a long life well into her eighties. No mention of any romance, but she didn't seem too concerned about that detail so we made suggestions for cool things she could invent—like ways to graduate school without actually attending and dishwashers that emptied themselves. To satisfy their curiosity, I'd told them the part about being surrounded by darkness and light and that I was going to get my heart broken. I thought they would get a kick out of that one. Not that they wanted me to get my heart broken…but better me than them, right?

I picked up the book and tried to read again. But two pages in (one page farther than I'd gotten the last time I'd picked up the book) I felt the headache coming on again. It occurred to me that I might need glasses—god forbid—and maybe I should see about making an appointment with an eye doctor. I tossed the book on the bed and closed my eyes. I thought again about Madame Jeanette's comment about my parents' impending divorce. I had already convinced myself that the mention of my brother was just a guess on her part—and a damned good one at that. I did have a brother. Nick was a year older than I and a freshman at the local community college. He had a girlfriend I hated named Abigail (not Abby but Abigail). If anyone dared call her anything other than Abigail, she would shriek like a total nut-job. Neither I nor my parents or friends could understand what he saw in her, but I guess the heart wants what it wants as they say. Anyway, it was true that my parents were getting a divorce. The strange thing is they seemed to get along just fine. I didn't get it. They didn't fight. They didn't seem to argue about money or parenting issues or communication problems or anything as far as I could see. All they had told me and Nick was that they had grown apart and this was nothing to do with us and blah, blah, blah. And they both said there was no one else, so who knows? It was maddening and made no logical sense to me so I tried hard not to think about it.

I went into the bathroom and brushed my teeth. The house was quiet. My dad wasn't home and Nick was with Abigail. My mom was downstairs watching television. I flipped off the bathroom light and walked down the hall, hesitating at the top of the stairs. I could hear the low roar of the TV in the family room.

"Good night, Mom!" I hollered down the stairs. She didn't respond so I yelled a little louder. This time she heard me.

"Good night, honey! Sweet dreams!" she hollered back.

Back in my room, I walked over to the window and glanced out to see the moon. It was huge and almost full, hanging low and gorgeous in the sky, a sort of a soft pink color. I could just barely make out a glimpse of the ocean in the distance. We used to have a great ocean view from our second floor until the numb-nuts across the street built a second story onto their house. How they were allowed to do that I still couldn't believe, but they were, and they had. But I could still catch a glimpse of the sea. When the leaves fell in the autumn my view would improve. I sighed and climbed into bed. I tossed Mark Twain to the floor and settled under my blankets for the night. I turned out the light and tried not to think about tomorrow and the first day of school. Morning would be here before I knew it.

I could tell something strange was going on the minute we pulled into the driveway of the school. I'd caught a ride with Lily and we were a little early so we could get a good parking spot. There seemed to be a back-up of cars. I craned my neck out the window to get a good look at what was going on. There were two huge black cars up ahead—they looked like Mercedes Benzes—idling in the drop-off zone in front of the school. We were too far back to see who or what was emerging from the cars. We waited our turn until we were finally able to move into a vacant space.

"What the hell is that?" Lily screeched. She was looking out the window and pointing at something up high. I looked up but didn't see anything.

"What? I don't see anything...what is it?" I asked. I kept staring in the direction she was pointing but everything looked normal. And then I saw something move on top of the building. "Oh! What *is* that? Is that a man up there...up on the roof?" I asked, incredulous.

"Looks like it," said Lily. "All dressed in black like a sniper. Good grief. Did the president move into town and enroll his kids at Portsmouth High while we were on summer vacation?"

"I highly doubt it," I laughed. "I'd like to think the president has more discerning taste in schools." We got out of the car, grabbing our book-bags from the backseat. As we neared the building it was clear that just walking in the front door wasn't going to be quick. There was a long line of students waiting to enter. Some goon with a wand was waving it up and over each student before allowing him or her to enter the building. We could hear the buzz and whispers of conversations as our fellow classmates speculated as to who was so important that it warranted this kind of security. I found it to be annoying and some-what demeaning. I'd made up my mind that unless it was the freaking queen of bloody England up there then there'd better be a damned good reason for this nonsense.

Every so often the wand would light on something sinister and make an annoying beeping sound. The poor kid then had to open his back-pack for inspection. I saw lots of iPods, cell phones and watches being inspected—for what? Who knew? Bombs? Nuclear weapons? Incendiary devices? This was beyond ridiculous. Lily asked some kids ahead of us if they knew what was going on and someone said it was some foreign dignitary from England. *Ha—maybe it* was *the freaking queen of bloody England after all*, I thought, with a quiet laugh under my breath.

We finally made it to the head of the line and the sniper-looking man waved his wand over me. Thankfully, it remained silent and I was allowed to enter. I told Lily I would see her later and I went straight to the office to try to find out what was going on. This was ridiculous after all.

The front office had about a gazillion people in it so I didn't even stop. I just kept going down the hall and around the corner to my locker. Students were everywhere, hugging and welcoming each other back to another year of insanity. I put my backpack away and pulled my schedule from my pocket. The first class was actually homeroom. I went into the class and sat in the back of the room. Maybe now we would find out what all of the hullaballoo was at the front doors.

Students filed in. I recognized everyone and I spoke to some of them. We all settled in and our homeroom teacher, Mrs. Handler, walked in and called us all to order.

"Good morning, class. Welcome to another school year at Portsmouth High. I hope everyone had a good summer and you're all rested and excited about another year of learning." She glanced around the room at all of us and then smiled a weird grin. Someone groaned loudly at the back of the room.

"I'm sure you're all wondering about the heightened security this morning. Rest assured that Portsmouth High School is a safe and secure learning environment and nothing has changed in that regard. But we do have a new student starting today and I'm asking you—as all of the teachers are asking all of the students this morning—to treat this new student as you would any other. His name is Andrew Easton and he will be attending Portsmouth High School this school year. I'm sure at some point, you will be meeting him or seeing him in the hallways or the cafeteria. Please treat him as you wish to be treated yourself—with the same respect you would afford any other classmate."

A voice from the back of the room interrupted Mrs. Handler's speech.

"Excuse me, Mrs. H., but just who the hell is Andrew Easton?" The voice belonged to Johnny Johnson. If there was going to be any trouble for the new kid, it would probably come from Johnny Johnson.

"For your information, Andrew Easton is a member of the royal family,'" she replied rather smugly. There were gasps around the room, mostly from girls. I could've sworn I heard some girl whisper Prince Harry's name. *Dumb twit*, I thought. Prince Harry finished school a long time ago.

People started asking questions all at once and Mrs. Handler finally put her hands up and shushed the room. "That's all the information I have. All we know is that Andrew is here for the school year. I'm sure he…or his family…had a reason for choosing Portsmouth but we don't know, and frankly, it isn't really our business. The only thing that's important is that we treat him with respect and make him feel at home here at Portsmouth High."

Mrs. Handler was starting to sound like an advertisement for the Portsmouth Board of Education. It was getting annoying. I couldn't help but think that if Andrew Easton wanted to be treated like one of us, then he should've arrived at school like us and not in armored cars with bodyguards and snipers on the roof. Unbelievable. I hated him already.

Mrs. Handler gave us some instructions for the day's schedule and the principal announced over the intercom how happy he was to have us all in school, ready to learn, learn, learn! "Yippee," I muttered to myself. The only mention he made of the new student was indirect: "Please be aware of the extra security today and be sure to welcome all of our new students to the school. I hope everyone has a fantastic and prosperous year."

The bell rang then and we were dismissed to our first class. For me that meant French and Mrs. Kneiffel (rhymes with Eiffel, just like the tower). And from there history, then math, U.S. government and finally lunch. Considering, or in spite of, the royalty in our midst, the morning went smoothly and I saw no one I didn't already know. Wherever the sniper dudes were, they were discreetly hidden now because everything appeared to be business as usual. The cafeteria was crowded and the food was still just as bad as last year. Science class was after lunch and I could already tell I would hate this class the most—even more than math—and that was a lot. Everything was perfectly and completely normal…just like any other first day of school anywhere in the good old U.S.A. until last period—English. That's when I first saw him: Andrew Easton.

He was tall. Even though he was already seated when I entered the classroom, I could tell he was tall—more than six feet I would guess. He had blond hair and was thin but not painfully so. He was sitting in the first row by the door, fourth seat back from the front. All of the seats around him were filling up fast. People—girls mostly—were staring at him. Some of them even said hello to him. He was polite and responded in kind in his British accent. I sat on the far side of the room and tried hard not to pay any attention to him. There was no way in hell I was going to be like the other girls and fawn all over this guy. But his novelty was compelling—no doubt about it.

Gretchen walked in and saw me. She waved and ran over to grab the seat in front of mine. As she sat down, she scanned the room and her eyes lit on the new guy.

"Holy crap," she barked a little loudly. I felt my face flush and I turned toward the window. "Is that…?" she started, and I was just about to shush her when somebody else beat me to it.

"Sorry," she muttered. I turned back just as the teacher walked in the door. Mrs. Clanton greeted us and welcomed us to class. Someone outside in the hall, dressed all in black, walked past the door and pushed it shut from the outside.

I tried to concentrate on Mrs. Clanton's voice. She asked how many of us had completed our summer reading and I couldn't help but glance toward Andrew Easton. I didn't know if he was really a prince or not but the irony of our required reading wasn't lost on me. Without warning, he suddenly turned my way and stared right at me. He looked at me for a moment and then dipped his head down toward his desk. I saw the corner of his mouth turn up ever so slightly. *What's that about?* I wondered.

We got through the rest of the class and forty-five minutes later it was over and the first day of school was history. Andrew Easton stood up and for the first time I could see just how tall he really was. He picked up his very fancy leather bag and slung it over his shoulder. I hadn't even noticed that it had been at his feet. A couple of kids spoke to him and he answered politely. As he left the room he looked back as if he were checking to make sure he wasn't forgetting anything. Once again he looked in my direction. I stared back and thought maybe I should smile or something but I just froze. He smiled at me and left.

"What the…?" Gretchen stared at me. "Did you have other classes with him? He seemed like he knows you already."

"Nope," I said. "Only this class. And I think he was smiling at you." I grinned at her and she gasped.

"Really? You think?" She looked like a stroke was imminent.

"Let's go, you goof. Lily's my ride and I don't want to keep her waiting." We left and headed down to the front doors. In the pick-up/drop-off zone, the black cars were back.

"Good grief. Is this going to be an everyday thing with this guy?" I muttered. "I mean, if you want to be normal, then don't announce with big black cars and henchmen that you're here. Sheesh!" I made my way down the few steps toward Lily's car. I could see her there waiting. She was talking to some classmates. She waved when she saw me. I waved back.

I had to walk past the two black cars to get down to the parking area. I couldn't see through the dark windows or tell if he was already in one of them. Then I reminded myself that I didn't care. As I passed the second car, I heard the sound of an electric window opening.

"Excuse me…miss?" Was the posh British accent speaking to me?

I stopped and hesitated before slowly turning around. I stared into the blue eyes of Andrew Easton. "Yes?" I replied, a little breathlessly, to my annoyance.

"You dropped something," he said in that maddening accent. I saw him point out the window to the ground behind me. I looked down, and all around, but at first I didn't see anything. And then I saw a glint of gold on the pavement near the curb. I must have dropped it—whatever it was—without even realizing it. I bent to pick up the object and glanced toward him. "Thanks. I didn't even hear it fall."

"You're welcome. You'd better hold on tight to it—it looks valuable." He smiled a disarming smile and then rolled up the window. The car drove away. I stood there dumbfounded and greatly annoyed. All I could think was that he would assume I had purposely dropped something in the hope that he would notice and tell me so I could speak to him. "Damn!" I muttered.

"Hey!" It was Lily calling me. "Hurry up!" She was frantically beckoning to me to get to the car. I stepped off the sidewalk and walked down the grassy embankment over to her car and opened the passenger side door. Once inside she pounced.

"Did the prince just speak to you?" she asked breathlessly.

"The prince? Oh, so he's the *prince* now, is he?" I shook my head in disbelief. You've got to be kidding.

"I saw you talk to him. What happened? What does his voice sound like? I cannot believe I don't have any classes with him! Life is so unfair! What did he say to you?" Her words came out in a long, breathy stream.

I laughed as I buckled my seatbelt. "Yes, the *prince* deigned to have a word with me. But don't get excited. He didn't ask me to marry him and move into the castle or go swimming in his moat. He just told me I dropped something."

"Oh, you sly devil! You dropped something on purpose just to get his attention? Brilliant! And it apparently worked! I should've thought of that! Way to go, Laura Calder! Or maybe I should start calling you Your Royal Highness!" She collapsed in a state of giggling hysteria.

I shook my head in horror. I *knew* someone would think that—if anyone else saw our short exchange I knew it would be assumed that I had orchestrated the whole thing. *Damn it!*

"I didn't drop anything! This isn't even mine!" I opened my fist and for the first time I actually looked at the round, gold shape in my hand. I stared at it. It was an amulet of some sort—a talisman—engraved with crossed swords on one side and a series of numbers and something like a coat of arms on the other side. It had a tiny hole at the top as if it had once been attached to a chain. It looked old and…valuable. It didn't look like anything that came from around Portsmouth, Rhode Island, that's for sure. It looked…ancient.

"What is that thing?" Lily asked. She looked like she wanted to snatch it out of my hands.

I closed my fingers over it and put it in my jeans pocket. "It's just some kind of coin, I think. Might make a nice necklace," I said. I looked out the window as Lily started the car and pulled out into the stream of departing traffic. I could hear her rambling on about her day and I know I should have paid more attention. But I was keenly aware of the weight of the talisman in my pocket. Not in the sense that it was heavy, but rather…its significance. My instincts were firing on all pistons. I knew I had not dropped any objects on the ground. This thing in my pocket wasn't mine. But why did I have the feeling it was intended for me? I shivered in spite of the heat of the day. Lily continued chattering away. I stared out the window, anxious to get home. I felt a headache threatening and once again I reminded myself to tell my mother I needed an eye doctor appointment.

Lily dropped me off at my house. I waved good-bye. There was no one home yet and I was glad to have the house to myself for a while. Mom worked at the bank and she wouldn't be home till after five. Dad was probably at his office—he was an architect and worked in Providence. Nick was undoubtedly at Abigail's.

In the kitchen I grabbed an Oreo from the package on the counter and poured myself some lemonade. Then I hauled my book-bag up the stairs to my room, glad there wasn't any homework tonight… other than that pesky required reading. I pulled the talisman out of my pocket and turned it over and over in my hands. It suddenly felt heavy. I knew it was a talisman because I had seen something like it in a movie once. But I couldn't remember just exactly what a talisman was. I grabbed my battered copy of Webster's Dictionary off my bookshelf and looked it up.

Talisman—noun—'*a stone, ring or other object, engraved with figures or characters supposed to possess occult powers and worn as an amulet or charm; anything whose presence exercises remarkable or powerful influence on human feelings or actions.*'

I ran my fingers over the surface of the object. I studied the symbols and numbers but they meant nothing to me. I looked at the hole in the top of it and sucked in my breath. Somewhere in my old jewelry box I had a gold chain that should fit perfectly through this hole. I looked around for the jewelry box and found it in my closet where it had been stashed for who knows how long—I had never been much of a jewelry wearer. I found the chain, dangled it over the hole in the talisman, and threaded it through. It fit as if it were made for it. I pulled it over my head and fastened the tiny clasp behind my neck. I looked down at where it lay on my chest and walked over to the mirror.

The afternoon sunlight danced over it and it seemed to sparkle for a moment. It was so pretty. I suddenly hoped that no one would report it missing and I had to give it up. And then a strange feeling washed over me. Somehow I knew, without a shadow of a doubt, that this talisman had been placed on the pavement waiting for…*me*. I don't know how I knew. I just did. I held its weight in my left hand for a moment and studied it. The sound of the front door opening made me jump. I quickly pulled out the neck of my t-shirt and dropped my new necklace down inside. I felt its coldness against my chest-bone just below the bottom of my bra and I winced at the sudden chill. I sighed deeply and then ran downstairs to start dinner.

Chapter Three

GYPSIES

With all the hoopla surrounding the arrival of Andrew Easton at Portsmouth High yesterday, it had escaped notice that Mr. Easton was not the only new kid in school this year. But the other new kids did not go unnoticed today. Oh, they were noticed alright—by the crack security team that followed His Royal Highness everywhere. Once again Lily and I were waiting in a long line just to enter the front doors of the school. I was staring off into space in the direction of the driveway, considering making a run for it and just going back home when a black Suburban drove up to the front of the school. It was about to enter into the drop-off zone in front of the building when one of the bodyguard/sniper/hitman/freaks suddenly broke rank from the security detail and dashed out in front of it. The Suburban slammed to a stop to avoid hitting the idiot. He walked around to the driver's side, where he appeared to exchange some words with the driver. I was unable to see inside the vehicle—its windows were tinted so dark that you almost couldn't tell where the doors ended and the windows began. I was standing on the pavement on the passenger side and not able to see who was driving or hear what was being said, but after a moment, Sniperman returned to his post by the black car, which was just dispatching His Royal Highness. I watched the Suburban slowly drive forward and continue on its way without even stopping to let anyone out. It drove around and entered the parking lot and parked way down toward the bottom of the lot.

What was the point of entering the drop-off/pick-up zone if you weren't even going to drop off or pick up anyone? I wondered. Maybe it was just a curiosity-seeker trying to push some boundaries. I watched the vehicle for a minute waiting to see who or what was going to come out of it when it was suddenly my turn to pass through security.

I got up to the sniper with his magic wand. He waved it over me and it beeped—loudly. I jumped back, shocked and looked down at myself. I was wearing the exact same jeans as yesterday and the same shoes—just a different shirt. What the hell was beeping?

"Empty your pockets, miss," said the sniperman in his annoying British accent. He glanced down at my jeans and made as if to reach for my backpack. I backed away and glowered at him. Now I was mad. I had spent kindergarten through the eleventh grade in the Portsmouth school system with never so much as a hint—not even a *whisper*—of a problem, and suddenly some English goon in a black suit with an earpiece was going to tell me what to do? I don't think so!

"No," I said firmly but politely. I stared the man down—or tried to. After about three seconds I felt ridiculous and knew embarrassment was going to start shading itself all over my face in rainbow hues. I never could handle conflict very well.

"I'm sorry, miss, but the wand has detected something potentially unsafe and I need to investigate. It will only take a moment and I do apologize for the delay and the inconvenience." He reached for the strap of my backpack hanging over my left shoulder and started to remove it. I jerked back and really gave it to him.

"Keep your hands off of me. I have—in this bag—exactly the same things I had yesterday and it didn't beep then. I think your equipment is malfunctioning. Now, if you'll excuse me, I need to get to class." I made to push past him but he blocked my way.

"Laura, come on. Just let him check your bag. You don't have anything to hide so what's the big deal?" Lily looked a little scared and tilted her head at me pleadingly. "Come on, we're gonna be late for class."

I noticed the line behind me and saw the faces of some of the other students waiting. Some were telling me to hurry up already. I looked at Sniperman and debated. I could let him search me and my bag and then when he found nothing I could give him a big old 'I told you so' and go on my merry way but…there was a principle at stake here. And I wouldn't back down.

"No," I said to Lily. And then I made to push past the sniper guy again. He grabbed my arm and stopped me, twisting me around harshly. And then something strange happened. The hot, late summer sun glanced across my face and Sniperman glanced down at my neck. Something had caught his eye. I tried to pull my arm out of his grasp but he held on tightly. He stared at my neck like a vampire contemplating taking a bite and then he suddenly let me go. He reached toward my neck and touched the gold chain showing above the collar of my t-shirt. It was sparkling in the sunlight. I automatically put my hand up to smack his hand away, wondering why no one was coming to my rescue. And then someone did.

"It's OK, Peter. There's no harm here." Andrew Easton was suddenly standing in front of me on the sidewalk. I hadn't even seen him get out of the car. He looked at me and smiled demurely. "I'm sorry, Laura. It's just a misunderstanding." He then looked at his bodyguard. "That'll be all, Peter." Sniperman Peter muttered "as you wish," under his breath and backed away.

Andrew looked at my neck, and a small smile played across his mouth. I suddenly had the feeling that the world was going all *Twilight* all over the place. I looked down and touched the chain. The talisman was buried down deep under my t-shirt where no one could see it. But Andrew knew it was there. I could tell.

"OK then," Lily coughed. I'd almost forgotten she was there. "Can we go inside now? Nothing like being marked tardy on day two of the new school year," she muttered.

"Of course," said Andrew. "Ladies…have a good day. And again— my deepest apologies." And just like that he walked into the school as if nothing had happened. Lily and I followed behind him. Once inside he disappeared into the sea of bodies. I assumed his henchman were trying to blend in somewhere in the vicinity.

"What the hell…?" Lily grabbed my arm and pulled me over by one of the other doors. "What was that about?" she gasped. "And how the hell did he know your name?" She looked stunned.

I hitched my book-bag up higher on my shoulder and shrugged. "I truly have no idea. This place has gone totally and completely nuts."

I started to walk down the hall but something made me look out the glass doors toward the parking lot. And that's when I saw them. And Lily saw them, too. She gasped loudly but I just held my breath—suddenly incapable of making my lungs work.

Walking up the front steps straight toward the sniperguard were three very tall, very dark, very ominous looking men. I leaned forward and stared through the glass doors wondering what the hell was happening and who were these men? The bodyguard contingent—six of them now—stood in a line, blocking their path. Words were exchanged and suddenly the sniper dudes broke rank and allowed the three guys to enter. They could not escape the magic wands though. But everything remained silent—no beeping—and they were allowed to enter the school. I turned toward the doors where they were entering—and so did Lily whose mouth was hanging wide open. Most of the other students still milling about in the front hall also stopped to stare. And then, upon closer inspection, I realized that these three people were not men. Not at all. They were boys—teenagers. They had olive skin and jet black hair and the darkest eyes I had ever seen. They looked like they had just walked straight out of central casting for a Hollywood action movie.

Many of the students hurried away to their classes—either in fear of being late or because they felt intimated by the Hollywood guys' sudden appearance. I watched as they spoke quietly to each other. Two of them smiled and turned to walk down the hall—seeming to know just exactly where to go. These two looked identical—they must have been twins. They said good-bye to the third guy as they sauntered off down the sophomore hallway. The other boy didn't move. He pulled a cell phone out of his pocket and pushed a button on it. A few seconds later it powered down and went dark and he put it back in his pocket. He had a backpack over his shoulder similar to mine. He patted the outside pocket of it as if making sure something important was still in it and then he finally looked up and took in his surroundings.

I was aware of Lily still standing next to me. She tugged on my arm, whispered, "I'll see you at lunch," and dashed off down the hall. I looked around and realized at that moment that the hall was empty. All of the students had gone to class. There wasn't a teacher or another adult in sight. All of the snipermen had disappeared. It was just me and this new boy standing here near the front doors beside the trophy case of the almighty Portsmouth Patriots.

He was tall and his hair was jet-black. His eyes were so dark I felt like I couldn't really see them—not the pupils anyway. His jaw was chiseled and his cheekbones were high-set. His nose was straight and perfect as if carved from stone. There was the tiniest hint of an indentation in his chin. He was big like one of those Portsmouth Patriot football players pictured on the wall of fame behind me. He was wearing jeans and a black t-shirt and black tennis shoes. He looked...otherworldly. And he was just staring at me. I felt like I couldn't breathe. My heart was pounding in my chest. I had no idea what was happening to me but it couldn't be good. We just stared at each other—waiting for someone to break the silence, perhaps? It seemed like time had stopped. He stared at me with the most penetrating of stares. I felt like I should say hello or run or something—anything but this weird, motionless nothing.

And then the spell was broken.

"Kids? Is everything OK here? You two need to get to class. You're already late." It was the front office secretary—Mrs. Oliphant. I hadn't even heard her come out of the office. She stared at us questioningly.

I blinked and nodded. With one more glance at the new boy, I turned and walked to French class. And neither of us had spoken a single word during that whole...whatever it was.

The morning flew by. I spent most of it somewhere else mentally. I couldn't concentrate and I had zero interest in anything the teachers were talking about. I felt kind of bad having this attitude so soon in the year—it was only the second day of school, for crying out loud— but I didn't care. I snapped back to awareness at lunch time when Lily pounced on me in the food line. Gretchen was already sitting at a table holding two seats for us. I could see her auburn hair across the crowded cafeteria. I glanced around the room slowly but there was no sign of either Prince Charming or the dark kid. Everything was business as usual. I put a cheeseburger on my tray and a salad. I grabbed a brownie from the dessert offerings and a bottle of water and moved ahead to the cashier to pay. I handed her my ID card and she swiped it in the register and it deducted an amount from my lunch account. Whatever we were paying for this stuff they called food, it was too much.

Over at the table I joined Gretchen. She and Lily talked for a moment about some assignment in their art class. Then Gretchen turned to me.

"So, I hear you and the prince are now on a first name basis...?" she said, mischief in her voice.

I grimaced. "Nope. I don't know what you're talking about." I said it matter-of-factly. I bit into my cheeseburger wondering if I could potentially get food poisoning from it.

"Lily told me he called you by name. He's in our English class. Maybe he heard the teacher say it yesterday and he remembered," Gretchen said excitedly. She popped a ketchup-laden French fry into her mouth and chewed slowly.

"Ha, ha, ha. Mrs. Clanton never said my name. He probably saw it on a paper or something or maybe he heard someone else say it and he just has a good memory...who knows?" I speared a cherry tomato and stared at it as if it had a message for me. I had no idea how Andrew Easton knew my name. But he had called me Laura today so, oh, yes, he knew it. And he hadn't said it casually. He hadn't stumbled over it. He had said it like he'd always known it.

We finished our lunch and I listened to them talk about other kids—gossiping and judging—like typical high school girls in a typical school cafeteria. I used to be like that, too. But today, I didn't feel like that any-more. I felt different—somewhat removed from everything around me. I zoned out for a moment until I heard Gretchen gasp loudly. I snapped out of my reverie and looked in the direction she was staring. Just enter-ing the cafeteria were the twin, dark-haired boys. They looked around the room and then got into the lunch line to purchase food.

"Who...are...they?" Gretchen asked in a whisper. She stared at the boys as they slowly moved through the line putting food onto their trays. Lily was quick to answer.

"They're the gypsies," she said, as if it were the most natural thing in the world to say. "They're both in my Chemistry class. I heard they just moved here from overseas—Portugal, I think I heard. They're very quiet. But I heard one of them speak and his English was flawless with only a hint of an accent."

"Wait, what?" Gretchen asked. "*Gypsies*? And you're just now telling us about them? By the way, they're *gorgeous*, in case no one's noticed." She stared at them and went into some weird lustful trance.

"Uh, oh," I laughed. "Colin better watch his back. He's got competition." I reached over and playfully chucked Gretchen on the shoulder. I hoped she was coming back down to earth.

Lily leaned forward and said in an almost conspiratorial whisper, "Well, if you think they're gorgeous, you should see the other one—the brother. He's in our grade." She looked glassy-eyed and deadly serious.

Gretchen gasped. "You mean there's *another* one?" *No...freaking...way!*" I thought she would fall over in a dead faint. Poor Colin. Maybe he should be warned about this gypsy fever setting in on his woman. But I couldn't really say anything about that. I had seen the other one myself. I knew what Lily was talking about. I was just about to tell them about my awkward encounter this morning with the brother when the bell rang. Lunch was over for us and it was time to get to class. We dumped our lunch detritus and went our separate ways in the hall. But as I walked to my next class something nagged at the back of my brain—a memory of some sort. Something I was missing. I couldn't figure it out but rather than make myself crazy about it, I tried to let it go for now.

The afternoon did not move as quickly as the morning but when it was nearing time for last period I got a strange sensation in the pit of my stomach. It was time for English and Andrew Easton would be there. I felt anxious and nervous and excited and I did not, for the life of me, know why. But I was in for a surprise. My stomachache was about to get even worse.

I had to walk past one of the dumb black-clad bodyguards to get into the classroom. Andrew was there, sitting in his chair—his copy of *The Prince and the Pauper* lying on his desk. I glanced at him and saw the book and I couldn't help but grin at the irony. He saw me look at him and he smiled back. *Oops.* If he only knew the smile wasn't really for him. Oh, well. Too late now. I felt his eyes on me as I walked to my seat over by the windows. I sat down and glanced his way and he smiled at me again. The other kids were slowly filing in and taking their seats. Mrs. Clanton was just calling the class to order when one more student walked in the door.

So, the gypsy boy was in my English class. He hadn't been here yesterday. Maybe he'd switched classes…or maybe he hadn't started yesterday after all. Mrs. Clanton said hello to him. She already knew his name. "Miguel, why don't you take the seat over there." She pointed in my direction. "Right behind Laura."

I swallowed a hard lump and my face reddened. He looked at me and even though his eyes were so dark I could barely see them, I saw the recognition in them. He remembered me from this morning. I could tell. He walked in front of the blackboard and turned down the aisle. I felt a strand of my hair loosen from the band of my ponytail when he walked past me. It fell down on my cheek as if it had a mind of its own. I caught Andrew Easton's eye. He was glaring at me. Or maybe it was at Miguel. I couldn't be sure. There was a coldness in his body language that had not been there before. I could hear and sense Miguel settling into the seat behind me. I heard the zipper of his book-bag opening. I could hear him take out a notebook and lay it on the desk. I heard the click of a pen. I wanted desperately to turn around and look at him but I was afraid. I didn't dare. And somehow, judging by the look in Andrew Easton's eyes, I knew he wouldn't like it either.

Somehow I got through English class though I never heard a word the teacher said. I had no idea if we had homework or a reading assignment or if we were ever even having English class again. Quite frankly, I wasn't even sure if American English was being spoken any more. Because in my mind, I was hearing British accents and Portuguese accents—although at this point I still hadn't heard a word out of the mouth of Miguel. For all I knew he was mute.

When the final bell rang I picked up my notebook and slid it into my backpack. I cautiously stood up and turned sideways. I saw Andrew stand and pick up his leather bag from the floor. He looked my way for a split second not letting his eyes linger. I dared to glance out of my peripheral vision to see what the gyp—*Miguel*–was doing. He was on his feet and waiting for me to move out of his way so he could get past me. I decided to look at him and maybe say hi. I didn't know where the urge was coming from but I really wanted to hear him speak. I was actually starting to feel a strange annoyance at the fact that this boy had not spoken a single word since I had first laid eyes on him. Granted, I hadn't been with him every second of the day and he had probably spoken many times away from me but…still…I found it maddening.

"Hi," I said. I think my voice cracked a little on the tiny word. *Oh my god. I hate myself.* I looked at him and tried to smile. I could feel my face reddening and I truly wished I would disappear into the floor.

He looked at me. I was close enough now to see that he did indeed have pupils in his dark eyes. I also saw stubble on his chin and upper lip and the hint of a five o'clock shadow on his jaw. My heart raced in my chest and I swear I felt the talisman shudder under my shirt. I lay my hand on my chest to calm my heart and the talisman, and decided I better just walk away. Maybe he really couldn't talk after all.

"Hello." Just one word. *Hello.* But a word, nonetheless. *The gypsy speaks*, I thought. I did hear an accent but it was subtle—so subtle as to be non-existent. His voice was deep and melodic—even with only one word I could tell. I wanted to hear more.

"Hi. I'm Gretchen Donovan. And you're…Miguel…?" Gretchen bumped me out of the way and smiled up at Miguel. "So, are you guys new in town?"

Holy cow. Gretchen was turning into Lily—acting pushy and forward. I closed my eyes in a slow blink and felt a charge in the atmosphere. He didn't answer immediately. He glanced across the room where Andrew Easton was taking a long time to get his bag over his shoulder. I could see one of his black-clad goons hovering outside the door waiting for him impatiently.

"Yes. I am Miguel Dos Santos. And yes, we are new here…sort of." He smiled slowly at Gretchen and then at me. His accent was hypnotic—subtle, refined. He sounded every bit as aristocratic as the prince with his posh accent.

"Sort of?" Gretchen asked, her eyebrows raised clear to her hairline.

"We moved here a couple of months ago. We've been here most of the summer." He stepped forward and we had to move out of his way out of the aisle so he could get by.

"Well, it's nice to meet you. I love your accent," said Gretchen. I couldn't believe it. What was wrong with her? It was like her mind had checked out and flown off to Mars.

He didn't seem to take offense. He smiled again and blinked a slow blink. "It's nice to meet you, too, Gretchen. And you as well, Laura. See you around." And with that, he walked across the classroom and out the door. As he passed Andrew, they eyed each other for the quickest of moments and then Andrew followed him out of the room. I hurried over to the door and stepped out into hallway but they were already gone—goons and all.

Gretchen chattered to me all the way through the halls and out the front doors to the parking lot where Lily was once again waiting for me. I immediately decided that tomorrow I would drive myself to school. I saw the prince's black cars drive away as Miguel and his brothers were getting into their Suburban. They drove out of the lot after the goon squad. At the end of the drive the English contingent turned to the right and the Portuguese group turned left.

"You getting in?" I didn't even realize that Lily was already in her car and had started the engine.

"Sorry." I hopped in and fastened my seatbelt. I felt weird… dizzy…not quite right.

"You wanna go to Newport Creamery for sundaes? Gretchen and Colin are going," Lily asked as she pulled out into the road.

"Actually I need to get home. I feel a headache coming on. Sorry, but I'll take a rain-check, OK?" All I wanted was to get home so I could be alone.

"Sure," Lily replied. She talked about the gypsies as she drove. I wondered who came up with the term gypsies? Were they really gypsies or was it just someone calling them that to demean them? I kept these questions to myself. In a few minutes Lily dropped me at my house on Topsail Road. I hopped out and grabbed my backpack.

"See you tomorrow. And, oh, Lil…I'm gonna drive myself tomorrow, OK?" I waved good-bye and watched her drive away.

I hurried into the house and stopped in the kitchen. Nick was sitting at the table drinking a Pepsi and reading the newspaper. He didn't even glance up when I walked in.

"Hey," I said. "What's up?" I grabbed a diet Pepsi from the fridge and looked for something to snack on. I saw the makings for turkey sandwiches on the counter near the sink and considered making one for myself.

"Not much. Just reading this article in the paper. Have you seen this?" He folded the paper back and pushed it across the table closer to me. He pointed to a headline that nearly made me choke on my diet Pepsi. It was just a short item—the headline was almost bigger than the actual article. Probably just enough information to satisfy people's curiosity and still preserve their privacy—the goon squad notwithstanding:

George I Branch of British Royal Family Moves to Portsmouth.

Several members of the British monarchy have settled on Aquidneck Island to foster relations between the sister cities of Portsmouth, Rhode Island, and Portsmouth, England. While here, Prince Ernst, Duke of Easton, and his wife, Duchess Beatrice, and their two children, Princes Tristan and Andrew, will be participating in local and state government, working with local businesses and Newport Hospital on health initiatives and engaging in local festivals, sporting and cultural events. The duke is a direct descendant of King George the First and is a member of the British royal family. It is not known how long the royals will be living in the area.

Holy crap. There were *two* of them? So Andrew had a brother. I wondered why I hadn't seen the other one at school. So this is why they were here. To foster relations? Wow. This is weird. I wondered where they were living. A family like that would be more inclined to live in one of the mansions in Newport. But then the princes would have to attend Newport schools, wouldn't they? So many damned questions.

"That's something, huh?" said Nick. "Can I have that back? I want to read the sports section."

I shuffled the pages and pulled out the sports section and handed it to him. I tucked the rest under my arm. Then something occurred to me.

"So…uh, Nick…? Have you seen the princes around town yet? Have you seen their ridiculous security goons?"

He laughed. "Like you could miss them. Actually the security people are very entertaining. You have to pass through their lame security before entering into the main hall at CCRI. Abigail beeps every time they wand her and it freaks her out. I love it! And that Tristan brother is a really nice guy. He's in my math class." He took a swig of Pepsi.

"You've met the brother?" I was astounded. "And what the hell is a member of the British royal family doing at podunk Community College of Rhode Island? Shouldn't he be going to Brown or somewhere prestigious like that?" This didn't make a lick of sense.

"Yeah, Tristan is actually at CCRI, but only for two classes. He told me his dad wanted him to go to Brown but he said—get this!—why waste money on an Ivy League education when he isn't planning to finish? Ha! Like he would even care about money to worry about the cost, right? So to please his dad he agreed to take a couple of classes at CCRI just for something to do. And I guess he got himself a job over at the polo grounds. I don't think he actually gets paid—it's not like he needs the money. He told me he's a horse lover like his cousin Zara. That's one royal I'd actually heard of—you know…Princess Anne's daughter."

"Wow. I had no idea you even knew who the British royal family was. I am impressed. And you had a conversation that long with this prince guy? Wow." Will wonders never cease.

"Yeah. We sit right next to each other. He's a cool dude." Nick drained the last of his Pepsi and sent the empty bottle sailing across the room into the recycle bin.

"Nice shot. Hey, where's Dad?" I asked.

"He's staying in Providence tonight. And Mom is going out with some friends after work so she'll be home later. We're on our own for dinner but I just had a turkey sandwich so don't worry about me." He grinned at me and winked.

"Right," I laughed. "But wait…Mom has *friends*? Since when?" Mom never went anywhere as far as I knew except to the bank, the grocery store and occasionally the beach.

"Apparently. Don't ask me, though. I don't know what's going on around here anymore."

I chugged the last of my diet Pepsi and said emphatically, "You can sure say that again." I heard him repeating himself as I headed up the stairs to my room. I would get something to eat later. Right now, I felt like I had a lot to think about and I needed the solitude of my room. I sat on my bed and pulled the talisman out from beneath its hiding place under my t-shirt. I turned it over and over in my hand and stared at it. It was so pretty…and mysterious. I closed my eyes and ruminated over the events of the day. And then I suddenly remembered what had been nagging at the back of my brain all day. It was something that the psychic had said…about my passport and where I was going: 'to the land of the gypsies.' I shuddered and felt my breath suddenly swoosh right out of my lungs…*gypsies*…

Chapter Four

THE BEACH

I couldn't sleep. I tossed and turned and watched the numbers on my bedside clock change slowly all night long. Finally sometime around four a.m. I fell into a deep slumber that was shattered at six o'clock when my alarm went off to the sounds of Adele singing about setting fire to the rain. I slammed my hand down on the snooze button and lay back against the pillow, exhausted. And then my stomach tensed and I sat straight up. Suddenly I couldn't wait to get to school. I hurried through a shower and blow dried my hair, pulling it back into a pony tail again. My blonde hair was sun-drenched from so much time at the beach: Gooseberry Beach and Easton's Beach. Wow. Andrew Easton. I wondered if that was a coincidence. One could only hope.

Nick was already up and eating toaster waffles drenched in maple syrup. Mom was standing with her back to the sink drinking a cup of coffee.

"Morning, honey," she said. "I feel like I never see you two anymore. How's school going?" She was asking both of us so I let Nick answer. He said something about the new people in town, referencing the article in yesterday's paper and then something about Abigail's upcoming birthday. When I didn't say anything, she prodded me.

"How about you, Laura? Is your senior year starting out on a high note?" She grinned over her coffee cup.

I sighed and nodded. "It's just peachy, Mom. Every day's a holiday. Every meal's a banquet. Every gathering's a parade. Every..." She cut me off with a laugh.

"OK! You're super thrilled to be back in school. I get it. Hey, I tucked the car keys into the outer pocket of your book-bag. I'm going to take a shower and get ready for work. You two have a good day. Love you both."

"You, too, Mom," we both said at the same time.

I went back upstairs and paced around in my room until it was time to leave. I checked my reflection in the mirror over my dresser and my hand automatically went up to my neck. The talisman wasn't there! Oh, it was hanging on my doorknob where I'd left it before getting into the shower. I placed it over my head and closed the round disc in my palm, feeling its smooth, cold weight. Then I tucked it into my blouse and bounded down the stairs. I couldn't wait to get to school.

It was a miracle! I was so early to school that I'd beaten the goon squad. Thank goodness. I parked my mom's green Jeep in the first space nearest the building. Only then did I wonder how Mom would get to work this morning. There were only about ten cars in the parking lot. I looked at my watch. Sheesh, I really *was* early. I'd have to be careful or I could get a reputation. I went inside and put my bag in my locker. I didn't want to go to my classroom yet but I didn't want to wander around the halls like a lost puppy either. I walked back to the front hall and pretended to study the main bulletin board, covered with notices about football games and Spanish Club and try-outs for the school musical. I nearly fainted when I saw that this year's musical was *Gypsy*. I had to blink hard and read the flyer again to make sure I wasn't imagining it. And then a bright yellow flyer at the far right end of the bulletin board caught my eye. I walked over to it and read it with interest.

Come Enjoy Portsmouth Polo Exhibition Matches Saturdays through September.

September 3: India vs. Spain

September 10: United States vs. England

September 17: Argentina vs. United Arab Emirates

September 24: England vs. Portugal
Glen Farm, Route 138.
Admission: $10; Gates open at 3 p.m.

"Good morning, Laura. You're early today."

I nearly jumped out of my skin at the sound of the voice so close to me. I turned, sucking in a deep breath.

"Oh. I didn't mean to startle you. So sorry." Andrew Easton looked down at me with a disarming smile. He was at least half a foot taller than I was. I had not been this close to him before and now I noticed for the first time how truly handsome he was. His hair was actually a darker blond that I'd thought originally and his lips were…nice. I felt my heart accelerate and my breathing threatened to stop altogether.

"It's OK. I didn't hear you." I looked around him to see where his 'protectors' were, but aside from some students arriving and teachers talking in the office, there didn't seem to be anyone paying much attention to us—no big men in black suits skulking around or waving magic wands. I saw a few girls give him the eye and big shiny smiles as they passed by us and I also saw their looks of apparent scorn thrown my way, but otherwise we were alone by the bulletin board.

"So where's your goon squad…oh, sorry…I meant to say your security detail?" I looked down and tried to suppress a grin.

He threw back his head and laughed heartily. "Goon squad! I love it. Sometimes I feel that way about them myself. They can be a bit… shall we say…intrusive."

"Ha. Well, that's one word for it. I mean…how do you stand it?" I shifted the weight of my bag on my shoulder and looked up at him. Oh, that accent…it was having an effect…I felt warmth seeping up my neck. Instinctively I touched my collar bone and felt the talisman nestled there under my top. His eyes followed my hand as I fingered the gold chain showing above the first button. He stared at my hand and I saw his eyes narrow. Then he looked at me strangely. I felt an unsettling blankness in my brain as if everything in it had just disappeared, never to be seen again.

"Well, actually, I've had seventeen years to get used to it so I don't really pay them much attention anymore—unless there's a need," he said.

For a moment I had no idea what he was talking about. Then I remembered we were talking about the snipermen. I was on the verge of a blonde moment and bit my lip to keep from saying something dumb. My brain wasn't working right. I was nervous and I had no reason to be. Some girls were suckers for a man in a uniform. But accents must have been my weakness.

I hesitated before asking my next question. "Is there...often a need? For their expertise, I mean?" The question was shifting into personal territory. I hoped I hadn't crossed any royal lines.

He looked over my head somewhere off down the hallway and sighed. "Not often, but sometimes...things happen." He looked like he was about to say something more but then the bell for first period rang and it was time to go. And I saw that the hallway was crowded. I hadn't even noticed the other students coming or going. I hadn't noticed noise or voices or anything at all...except Andrew Easton. I saw a hint of sadness wash over his face. He took a step backward, said, "I'll see you later then," and was gone.

I remained frozen next to the bulletin board and may very well have stayed there all day except that Lily and Gretchen ran over and greeted me exuberantly. We walked to our first period classes and planned to meet in the cafeteria at lunch time. I went into French class and sat in my usual spot. This was my favorite class and I excelled at it, but today I couldn't even remember what French sounded like.

Lunch was uneventful—for the most part. I had not seen Andrew Easton at all since this morning. And I had not seen any gypsies either. But Lily had.

"Those gypsy twins are smart. They're supposed to be like, sophomores, but they're taking senior level science. We had to do this dumb formula in chem class and they were the only ones who got it right. Would you have ever thought a gypsy would know anything about chemistry?" She talked around bites of her pizza.

My eyes widened in surprise. "Wow, Lily. Isn't that kind of harsh? Why can't a gypsy be good in science? And for that matter, why do you keep calling them gypsies? Isn't that kind of...racist or something?" I was actually getting a little heated on this topic but not sure at all why I would care. Well, I always did have a soft spot for the underdogs of this world. My protective side must be coming out. It could be the Sagittarian in me—we Sags had a serious thing for social justice.

"*I* didn't coin the term. That's what everyone calls them. I don't think it's meant to be discriminatory." Lily defended herself through more bites of pizza.

"Well, whatever they are…they sure are…hot," sighed Gretchen.

"Excuse me…but don't you have a boyfriend?" I teased Gretchen. "Maybe we should talk Colin's parents into moving to Portsmouth so he can go here and keep a closer eye on you. Middletown can find another quarterback for its football team."

I listened to them banter back and forth and when lunch was over we went our separate ways. I was counting down the minutes until English class. The funny thing was…I wasn't sure who I was more excited to see: the prince…or the gypsy.

As it turned out, English was a bust. Neither Andrew nor Miguel was in class. I felt bereft and just wanted it to be over. It seemed a little reckless to be absent from class already on only the third day of school. I even missed the sniper dudes a little bit. Wow. I really was losing it.

The next two days were more like normal. The goonies were back but not wanding people anymore. We could come and go normally and they stayed in the background—well, as much in the background as six hulking men in black could be. And Miguel was back in English class, too. He was quiet as usual. Always the last one in the class and when the bell rang he was out of his seat and out the door before any-one else had even moved. Andrew acknowledged my presence with a smile both days and sometimes I caught him staring at me but we didn't talk again.

I was happy it was Friday, the start of a three-day weekend—thank goodness for Labor Day. And I finally had an appointment with an eye doctor. Once and for all I was going to get to the bottom of my weird headaches. They weren't bad headaches, just a small annoyance—not the kind that cripple you like migraines, when you need darkness and silence and you feel like knives are stabbing your eyeballs. Mom had made the appointment for 4:30 after school today. She'd let me drive her car again so I could take myself there, which reminded me that I needed to ask her how she was getting to and from work every day. She certainly wasn't walking—it was at least four or five miles away.

School got out at 3:30 and even though it would only take a few minutes to drive to my appointment, I decided to head straight there rather than going home first. I figured I would stop at the little book-store down the street from the eye doctor and see if I could find any treasures to read in the waiting room. I drove north on highway 138, past the Red Rooster Vineyard and Winery and the polo fields. The day was overcast as the sun shifted in and out of the clouds. It was also hot and I considered turning on the AC but decided an open window was better. I rounded a sharp curve in the highway just as a large, black Suburban was pulling out of a hidden drive. I slowed for it and was now directly behind it. The windows were so dark I couldn't see any-thing inside but I thought I could make out at least three heads in there. The vehicle was driving the speed limit and I realized I was too close to it so I braked and held back a little. I studied the license plate for a second—just a normal Rhode Island license plate. I leaned forward and bent over the steering wheel to try to peer into the back window but it didn't help. Suddenly the Suburban slowed and pulled over to the side of the road. I slowed, too.

Now I had to pass them. Why had they pulled over? Were they having mechanical trouble? Was I supposed to stop and see if they needed help? My heart pounded as I drove slowly past them. I glanced out my passenger window and looked, for a millisecond, into the dark eyes of Miguel Dos Santos. His window was down and he was staring at me. He didn't smile or wave or anything—he just stared at me. I felt my mouth fall open in an 'o' and I gasped, stepping too hard on the gas. The Jeep jerked forward and it scared me. I calmed myself and slowed the car and continued on down the road. Behind me I saw the Suburban make a U-turn and disappear from view.

I pulled up in front of The Red Door Book Store and sat there. A few customers browsed idly inside. I had intended to go in, but I couldn't move. I couldn't figure out why the sight of Miguel Dos Santos had me so unnerved. Between him and the damned prince I was going to go crazy. And I had no idea why. After a few minutes in the car I decided to forgo the bookstore and get to my appointment. Maybe they could see me early.

An hour later, with a prescription for eyeglasses in hand, I headed for home. Great. I needed glasses. Wasn't that just fabulous. I guess I would go eyeglass shopping tomorrow. And then I remembered my other weekend plans. Lily and I were going to the beach tomorrow. Gooseberry Beach—my favorite beach on Aquidneck Island.

As I drove past the hidden drive where I had seen the Suburban emerge earlier, I slowed the Jeep and stared down the drive. It was endless. All I could see were tall pine trees down both sides. I couldn't see a house or any sign of life at all. I wouldn't have even guessed there was a house back there. Come to think of it, there wasn't even a mailbox on the highway indicating that anybody lived back there. Weird.

I drove home and was surprised to see that my father had returned from Providence or sailing or wherever the hell he was these days. I pulled the Jeep into the driveway and parked next to his Toyota and sighed. I hoped it was going to be a quiet evening. I knew my parents were talking divorce but they didn't act like a divorcing couple. I didn't understand them. Now that I was thinking about it, there was a lot I didn't understand these days. I sighed again and went inside.

I finally found out how my mother was getting to work every day. She was being picked up by the manager of First Federal Bank of Rhode Island, where she worked as a loan officer. I had met Mr. Aldean a few times when I'd visited Mom at work but I'd never given him a second thought. But apparently my mother had. He drove up to our house at 8:30 Saturday morning and she seemed in a big hurry to join him in his fancy Land Rover. And what really made it weird was seeing my dad walk out to the car with her and greet him like they were the best of friends. I saw them shake hands and talk a minute and then he stood back and waved as they drove away. Back in the house, Dad helped himself to a piece of bacon off of my plate and patted me on the head, acting if everything were totally normal.

"Hey baby. What're you up to today?" he asked. He poured himself a glass of orange juice from the carafe on the counter and drank it in one long gulp.

"Going to the beach with Lily," I sipped my juice and glanced over at him."What are you up to today?" I asked. "Going sailing again?"

"Yep. I'm meeting Tim and Ed down in Newport. We're taking Tim's new boat out today—the maiden voyage of the *Lonely Lady*. Can't wait." He refilled his glass of OJ and came over and joined me at the table." Hey, where's your brother?"

"No idea. He probably spent the night at Crabigail's."

Dad laughed. "Ha! Yeah, she is a piece of work, isn't she? That relationship's a mystery if I ever saw one."

I cleared my throat. "Uh...so is yours...and Mom's." The words came out quietly. I hoped I wasn't opening a huge can of worms here.

Surprisingly Dad laughed. "Oh, honey. There's no mystery there. I love your mother, but like we told you and Nick before, we've just grown apart. There are no hard feelings on either side. I know I've been spending a lot of time in Providence working a lot, and when I'm home, I'm sailing. And I know I need to spend more time with you and Nick. But you guys are teenagers and I know how teens like their privacy. I certainly don't want to cramp your style. And you know if you need me all you have to do is call."

"But...is she dating...her boss...Mr. Aldean? Are *you* dating someone else? I mean what are your rules with each other? Anything goes?" I was confused and not entirely happy with their modern take on marriage.

"I don't know...maybe she is," he replied. He stood up from the table and put his glass in the sink. "But, Laura, if she is, I'm OK with it. Really. If she's happy, I'm happy. Now, my dear, I've got a boat to christen. See you later." And with that, he was out the door and gone.

"Wow." I said aloud to the vase of gerbera daisies in the middle of the table. "Love how you didn't answer the rest of my questions. Have fun sailing."

I put all of the breakfast dishes in the dishwasher and ran upstairs to put on my swimsuit and pack a beach bag. I contemplated my new necklace in the mirror. It didn't seem like a good idea to wear it to the beach where it could get lost, and I wasn't sure if salt water would hurt it, so I decided it would be better to leave it at home. I placed it gently in the top drawer of my nightstand and reached under my bed for a pair of flip-flops. I slipped them on and headed down to the Jeep. Lily had originally planned to pick me up but I'd called her last night and told her I would meet her at Gooseberry Beach. I needed to run an errand first. I figured I may as well stop at Middletown Optical and order myself some new specs. Yippee.

Well, that wasn't so bad, I decided. I'd ordered the glasses—cute, smallish, navy blue plastic frames, and they would be ready for pick-up next week. And now I was pulling into the mostly empty parking lot of Gooseberry Beach. I didn't see Lily's car anywhere so I waited in the Jeep and listened to a Coldplay CD to pass the time. Fifteen minutes passed and still no Lily. I checked my cell phone and there were no messages or texts. What was keeping her? No one loved the beach more than Lily and it wasn't like her to be late. I waited another five minutes and then decided I would go on down to the water and find a nice spot to spread out.

It was a bit of a hike from the parking lot to the water's edge—a round-about sort of hike around a huge mound of rocks that towered way over my head. This rocky outpost was part of the inlet that formed Gooseberry Beach in Newport. It was situated off Ocean Drive and was a peaceful secluded beach away from the mass of tourists who preferred bigger areas for sunbathing and swimming. As a matter of fact, most tourists didn't even know it existed. Today I was pleasantly surprised to see only one other family, a mom and her two kids splashing in the shallow water. A couple of hundred yards or so from the rocky beach was a little island. You could walk to it—the water never got more than waist high—but there were rocks of all sizes between the shore and the island and it was slow going. I'd been over there a lot with friends over the years, just hanging out and enjoying the tranquility. It helped to wear water shoes to protect your feet from the sharpness of the rocks.

I spread my big beach towel out on the sand and was just about to plop down on it when my phone pinged. It was a text from Lily: *Sorry, can't make it. Mom slipped in the driveway and may have a broken ankle. We're at the ER now. Call you later.*

Bummer. I sat down and looked around. I watched the mom and her kids playing in the water and debated whether to go back home or stay for awhile. I texted a response to Lily wishing her mother well and then decided I would go back home. But when I heard the mom tell her kids it was time to go home for lunch and naptime I changed my mind. If she and her tots were leaving, who was I to miss out on having my favorite beach spot all to myself for a while? This was too good to be true. They gathered their blanket, towels and toys and left the beach to me. I pulled out *The Prince and the Pauper* from my tote bag (I'd brought it along just in case I felt like being a responsible student) and dropped it next to my feet. I sat with my knees pulled up to my chest, my arms wrapped around them and stared out at the beautiful water. The view of the ocean was partially obstructed here because of the large rock formations and the little stony island just offshore, but I could see around it enough to admire the gorgeous ocean. The sun was darting in and out of clouds and the waves were wild. It almost looked like a storm might be coming. It was warm though and that was nice. I hoped my dad was safe out there in these choppy waters. I was enjoying the peacefulness and thinking how much I didn't feel like reading after all, when a movement to my right caught my eye. I slowly turned my head but I didn't see anything at first. I felt a sudden rush of goosebumps forming along my arms. And then I saw it again—a flash of black at the top of the rocks. My breath caught in my throat and I felt a hammering in my chest. I wasn't alone out here.

I tried to remain calm. I slowly pulled my cell phone from my bag and slid it closer to my body. I didn't know who I was going to call or if I even needed to call someone but it felt like the right thing to do. I stared up at the rocks and contemplated making a run for it when the black figure appeared again at the top of the rocks. It was one of the goons.

Holy crap, I thought. *What the hell are they doing here?* My heart was racing and I wasn't sure if I should acknowledge them, leave the beach entirely or just mind my own business. I had every right to be here and they had better not even think about asking me to leave. If they did, I would call my Congressman. I wasn't sure who that was but I would Google it when I got home and find out. They'd be sorry they ever messed with me—again.

And then around the side of the rock formation walked his royal highness Prince Andrew. To say I was shocked to see him here was an understatement. I felt self-conscious all of a sudden and very glad I still had on my shorts and tank top hiding my pink one-piece. I would hate to be seen in a bathing suit by a member of the royal family even if he was a gazillion times removed from the top of the royal food chain.

"Hello, Laura. Fancy meeting you here," he said in his lovely posh accent. He walked slowly through the sand toward me. He was wearing khaki shorts that came to his knees and a dark gray t-shirt advertising a rock band I'd vaguely heard of. Was it normal for princes to wear shorts—and flip-flops? Wow. This seemed unusual. "May I join you?" he asked.

"Uh…sure," I replied nervously. I hoped he couldn't hear the uptick in heartbeats coming from my chest. It was ridiculous to feel this weird every time he was near. I was sure I wouldn't react this way internally if he were just a normal every-day boy. The whole royal thing was rather unsettling. "What brings you to this part of town?" I asked him as he joined me on the blanket. He sat Indian-style to my left with his body turned partially toward me.

"Actually, I live near here." He pointed over his shoulder somewhere past the sniper man seated on top of the rocks behind us. "It's not very far. We walked here."

"I see you brought your goon squad with you." I couldn't resist the jab. These guys really annoyed me—seriously—this was overkill.

He laughed. "Yes, just a couple of them. That's Peter up there. I think you met him the other day."

"Ah, yes, Peter." I turned toward him and waved. "Hi, Peter!" I yelled loudly. He nodded his head in acknowledgment and then turned his attention elsewhere. To Andrew I said, "Sorry—I couldn't resist."

He chuckled. "It's OK. You probably made his day." He hesitated a moment and spoke again. "It's a nice surprise seeing you here today. Unexpected."

"This is my favorite beach actually. But…did you say you lived near here? In Newport?"

"Yes. Just a little way up the road."

"But…if you live in Newport, how can you be in the Portsmouth school system? You generally have to attend the school in the town you live in. I think it's a law or something."

A look of embarrassment washed over his face. "Well, the houses were unsuitable in Portsmouth so my father thought Newport would be better." He looked down and stuck his long fingers in the sand and twirled them in a circular pattern.

To say that his words offended me was an understatement. I was not quite sure how to respond or even if I could without losing my temper. But I knew I couldn't let this go. "By unsuitable, do you mean too small? Do you mean not 'mansion' enough?" My tone was borderline rude but I couldn't help it. This was ridiculous and so…elitist!

Andrew looked out toward the island. "Please don't misunderstand, Laura. I think the homes in Portsmouth are quite lovely. But I didn't have a say in where we live. It was my father's decision and he is a bit of a…" He didn't finish the statement. "What I mean to say is… please, Laura, don't judge us…me." His voice sounded so sad that I immediately felt a stab of guilt in my conscience.

"I'm sorry," I said. "But you're right. There are lovely homes in Portsmouth. And Newport, too." I decided I would let him off the hook this time. I guess it was obvious that when you were royal you could break rules that we civilians wouldn't ever dream of challenging. So he lived in Newport and attended school in Portsmouth. I guess that wasn't such a crime after all.

We sat in silence for a few minutes as a thousand questions ran through my head, but I didn't want to be nosy or annoying so I kept my mouth shut and waited for him to break the silence.

"So, tell me, Laura Calder, tell me your life story." He looked at me with something in his eyes I couldn't read. He knew my last name. My goose-bumps came back and my heart did its weird thud thing again. I became acutely aware of his nearness to me, noticing the fine hair on his legs and arms and the curve of his jaw. He had a full lower lip and a thinner upper one and his nose was long and straight—but not too long—it was just right. His eyes were the color of Newport Bay when the sun was shining—not cloudy like today. And so I told him about my life. My parents and their weird marriage and my brother and his nasty girlfriend. I even told him I was getting glasses. I was amazed at how easy he was to talk to. And he was a good listener. He only interrupted me occasionally for clarification about something I'd said. After a while I decided I'd been talking way too much and I stopped. I bumped his arm with my elbow and smiled. "OK, Prince Charming. Your turn."

He grinned and leaned back on the blanket and put his hands behind his head for a pillow. I remained upright and turned slightly toward him and waited for him to speak.

"Well, there's really not much to say," he started. I immediately burst into laughter.

"You're hilarious! Not much to say? Other than you're a descendant of George the First and the Queen is your…something or other… there's not much to say? Awesome! I love it!" I couldn't help myself. This was too much.

"OK, OK. So maybe I do have a colorful history and an interesting and somewhat well-known family—I'll give you that. But for the purpose of being here in Rhode Island in America, I'm just Andrew Easton. I have an older brother named Tristan who is crazy about horses and a sweet and loving mother and a rather domineering father. I'm sure he means well. Oh, and I'm a Scorpio if that tells you anything—November 12th." He sat up and looked at me. I saw him glance at my chest and I felt self-conscious. Was he checking me out?

"You're not wearing the necklace." He looked so serious all of a sudden.

"The necklace?" I knew what he meant but the way he said it made me suspicious.

He cleared his throat and glanced out at the water for a moment, then back at me. "I noticed you've been wearing a gold chain. It looks nice on you. You should always wear it. It matches the gold in your hair."

Wow. So he'd noticed my hair, too? I didn't know what to make of that. But I couldn't pass up this opportunity to get clarification on this talisman thing that I'd supposedly dropped. I knew there was more to this and now was my chance to find out. I was just about to ask him about the gold coin/talisman/amulet—whatever it was—when we were interrupted by Sniperman Peter.

"Andrew. We have to go now. We have to get you to the polo field." The goon was standing nearby and looking down at us.

"I'm sorry. I've got to go. But I'll see you Monday, yes?" Andrew stood up and stepped off the blanket.

"No. Monday's a holiday in this country. You'll see me Tuesday." I started to get up and he held his hand down to me. I looked up and hesitated briefly and then put my hand in his. It was big and warm and…nice. I felt a rush of heat wash over me. He didn't let go of my hand immediately after I got to my feet. He continued to hold it for what was only a couple of seconds but seemed much longer than that. Then he gave it a gentle squeeze and let it go.

"Right then, until Tuesday." He said it so quietly I barely heard him. And then he turned and walked toward the rocks and disappeared. I didn't realize I'd been holding my breath until it suddenly came out in a puff. I put my hand to my chest and felt my heart pounding. And I suddenly had the urge to hurry home and put my necklace back on. I needed to feel its weight and comfort around my neck. I gathered my things and headed back to the Jeep and home.

C h a p t e r   F i v e

DAПGER

With my talisman back around my neck, I felt a strange sense of security. I was in my room staring out the window thinking I should do some math homework but I wasn't really feeling math at the moment. I was thinking about Andrew Easton. There was something sad about him—and a sense of innocence about him, too. I was also thinking about how cute he was.

"Get a grip, Laura," I scolded myself. I sat down at my desk and pulled out my laptop. While I waited for it to boot up, I dashed downstairs to get a piece of the cake that Mom had made earlier in the day—she always liked to bake goodies on the weekends. I brought the lemon cake and a glass of iced tea up to my room and ate several bites and took a long pull on the iced tea. I set the plate and glass down and opened up Internet Explorer thinking I would Google some stuff for my history class but then another idea popped into my head. I ran back downstairs to Dad's study. I knew he had a magnifying glass somewhere—I'd seen him use it when he was studying nautical maps for fun. I found it easily enough under a pile of papers on top of his desk and took it with me back to my room.

I sat down at my desk and removed the chain from around my neck. My desk was by the window and with the afternoon sun streaming in, coupled with the lighted magnifier, it was easy enough to see previously unnoticed details on the round gold disk. I opened the clasp and slipped the disk off the chain and then turned the talisman over and over in my hands, feeling its weight and coolness. I could feel the grooves from the symbols as I studied the side with the crossed swords first. The swords, slightly raised, were long, reaching almost to the edges of the circle. Around the perimeter were inscribed some letters in a foreign language—I was guessing Latin or maybe even Greek, but I wasn't sure. I grabbed a pen and a piece of paper from a spiral notebook and copied down the letters. Then I went to a translation engine on the Internet and held my breath as I waited for the results. It took only a second. Seven words appeared on the screen:

Royal Birth—Gypsy Death—In Darkness, Light

I couldn't breathe. My hands began to shake. I felt like I was hyperventilating. What does this mean? A feeling of dread snaked its way through my body. I closed my hand around the talisman and squeezed it tightly. After a few seconds I exhaled and opened my hand. I turned the coin over and studied the other side under the magnifier, which revealed a symbol that looked like a coat of arms—it had a crown at the top and an X shape under it with five small shields on the X, each of which was inset with five tiny circles. There were two sets of numbers on this side of the coin—one set above the coat of arms and one set beneath it. I studied the numbers with great interest.

121219931
031220122

My stomach seized. I felt a pounding in my head that aspirin could not cure. The taste of bile rose in my throat. I pushed back my chair roughly, knocking it into my bed. I dashed to the bathroom across the hall and shoved the door shut as I knelt before the toilet and vomited the lemon cake and iced tea. I wiped my mouth with toilet paper and stood up shakily. I looked in the mirror and barely recognized my own face. Beads of sweat covered my forehead and I was pale under my summer tan. I gripped the sides of the sink and concentrated on getting my breathing under control. When I felt like I could move again, I walked on shaky legs back to my room and put my chair back in front of the desk. I forced myself to look at the numbers again under the magnifier. There was no doubt. No doubt in my mind that the first set of numbers was my birth date followed by the number one. And that left no doubt as to the meaning of the other set of numbers. I was going to die on March 12, 2012. But what was the significance of the number two after my date of death? I closed my eyes and then suddenly opened them again. Two. I would not die alone. Two would die. But who would die with me?

I spent the rest of the day and Sunday in my room pretending to do homework. Both Lily and Gretchen called and texted about going to the mall or a movie. Lily was done with her mom-sitting duty, now that her mother was getting around OK on her crutches and she wanted to hang out, but I didn't feel like I'd be good company. I begged off with a different excuse each time they asked—headache, stomach-ache, toothache. I loved my two best friends, but luckily they were too self-absorbed to notice that I was blowing them off.

As the time passed, my emotions ran the gamut from fear to flat-out ambivalence. I finally convinced myself that those damned numbers on the gold coin thing were nothing but that—just numbers. I could not believe that I had made myself sick over a necklace! I must be losing it. Ha! Maybe I really had a head problem after all—a tumor growing at the speed of sound. Any minute I would keel over. I actually felt foolish for thinking that those numbers referred to my birth and death dates. Wow. Talk about an overactive imagination.

I became studious and read *The Prince and the Pauper* all the way through to the end. It was actually pretty good. I even finished the rest of my homework and by Monday afternoon I was antsy and itching to get out of the house. Mom was on the back deck reading and Dad was off sailing again. I assumed Nick was at Abigail's. I asked Mom if I could use her Jeep to go to Barnes and Noble in Middletown and she didn't even look up from her book. She just waved toward the hook on the kitchen wall where we kept spare keys and I grabbed them and dashed out of the house.

As much as I loved going to Barnes and Noble—I could *live* there— I didn't really want to go there today. I had been thinking about Andrew Easton a lot this weekend and I was considering driving into Newport back near Gooseberry Beach to see if I could spot a goon on patrol and thereby figure out which mansion he was calling home. But…and this was a big one…I actually was more curious about something else. I don't know why I felt compelled to drive back down the road where I saw the black Suburban, but something was pulling me there.

I drove slowly along the north-bound highway. For a holiday, the traffic was surprisingly light. I had the road virtually to myself. Much of the highway was lined on either side by trees—a mix of tall pines and leafy trees—some of which I was horrified to notice, were starting to change ever so slightly into their autumn colors—just the merest hint of yellow fading into green around the edges here and there. I shook my head at that. I wasn't ready for cold weather. Every so often there would be a break in the trees and a house would appear or an antique shop. I passed a florist shop and a convenience store. As I neared the area where I thought the hidden drive was, I slowed even more. I wasn't really worried about getting caught. The chance of any of the gypsies being out and about at this exact moment was slim to none. I slowed my car and hugged the side of the road as I neared the entrance to their drive. I looked down it and saw absolutely nothing. Just an endless row of trees into which the drive curved slightly and disappeared. *Well, isn't this anti-climactic*, I thought. I suddenly felt stupid. What did I think I would find here? More to the point, what was I looking for?

I pulled back onto the road and headed into Portsmouth's main square. I saw an empty parking spot in front of Skippy's Old-Fashioned Ice Cream stand and decided to indulge myself. It wouldn't be long before Skippy's would be closed for the season so I'd better get my fix while I could. I parked and walked up to the window. When my turn came I ordered a cappuccino chocolate chunk cone and sat on a picnic bench to eat it. I watched traffic go by—back and forth on the highway—and I realized that I was watching for it—the black Suburban. I sighed and questioned my sanity. I pulled my necklace out from under my t-shirt and turned the disk round and round in my fingers as I continued to stare out at the road. Every so often the sunlight glanced upon the disk and I noticed that the crossed swords seemed to glow, throwing intermittent rainbows of light beams into the air around me. It was pretty and hypnotic—a little girl at the table next to mine couldn't take her eyes off of it. I smiled at her and then dropped the necklace back down my shirt where it belonged.

I finished my cone, tossed my napkin into the trash can, and got back in the Jeep. Enrique Iglesias was singing about heroes on the radio so I turned it up and sang along as I headed back toward home. Once again, I glanced down the hidden drive as I passed but there was nothing to see. I drove on and as I neared the 7-Eleven, I decided to stop for a drink. There was only one other car there and it was at the pump getting gas, though its driver was nowhere to be seen. I parked in the spot at the corner of the store and hopped out of the Jeep. The store's door made a jingling sound when I entered. I didn't see anyone inside, not even the clerk who was usually seated behind the counter. I had been in this store many times over the years and I had seen lots of employees come and go. But at the moment there didn't seem to be a single soul in the place. I walked over to the far wall where the refrigerated cases were located and perused the many beverage choices. I coughed and even faked a sneeze thinking that if I made enough noise the clerk would hear me and come out of the back room or the bathroom or wherever he or she was.

I heard the door jingle again—another customer was coming in. *Good*, I thought. *At least I'm not alone in here now.* I opened the refrigerator containing the Fanta products and selected an orange pop. I sincerely hoped the clerk would show up—I was actually starting to get a little worried and I was really thirsty. I turned toward the front of the store and saw the other customer. It was none other than Miguel Dos Santos standing just inside the door. But he didn't look right. I froze in place. I stared at his face and the expression on it frightened me. Suddenly, without warning, he charged toward me as if to attack, just as a strong arm clamped around me from behind and dragged me backward. I felt my knees buckle and I started to slump against whoever was holding me so tightly that it was hurting to breathe. A hand smelling of gasoline came around in a flash and covered my mouth before I could muster a scream. *What was happening?* I tried to twist away but the man—I could tell it was a man now—held me too tightly. I turned wild eyes toward Miguel who had his hands up as if in surrender. Then he spoke.

"Let her go," he said. I watched as he seemed to inch slowly toward me. But there were at least three aisles of merchandise between us. I didn't see how he could get to me in time. "You don't want to hurt her."

"Shut up, gypsy!" the man yelled. His face was so close to mine that I could smell his beer breath and feel the brush of his stubble across my temple. "And stay back. I didn't come here to hurt nobody but nobody ever listens. And stand still. I see you moving. Stop it!"

The man removed his hand from my mouth for a moment, long enough for me to take a gasping breath. I was about to yell or beg for mercy—I wasn't sure what words would come out of my mouth, when he whispered in my ear. "Don't make a sound. No screams. I don't want to have to hurt you." I felt him digging into the waistband of his pants reaching for something. I saw Miguel watching him, his expression dark. The man clamped his hand back over my mouth and pressed down.

I didn't understand why Miguel didn't make a run for the guy. He didn't have a weapon. I decided right then that I was going to fight back and get away on my own. The man wasn't expecting me to try anything so I was sure I had the element of surprise on my side. Just as I was about to elbow the guy, I heard Miguel say, "Put the knife down. You don't want to do this. She's an innocent girl—let her go." And then I saw the knife as it came slowly up to the side of my face. I gasped and shook with fright as a damned tear slid out of the corner of my eye. His arm squeezed tighter around my body and I felt dizzy with fear.

"You, gypsy boy—get over here." I felt the man jerk his head in the direction of the stockroom. "Slowly." I was frozen with fear. I could see the tip of the knife in my peripheral vision and for a moment I had the distinct feeling that this could be it—the end of my life.

I watched as Miguel slowly made his way around the end of the candy aisle toward us. As he walked, his eyes darted back and forth between me and the robber. I felt the knife point touch my temple and I gave another muffled cry under the man's stinking hand. My knees were buckling. I was going down, I could feel it. I was going to faint. The man jerked me up to prevent me from falling. His arm was pressing so tightly against me that I thought my chest would crack. He looked down over my shoulder and whispered ominously, "what's this?" I felt his knife hand slip under the collar of my t-shirt and I let out a muffled protest and tried to thrash away from him. His arm tightened around me even more. Using the tip of the knife he lifted the chain up from my collar bone and ran the knife along the chain, lifting it from my chest. He saw the golden coin dangling there and made a sniggering sound in his throat. "Nice," he said, and gave the chain a hard yank with the knife. It snapped, digging into my neck, as the coin broke free and flew across the aisle, rolling to a stop near Miguel's feet. Miguel acted like he didn't even notice.

"Please," said Miguel softly. His eyes never left the robber's hand, which was now back against my cheek, the knife lightly touching my jaw. I could feel its cold hardness and I was afraid that if Miguel tried anything, the man would not hesitate to plunge it into my face. Miguel tried again. "Let her go. You can have me. She didn't do anything to you—let her go."

His pleading was quiet and intense. He continued to move in careful, deliberate steps toward us. Just as he came to within ten feet of the robber, a muffled sound came from the stockroom. It was just enough of a surprise to cause the robber to lose his focus for a split second. And that was all Miguel needed.

"*Move, Laura*!" he screamed as he lunged for the man, knocking the knife out of his hand and knocking me to the floor in the process. The knife flew back against a refrigerated case full of milk and eggs, colliding with enough force to crack the glass. I slammed into a row of shelves and a display of canned goods fell on top of me. I struggled to my hands and knees and crawled through the cans toward the door. I searched my pocket for my cell phone to call for help and realized that, like an idiot, I had left it on the passenger seat of my car.

Miguel was on top of the man now and they were wrestling and cursing. Merchandise was falling off the shelves, littering the floor. The man tried to throw a punch but Miguel blocked it and clocked him in the face. I heard a cracking noise and blood spurted from the robber's nose and he fell back in a heap and stopped struggling. Miguel was on top of him again and kept him in a tight hold as he looked over his shoulder at me. "Laura! Kick the knife away—it's too close!"

I scrambled to my feet and gave the knife a swift kick. It slid to the back of the store far out of the robber's reach. "I'll call for help—my phone's in my car." The words came out of my mouth in a whispered rush.

"No—just take mine. It's in my back pocket." I saw the shape his phone made in the pocket of his jeans. I reached in and pulled it out. I was so nervous, though, that just dialing 911 seemed nearly impossible. My hands were shaking so badly that I couldn't push the correct numbers. I got it wrong the first time and had to dial again.

"It's OK, Laura. Just breathe," Miguel said. He continued to restrain the robber who was trying hard to break away from Miguel's strong grasp.

I nodded and leaned back against the shelves across from him and sank to the floor. The dispatcher answered and I yelped into the phone. "Police, please! At the 7-Eleven in Portsmouth—there's been a robbery. Please hurry!" My words came out in a jumble. I wasn't even sure that I'd said the right thing to make help come. The dispatcher asked me some questions and assured me that officers were on the way.

The man tried again to break free of Miguel's strong arms. He nearly rolled them both over in his effort to get out from under Miguel's hold. "Let me up, gypsy boy. You broke my nose, you son of a...," and just as the robber jerked his knee up into Miguel's hip, he hit him again. The robber went silent.

Another sound came from the back—a muffled whimper. I was still holding the phone, not sure if the dispatcher was still on the line. In the distance I could hear the sirens.

"Laura—go check on the clerk—in the backroom," Miguel ordered. I nodded and ran to the stock room and found the clerk tied up and propped against boxes of paper towels. It was one of my classmates—Scotty Jameson.

"Scotty! Are you alright?" I cried. I put Miguel's phone in my pocket and untied Scotty as he struggled to get up. He shook out his legs and hands to get the circulation flowing again. He paced around the stacks of paper towels and cleaning products in a frantic march.

"Did he get away? Did you call the cops?" Scotty was going into shock, if he wasn't there already. We ran back into the main part of the store where Miguel was still holding down the robber. At that moment I saw two squad cars fly into the parking lot. The cops emerged from their vehicles with their weapons drawn. I felt afraid all over again.

Scotty was snapping out of it and he was getting mad. He stalked toward Miguel and the robber and looked like he wanted a piece of the guy himself.

"Don't do it," said Miguel. "Just let the cops know it's OK to come inside. I've got him."

Scotty hesitated. Clearly he wanted to get in a punch of his own on the criminal's face, but he obeyed Miguel, nodded, and then turned toward the windows to wave the cops inside. Four of them came in quickly and within seconds they had relieved Miguel of his burden and proceeded to place the man under arrest.

I was still standing near the stockroom door, feeling suddenly weak. I slid down the wall to the floor and felt the jab of Miguel's phone in my thigh as I hit the floor. I pulled the phone out of my pocket and then covered my face with my hands. Miguel came over, slipped the phone into his pocket, and then I felt his arms circle around me. My shoulders shook and I tried to subdue my sobs.

"Shh," he whispered. "It's over. You're safe now." I leaned into him and pressed my face against his chest. He rubbed my back softly and comforted me until I felt myself begin to calm and my breathing started to return to normal. His chest was hard and I felt so small in his arms. I could smell his skin—it smelled like pine. And I could not believe that after all we had just been through that I would even notice such a detail as his scent or his touch.

A police officer walked over and began to question us. We both gave statements and provided them with our contact information. Scotty also gave a statement. Miguel showed the officers where the knife had landed when I kicked it out of the robber's way. We watched as they collected evidence and took the criminal away. They had Scotty call his boss to tell him what had happened and they told him he had to close the store down for the rest of the day. I was afraid the policeman questioning me would make me call my parents and I was so relieved when it didn't come up. No sense freaking them out before it was necessary.

After what seemed like forever, we were all allowed to leave. Miguel and I walked out together while Scotty went about his locking-up procedures.

Miguel walked me to the Jeep. His Suburban was parked just on the other side of it. My mind was racing with confused thoughts—about what had just happened and Miguel's bravery. I had so much to say and I didn't know how to start. But he spoke first.

"I'm sorry," he said. He stared over my head toward the highway. I heard him sigh.

His words surprised me. "*You're* sorry? You saved my life—and Scotty's!" I said. I reached out and touched his arm. I wanted him to look at me.

He gave me a half-smile. "I'm sorry I knocked you down. I only had the one moment and I didn't want to miss it." He sounded…torn up over it. I noticed that his accent was more pronounced now.

"It's OK. I'm fine." I saw him look down to where my hand was still on his arm and I felt embarrassed. I dropped my arm to my side. "Thank you."

"I would say it was my pleasure, but actually…it wasn't." He smiled at me, the most disarming smile.

I couldn't help but emit a quiet chuckle at his words. And then something occurred to me. "Did he hurt you—that guy?" I studied his face and hands checking for obvious injuries.

Miguel shook his head. "No. Look at me…not a scratch," he smiled again. Then he put his hand in his pocket and pulled something out—my coin and the broken chain. I gasped.

"My necklace! Thank goodness he didn't steal it. And thank you— again. I guess I forgot about it in all the—drama." I reached for it and he placed it in my hand and I felt him curl my fingers around it and squeeze tightly, as if to make sure I had a firm hold of it.

"Your chain's broken. You'll need a new one…but make sure it's stronger so it can't break," he advised, almost pleadingly.

I nodded. "I will," I promised. I realized that his hand was still enveloping mine. My pulse quickened. He let go of my hand and cleared his throat, then took a step back.

"Are you going to be OK to drive home? Because in a few minutes this is going to hit you hard and you could go into shock." He sounded genuinely concerned.

"I'll be fine…if you'll be fine," I said, hoping it would be true.

"Well, that's a deal then," he said. And without warning, he suddenly pulled me into his arms and held me close for just a moment. Then he whispered, "Be safe, Laura."

And with those words, he got into his Suburban and drove away. I climbed into my car and headed for home. In spite of the late summer heat, I felt goose-bumps rising on my arms. My stomach was in knots and I felt like I couldn't breathe. I had just witnessed a convenience store robbery. And now I had to go home and tell my parents. It would probably make the police blotter in the local paper and possibly the evening news so it wasn't like I could keep it a secret. But beyond all that, something had passed between me and Miguel Dos Santos. I didn't know what it was or if it even meant anything. But it was something— and that was what was on my mind when I tried to sleep that night.

Chapter Six

FIRST DATE

Stories were spreading like wildfire around the school on Tuesday. I couldn't believe the outrageous versions of what my fellow students thought had happened at the 7-Eleven. I heard that I had stabbed a man and put him in intensive care in Newport Hospital. I heard that I was in a coma and not expected to live. I heard that Scotty Jameson had robbed his own store in a desperate plea for attention. I even heard that Miguel Dos Santos had robbed a convenience store and thanks to me I'd saved Scotty Jameson's life from the evil gypsy boy. That one hurt. And it made me mad.

"I wish people would just shut the hell up already," I complained to Lily as I pulled some textbooks out of my locker. I hated all this attention and the obvious lies.

"But you must have been out of your mind with fright!" Lily was practically hyperventilating. "I knew those gypsies were trouble—it must have been so awful for you." She actually looked scared for me even though she sounded like she wished she'd been there, too, for the thrill of it.

I was close to exploding. "Miguel Dos Santos saved my life—and Scotty's, too. He did nothing wrong. If it hadn't been for him, then some of the stupid rumors going around school might be true. Now if it's all the same to you and everyone else, I don't want to talk about it anymore." With that, I stalked off to science where I had the misfortune of having to hear Scotty brag about his bravery to the class and

85

how he helped saved the day. He caught my nasty glare and immediately shut his mouth.

I was keenly aware that though the goon squad was here, roaming about in the hallways, I still had not seen Andrew. Nor had I seen Miguel. I hoped that wherever he was, he was OK and not suffering from post-traumatic stress disorder. I didn't have to worry about suffering from any long-term effects of the robbery myself because my mother was taking care of that for me. When I told her what had happened she nearly stroked out. My father went so far as to call the police station to get more information and to make sure the guy was really in jail and not getting out any time soon. Of course, Nick thought it was the coolest thing ever. For a kid in college, he could be so immature sometimes.

Finally it was last period and as usual, my stomach tied itself into knots as I walked there with Gretchen chattering beside me. I rounded the corner and saw Andrew standing outside the door, one of his henchmen standing a few feet away, pretending to be invisible.

"Laura!" he cried. "What happened? I've been hearing awful rumors all day." The look of concern in his eyes was touching. He stepped closer to me and put his hand on my arm.

I told him the quick version of the story. When I mentioned Miguel's name, he stiffened.

"Yes, I heard that Dos Santos happened to be in the shop. Lucky break for you," he said. I thought I heard an air of contempt in his voice—but maybe it was just jealousy that he hadn't been the one to 'save' me. "In any case, I'm glad you're safe," he smiled.

"Thanks," I said and returned his smile. We walked into the classroom and he took his usual seat in the first row and I walked to the far side of the room to my own. I felt apprehension in my gut, wondering if Miguel would show. I hadn't seen him or his brothers all day. And then, right on cue, entering the classroom one second before Mrs. Clanton, came Miguel. He kept his eyes down as he crossed the room and took his seat behind me without so much as giving me a second glance. I heard his book-bag thud softly onto the floor and his chair creak as he settled into it. My heart was beating so hard I feared the whole class could feel the vibrations. I took a deep breath, slowly turned in my seat and looked at him. His eyes met mine but he did not smile. His face had no expression. I tried to smile but my facial muscles wouldn't work. I croaked out a soft "hello," to which he responded in kind and then he opened his copy of *The Prince and the Pauper* and proceeded to ignore me. I turned back in my seat and felt my face redden. I saw Andrew shift in his seat out of the corner of my eye so I stole a glance his way to see if he was looking at me. But he wasn't. He was looking at Miguel. His eyes looked menacing. I shuddered and prayed that this class would end quickly so I could go home.

The rest of the week sped by in a blur and I was happy to have it over. Miguel had proceeded to ignore me all week and Andrew continued to be his sweet but quirky self. Whenever Miguel was anywhere near, Andrew acted cold and distant but when Miguel was not around all seemed well in his world. I was beginning to wonder if they knew each other outside of school but decided that was impossible. Wouldn't I have seen them talking or something? I had tried a couple of times to talk to Miguel before and after class, and though he was polite, he didn't say much. I couldn't for the life of me figure out why he was acting this way. It bothered me but I knew there was nothing I could do about it, short of confronting him after school. But he always disappeared so fast that it was like he hadn't even been there.

After English class on Friday, Andrew walked with me and Gretchen to the parking lot with his security following along behind us like little puppies. It was so silly—those guys following him around everywhere—and so unnecessary. Andrew had settled in nicely to the school and no one even seemed to care anymore that he was a royal. The girls still flirted mercilessly and a few brave guys were often seen trying to chat him up in the halls, but he kept a cool distance from everyone, though he was always polite and congenial. Only with me did he ever talk at length. And when we exited the school and walked out into the sunshine he stopped me before I could walk down to my car. I waved good-bye to Gretchen and turned to Andrew. We were standing next to one of his fancy cars. He looked…nervous. I waited and waited and was just about to say something—anything—to break the silence when he beat me to the punch.

"Laura." He said my name through a puff of nerves—I could tell he was suddenly uncomfortable. "I was wondering if you would do me the honor of going on a date with me tomorrow night?"

I raised my eyebrows and smiled slowly. So the prince was asking out the commoner, huh? Wow. I kept that thought to myself and answered him without hesitation. "I would love to. What did you have in mind?" I felt my stomach begin a series of flip flops that threatened to make me swoon. Of all the girls at Portsmouth High School, somehow the prince was asking *me* out on a date. How utterly absurd.

"Have you ever been to a polo match?" he asked.

"Actually I have, but not in a long time," I answered. "My brother thought polo would be fun but unfortunately he found out he was allergic to horses so he tried jai alai instead. That lasted about a week. Now he surfs." I suddenly had a case of 'too much irrelevant information.' "What I mean is, when he played, my mom made me watch."

"Ooh. It sounds like polo isn't your cup of tea then," he said, looking a little dejected.

"Oh, no! It isn't that. I would love to go. It might be nice to see it played by professionals."

"Well, I thought we would watch the match and then perhaps go to dinner in Newport. There's a restaurant there my family has discovered and we've fallen in love with it. Maybe you've eaten there. It's called the Dancing Pony Club...?"

I was not expecting him to say that one. The Dancing Pony Club. Wow. "Uh, yeah, I've heard of it. But I've never been there. You have to be a *member* to go there. I'm quite sure they won't let me in." Now I felt embarrassment creeping in. The Dancing Pony Club? Really? I made fun of that place. Any place of exclusivity made me gag in disgust. But I kept that thought to myself. I was quite sure that his royal highness had spent his entire life dining in exclusive establishments.

"Of course they'll let you in. You will be my guest...unless...you would prefer to go elsewhere?"

The tone of his voice made him sound open to a different option. I personally couldn't bear the thought of being seen anywhere near The Dancing Pony Club. So I made a suggestion. "How about the Brick Alley Pub?"

"A pub? Oh, yes! I love a good pub. Let's go there then, shall we?" He seemed excited so I was glad I'd made the suggestion.

We set a time for him to pick me up and when I reached into my bag to get a piece of paper and a pen to write down my address, he stopped me.

"No need, Laura. I already know where you live. I'll pick you up at three o'clock for the match and then dinner after. Does that sound good for you?" He looked so darned earnest that I had to bite my lip to keep from cracking up.

I kept a poker face and did not even act like I'd heard what he'd said just before telling me he would pick me up at three. I agreed and we said good-bye before he drove off in his fancy car with his goons. I walked to the Jeep and climbed inside and sat there astounded. He already knew where I lived? Really? I didn't even dare think what that might mean. I started the car and headed for home.

Gretchen was giving me advice on what to wear on a date with a prince—as if she were an expert in the field.

"I've read enough *People* magazines about Prince Harry to know that there is a certain look for a polo match," she said, perusing my wardrobe, which consisted mostly of t-shirts and jeans. "Do you have any hats?"

I raised an eyebrow at her in disbelief. "Really? Hats? You mean like a fascinator? Oh, yeah, that sounds awesome!" I screwed up my face into a gleeful contortion.

"Seriously? You'd wear a hat to the polo match?" Gretchen was impressed.

"Of course—I will get right on the hat bandwagon—just as soon as hell freezes over." I shook my head at her. "Gretchen! This isn't the Kentucky Derby. Did you really think I would be caught dead in a…*hat*!?!"

"Well, I would totally wear one if I were going out with a prince," she sighed exasperatedly.

We finally found something suitable that didn't seem like it would be too out of place for polo. I would wear a pair of khaki dress pants and a navy blue blouse with a pair of cute taupe peep-toe sandals. As a concession for not wearing anything on my head, I let Gretchen paint my toenails a lovely shade of pink. As she was giving me the once-over she commented on my new piece of jewelry.

"That's a pretty medallion you have there. Is it new? Where'd you get it?" She leaned closer and reached out as if to touch it. Instinctively I moved backward a tiny bit and grasped the disk in my hand. I felt very protective of it and it didn't feel right for anyone else to touch it besides me.

"I…uh…sort of found it. It's just some fake coin and I put it on a new chain that I bought at Casey's Jeweler's this morning. Oh, hey! Did I show you my new glasses?" I turned around to my dresser and hoped Gretchen wouldn't notice the abrupt change in subject. I had no idea why I didn't want to talk about my necklace but I didn't question my feelings on the matter. I turned around and grinned at Gretchen, striking a pose. "What do you think?" My new navy blue specs were perched on the end of my nose. "Do I look like a major librarian now or what?" I laughed.

She laughed, too, and said I looked sexy, so I accepted her ringing endorsement and pushed my glasses into place and succumbed to having my fingernails painted as well. Then we discussed the pros and cons of my wearing my hair up or down.

"Definitely down," said Gretchen. "When he zooms in for the good-night kiss, he's gonna need something to grab onto—may as well be a handful of your silky blonde tresses—well…unless…you'd rather it be something else." I saw the wicked grin on her face and shrieked.

"Gretchen! You little tart! Bite your tongue!" I laughed. "Princes don't behave that way!" I tried to act disgusted but it was actually rather funny.

"Oh, Laura! You need to read more magazines and watch *E!* TV. Those royals are a randy bunch of savages!" She had a knowing look on her face—probably from years of reading *Us Weekly*.

I shook my head at her and laughed. I seriously doubted I would have to fend off Prince Andrew. He struck me as being the model of decorum.

Gretchen left around two o'clock and I began a nervous pacing around my room. As usual, my father wasn't home. He said he was sailing but could someone really sail that much? I wondered if maybe he was the one having a 'relationship' and not Mom. A little before three o'clock I went downstairs to wait for Andrew. Mom was in the living room pretending to read but I knew she was waiting to meet the prince. I had told her about Andrew and she was nothing short of impressed. I had a feeling she was looking at me and seeing Kate Middleton's face.

I saw two black cars coming up the street. I sighed in frustration. "Looks like he brought the goon squad as usual," I muttered.

"The goon squad?" Mom questioned. "You mean a chauffeur?" She looked puzzled.

I gave her a half-grin. "Something like that."

A few moments later, the doorbell rang. I answered it, keenly aware of my mother hovering somewhere behind me. There at the door was Andrew looking very dapper in dark pants, a dress shirt and tie. I immediately felt embarrassment at my choice of outfit.

"Hi, Andrew," I said a little breathlessly. "You look…very handsome and…I think I'm under-dressed!" My words came out in a nervous rush.

He said hello and leaned toward me, planting a kiss on each cheek, European style. "No, no. You look perfect just as you are." He suddenly reached for his tie. "Will it make you feel better if I lose the tie? I almost didn't wear one to begin with." He untied the knot and left it loose around his neck. I saw my mother smile and nod.

"That *is* better—it makes you look more relaxed," I said approvingly.

I introduced him to my mother and sent a silent prayer to the gods of discretion that she wouldn't say anything we would both regret later. But she didn't and Andrew was very gracious with her. I said good-bye to her and we headed to the cars. One of the goons standing by the first car opened the door for me and said, "Good afternoon, miss." I smiled in greeting.

It was a short drive to the polo field and we were there in only a few minutes. On the way, Andrew and I talked about inconsequential things like school and sports. He told me that his brother Tristan would be playing in the match. I was surprised to notice that the butterflies I had been feeling while waiting for Andrew to arrive, quickly disappeared once we were in the car. I felt very comfortable with him and even the security guys didn't rattle me too much. It was actually easy to forget they were even there.

Once at the field, the car was waved through the gates and we entered a parking area reserved for VIP's. I felt a knot form in my stomach at the thought that someone from school could be here and see me getting out of the fancy car with the prince. I had the feeling that it would mark me in some way as being superior and haughty and I would hate that. But since what other people chose to think was totally out of my control, I let the worry go and planned to enjoy myself... until we got to our seats.

One of the security men led us to the stands where we were taken to a private area away from other spectators. *Uh, oh*, I thought. *Here we go with the special treatment.*

A distinguished-looking couple and a boatload of new goonies that I had never seen before were in the stands. The woman waved excitedly at us and we went up the steps to join them. Andrew whispered to me from behind that I was about to meet his parents.

He put his hand at the small of my back as we climbed the last few steps. Once on the viewing platform, he made the introductions. I shook their hands and hoped that they couldn't feel how badly mine were shaking. Andrew's mother seemed sweet and she was quite lovely. But his father, the duke, scared me a little.

"Andrew. Nice of you to come cheer on your brother. And, Laura... it is Laura, yes?" I nodded and he continued. "Thank you for coming. If there is anything you need let one of my detail know. They will be happy to oblige." His words were friendly enough but the way he said them was less than sincere. I saw him give me the once over, too, though I didn't think Andrew had noticed.

"Andrew. Can I speak to you for a moment...alone?" he asked, giving me the quickest of glances.

"Excuse me, Laura. I'll be right back," Andrew said, giving me a smile that didn't reach his eyes. He and his father walked away toward the end of the viewing section where a mini bar had been set up to cater to the VIPS. They spoke for a few moments and I tried not to pay attention to their evidently tense conversation. When Andrew returned his face looked pinched and I could tell that his father had said something to anger him. I was sure it was about me. He dropped the frown and sat down by me and handed me a program about the upcoming match.

The duke seated himself at the end of the aisle with a drink in hand. Andrew's mother leaned over and asked me questions about my family and school. Soon the match began. I felt a little awkward about the match because it was England versus the United States. I had the strangest feeling that this date could be good or bad depending on who won. I personally didn't care one way or the other but I knew royals took their polo seriously.

Once the game was underway, Andrew pointed out his brother, Tristan. I could tell he was as tall as Andrew even though he was on horseback. I could see blond curls billowing out from under his hat. The novelty of the sport made it interesting to me—for about the first half hour. And then it was just a bunch of men riding horses and hitting a ball with sticks. Andrew tried to keep me informed as to what was happening and he spouted some terms like 'ride-off' and 'hooking' but it was all Greek to me. Every so often something would happen on the field that angered the duke and he would yell and curse like a mad-man. Andrew tried hard to ignore him—he even made a joke about his father's polo temper but no matter how you cut it, it was awkward.

Andrew went to the bar and brought us back Cokes. The game continued and after about two hours give or take, it was over. The United States had won. And the duke was not happy. He was yelling and swearing and making such a spectacle of himself that one of his own security guards even tried to calm him. The duchess looked stricken and said a hasty good-bye to Andrew and me and asked one of the goonies to take her to the car. Andrew took my hand and led me away from his father's tirade down to the car park. I was absolutely astounded at his father's behavior. I had never seen anyone act like that, not even two-year olds I'd babysat in the past.

Once inside the car, Andrew turned to me, embarrassed, his face pale. "I am so sorry you had to see that. I should have known something like this would happen. Father had placed a large bet on the match and if there is one thing about my father, it is that he hates to lose at *anything*. I am truly sorry and I sincerely hope you won't hold his actions against me."

I reached over and took his hand. It was trembling. I was keenly aware that the driver was listening—I saw him look at me in the rear-view mirror and I felt annoyed by the intrusion. "It's OK, Andrew. These things happen. Some people take their sports a little too seriously. Of course I would never hold that against you."

He squeezed my hand gently and I felt him relax. "You're very kind. As it happens, my father takes *everything* seriously. I don't think he has any joy in his life." He turned my hand over in his and rubbed his thumb gently across my palm. My heart's pace picked up and my friends, the goose-bumps, returned immediately. I felt a dizziness setting in. I saw the driver's eyes in the rearview mirror again and I noticed his expressionless face. *It's like they're some kind of robots*, I thought.

"Does the driver know where we're going?" I asked.

"Yes, but, I was thinking…it's a little early for dinner. Would you like to come to my house for a little while before we go to the pub?"

I hesitated. If it meant running into the duke I'd just as soon not. Andrew picked up on my hesitation and guessed correctly what had precipitated it.

"Don't worry, Laura. My parents won't be there. They're having dinner at one of the mansions tonight. But my brother will be there eventually and I would love for you to meet him." He stopped rubbing my palm but held onto my hand with both of his as if it were a lifeline.

"Alright then—sounds good," I agreed. I had not expected to see where the royals were making their home so this would be a bonus. He leaned forward and told the driver to go to the house. The driver nodded. "Yes, sir," he said. Really, this formality and subservience were almost more than I could stand.

We drove through Middletown, on into Newport, and entered Ocean Drive. The sun was just beginning to set and the colors on the horizon were turning a soft peachy pink. The ocean was dotted with a smattering of sailboats and the waves crashed upon the rocky coast. We drove a couple of miles and passed the entrance to Gooseberry Beach. About a quarter-mile after the beach, we turned right into a long driveway. I could see the house sitting atop a hill. It was white with black trim and it was huge. Lights were blazing from nearly every window. "Looks like someone's home," I said glancing at Andrew.

"Not really," he said. "Just the staff." He let go of my hand and we got out of the car and walked up the steps to the double-wide front doors. As we reached the top step, the door suddenly opened. I saw a woman—a maid, perhaps—dressed in black and white, standing behind the door, her hand on the knob.

"Good evening, Prince Andrew," she spoke quietly, dipping ever so slightly in a curtsy.

"Hello, Jane," he said. "How are you this evening?"

"Fine, thank you," she smiled at him. Andrew introduced me to her and I offered my hand in greeting. She seemed surprised by my gesture but took my hand and shook it limply. "Shall I have Robert get you and your guest some refreshments, sir?"

"Nothing for me. Laura, would you like something to eat or drink?"

"No, thanks. I'll wait till we get to Brick Alley. But thank you," I directed my thanks to Jane. I finally took a moment to take in the decor. We were in a front hallway lined with long narrow tables along each wall. I could see into the rooms to my right and left—they were both lined with books and I thought I could be happy living in those two rooms alone.

"Come, Laura, let me take you on a tour," Andrew took my hand again and we walked from room to room, each one more beautiful and austere than the next. The living room, which Andrew called a salon, was decorated with dark cherry bookcases, heavy pine end tables and Tiffany lamps. The sofas were narrow but appeared over-stuffed and seemed very formal. They didn't look like the kind of couch you could lay on and eat popcorn while watching a movie. And then I noticed there was no TV in here so forget about watching a movie—maybe their entertainment was conducted elsewhere in the house. The dark draperies were heavy but pulled back to bring in the views. The kitchen was huge and there were people in there doing some kind of prep work. Andrew asked me again if I would like a drink but I declined. We walked back to the main hall just in time to see Jane opening the front door. A tall blond boy walked in carrying a large gym bag. A security guy came in behind him carrying another large bag.

"Tristan!" Andrew walked over to him and clapped him on the back, grinning wickedly. "So…the match…it didn't go exactly according to plan, eh?"

"You don't say," said Tristan, looking at me. "Hello," he said.

"Hi." I was about to introduce myself but Andrew cut in. "Tristan, this is Laura Calder. We have English class together."

"Nice to meet you," he said, proffering his hand which I shook firmly. "Your country killed us today." He grinned sheepishly.

I laughed. "I'm sorry about that. Maybe you can ask for a rematch or something." I wondered if I should feel badly about England's loss.

Tristan shrugged and his grin suddenly disappeared. He turned to Andrew. "I suppose Father didn't take our loss well." It was more a statement than a question.

"Unfortunately, no," Andrew replied. "But what else is new." The brothers talked a moment more and then Tristan ran up the stairs. At the top he stopped and looked down over the railing. "It was nice to meet you, Laura," and with that, he waved and disappeared down the hall.

"I'd take you upstairs but it's just a bunch of bedrooms and bathrooms. And I'm feeling a bit famished. Shall we head over to the pub now?" Andrew asked, suddenly in a hurry.

"Ready when you are," I said. And without his having to say a word, a goony appeared out of nowhere and opened the door and followed us out to the car.

"How do they *do* that? Just appear like that?" I whispered as we settled into the car. "Are they even real people? No offense intended, I promise."

Andrew nodded and I could tell he was suppressing a laugh. "Ha, ha…they're real…and very intuitive—most of the time."

In the car, Andrew sat closer to me. It was getting quite dark now and I could feel his presence in every one of my pores. And again my heart threatened to burst out of my chest cavity. I decided that dating a prince was hazardous to my health. We talked quietly about favorite foods—I didn't even know how the subject came up—and soon we arrived at the pub. Andrew leaned forward toward the driver and touched his shoulder. "I would prefer that Laura and I go into the restaurant alone. You can come back in a couple of hours. We'll meet you out front here at the corner. I don't need any…help… tonight." The driver nodded and we exited the car. Andrew took my hand again and we walked into the crowded pub. I wondered what he'd meant when he'd said 'help' but I didn't feel right asking him to explain.

We put our name on the waitlist—I used my name—and we were told it would be thirty to forty-five minutes for a table. Andrew was shocked.

"Did she say we have to wait forty-five minutes for a table?" he asked incredulous. "I'm sure we can do something about that." He started to approach the hostess but I grabbed his arm and stopped him.

"No!" I whispered. "It wouldn't be fair to the others who were here before us. We have the time…don't we? Or are you in a hurry?" I was a little peeved that he would use his name to help us jump the line and I think it showed in my tone.

Andrew looked sheepish. "I'm sorry. You're right. There is absolutely no hurry at all." We sat on a bench by the front windows talking while we waited. Every so often one of the security guys would walk past the windows and pretend not to look inside. A few people stared at Andrew with familiarity in their eyes but aside from a few classmates who came over and said hello, no one seemed to pay us much attention. I was thankful for that.

Finally we were seated and given menus. Andrew was amazed at the menu. I didn't think this was quite the kind of pub he was expecting—not like a typical London pub anyway. We ordered an appetizer of spinach-artichoke dip and tortilla chips and sodas. The restaurant was very crowded and noisy but I loved the atmosphere. Andrew was impressed by the large television screens near the bar playing sports on all the channels. We both ordered steaks and potatoes—French fries for him and a baked potato for me. As we ate I realized how hungry I actually was. He said he loved the food and asked if I wanted dessert.

"Ah…I would love some…but I can't eat another bite," I leaned back in my chair and sighed. It was a testament to how comfortable Andrew made me feel that I could eat as much as I did on a first date. The waitress brought the check and Andrew paid with a platinum credit card. I thanked him profusely for the meal and also the polo match. We walked through the crowded restaurant and out into the night. I was surprised to feel that the heat of the September day had turned to a chilly evening and shivered.

"Cold?" Andrew asked. He stepped closer and put his arm around my shoulders. We walked to the corner where the car would meet us and he kept his arm around me and rubbed the length of my arm for warmth. I saw his car coming down the street. And I saw another familiar looking car behind it. My breath caught in my throat. I looked at the Suburban but the windows were too dark to see inside even under the street lamp. Andrew's car pulled up and he opened the door for me. As I stepped into the back of the car I glanced backward at the driver of the Suburban behind us and was certain it was Miguel behind the wheel. And perplexingly, I felt a massive stab of guilt cut through me.

We drove out of downtown and headed toward the water. I couldn't resist turning around once to glance out the back window. But there was no one behind us—just the dark road. I saw the driver staring at me in the rearview mirror and I felt embarrassed as if he had caught me stealing. Andrew was talking about boats or something nautical beside me but I wasn't concentrating. I realized I was being rude, though Andrew hadn't noticed, and so I gave him my full attention. Then I started to ponder the whole goodnight kiss thing and wondered if or how it would happen considering we weren't alone. Once we arrived in my driveway where my house was dark except for the porch light, the car stopped and idled. I saw Andrew make eye contact with the driver and then a button was pushed and suddenly a dark screen that separated the front seat from the back seat closed with a quiet hum leaving us alone.

"Whoa," I whispered. "Slick," I grinned in the darkness. Andrew scooted closer to me and took my hand.

"Don't worry. He is very discreet. He can't hear us and it's too dark to see—if it were daylight…maybe."

He turned his body toward me and reached up and touched my hair. "I'm glad you're wearing your hair down tonight. It's beautiful." His fingers tangled themselves gently in it and he looked at me with something akin to desire in his eyes. I felt the familiar tingling and shivered. I sent a silent thank you to Gretchen for suggesting I wear it down tonight instead of in my signature pony tail.

"Laura," he whispered. "May I kiss you?" he asked politely. As he asked he leaned ever so slowly toward me.

I gulped. "Yes, you may," I could barely get the words out. He closed the distance between us and his lips touched mine softly. His hand came up and caressed my cheek. I kissed him back tentatively, not sure if there was some sort of royal kissing protocol I should be following. He shifted his body closer and put his arms around me and pulled me into his chest. A slight gasp escaped from me as his kissed deepened. It was tender and sweet and I felt that swooning feeling again. He stopped for a moment and leaned back the slightest bit so he could look into my eyes.

"You are very beautiful, you know that, right?" He smiled at me, his eyes twinkling in the tiny bit of moonlight that filtered through the window. "So beautiful." He glanced down at my neck where the new chain of my necklace was visible in the V of my blouse. "You're wearing the talisman."

I leaned back and stared at him. "Talisman? How did you know it was a talisman?" I put my hand over my heart and felt the outline of the coin under my blouse. Andrew dropped his arms away from me and glanced out the window. After a moment he turned back to me and claimed my hand again.

"Well, I saw you drop it, remember? And I've seen you wearing it at school. The chain is nice."

"Thanks. It's new. The other one broke during that robbery at the convenience store." I watched him carefully as I said this, gauging his reaction. His face was unreadable. I half expected him to ask me to show him the whole necklace but he let the subject drop. I was just about to ask him if he had really seen me drop it that day at school when I heard a sound from the front of the car.

"Uh, oh." I said. "Is that a hint that it's time to go home?" I felt a blush of embarrassment high on my cheeks.

Andrew put his arms around me again and pulled me close. "No, don't mind him. But I should let you get to bed. I had a fantastic time tonight, Laura, and I hope you'll go out with me again."

"I would love to. And thanks—for the polo and the dinner and the company and everything." I turned my face to him and he kissed me again. His lips were soft and the kiss tender. And this time I noticed that he smelled so amazing—like the ocean mixed with a citrusy aftershave. He held me tightly and kissed me one more time and then we got out of the car and we walked to my front door. He waited to make sure I was safely inside, then he waved and got back in his car and he and the goony drove off into the night. I stood at the window in my darkened living room and watched the car disappear. Just as I was about to turn from the window to go upstairs to my room, I saw a big black car drive past my house. It looked like a Chevy Suburban. I shivered and flipped off the porch light and dashed quietly up the stairs.

Chapter   Seven

THREATS

A new pattern quickly developed at school. Andrew became a constant presence in my life. Every morning he—and at least one bodyguard—were waiting for me at school. We even had a special meeting place. It was near the north entrance doors closer to where my locker was located, nearer to where the school backed up into the woods behind it. He would be leaning against the brick building, one foot up behind him, planted on the wall, his book-bag usually on the ground beside him. He was devilishly handsome and now my every morning began with heart palpitations—a new friend to join the goose-bumps that seemed to live on my skin no matter what the temperature was. I was definitely in full-blown crush mode.

Andrew walked me to every one of my classes even when his class was at the opposite end of the building. And when class was over, he was always there waiting for me. And after English we always walked out together to the parking lot where his car would be waiting with Sniperman Peter at the wheel. My friends were being very patient with me. They didn't hold it against me that my head was in the clouds most of the time. I was fairly sure their patience was down to their both having visions of a royal wedding in their heads and hoping they would both get their Pippa Middleton moment in the sun. And one day, Andrew offered to pick me up for school in the morning and that was the end of driving myself. My mom got her car back and I rode to school in style—whether I liked that aspect of it or not.

But in spite of my happiness from growing closer to Andrew, there was always something nagging at the back of my mind. I was worried about Miguel. He came to school every day as normal, and though he was always polite, he kept his distance from me. I'd thought that we had somehow formed a bond that day of the robbery, but he acted as if it had never happened—that he had not saved my life. And though I didn't want to admit it to myself, his aloofness was hurting my feelings.

This afternoon Andrew seemed especially different. He seemed fidgety as if he had a lot of excess energy that needed to be expended. I asked him if he was OK.

"Fine, yes. I, uh…was wondering if you would have dinner with me tonight. I know of a place—and don't worry—you don't have to be a member to eat there. As a matter of fact, I think you'll like it—you've probably even been there before—it's in Middletown. It's called Joe's Clam Shack."

I laughed. "Oh, yes, I know it. Would you believe I used to work there? Last summer I tried my hand at waitressing there and it was a total disaster. I didn't last through the end of June." I blushed at the memory of that nightmare.

He laughed, too. "Well, alright then. So it's a date?"

We agreed that he would pick me up at six o'clock and we would have a stroll on the beach after dinner. He dropped me off at home, promising to return in a couple of hours. I was really wishing he would leave his 'friends' at home so we could do something alone just once but I figured that would never happen in a million years.

Nick was home, in the kitchen talking on his cell phone—to Abigail, I assumed. He hung up quickly when I walked in the room. I saw the serious look on his face and immediately felt a tensing in my gut. "What?" I asked, afraid of what he was going to say.

"Hey…I've been waiting for you. I want to tell you something kinda crazy." He swigged from a can of Pepsi and kicked the chair out next to him so I could sit down.

I remained standing though I felt a strange dizziness coming on. "Is something wrong with Mom? Dad? Are they going ahead with the divorce?" My stomach churned with worry. But if this was finally it and they were breaking up, it could be a good thing in the end—for everyone. I tried to convince myself of this as I waited for Nick to speak.

"No, as far as I know, Mom and Dad are still as weird as ever. This is about the royals. I know you and the prin…*Andrew*…have been spending a lot of time together…which is fine and all, but something happened today and I just thought you should know." He had a weird look on his face and it made my uneasiness even more pronounced. "I saw something…well, heard something…kinda freaky at school. And maybe it doesn't mean a damned thing but in any case I thought you'd want to know."

"Spit it out, Nicholas. You're giving me a stomachache already!" I cried. I finally sank into the chair beside him, just in case whatever he was about to tell me didn't sit well with me and my suddenly weak stomach.

"Well, you know how I told you that Tristan, Andrew's older brother, takes a couple of classes at CCRI. I still can't figure that out—seriously—the kid's rich enough to go anywhere—Brown, RISD, whatever…"

"Focus, Nick. Come on." My patience was wearing thin.

"So anyway, I was in the library today trying to study for a quiz and I was sitting in one of the carrels. I was way in the back and I thought I was alone back there but then I heard a British accent and realized that Tristan was somewhere nearby. I looked around and saw just the back of his head in another carrel near me. I was close enough that I could hear his conversation—his side of it anyway. It kind of freaked me out."

As much as I didn't think I really wanted to know, I had to ask. "What did you hear?" I closed my eyes for a brief second and then looked at Nick. I don't know why I was so sure that I was going to hear something bad but I was convinced that it couldn't be good.

Nick continued. "I heard Tristan say over and over, 'I won't do it. I won't do it. It's not fair. If this means so much to you, you do it.' It was something like that. Then a few seconds later he said—and this is the part that really freaked me out—'if you try to make me do this I'll kill myself. I mean it, Father. I will.' Then he was quiet for a minute or so—listening, I guess, to the duke—and I heard him whisper, 'don't you dare put this on Andrew. I don't care what the decree says—if you're so hell bent on carrying out this damned vendetta then be a man and do it yourself.' Then he hung up. He moved his chair back and I hurried up and buried my face in my book. And then he walked right past me and didn't even seem to notice I was there—I don't know how he didn't see me—and I swear I saw tears on his face. It was the freakiest damned thing ever." He stopped and finished the last of his Pepsi, then crushed the empty can in his hand.

I didn't say anything for a minute. I sat stone cold still and tried to make sense of his words. Then I thought that maybe Nick had misheard. "Are you sure that's what he said? That he would kill himself?"

"I mean, I may not have told you everything word for word, but it's close enough that I didn't tell you anything wrong. And, yes, he definitely threatened to kill himself. My question is, should we do something about this? Seriously—we hear all these stories on the news about people—teens especially—crying out for help and no one helps them and then they go and off themselves. I don't want that on my conscience. I told you before he's actually a cool guy. Somewhat obsessed with horses, but whatever—to each his own, I guess."

I didn't know what to make of this. It seemed like a personal issue and I wasn't sure if we should interfere with a...royal...problem. "I mean, come on, Nick. Kids threaten to do all kinds of crazy things when they're upset with their parents. You know that. I don't think he really meant it."

"Well, maybe you should talk to Andrew next time you see him and try to feel him out about Tristan—you know—just to be safe." He was so damned troubled by this that I was actually touched. Who knew my brother had a heart?

"I'm going to be seeing Andrew in a couple of hours—we're going to Joe's Clam Shack for dinner. If I can find a way to broach the subject without seeming nosy, I will." That was the best I felt I could do. As close as my relationship with Andrew was becoming, I still didn't feel like I could pry into his family matters. I thought of his father, the duke, and suddenly it didn't seem so shocking that Tristan would be upset by something the duke wanted him to do. From my limited exposure to him, the man seemed like a tyrant of the highest order.

I squeezed Nick's arm, told him I'd see him later and then headed upstairs to my room. I sat on my bed and thought about what Nick had told me about Tristan. It was troubling for sure. He couldn't possibly mean it—that he would kill himself—there couldn't be anything so bad that it would be worth committing suicide over. Was there? No... that was just absurd.

I pulled out the talisman and stared at it. What was it about this thing that made me feel…different? I still felt there was a connection between it and Andrew but I was too afraid to bring it up. And then I remembered Miguel's telling me to get a stronger chain for it—which I had—and wondered about that, too. I considered taking it off and leaving it at home tonight just to see if my mood would somehow be different without it, but when I took it off, I actually felt bare and… bereft. As it was, I only took it off for showers and when I slept at night. And though the chain was visible above my neckline, I always kept it tucked down inside my shirt, near my heart, for safekeeping. I remembered the definition of a talisman: *anything whose presence exercises a remarkable or powerful influence on human feelings or actions* and thought to myself, *well, isn't that the truth!*

A few minutes before six, I heard a ping on my phone–a text from Andrew. We had started texting each other now and he often sent me messages throughout the day—just funny things that happened at school or something he thought I would get a kick out of. And sometimes he texted me just to tell me he missed me. It was sweet and it always had the desired effect on me—swooning and dizziness often set in. This text said that they'd just left his house and would be here soon to pick me up. I noticed the word 'they' and sighed deeply. Just once I wish the world would open up and swallow the entire goon squad. They were so…redundant.

When we arrived at Joe's Clam Shack, I was shocked to learn that the security dudes were dropping us off for the evening. As in, letting us out and then driving away. "So they're not going to hang around outside and pretend to be invisible? Which, by the way, they're not always good at, you should know." I sounded a little cocky but I just couldn't help myself.

"You are so funny, Laura. I gave Peter instructions not to come until I called him." Andrew grabbed my hand and we walked inside the restaurant. I was surprised to see that it wasn't as crowded as usual, but then again, summer was officially over so business would die down with the departure of the tourists. We were seated right away at a corner table by the front windows, which offered a spectacular view of the beach and the wild Atlantic Ocean across the street. The weather had been overcast and misty earlier today but now it was cloudy and cool, and the sun, what could be seen of it, was casting beautiful colors of lavender and pink on the horizon. We placed our orders—fish and chips for Andrew and the shrimp basket and onion rings for me, which caused Andrew to laugh at me.

"What's so funny about onion rings?" I asked, obviously not getting the joke.

"Well, am I going to be tasting them later?" he asked, a mischievous glint in his eye.

I felt my face redden. "Oops." I stifled a giggle. "So you're saying there could be a problem with my breath, huh?"

"Well, if you share them with me we can call it a draw—how about that?" The waitress brought our drinks then and we turned our attention for a moment to the view of the ocean. It was quite spectacular. Then I remembered something.

"Andrew! Did you know that the name of that beach over there—" I pointed across the street toward the water, "is Easton's Beach?"

He glanced toward the beach and nodded. "Actually, I did. I doubt there's any connection to my family but it's nice to think I have my own beach. After dinner I'll let you walk on it, if you want." He gave me a wink. Our dinner arrived and he immediately reached for one of my onion rings. "May I?" he asked.

"By all means," I responded. His sharing of my onion rings signified that a kiss was coming later and I was totally alright with that. My stomach flipped at the thought. I had to be careful about thinking of being in Andrew's arms and feeling his lips against mine—thoughts like that messed with my appetite and I really loved fried shrimp.

When we were finished with our dinner we agreed to share dessert—chocolate cake. And then Andrew paid the bill and we left the restaurant. I shivered in the evening air though I was wearing a sweater—I hoped it would be enough to keep the evening chill away.

"You're cold?" Andrew asked, concerned. "Come here." He pulled me close and wrapped his arm securely around me. It was dark out now but the moon was full and rising in the night sky. We crossed the street and entered the parking lot. Ahead and down the beach a ways was a large sand dune. We walked hand in hand now, toward it, and entered the flattened area of Easton's Beach. I had to stop and remove my shoes. Andrew took note and did the same. I bet he was wishing right about now that one of the goonies was here to hold our shoes. I shuddered at the thought. We took in the majesty of the ocean and I was happy that we were the only souls on the beach right now. We had it all to ourselves. Stretching out in front of us were the choppy waters of the dark blue Atlantic. To the right, off in the distance, was the entrance to Newport's famous Cliff Walk, winding uphill with jagged walls of rock cutting into the sea below it to its left. Beautiful mansions were situated on the right of Cliff Walk spaced far apart. Some of the grand homes were visible while other, more private ones were concealed behind large fences or shrubbery to discourage prying eyes. To our left, up the beach just beyond Joe's Clam Shack, but on the ocean side of the road, was the Easton's Beach Club and Hotel. Unlike the Dancing Pony Club, this 'club' was not exclusive—anyone could swim and sunbathe here and the hotel's restaurant was open to the public. They also had a bar at one end and a coffee shop at the other. I had eaten in the restaurant many times with my parents over the years and Lily and Gretchen and I had had many breakfasts and lunches in the coffee shop.

Now Andrew and I were walking hand in hand along the water's edge, just far enough from the tide to keep from getting our feet drenched. Andrew was quiet and I wondered what he was thinking. I thought back to my conversation with Nick earlier and tried to figure out a way to talk about Tristan without sounding any unnecessary alarms. Finally I broke the silence.

"So…your brother seems quite nice. What's he like?" I asked, trying to sound as casual as possible. We walked slowly along the path of the moonlight's line in the sand in the direction of the Cliff Walk. Way up ahead of us I noticed someone coming down the Cliff Walk heading in our direction. Most of the Cliff Walk was in darkness but the moon highlighted parts of it as did intermittent lighting from the properties and streetlights glowing along Memorial Boulevard, the road leading from Middletown into Newport.

"Uh, oh," laughed Andrew. "Should I be worried?" Though he'd laughed when he'd said it, I thought I detected a note of jealousy in his voice.

"Of course not. I was just curious, that's all. Your family seems so lovely. I enjoyed talking to your mother at the polo match. And your father comes across as very…passionate." That seemed like a safe word to use to describe the tyrant. "So I just wondered about your brother's personality. Are you two alike?"

Andrew considered the question. "Yes and no. We are alike in most ways but Tristan is more apt to defy our father about…things. I've always tended to just do whatever Father wants. It seems to make life easier to bear."

"Oh…like…what things?" I asked quietly, suddenly feeling nervous as I tried to steer the conversation in such a way as to get information about Tristan and the threat Nick overheard him make to his father about ending his own life over something he didn't want to do.

Andrew started to speak then hesitated. Finally he seemed to formulate an answer to my question. "Let's just say that my father has an unnaturally strong sense of history and tradition—you know, like carrying on family legacies and such. But Tristan doesn't care about that stuff. He pretty much just cares about horses. He doesn't want to go to college. Father is making him go but Tristan insisted on attending the little college here on this island, much to my father's chagrin. Some of those horses you saw at the match are Tristan's. He trains them and rides them and lives for them. He just wants to be left alone to live his own life. Father, of course, has other plans." Andrew sighed and stopped walking. He looked out at the horizon. We could see the distant lights of a passing freighter making its way to Europe or Bermuda or some other far-flung place.

"How old is Tristan?" I asked. "I mean, isn't he old enough to move out from under your father's roof and start his own life? He could do something with horses, I bet, like breeding or racing or something." I had the sense that I was trying to save Tristan now—but from what, I still didn't know and didn't dare ask.

"Tristan's nearly twenty and don't think he hasn't thought about that." Andrew said it with a fierceness that took me by surprise. Obviously I had touched on something sensitive. I was afraid of pushing him too far. I looked ahead into the distance and noticed that the person I'd seen earlier, coming down the Cliff Walk, was getting closer. It looked like a man—I could make out the shape of him in the moonlight.

"What's holding him back?" I asked softly. We were still holding hands and I felt his tighten around mine. Suddenly he stopped and pulled me close, into his chest. Though I was tall, he was a head or more taller than I. He wrapped his arms around me and pressed his cheek into my hair. I felt breathless—with both a strange fearfulness and the attraction I felt for him.

"Oh, Laura," he whispered. "My family is so messed up. I wish I could explain it to you. But in a few months this mess will be over and we can all get back to some semblance of a normal life."

I was stunned. He had suddenly said so much in so few words. So there *was* something wrong in Andrew's family—possibly having to do with Tristan. I wondered if I could help somehow.

"What's going on? What can I do to help?" I breathed the words into his chest. He crushed me closer to him and I felt the breath rush out of my lungs. My arms were around him but I loosened them now to try to give myself a little breathing space. "What is it?" I whispered into the darkness.

When Andrew answered me his voice had changed. He sounded angry and frustrated but I knew it was nothing to do with me, so I let him vent.

"I'm sorry, Laura. I can't talk about it. Everything will be fine. As long as my father gets what he wants then everything will work out according to plan—that's the important thing. Let's change the subject now…please…I've already said too much."

"Yes, you have," said a husky voice from behind Andrew. I jumped in fright and Andrew, caught off guard by the unexpected sound, whirled around toward the speaker, inadvertently knocking into me, causing me to lose my balance. I stumbled backward and felt myself falling into the sand.

"Ooh," I gasped as I fell, instinctively putting out my hand to break my fall. I stumbled a few steps in the sand trying to remain upright but it was impossible with my feet sinking into the wetness. I toppled over backward in a heap onto the wet sand.

"Laura!" yelled Miguel, dashing toward me. As he reached down to catch me, Andrew shoved him hard away from me and Miguel fell backward onto the sand.

"What the hell are you doing here, Dos Santos?" Andrew spat out the words between clenched teeth. He towered over Miguel who immediately sprang cat-like to his feet. Miguel turned to me and once again offered his hand to help me up, but again, Andrew shoved him away. He started to fall backward but was able to regain his balance and remain on his feet. Miguel glared at Andrew, not taking his eyes off of him this time. His hands formed into fists defensively in front of his body. "Keep your hands off of me, Easton," he hissed.

Andrew advanced toward him, his face fuming, his breath coming out in hard, fast puffs. "I ought to take care of things right here, right now…and save my brother the trouble," he hissed, his voice dripping with venom. I heard the violent undertone in his words and feared he would hurt Miguel. He sounded so much like the duke that I shook with apprehension.

"You'd like that, wouldn't you?" Miguel responded in kind. They circled around each other like gladiators in the ring, each one gauging the other, ready to fight to the death.

I pushed myself out of the sand and got to my feet, wiping my hands down the front of my sweater as I stumbled toward them. "What the *hell* is going on here?" I cried. "Do you two *know* each other?"

"Stay back, Laura," Andrew demanded. He put himself between me and Miguel and kept me from getting too close. "It would appear that *Miguel…*," he spat out the word, "has a problem with his temper."

"I can handle my temper just fine…unlike some members of your family," said Miguel tauntingly.

"You son of a bitch!" Andrew shouted. With those words he was on Miguel in a flash, taking him down into the sand. They rolled each other over several times, attempting to throw punches, which each one was able to block like professionals in the ring.

"Stop!" I screamed. "Please!" I was crying now and looking frantically up and down the beach hoping to find someone to help—to stop this insanity. Where were those damned snipers when you needed them? "Andrew! Miguel! Please!" I begged, hysteria threatening to overwhelm me.

Miguel seemed to be gaining the upper hand. He had Andrew pinned down and as Andrew struggled to get up, I felt the sudden need to intervene—to save Andrew from being harmed. I grabbed a handful of sand and ran over toward them. When I had a clear shot, I threw the sand hard, directly into Miguel's face. Immediately he loosened his grip on Andrew's body and fell backward.

"Damn it, Laura!" he yelled at me. He got to his feet and swiped at his eyes and spat a mouthful of sand onto the ground. "What did you do that for?" he yelled at me.

Andrew got to his feet and once again placed himself between me and Miguel protectively. "We're done here, Dos Santos. So why don't you go back to your gypsy camp where you came from," he said tauntingly.

Miguel clenched his jaw. Even in the darkness with nothing but a thin swath of moonlight for illumination, I could see that Andrew's words were having the desired effect. I shrank back behind Andrew, expecting Miguel to lunge for Andrew's throat, but he surprised me. He remained still, a dark statue in the sand. He stared menacingly into Andrew's eyes. "Yes, we *are* done here." He moved then, taking a step back.

"For now," Andrew hissed through his teeth. With those threatening words, Andrew turned around to me and grabbed my arm, pulling me roughly across the beach back toward the parking lot. At that moment, two members of his crack security team appeared around the corner of the sand dune.

"You're late, guys," Andrew admonished them angrily. "But I handled it." The goons looked horrified. I bet they were scared for their jobs more than for Andrew's safety—I hoped I was wrong about that. As we rounded the dune, I looked back over my shoulder to where Miguel had been standing, but all I saw was the churned up sand where they had fought in the moonlight. Miguel was already gone. I heard the waves crashing menacingly over the shore as if they, too, were angry.

In the parking lot, the goons fussed over Andrew but he waved them off and told them to get back in the car. "We'll be there in a minute. I need to talk to Laura alone," he said authoritatively. Then, noticing that neither of us had our shoes, he asked one of the guards to go back to the beach to find them.

Andrew turned to me. He pulled me roughly into his arms and hugged me tightly. "I'm so sorry. That was…a mistake…but it won't happen again."

I brushed sand from my clothes and hair and tried to calm my breathing. "Andrew…what *was* that?" It had all happened so fast and none of it had made sense. "You know Miguel?"

"I know him, yes. But don't worry about it—don't worry about any of this. It's just a misunderstanding—something that happened a…while back…nothing to concern yourself with, OK?" He brushed his hands over my hair and pulled me in close and kissed my forehead tenderly. I pulled back and frowned.

"No…it's not OK. I want to know what that was about. Miguel knows something about you. What? What's going on?" I sounded desperate. I could not accept that there was any kind of bad blood between them. How did they know each other well enough to have anything to even fight about?

He changed the subject abruptly. "Are you hurt?" He looked me up and down and when I shook my head he pulled me back into his arms. He bent down and kissed me and I wanted to resist. I wanted to put him off until I had some answers but his kisses were making my head spin and I couldn't think straight.

"Andrew…stop," I whispered against his mouth. "Please tell me what's going on. Maybe I can help." My hand was behind his head, my fingers gently grasping his hair into loose bunches. I held him close, trying to pass some sense of trust into him.

He stiffened and pulled my arms away from him. "You need to let this go. It's just a misunderstanding, like I said. I need you to let this go—to forget this…*please*."

Andrew waved a hand toward the cars and one of the bodyguards instantly opened the back door. He took my hand and pulled me gently toward the car. I climbed in and he got in beside me. The guard closed the door and got behind the wheel. We were silent on the ride back to my house. I had so many questions—so many worries. But I could tell by the set of his jaw and his steely-eyed gaze that there would be no answers tonight.

At my house he walked me to the door and we stood under the porch light. We were both a mess—wet and covered in sand. If my mother saw me like this she would get the wrong idea. I knew what she would think we had been doing in the sand. I fervently hoped she would either not be home or at least not hear me come in. I didn't feel like explaining…considering I didn't even know what had happened myself.

Andrew kissed me softly and wiped more sand from my hair. "Good night, Laura. Don't let the way this night ended change your feelings for me. I love…being with you." And with those words he pulled me swiftly into his arms and kissed me hard on the mouth. The kiss was rough and left me shaking. He released me and walked back to his car. I let myself in the house and watched through the front window as his car drove away into the night. I heard my mother call my name but I pretended I didn't hear her and I quietly raced up the stairs to the bathroom to shower and wash away the sandy evidence of this night—evidence that proved nothing.

C h a p t e r   E i g h t

Against the Wall

It was as if time had stopped. The rest of the weekend dragged. I was worried about the fact that I hadn't heard from Andrew. I puzzled over the events of that evening and couldn't even formulate a theory as to what had led to the confrontation between him and Miguel. Why was Miguel on the beach? Did he know Andrew would be there? If so, how could he have known? And what was the connection to Tristan? What did Tristan not want to do that Andrew seemed willing to do for him? And something else bothered me…I was shocked at Andrew's anger. It had reminded me of his father and that left a tension in my stomach that wouldn't subside. And then my parents chose today of all days to tell me and Nick what we both already knew.

Nick and I were in the living room sitting awkwardly on the couch waiting for this to be over. My mother was explaining—again—about how much they both loved us and loved each other but they had grown apart and had decided that divorcing was the best option and blah, blah, blah. Any other day I'm sure this news would have affected me more deeply than it was affecting me now. We had known it was coming so I guess that prior knowledge helped to soften the blow. My father would be moving into an apartment in Providence closer to his office. I wondered if this would affect his sailing schedule—I sometimes thought he spent more time sailing than working anyway. And my mother assured us that she would be here at home with us like always and nothing would have to change. Nick wasn't even fazed. He hugged them both and asked if he could leave. My father pulled me into his arms in a bear hug and asked me if I was OK.

"I'm fine, Dad," I said. "It's not like we didn't see this coming. As long as you two are happy, that's the main thing." And I really meant it. At the forefront of my mind was the situation with Andrew and Miguel—it was numbing me to any fallout I might be feeling about my parents' divorce. But I was sure this would hit me later when I least expected it. Finally I was able to go to my room but not before my father gave me a great piece of news.

"Laura, earlier this morning I talked to an officer at the station about that robbery. The perp pleaded guilty and is going straight to prison. He isn't passing go or collecting two hundred dollars so at least we don't have to worry about this anymore. Turns out he had a string of priors."

I couldn't help but laugh at Dad's words. It was as if he were repeating lines straight out of an episode of *Law and Order*. And it did make me feel better. I hugged them both and went up to my room. I was kind of hungry but the thought of eating anything made me nauseous.

I decided to contact Andrew. I really wanted to talk to him before school tomorrow. I wasn't even sure if he was going to pick me up in the morning as usual. I hadn't heard a word from him since that mess on the beach. I opened my phone and sent him a text. *Hey there…how are you today? Haven't heard from you so just checking in. See you tomorrow?* I pressed send and then proceeded to stare at my phone willing it to answer. After ten minutes of this I realized how foolish I was acting and I tried to do some homework. Time passed. I finished my homework and even attempted to read for pleasure. And I finally decided I needed food, whether I wanted to eat or not. I went down to the kitchen and heated up some leftover chili in the microwave, and sat at the kitchen table eating in the silence of the house. I didn't know where everyone had gone but I was glad for the solitude.

I finished eating and as I was walking up the stairs I heard the familiar ping of a text message on my phone. I pulled my phone out of my pocket and held my breath before looking at it. It was from Lily. I sighed in disappointment and walked into my room, sinking down onto my bed. Lily wondered what I was doing and did I want to hang out? I texted her back and told her I wasn't up for company at the moment. I mentioned my parents' divorce in my reply text and a few seconds after hitting send, my phone rang.

"Oh, my gosh, Laura," said Lily. "I am so sorry. I know this is hard right now but it gets better, I promise. Keep in mind my parents have been divorced—twice. Why they remarried I will never know. I mean if it didn't work out the first time…right?"

I listened to Lily give me advice on how to survive divorce for a minute or two but soon my mind drifted. She was still talking when I heard the sound of an incoming text message. My heart immediately went into overdrive as I pulled the phone away from my ear. Andrew's name appeared on the screen.

I waited a beat for Lily to take a breath and then jumped in. "Hey, Lil…my mom needs help with something. Can I call you back later?" I'd crossed my fingers as I'd told my little white lie. We hung up and I took a deep breath and opened Andrew's text: *Sorry I didn't call. And sorry again about the other night. I'll pick you up in the morning… usual time. I miss you.*

I hugged the phone to my chest and sank down into my pillows, grinning foolishly from ear to ear. Thank goodness he was still speaking to me. Getting this text reinforced just how much I had been missing him. I sighed with relief and texted him back quickly. *It's OK…no worries. Yes, same time tomorrow…and I miss you, too.*

I felt so much better—like I could survive the rest of the evening without going crazy. I eventually went downstairs and joined my mother in the kitchen for a late dinner. It seemed like it had been forever since I'd eaten a meal with one of my parents. Nick was out as usual and Dad had gone to Providence. Mom seemed happy to have my company. I made a point of paying careful attention to her just in case this whole divorce thing was affecting her more negatively than she was letting on. But I was happy to note that she seemed just fine—her usual jovial self. When we finished dinner I complimented her on the delicious chicken and broccoli casserole she'd made and told her to go relax. I stacked the dishwasher, put away the leftovers and flipped off the kitchen light. Then I went upstairs to my room and read myself to sleep.

The next morning Andrew arrived right on time. As I walked down my front steps he got out of the car and met me half-way. He had the sweetest expression on his face—sheepish almost. He opened his arms and I walked right into them. He kissed me gently and held me for several moments before walking me to the car and opening the door. We got in and the driver backed out and we headed to school. We talked quietly about neutral subjects like what we each had done the rest of the weekend. Ironically, he'd gone sailing with his father and brother. I told him about my dad's obsession with that pastime and then mentioned homework and reading. I didn't say anything about my parents' divorce—I didn't want to bring us down. Nor did I tell him how much of the weekend I'd devoted to agonizing over the beach incident and missing him and worrying about him. We both just acted like it hadn't happened, though it was never far from my mind.

"Oh, Laura...before I forget...I have to leave early today. My father is giving a speech at some fundraising tea on Goat Island and we all have to go. But I can arrange for one of my drivers to make sure you get home. I won't leave you stranded."

"Oh, no...don't worry about that. I can catch a ride with Lily. She's been on my case for ignoring her lately anyway. You go support your dad." I didn't let him see my disappointment. Already I was getting so used to his company that being too long apart made me anxious. He walked me to class and the morning sailed by. Getting through boring class after boring class was so much easier now that I had Andrew waiting for me after each one. After lunch he said good-bye to me at my locker and gave me a quick hug.

"I'll call you later," he said. He smiled and touched his hand to my hair for a second and then he and Peter left the building through the back doors. The afternoon didn't pass as quickly as the morning had, probably because I knew Andrew wasn't here. But finally it was time for English class—the day was nearly done. I suddenly remembered that I'd forgotten to ask Lily for a ride home when we were at lunch. *Oh, well...*I thought. *I'll catch her after school in the parking lot.*

I was in for a surprise when I got to English. In a strange change of pattern, Miguel Dos Santos was already in class when I got there, seated in his chair behind mine with his notebook open on his desk. I knew he noticed my visible shock at seeing him. My stomach tightened as I walked nervously across the room and stood beside my desk. I looked down at him. There was no way I could act normally with him. I glanced around, noting that there weren't too many kids in the room—the teacher hadn't even arrived yet. I had to say something. I cleared my throat and looked at him. He stared at me silently, unmoving. I suddenly felt a little afraid of him. But I had to try to get to the bottom of this.

"Miguel," I said his name quietly. "What was that about—the other night at the beach?" I spoke in a low voice so that the few students in the room wouldn't hear. I waited for an answer, not sure if he was even going to speak.

"Hello, Laura," he said softly. "You owe me an apology." He continued to stare intently at me. There was a firmness about the set of his mouth, though his eyes looked warm…not unfriendly.

I leaned down toward him a little. "Are you kidding me?" I whispered. "*I* owe *you* an apology? After you show up on the beach out of nowhere and scare the crap out of us and then proceed to beat up on Andrew for no obvious reason…yet *I* owe *you* an apology? How do you figure?" I was livid now.

"You threw sand in my face…and after I saved your life, no less," he grinned somewhat wickedly. "I'm hurt."

I didn't even know how to respond. I tried to reply but realizing that nothing sensible was likely to come out of my mouth I just stared at him with an expression of astonishment on my face. And then the teacher arrived and called the class to order so I had no choice but to take my seat and attempt to calm myself and concentrate. It seemed as if this class would literally never end. For the whole fifty-minute period I was keenly aware of Miguel's presence behind me. It was all I could do to keep from turning around to look at him. With my mind zoned out anyway—I couldn't even remember what class this was—I tried to analyze Miguel's words—and his demeanor. He didn't seem angry or contrite—none of the things a normal person would feel who had acted as he had the other night. What was his deal? I determined that after class I would not let him make his usual quick escape from the room. I would stick out my foot and trip him if it came down to it.

Eventually class neared its painful end. And the closer the clock ticked toward dismissal the more nervous I got. My stomach felt queasy, my peripheral vision turned black and even my lungs threatened to malfunction. *What the hell is wrong with me? I will not let this gypsy boy bully me. Just because he saved my life it doesn't mean I owe him anything…does it? He owes* me *the apology—and he owes one to*

Andrew, too. This is ridiculous. These thoughts were running through my head as the final bell rang, signifying the end of the school day. I heard Miguel putting his books away and then he was standing up behind me but not moving. I stood up in front of him and turned toward him, blocking his path to the exit. He just looked at me…waiting.

Finally I mustered the courage to break the awkward silence between us. "Miguel…can we talk somewhere…privately…outside or somewhere?" I heard the breathiness in my voice and felt embarrassment staining my cheeks pink. Why was it so hard to have a normal conversation with him?

"Of course," he said, his voice even. His gaze was steely but not too threatening so I figured we would be able to have a calm discussion. We walked out into the hallway toward the back exit doors. I led the way. I didn't really know where we were going so I just went out the back door and stopped by the side of the building. A few other students exited with us but didn't pay us any attention. Miguel hoisted his bag higher on his shoulder and leaned against the brick wall. I stood a couple of feet away, my back to the woods that butted up close to the rear of the school. It suddenly occurred to me that he could potentially subdue me, drag me into the woods and kill me and no one would be able to help me. And then the absurdity of that thought nearly made me laugh hysterically. I took a deep breath and spoke.

"So, Miguel…what was that about…the other night?" I asked, my nerves on edge.

He brushed his hand through his black hair and sighed. "What did Andrew tell you it was about?"

"Andrew didn't tell me anything, really. He said that it was just a misunderstanding. Something that happened a while back…nothing to worry about." I saw his jaw tense and he looked off into the woods, considering his response.

"Well, he told you the truth. It was nothing that can't be resolved peacefully—nothing at all for you to worry about." He turned his dark eyes on me. I thought I saw a pleading look in them.

"But that doesn't answer my question. At least tell me this…how do you know Andrew? Did you know him before? I mean before school started?" This didn't seem like too much to ask.

He hesitated. I saw him work his jaw again. He seemed to be weighing his words before speaking them. "Yes. We knew of each other before. We moved here about the same time and had an occasion to meet. And just so you know…I don't have a problem with…your *prince*."

I gasped at the implication in his words. "*My* prince? But what about his family? Do you have a problem with them?" I felt myself getting agitated. I had no doubt now that something was amiss.

"Laura…listen to me. Whatever…*problem*…I have with anyone is my business. If you're smart you'll listen to me when I tell you to butt out—for your own good. Trust me." His face was tense and his eyes sparkled in the late afternoon sun. He looked both menacing and valiant at the same time. Was this the same person who had saved my life so bravely not so long ago?

I felt a wave of anger course through my body threatening to erupt like a volcano. I stepped closer to him and tried to stare him down—not an easy task—his eyes were so dark and endless and he was at least half a foot taller than I was. "Are you threatening me, Miguel?" I whispered. I would not back down. No way would I let him see any fear.

All of a sudden, with no warning, Miguel pushed himself off the brick wall and circled around me. He placed his hand on my shoulder and pushed me back against the building—but softly so I didn't bang into it. He leaned down close to me and put his face beside mine, his mouth to my ear. "Laura, I would never threaten you. I care about your safety. I saved your life, remember?" I felt his breath cause strands of my hair to loosen from its clasp and float down to my cheek. I couldn't tell if I was breathing—I couldn't feel anything except his breath on my cheek. I could hear his accent, more pronounced now. "But listen to me now. Sometimes things aren't what they appear. Be careful who you trust, Laura. Didn't anyone ever tell you that sometimes you're safer in the darkness than in the light?"

His hand was still on my shoulder, holding me in place. I felt my heart thudding in my chest and feared he could hear it, too. I heard his words—I heard a familiar ring to them. And any fear I had of him seemed to fade of its own volition, though not completely. I turned to him—our faces were only a couple of inches apart. My breathing quickened. I saw the stubble on his chin and the fullness of his lips. I felt dizzy, sure I would slide down the wall any second into a heap on the ground.

"Miguel, I…" I tried to speak though I had not formed a cohesive thought. I didn't know what words would've come out of my mouth. But he put his warm finger to my lips and shushed me quietly. His mouth was so close to mine and everything about him threatened to overwhelm me. My pulse raced. I didn't understand why I wasn't pushing him away or running or doing something defensive. Shouldn't I want this to stop—whatever it was?

"It's OK, Laura. I forgive you for throwing sand in my face. We'll just call it a misunderstanding," he whispered. My breath caught in my throat as his mouth began to close the distance to mine. I closed my eyes and felt his lips brush mine feather-lightly.

"Miss Laura!" a British voice yelled. "Are you alright?"

Miguel jumped back immediately and dropped his hand from my shoulder. He turned away from the speaker. It was Peter, Andrew's chief goon.

I took a deep breath—my first one in I didn't know how many minutes. My face was red and I felt my whole body shaking. I croaked out an answer. "Yes, Peter. I'm fine. Why are you here? Is Andrew here?"

Miguel kept his back to the bodyguard and moved away, closer to the trees. I looked at his slowly retreating figure and felt utter confusion. The world didn't seem to make sense any more.

"No, miss. But he was worried about your getting home and asked me to check on you and get you home safely." He looked at Miguel's back when he said the words and I saw the contempt in his eyes and I heard it in his voice.

Miguel turned sideways to me then. "Bye, Laura. You have a nice evening." And then he walked away—taking the long way around the back of the school to the parking lot.

Peter came over and removed my book-bag from my arm and hoisted it over his shoulder. "Shall we go, miss? The car is waiting."

I nodded and walked with him around to the parking lot. The car was there, another goon in the driver seat. Peter opened the door for me and I climbed in and he handed me my bag. I hugged it to my body tightly. He got in the front passenger side and the goons drove me home. The ride to my house was blessedly short though I didn't really notice it. I'd remained trance-like for the duration of the trip. When we arrived, I was out the door before Peter could open it for me.

Instead of going into the house right away, I sat down in the wicker chair on the porch and tried to collect my thoughts. Miguel was about to kiss me. There was no question that if Peter hadn't suddenly appeared out of nowhere, then Miguel would have kissed me. I touched my fingertips lightly to my lips and wondered…that almost kiss…what it would have felt like…tasted like…I felt dizzy and was thankful I was sitting down. I reached for my pendant. I pulled it out from under its hiding place inside my shirt. It was warm and hard, yet smooth and comforting, too. It seemed as if the world were getting more insane every minute. I wondered what Peter would tell Andrew. I had a feeling Andrew might be the jealous type. It probably wouldn't go over well. I sent a silent prayer to whoever was in charge of the universe that Peter would use discretion in this matter. I pressed the disk to my cheek and felt its warmth against my skin. Then I put it back into my shirt and went inside the house.

Chapter Nine

Accident

When Andrew and his crew picked me up the next morning, I was wary. I had no way of knowing if Peter had given me away, but I took it as a good sign when the car showed up on time. I was already on the front porch waiting and I dashed down the drive quickly so Andrew wouldn't feel like he had to get out of the car and escort me, like he usually did. But he seemed completely normal and greeted me with a smile and a kiss. Peter, who was in the driver seat, looked at me in the rearview mirror. His eyes gave nothing away but judging by Andrew's demeanor, I had to believe that Peter had not told Andrew about Miguel. I sent him a silent thanks with my eyes and turned my attention to Andrew. He was talking about polo. *Imagine that*, I thought.

"It's the last official international match of the season and even though our last attempt at watching polo wasn't the best, I was hoping you'd be willing to give it one more try. What do you think?" Andrew was asking me.

"Is England getting another chance at the United States then—are they getting their rematch?" I laughed.

"No such luck." Andrew gave me a crooked smile. "It's England versus Portugal actually. Should be a good match. Last time I saw those two teams play—this was back in England—we beat them senseless. It was amazing. My cousins William and Harry played in that one." He seemed very excited. Though I didn't necessarily feel his passion for the sport, the irony that the opposing team was Portugal was not lost on me. It gave me cause to wonder who might be in attendance to cheer that team on.

"Sounds like fun," I said. I only hoped it would be.

The rest of the week went by in a blur. I was always a little fearful just before English class, but Miguel was back to his usual pattern of being the last one to arrive to class and, somehow, the first one out the door when it was over, in spite of the fact that he sat on the far side of the classroom from the exit. Andrew ignored him completely—didn't even make eye contact with Miguel, as far as I could tell, so I determined that whatever had happened between them in the past would always remain a mystery to me and I would just have to accept that.

The day of the polo match was sunny but cool. It was officially autumn now and I could feel it in the air—cold was coming whether I liked it or not. The leaves were changing to soft orange and yellow and there was a hint of crispness in the afternoon air. I stood on the front porch waiting for Andrew. Even from this distance I could hear the Atlantic Ocean crashing onto the shore in a rhythmic cadence. I once again silently cursed the neighbors for building that damned second-story addition onto their house as Andrew and company drove up the drive.

"Hello, love," Andrew said, kissing me lightly on the lips and pulling me into his embrace. I settled into his arms in the back seat and we headed off to the polo fields. Andrew seemed almost giddy with excitement. I could hear the driver talking quietly to his goon partner up in the front seat. They, too, seemed excited. *This match must be a really big deal, if it's getting everyone this jazzed up*, I thought.

We pulled into the VIP section and parked. There was already a lot of cars in the parking lot—most of them Mercedes, BMWs, and Jaguars, even a couple of Rolls Royces. I was beginning to understand why they called polo the sport of kings. And then I saw one black car that stood out somewhat from the others. I felt the familiar roiling of my stomach and the hairs on the back of my neck stood up. There was no mistaking the familiarity of the big black Chevy Suburban parked in the last row. I scanned the lot and then looked toward the field and the stands. It seemed that hundreds of people had turned out for this last official match of the season. The stands were filling up and Andrew took my hand and led me from the parking lot to the VIP area. My nerves were tingling as I settled into my seat and again scanned the area around me. And then I heard Andrew mutter profanely under his breath.

"What the hell are *they* doing here?" he mumbled to himself.

I looked in the direction he was facing and saw them—Miguel and his brothers and another man who looked like them. They were also in the VIP section but farther back and near the aisle. I looked at Andrew and the expression on his face made me shrink back into my seat. I was glad that my sunglasses were hiding the apprehension in my eyes.

"I can't believe they let those damned gypsies in here—this place will go to the dogs," Andrew groaned.

"Hey, now," I admonished him. "That's not nice." I said it as lightly as possible so as not to aggravate him. I was already worried enough about how his father would behave today—I didn't want to have to worry about Andrew going ballistic as well. I could see his parents making their way toward us, goons in tow.

Andrew swallowed visibly and grabbed my hand. "Uh, oh. Here he comes. I hope this match goes well so Father has no reason to explode." I heard the tension in his voice and I gave his hand a comforting squeeze.

"Even if England doesn't win, that's no reason for him to explode. Losing is as much a part of life as winning. It's losing from time to time that makes us appreciate the victories." I leaned into his side and he slipped his arm around me and kissed me.

"I know, love. You're preaching to the choir—it's my father who doesn't understand the concept of balance. I'll be right back—I'm going to go get us some drinks."

He passed his parents in the aisle. The duke and Mrs. Easton greeted me warmly as they settled themselves into their seats. His father seemed happy enough today but I couldn't help but notice the wary expression on his mother's face, as if she were hoping for the best but preparing for the worst.

With Andrew away for a moment, I stole a glance back to where Miguel was sitting with his brothers. He was looking at me—or in my direction anyway. I was tempted to wave but somehow it didn't seem appropriate. I wondered where his parents were…who they were… did he even have parents? He was such a mystery. After a moment he looked away toward the field and I turned my attention there as well. The horses and riders were coming out onto the field. The bright red and green shirts of the Portuguese team stood out against the bright blue sky, contrasting sharply with the red and blue stripes of the English team.

Andrew returned with our Cokes. He pointed out Tristan on his russet-colored mount—easy to distinguish because of the longish blond hair curling around the bottom of his cap. There were eight players on the field and though they seemed small from this distance, I knew the men were big—tall and broad-shouldered. The horses looked massive, too, and beautiful, and I couldn't help but feel a pang of sympathy for them.

After the pre-recorded anthems of each team were played over the loud-speakers, the players moved into their positions. The horses were frisky and ready for action. The air was electric with tension and excitement—this game had a distinctly different feel from the previous match we'd attended. Then, I suddenly noticed an oddity on the scoreboard. It appeared that the Portuguese team already had one point on the board. I felt a rush of nerves—there was a mistake on the board and no one but me seemed to be noticing. I glanced around at the faces of the spectators and then at Andrew. He seemed oblivious. I had to do something before the duke noticed. He would go postal and accuse the Portuguese of cheating. That would be bad.

"Andrew," I whispered. "I think the scoreboard is broken. Look!" I pointed to the board. "They've accidentally given the Portuguese a point and the game hasn't even started yet. Someone should tell them!"

Andrew pulled me close and kissed the top of my head. "It's OK, Laura. That's normal. It's one of the rules of polo. Our team has a higher handicap than theirs by one point, so they automatically get the extra point to make it even. It's normal."

"Wait…they get an extra point just like that? That doesn't seem fair to England." I was perplexed. A rule like this would never fly in an American sport, that's for sure.

"It's OK. Quite simply, it just means that we're better than they are—that extra point won't hurt us one bit." He sounded quite confident so I let it drop, although I wasn't sure that I agreed with a silly rule like that. Andrew seemed to make more of an effort this time to explain things to me, telling me there would be six chukkers in the game. I laughed at the silly word.

"A chukker is a playing period. They're only about seven minutes long but with fouls and boundary outages, it will seem longer—kind of like your American football. I've seen a few of those games—they seem to go on forever." He grinned.

"Tell me about it," I laughed. The game was now officially underway and the crowd was cheering. I made a careful point to pay attention but I occasionally stole a glance in Miguel's direction to see if he seemed to be enjoying the game.

After three playing periods, the score was seven to six in favor of England. It was quite a sight to really pay attention and see the horses racing up and down the field, sticks flying, the little white ball sailing up and down the field. And so far, the duke had remained calm even when Portugal had scored points, so all in all, it was turning out to be a great match and a lot of fun. There was a short break in the game and spectators stood to stretch and refill drinks. Andrew was excited and I hoped for everyone's sake, that England would maintain its lead all the way to victory.

The second half began and it was just as exciting as the first. Both teams were playing well and defending their goals strategically. Eventually Portugal scored another goal and tied the score. The game was nearing the end now and England had control of the ball. It was Tristan now, galloping down the field after a nice straight shot down the line. Portugal rallied and blocked the goal. Back up the field they flew, the horses galloping, the players moving in perfect sync with their mounts. It truly was a sight to behold. Back and forth they rode up and down the field. Suddenly a Portuguese player hit a hard shot that sent the ball tight down the line straight into the goal—they were now ahead by one point. I looked up at the clock and my heart sank. England was going to lose.

I stole a quick glance at Andrew, who jumped to his feet with a shout. His father also stood and yelled something unintelligible. *Oh, no, here we go again,* I thought. A jolt of dread shot through my nerves strong enough to make the hairs on my arms react. Just as the last seconds ticked away, an English player, in a rush to beat the clock and to keep the ball in play, pushed his horse hard and it made contact with a Portuguese player. The horses crashed into one another sending the English player flying into the air—his horse nearly crushing him as it tried to remain upright. The Portuguese player struggled to stay on his horse as it stumbled sideways but he was able to hold on. Referees charged onto the field and called a halt but the clock had already run out before the horses had even made contact. The game was over. England had lost. Someone was hurt. And the duke was mad.

"Tristan!" It was Andrew shouting next to me. "That's Tristan!" He jumped up and started making his way down the stands following along behind the duke who was fuming and looked ready to kill.

The duchess glanced at me and shook her head. "I hate this bloody game," she muttered. I thought she would want to go down to the field to check on Tristan, but she remained behind with a security guard. I wasn't sure what to do. People were leaving the stands—many of them heading down toward the field to get a closer look. I stayed put, weighing my options. I glanced up at Miguel's seat but he and his brothers were already gone.

I decided I had to go down to the field and see if I could find out if Tristan had been badly hurt. Without asking permission or clearing it with the duchess I stood up and made my way down to where I could see Andrew's head higher than most. When I got closer, I could hear the duke. He was clearly out of control. Screaming about the "damned thieving gypsies" and how they were trying to kill his son for the sake of a victory—an unbroken stream of outrageous utterances and awful cursing. I had seen everything that had led up to the moment of Tristan's fall and if I were a referee I would not be blaming the Portuguese. The duke's wild accusations were all wrong. I hoped no one would pay any attention to his ranting.

Paramedics were on the field tending to Tristan. I could see his arms and legs moving and took that as a good sign. He was placed on a stretcher and taken away in an ambulance, accompanied by one of his security guards. The crowd was starting to thin now that most of the drama was over. Andrew turned and saw me standing back near the seats. He came over to me. His face was white and he was shaking.

"Laura," he said, pulling me into his arms. "I could kill my father."

"Is Tristan alright?" I asked, ignoring that statement for the moment.

"He's going to be OK. The paramedics don't think he broke any bones but he's going for x-rays to be sure and to get checked for a concussion. But my father...*ooh*." Andrew dropped his arms from me and paced around in front of the stands. I could clearly see that he was trying to get his emotions in check. Finally he walked back to me.

"My father has no ability whatsoever to control his temper or his tongue. I understand his frustration, but he has no tact. His behavior is embarrassing and childish." Andrew put his hand at my back and guided me toward the car park. He continued as we walked. "Those Portuguese are a wild bunch of animals though, that's for sure. Thankfully Tristan will be OK—this time."

I bit my tongue—not quite sure how to respond. I had seen the play on the field. I had seen Tristan charge at the Portuguese player—this was clearly Tristan's mistake. But I thought better of sharing my viewpoint with Andrew. Something told me it wouldn't go over well.

In the car, Andrew turned to me. "Laura, do you mind if I take you home? I think I need to go to the hospital just to make sure that Tristan's alright and my mother, too. And to make sure my father hasn't done anything stupid that we'll all regret tomorrow when it winds up in the papers."

"Of course," I said quickly. "Absolutely. You should go." I actually didn't mind. I needed some time alone to decompress the bad ending of an otherwise exciting match. In a few minutes we were at my house and Andrew walked me to the door. On the porch, he pulled me into his arms and held me close. I breathed in the scent of his skin—musky and sweet at the same time. These were the moments when I wished I could stop time. He leaned down and kissed me softly and then he let me go and waved over his shoulder as he left for the hospital.

Just as I walked into the house, my phone beeped with an incoming text message. I didn't recognize the number. I opened it and read: *Laura...do you know Red Tide Beach on Narragansett Bay?*

I gasped. Who the hell was texting me? I sank down onto the bottom step and my hands shook as I tentatively typed a response: *Who is this?*

A minute later I got my answer: *Miguel. Please. It's important. Come alone. And don't be afraid. You're always safe with me.*

I was stunned. Miguel? How did he get my cell phone number? And come alone? He had to be kidding. I quickly sent a reply: *How can I be sure it's safe? Why do I have to come alone? Maybe I should bring Andrew.*

A few seconds passed and then his reply: *No! Come alone, please. Seven o'clock. Red Tide Beach on the bay. I'll be waiting.*

My instincts were firing on all pistons and I could feel my imagination going into overdrive. This was some kind of trap. Miguel scared me sometimes. I thought back to our almost-kiss at school. I had felt frightened then, but I had to admit it had been a good kind of frightened. Could I trust him? He had saved my life after all. The few times I had been near him I had felt something almost electric pass between us. I went into the kitchen and spoke to my mom a few minutes about nothing of importance. I didn't even mention the drama at the match—I really didn't want to get into it. I just wanted to get to my room. I had to think. Should I do this? Was it safe? Could I trust Miguel? Should I tell Andrew—or someone? Maybe I should tell my mother where I was going so that if I didn't come back within a reasonable amount of time she would know where to send the cops. What if they never found my body? What if he dismembered me and dumped my body parts in Narragansett Bay? Oh, geez. Now I was losing it and just being absolutely ridiculous.

I looked at my watch. It was 6:30. I peered out the window and saw that the afternoon light had long since faded into evening. It wasn't completely dark yet but it would be soon. I paced around my room and considered my options. I could go and get kidnapped or murdered or who knows what. Or I could not go and ignore any and all texts I got from Miguel. I could even call Andrew and get his advice. I was sure he would tell me not to go and then go in my place and beat the crap out of Miguel. Or I could go and see what Miguel wanted and everything would be OK and I would be safe. I could even take a knife from the kitchen with me in my purse just in case I had to fight him off. I pondered all of this as the clock ticked. Finally, at quarter till seven I made my decision. I would go see Miguel and trust that everything would be fine. If I thought about it logically, I had no reason to fear him. He had only ever been kind to me—well, except for when he ignored me every day at school. He must have a good reason for being so cryptic. I would see this through and have faith that I would be safe. I squeezed the strong chain of my necklace—it would protect me from anything.

Chapter Ten

RED TIDE BEACH

"Mom," I called out as I ran down the stairs. "I'm taking the Jeep to run an errand, OK?" I stuck my head in the living room where she was reading.

"OK, but I need it back around nine. I'm going to a late movie—the new George Clooney film," she said, looking up from her magazine.

I was stunned. "You're going to a movie? I didn't know you liked George Clooney." Wow. My mother never did anything for fun except read as far as I knew.

"What? I can't go out every once in a while? And who doesn't like George?" She looked at me like I had three heads. "Where are you going?"

I hesitated. Tell the truth or lie—the age old dilemma when dealing with parents. "I'm just going to meet a friend at Red Tide Beach for a chat. I'll have the car back in time for you to get to your movie—promise." I crossed my fingers and hoped she wouldn't ask what friend.

She returned her attention to her magazine. "OK, fine. As long I leave here by 9:15 I won't miss the previews."

"Thanks, Mom," I waved and dashed to the kitchen, grabbing the car keys from their hook and I was out the door in a flash. I headed down the road and turned onto the main highway. Red Tide Beach was on the west side of Portsmouth so I headed north to route 114, where I turned left on to a country road and headed toward the bay. This part of Portsmouth was slightly more rural, the houses spaced farther apart.

It was quiet out here and peaceful. I drove down the road, surrounded by woods on either side, noticing the occasional house and one gas station. I passed Binder's Orchard on my left and Gilley's Greenhouse just past that on the right. Finally I could see the sparkling waters of the bay in the moonlight up ahead. The encroaching darkness still left just enough light to see clearly. When I reached the end of the road I turned left and drove about a half-mile to the entrance of the parking area for Red Tide Beach. I saw the Suburban immediately. I pulled into the lot and parked a couple of spots down from Miguel's car and turned off the engine. I had never felt so nervous in my life. Between my quaking stomach and the adrenaline coursing through my veins, I was amazed to find I could still breathe if I concentrated hard enough. I opened the car door and got out on shaky legs—everything was shaking for that matter. I looked around and saw Miguel near the rocks that jutted out into Narragansett Bay. He stood up and turned toward me. I swallowed hard and went to meet him.

"I didn't think you'd come," he said quietly. He took a few steps toward me, his hands in his pockets. He was wearing jeans and a long sleeved, white, button-down shirt, the sleeves folded up to the elbows. His hair was slightly mussed from the breeze coming off the bay. He looked…breathtaking.

I swallowed my nerves and glanced past him at the churning waters of the bay. The sun was setting now and soon it would be too dark to see out here. I noticed that the moon had gone into hiding behind cloud cover. But I could see Miguel alright. He seemed larger than life. Tall and imposing. It must be an optical illusion making everything seem more defined than it was—bigger somehow and surreal. I had the feeling I was in some Hollywood movie and the director was waiting for the actors to get the scene just so before the natural light faded.

"Why am I here, Miguel?" I asked softly. I crossed my arms in front of my chest protectively or maybe it was just self-consciousness. I felt exposed—vulnerable—and strangely excited.

"Because I asked you to come," he replied. "Will you sit with me on the rocks over there?" He pointed down near the water where a large, waist-high, flat-topped rock stood like a mini monument on the beach. I nodded and followed him to the rock. In the blink of an eye he was standing on top of it, reaching his hand down to me. I looked at the rock and wondered how he had gotten up there so fast and how I would manage. I hesitated a second and then placed my hand in his, planting my right sneaker-clad foot on the side of the rock and pushing myself up. He pulled me up in one swift motion and I was on the rock beside him. I wobbled, out of balance for a second, and he steadied me with his hands. Then we sat side by side facing the bay and I waited for him to speak. Strands of my hair loosened automatically from my pony tail, as they always seemed to do when I was near Miguel, and floated about my face. I was surprised when he turned his body toward me and reached up to smooth the hair back from my face. I held my breath, waiting, wondering, watching, wanting…*ooh*, I stopped my thoughts in their tracks before they could formulate into something I didn't need to hear in my head right now. Finally he spoke.

"So, what's with you and his royal highness?" he asked, a slight smile playing at the corners of his mouth. His eyes were dark and mysterious—I couldn't read them. But his question certainly caught me off guard.

I shook my head in disbelief. "Let me see if I've got this right. You called me out here to ask me about my love life?" Unbelievable. This guy made no sense at all.

"No, actually, I asked you here so we could talk…," he hesitated, sounding more cryptic than ever.

"About?" I waited. A seagull flew past us then, unusually close, as if it wanted to hear his answer, too.

"About you. I just wanted to get to know you. I feel like, having saved your life and all, I should at least get to know you a little better."

"You bring that up a lot, you know—about having saved my life. I appreciate what you did, Miguel, but am I forever in your debt because of it?" I realized after the words came out of my mouth that I sounded like a bitch for saying it. But it was a fair question just the same.

"Of course not, Laura. I just like to tease you. And don't even get me started on the whole sand-throwing incident," he chuckled. He pulled his feet up and wrapped his arms around his knees and looked at me sideways.

"Well, I'd like to say I'm sorry about that, but, as no one will tell me what that night was all about, I have to stand by my actions. I felt a threat and I reacted to that feeling." I knew I sounded a little cocky but I couldn't help myself. It was maddening not knowing the whole story.

"I'm sorry…about that night…and I understand your frustration. I will tell you this…I know Andrew Easton—and his family. We have a past connection and the fact that we both suddenly live in this tiny Rhode Island town at the same time isn't exactly a coincidence. It's just business, though, that's all—nothing for you to worry about." He stopped speaking a moment and stretched out his long legs over the rock again. "And I don't know how much you know about the duke or how much time you spend around him—realizing it's none of my business anyway—but I just wanted you to know that the duke isn't a nice man. He hurts people. And I don't want him to hurt you."

I turned my body more toward him so I could see his face. Was he warning me about something? Dare I even ask him to be specific? I had to try to get more information so I wouldn't be swimming around in the dark—maybe he knew something that would help me understand Andrew's family better. "Why would the duke hurt me—or hurt anyone, for that matter? I mean, I know he has a terrible temper—I've seen it in action. But I don't think he can help himself. I think he could do with some anger management therapy, if you ask me."

It was quite dark now and getting chilly. I shivered a little and rubbed my hands up and down my arms for warmth. I should've brought a jacket but it hadn't even occurred to me.

"The duke doesn't care if he hurts people. He hurts his own family, but that's not my concern. I'm just saying that if you're going to… *date*…the prince, then you should be aware of what you're getting yourself into." I saw him look at the chain of my talisman then, and he reached over and picked it up from my collarbone. The feel of his warm fingertips against my skin made me shiver. "Where did you get this…necklace?" he asked quietly. As he asked, he pulled the chain up and brought the medallion out from under my shirt. He leaned closer and held it in his hand. In the light of the half-moon, finally visible again now that the clouds had moved on, he studied it closely. His face was mere inches from mine and I involuntarily stopped breathing, even as my pulse quickened.

"I…found…it," I whispered. My voice was suddenly not cooperating. It was hard to talk when I couldn't breathe—when he was this close.

"Really." It was a statement—not a question. "It's valuable, Laura. I can tell. We used to have something similar to this in my family—an heirloom. You should always wear it—for good luck." He laid it back down on my chest and dropped his hand.

"I do—wear it all the time. And I got this chain—it's stronger—like you told me to."

"Good. Protect it, Laura. I have a feeling it's going to bring you something good—at least I hope you'll think so," he said. He suddenly turned away to look at the dark bay and cleared his throat—almost as if he'd misspoken.

"You say that like someone who knows more than they're letting on," I said. "Do you…know something you're not telling me?"

"No…but, hey, you're supposed to be telling me about you, remember?" The abrupt change of subject didn't even surprise me. Being cryptic was, apparently, just a part of his nature.

"Actually, Miguel—I'd rather hear about you—you always seem so…mysterious. And your accent—it's more pronounced when you're…I don't know…agitated, maybe."

"You think so? Perhaps. In any case, you're trying to turn the tables on me. I want to know about you. What's your favorite color? What are your plans for after graduation? When is your birthday? What did you have for dinner last night?" He smiled at me. I could see his even white teeth gleaming in the half-moon light and I thought I saw a twinkle in his eyes.

I shivered again—as much from the cold as from his nearness. Without warning he inched closer to me and I felt his arm slip around my back, his hand taking hold of my arm. I stiffened—not sure what this meant—but he did not remove his arm.

"It's OK, Laura. You're cold. I'll keep you warm while you tell me about yourself. I promise I won't bite." He held me a little tighter as he said the words. I could smell his shirt—a dryer sheet mixed with an ocean breeze—and I felt every one of his fingers as his hand pressed lightly into my arm. *Can he feel the rapid racing of my blood under his hand*? I wondered. I relaxed my posture a bit, but in the back of my mind I knew that Andrew *would* bite if he saw this—probably in the form of a fist to Miguel's face. Andrew…I could see his face in my mind. This seemed wrong somehow…was I cheating on Andrew? I swallowed and tried to decide if I should talk or leave before something happened that shouldn't be happening. And I realized that, deep down, for whatever reason, I didn't want this to be over yet so

I answered his crazy questions. I couldn't remember what I'd had for dinner last night, I told him. I had a December birthday, the 12th—a Sagittarius—to his Libra—October 12, he'd told me—exactly two months older than I.

We continued talking for a long time—well, I talked mostly—he listened. His arm stayed in place around me the whole time and sometimes he softly rubbed his hand up and down my arm. I liked the feel of his hand there—it made me wonder…and then Andrew's face popped into my head again and I knew I should probably go. I suddenly wondered about the time.

"Oh! What time is it? My mother needs her car back by 9:15." Before I could pull my cell phone from my pocket, Miguel had his out, its face glowing in the darkness.

"It's just nine now," he said. He dropped his arm and stood up. He reached down and pulled me to my feet. He jumped down off the rock and reached up to me. "Jump, Laura. I won't let you fall."

I stepped off the rock and hit the sand with a soft thud. Miguel caught me in his arms—and didn't let go. We stood in the darkness, his arms around me, his face against the top of my head. I could hear him breathing. I kept telling myself to move…to go to the Jeep…to do something before I ended up regretting coming here. Before I did something that could hurt Andrew…if he knew. But I couldn't move.

"Thank you for meeting me tonight, Laura." Miguel whispered the words into my hair. He reached up and brushed back the errant strands. He leaned away slightly and looked down into my eyes. I needed to look away—to run—to do something—anything—but I was frozen in place. "Always remember…if you ever need anything—ever—all you have to do is call. My number is still in your phone, isn't it?"

I nodded, not looking away from his face. I should have asked him then how he got my number but I realized I didn't really care. I marveled at his jaw-line, his full lips and dark eyes and I had that weird dizzy feeling that liked to wreak havoc on my central nervous system. And then, as if it were meant to be, with no power to stop it, he kissed me. He pulled me closer, bent his head down and placed his warm lips on mine. My knees threatened to buckle so I reflexively grabbed him to keep from falling. My arms went around him and I felt myself returning his kiss almost against my own will—knowing it was wrong—and yet so right. I felt his tongue touch my lips and a moan escaped me. The kiss deepened and I didn't want it to end. And then his lips moved to my jaw and he kissed it tenderly.

"You'd better get home—your mother's waiting." He whispered the words against my cheek.

"Yes," I breathed. We walked back to the parking lot, his arm still around me. At my car, he pulled me close again and hugged me to his chest tightly.

"Be safe, Laura, *minha querida.*" The sound of his native tongue threatened to derail me—my senses were a tangled mess. Then he walked over to his Suburban and climbed inside. I got in my car and started the engine.

He waited for me to pull out first and then followed close behind. He continued to follow me until I turned back onto the main highway that would take me to my neighborhood. He turned the opposite direction and my eyes never left my rearview mirror until his taillights disappeared. I arrived home just in time to see my mother coming out onto the front porch. I parked and left the car running.

"I was wondering if you were ever going to get here," she said, sounding slightly annoyed.

"Sorry, Mom. Have fun with George—and don't eat too much buttery popcorn. You know how movie theater popcorn always gives you a stomachache." I punched her lightly on the arm and grinned at her as we passed in the driveway. She laughed and got in the car and drove away. I went straight to my room and collapsed on my bed. I was one massive bundle of nerves and confusion—and thankful I'd had the presence of mind to act normally in front of my mother so she wouldn't question why I looked like a volcano about to blow. I grabbed my extra pillow and squeezed it hard. And I was surprised to feel a tingling sensation in my eyes that signified tears were coming. What did I have to cry about? I must surely be losing it. I closed my eyes against the wetness and saw Miguel—his face, his lips, his hair— everything about him was like a myth. I forced myself to think about Andrew. Beautiful Andrew—so sweet and also mysterious in his own way. And then my phone rang. I dropped the pillow from my grasp and pulled my cell phone out of my pocket. It was Andrew.

"Hey, you," I said a little breathlessly.

"Laura! Hi. What are you up to?" he sounded normal—like himself—like he couldn't somehow telepathically know that I had kissed someone else tonight. I settled myself into my pillows and Andrew and I proceeded to talk for the next hour about anything and everything—as if the whole episode with Miguel was a figment of my imagination—something that would stay in its place, secreted away from Andrew, forever. I listened as Andrew told me that Tristan was home and aside from being sore all over, he was going to be fine—good news indeed. And as he talked about everything under the sun, including telling me how much he missed me, I resolved that what had happened with Miguel, would not—could not—ever happen again.

Chapter Eleven

Sensations

The weather turned cold and frost began to cover the ground in the mornings. I reluctantly swapped out my summer wardrobe of flip-flops, shorts and tank tops for jeans, sweaters and long-sleeved shirts. School had officially settled into a boring rhythm, punctuated with evenings with Andrew doing homework together or out walking on the wooded trails of Pilgrim's Park or on the beach. His goon squad had finally loosened up a bit and I no longer had the feeling that we were being babysat every day. Andrew came to my house from time to time and he even had dinner with me and my family one night. I was nervous about that, especially with Nick—you never knew what would come out of his mouth—but it had gone fine. My dad had come down from Providence to join us and my parents had acted like everything was normal between them. Dad and Andrew had even bonded over sailing—what else?

I had finally told Andrew about my parents' pending divorce and he was supportive and also surprised. He couldn't imagine how a divorcing couple could get along so well like that—it defied everything he knew about divorce. I had laughed and told him to hush and not jinx it—that everyone seemed happy and at peace and that was the main thing.

At school, Miguel was his usual polite self. He spoke to me if we passed in the halls and he always said hello in English class. He and Andrew ignored each other completely, to the point of being obvious about it. No word was spoken by either one of us about that night at Red Tide Beach—it truly was as if it had never happened. Sometimes I could feel his nearness, even before I saw him—and when I looked at him I would feel an internal shift, as if a magnet were trying to pull me toward him—physically and emotionally. I ignored it as best I could and immersed myself into my relationship with Andrew.

Lily and Gretchen had all but given up on me. I knew I was neglecting them—they were my best friends after all, but I was so happy with Andrew that I couldn't imagine not being with him every chance I had. And anyway, Gretchen had Colin and Lily had told me recently that a really hot junior named Brent had asked her out. I had teased her about robbing the cradle, to which she'd responded with something about stealing the crown jewels. I didn't touch that flip remark with a ten-foot pole but I thought it was funny just the same.

One night Andrew sent me a very surprising text: *Can you come for a ride with me?* I quickly typed back: *Sure…where are we going?* His reply was instant: *It's a surprise. See you in five.*

Five? Minutes? Holy cow! I quickly filled the dishwasher and dashed upstairs to grab my jacket. I checked my face in the mirror—already flushed with excitement. I ran a brush through my hair and started to pull it back into a pony tail, but thought better of it, remembering how much Andrew liked my hair down. I went downstairs and told my mother I was going for a ride with Andrew. She never minded my being with him. She knew she didn't have to worry—with the goon squad, we were never alone anyway so it wasn't like anything would happen that would cause her to be concerned. In any case, Andrew was always a gentleman, so I knew my virtue was safe with him—funny, because I wasn't sure how I felt about that. I saw the lights from his car coming up the driveway and I ran out, automatically going to my usual spot on the rear passenger side. But when I came abreast of the car, the front passenger window hummed down. I peaked inside and was shocked to see Andrew at the wheel.

"Whoa! You're driving?" I was flabbergasted. "Did you steal this thing?" I laughed. I heard the automatic lock click and I opened the door and got in. "Where are the goo—the guys?" I asked, incredulous.

"Ha ha. No, I didn't steal it. I just informed Peter that it was high time you and I got to be completely alone. I just hope they don't get the bright idea to follow us. I've been checking the rearview mirror but I haven't seen any of them. And I ordered him not to tell Father I was ditching security tonight." He reached over and touched my hair and leaned in for a kiss. "You smell divine," he breathed against my cheek. He leaned back into his seat and put the car in gear and we headed out.

"Andrew?" I'd been wondering about something for as long as I'd known him and now seemed like the perfect time to ask. "Exactly why are you accompanied by security all the time? Is it something to do with your father?" I hoped he didn't get the impression that I thought his life wasn't worth protecting—he had to know me better than that by now.

"Yes, it's my father. He is all about security. But if you think it's bad for me, you should see what my brother has to deal with. Poor Tristan can't get a break from the goons—as you like to call them," he laughed.

"But what exactly are they protecting you and Tristan from? Are you in some kind of danger here?" I knew I was prying—and not even sure of my motive for asking or what I was trying to find out.

Andrew sighed. He considered the question for several beats before giving me an evasive answer. "You never know, Laura, who out there would wish one harm. Better to be safe than sorry. But tonight is about you and me. And, hey, speaking of safety, keep an eye on my driving. Every once in a while, I have an urge to drive in the left lane—it feels really strange to be sitting on the left side of the car and driving on the right side of the road, especially when making turns. It's completely foreign to me."

I assured him I would pay attention to his driving. "So where are we going anyway?"

"I discovered a cool beach recently when I was with the goon squ—I mean, my drivers. Ah…you've got me calling them that all the time now! Anyway, it's called Red Tide Beach. Have you ever been there? Surely you must have since you live here." He made a turn onto route 114 and we drove into the waning light.

I didn't answer immediately. Of course I had been there—many times over the years, but the last time I was there was still fresh in my memory even though I tried not to think about it. Sometimes the memory of that night invaded my dreams and I would wake up, the feel of Miguel's lips imprinted upon mine so deeply that it was as if he had only just kissed me moments before I awoke. *Holy crap, where was this coming from? Stop it*! I chastised myself. I cleared my throat.

"Uh, yes, of course," I said. "It's a nice beach." But I didn't want to go there tonight. Of course, I couldn't tell Andrew that. We arrived at the beach and I was surprised to see a lot of cars in the parking lot.

"Well, damn!" Andrew swore. "I was hoping we would have this place to ourselves." He drove through the parking lot, looking for a place to park. "Why are all these people here? Didn't they get my memo that I wanted to be alone with you here tonight?" He gave me a crooked grin.

I was relieved. "It's OK. Maybe it's a private party or something. Let's go somewhere else. I know a place."

"Great," he said, and drove on through the parking lot and back out onto the road. "Where to, my lady?"

I directed him north toward Tiverton, to a little park that was nestled in the woods. The Sakonnet River was nearby but it was too dark to navigate the woods leading down to the water's edge so I suggested we stick to the paths. There was enough moonlight that we wouldn't get lost and the park wasn't that big anyway. But Andrew had a different idea.

He pulled into the last spot by the edge of the woods, turned off the headlights and we were in near total darkness except for a parking lot security light nearby. There wasn't another soul around—it was just the two of us. He turned off the car and unbuckled his seatbelt. "Is it OK with you if we just stay in here and talk...or maybe...this..."

My breath caught as he leaned over and unbuckled my seatbelt. When I was free of it, he slid toward me a little bit and then pulled me into his arms. His lips were on mine so fast I didn't have time to feel self-conscious. His hands tangled in my hair and his lips made a trail along my jaw toward my ear and back again. I shivered and I must have moaned or made some sound because he brought his lips back to mine and kissed me deeply. I heard a soft groan coming from the back of his throat and I felt his tongue move tentatively against my lips—and once again, I was enveloped in that familiar swoony feeling.

"See how much better it is when we're alone? No one watching in the rearview mirror—just me and you," he whispered. He ran his hand down my arm and took my hand, bringing it up to his face and kissing my palm. Then his hand was back in my hair and he was kissing me again with a passion he had not shown before—because we'd never been this *alone* before. I felt his fingers at my neck, touching the chain of my talisman, holding it a moment and then letting it go. He dropped his hand to my waist and I felt his hand slip under my jacket. My heart was pounding madly and I was breathless. Every nerve was on fire, my senses muddled. I returned his kisses, reveling in the taste of him.

"You're so beautiful, Laura. You've made my every day here in America—since I've known you—better. I can't imagine not being with you." He whispered the words to me softly, his mouth now close to my ear. His hand never moved any more than where it was now, just under my jacket, lying lightly against the cotton material of the shirt covering my stomach.

"I feel the same," I whispered back. But even as I said the words, I felt a strange negative impulse hit me, like a stabbing sensation in my neck. I put my hand up to my throat and gently rubbed the area around my collar bone. The chain of my necklace felt hot against my throat. I did feel that way about Andrew—I was sure of that. I pushed the tiny doubt away and nestled my head into his shoulder. I breathed in his heady scent. He held me and then brought his hand out from where it rested on my stomach and embraced me tightly. And then his cell phone rang.

"Damn it!" he cursed. He sat back and pulled the phone from his pocket. He said hello and spoke for a minute or so. I could hear the voice on the other end though I could not make out the words. After another moment he snapped the phone closed and cursed again.

"Damn! I've been found out. Father wants me to come home." He laid his phone down on the dashboard and pulled me back into arms. He kissed me again and put his hand behind my head and pushed it gently into the crook of his shoulder. He held me like that for several moments and then the next words he spoke startled me. "Laura, when this is over and we go back to England, I want you to come with me."

I froze in his arms for just the tiniest of seconds and then slowly straightened up so I could look into his eyes. Though it was dark outside, I could still see his face from the parking lot security light. I frowned. "When what's over, Andrew?" I asked softly.

He made a sharp intake of breath and turned his head away from me for a moment but he kept his arms around me. Then he turned back to me and nuzzled his nose and mouth into the hair above my ear and whispered, "I mean, when my family's cultural exchange or whatever my father calls it, is over, I want you to come to England—after graduation. You could go to school there. I know you love reading and want to be a writer and even work in publishing. You could do that in London."

I gasped in shock. "How did you know I wanted to be a writer? I don't remember ever telling you that." I was truly puzzled. I hadn't ever really told anyone that. My post high school plans were still mostly a mystery—even to me.

"You must have mentioned it once—how else would I know?" he spoke quickly. "In any case, it's something for you to think about and consider. All I know is—I don't ever want to lose you."

I kissed him then and clasped my hands in his thick blond hair. "You won't," I promised. As soon as I said the words I felt the sensation in my neck again—a heat running just under the chain of the talisman. I put my hand against my collarbone and pressed down.

He sighed and returned my kiss, then turned his attention to the car and the drive home.

We were quiet on the ride back to my house. He played the radio— a classical station—and we held hands as I reminded him to stay in the right lane.

At my house he walked me to the door and kissed me good night. And then he surprised me again. "I love you." He cupped my face in his hands and kissed me before I could take a breath.

He didn't even wait for my response. He was back in his car and down the drive and gone before I had fully processed those three little words. I opened the door, floated up the steps and went straight to my bed. I never changed into pajamas or brushed my teeth or did any of the things that made up my night-time ritual. It was as if I were in an emotional coma. The only thing I could feel was the weight and the heat of my necklace as it tingled against my chest.

C h a p t e r   T w e l v e

OMEN

Andrew texted me several times throughout the day on Sunday. He had an engagement with his family so I wouldn't be seeing him today. I had plenty to do to keep me busy, though, so I didn't dwell on his absence. Tomorrow there was no school because of Columbus Day so we'd made plans to go to dinner and a movie in the evening. Today I helped my mother clean the house and do laundry. I ran the vacuum, finished my homework and even baked a vanilla cake from scratch. While I was mixing powdered sugar and cream cheese in the mixing bowl for the frosting, I recalled suddenly that Miguel's birthday was this week. We'd told each other our birthdays that evening at Red Tide Beach. He would be eighteen. Suddenly this cake took on a new significance. I had no intention of giving him the entire cake, but giving him a piece of it would be a nice gesture. Just the thought of contacting him about a piece of cake made my stomach churn and my nerve endings twitch. I was fairly certain he would think I was crazy for giving him cake. But the longer I mixed the frosting the more certain I was that it was the right thing to do. Once the cake was frosted, I cut a generous piece from the corner and placed it into a disposable plastic container. I even slipped a plastic fork inside with it. I shook my head in disbelief at my actions, thinking I must be nuts—and totally unsure of the effect it would have. What if I were giving the wrong impression? Would he read more into my little acknowledgment of his birthday than I'd intended? Did I even care? So many questions—so few answers.

In my room I sat down at my desk and scrolled through my phone looking for the texts he'd sent me the night of our meeting at Red Tide Beach. I initially had planned to call him on the phone, but after careful consideration, I realized I didn't have the guts to actually speak to him directly—thank goodness for texting. I gathered my courage, took a deep breath, and with very shaky fingers I typed a text message: *Hi, Miguel. Just wanted to wish you a happy birthday—this week—18! I've even got cake…if you'd like some…?* I waited five whole minutes before I had the nerve to press send and as soon as I did I threw my phone down on my bed as if it were on fire. Then I ran from the room to put some distance between it and me—who knew that a cell phone could be the most frightening thing in the universe?

In the kitchen I poured myself some iced tea and quietly paced around. I didn't want my mother to wonder why I suddenly seemed nervous and keyed up. Then I remembered she wasn't even home right now. She'd gone to the store to get groceries—lucky for me. I thought I heard a faint pinging sound in my room but I was too afraid to go up to check. I walked into the living room and looked out the window at the front lawn. Yellow oak leaves and red and orange maple leaves were scattered about the yard, a brisk wind causing them to swirl about in colorful miniature tornadoes. It was overcast today, the sky threatening to rain any minute. I watched a couple of cars pass on the street and finally decided I'd avoided my room and the phone long enough. As I slowly trudged up the stairs I tried to figure out what my problem was. What was I afraid of? Miguel? Or Andrew finding out I'd texted Miguel? I pushed these questions from my mind as I picked up my phone and looked at the number on the screen.

Miguel. With trembling fingers I opened the text and read his words: *Thank you for remembering. Yes, 18. Old, huh? You have cake? I'd love some. When do I get it?*

Again I threw the phone onto my bed as if it were a bomb. Did this mean I would get to see him today? Excitement bubbled in my stomach even as a wave of guilt washed over me. It wasn't right to feel this way. I had Andrew. I loved Andrew. So why this reaction to someone who scared me just as often as not? I hit reply and stared at the blank screen. There was no turning back now. I texted: *You can have it any* *time…tell me when's good for you…*I hit send and…waited. His reply was immediate: *Now.* It wasn't even a question.

Holy cow. I wasn't ready for this. I thought I would have had more time to mentally prepare myself. He was available *now.* I paced around my room in a panic. I grabbed my make-up bag and stared at it like it was a new invention I'd never seen before. I shook my head back and forth, trying to clear my addled brain. With shaking hands, I put on a little foundation and some mascara. I added some pink gloss to my lips and contemplated blush—no—there was no need for that—lately I'd become the queen of pink cheeks and it was all natural, considering lately I always seemed to be in some weird, over-hyped state of being. I ran a brush through my hair, not bothering with a pony tail. I grabbed my heavier jacket—another check of the weather confirmed the rain and wind—and ran downstairs.

What the hell was I thinking? I couldn't go anywhere. I didn't have a car and I hadn't even texted Miguel back. I was getting way ahead of myself and not thinking straight. I stood by the front door and did some deep breathing exercises until I had myself under control enough to reply to Miguel's text: *Now would've been good but I don't have a car at the moment—my mom has it—sorry.* I sent the text and felt… bereft.

In a moment his reply came: *Not a problem. I can pick you up.* I read his words and nearly dropped the phone again. Without hesitating to consider the consequences, I replied: *OK. You're sure you don't mind? I'm not interrupting anything?* Another quick response: *No, never. I'll be there in a few minutes.*

My nerves seriously couldn't handle this. He would be here in a few minutes. I looked at my reflection in the front hall mirror. "Laura—what the hell are you doing? Are you crazy? This is wrong— you know it is. You're playing with fire. You're gonna get burned." I said the words in a low whisper to my face in the mirror. And then I instantaneously felt a slow heat at my neck and under my sweater where the talisman lay against my chest. "*Ooh,*" I gasped. "What the hell…?" I quickly pulled the necklace out from under my sweater and leaned forward, letting it dangle down in front of me. I watched it swing back and forth as I stood at the bottom of the stairs, bent over at the waist, shaking my sweater to move the air around. I rubbed my neck and then straightened and stepped back to the hall mirror. I pulled the collar of my sweater down and looked closely at my neck. There was no mistaking the slight red discoloration of my skin under the area where the chain lay. I sank down onto the bottom stair and grasped my knees tightly to my chest. What was happening? I couldn't possibly be imagining this, could I?

With trepidation, I picked up the talisman and studied it closely. It looked the same as it always did. "What are you trying to tell me?" I asked it quietly. "Are you sending me a message?" I was thankful there was no one around to hear my insane muttering. I held the disk tightly in my hand and closed my eyes. I was literally going nuts—no question. And then I heard the sound of a car coming up the driveway. I jumped to my feet and nearly lost my balance. I had intended to leave my mother a note telling her I was out on an errand but there was no time. I would just have to send her a text when I had a chance. I slipped on my jacket and stepped out onto the front porch. And then I realized I'd left the damned cake in the kitchen sitting on the counter.

"Oh, my god, I'm so dumb," I mumbled. I held my finger up to the dark windshield, hoping Miguel would see my signal to hang on a minute. I ran to the kitchen and grabbed the cake, then ran back outside and, with a deep breath, I ducked my head against the rain and dashed to his car. He leaned across and opened the door for me just as I got there. I hopped into the Suburban and settled into my seat and let out a slow, quiet breath. Then I turned to look at Miguel, knowing my face was all kinds of red. "Hi," I breathed. It was only one word but even I didn't recognize the sound of it coming from my own voice box.

"Hello there, Laura. This is an unexpected surprise," he said. I tried not to stare at him. He looked…devastating. His hair was damp from the rain and slightly mussed and his jaw-line was unshaven. His eyes were dark and penetrating. He truly did look like the gypsies I'd read about in books and seen in movies. I felt like I was seeing him for the first time. And then I realized that I had not given him my address, yet he knew where I lived. I remembered back to the night I had seen a car like his drive by my house and I knew now for certain it had been his car. But I didn't say a word.

I held up the plastic container. "Cake—as promised." I was amazed at myself. I'd gotten three more words out of my mouth without passing out.

"I can't wait to try it. Would you like to come back to my house? Although there's no one there at the moment—if that's a problem for you…?" I heard the question in his voice and I wondered why it would be a problem. Then I blushed even more. Alone in a house with Miguel—in the mystery house that I couldn't see behind the trees. I was quaking now. I would never survive this—not because I was in fear of my personal safety. But because the powerful attraction I felt for him was palpable—almost crippling.

I managed to breathe out an answer as I buckled my seatbelt and then took in the interior of the car. "No, of course not." I held the cake in my lap as I noticed the dashboard. It was crazy—high tech didn't begin to describe what I was seeing. There were monitors, a phone and a built-in GPS system and knobs and buttons and red and green lights and I didn't understand any of it.

"Wow," I said, my eyes wide. I glanced over my shoulder and saw the two rows of black leather seats. I noticed the scent in the car—new car smell mixed with pine and mint. And suddenly there came the low sound of plaintive music playing all around me in surround-sound. I didn't recognize it but it sounded like fado music. "Nice car," I breathed.

"Thanks. It's my uncle's. He has another just like it, only white." He turned the car around in the driveway and pulled out onto the road.

So he has an uncle. One more detail of his life revealed. And now I just had to ask. "What about parents? I mean, do you have parents?" I realized how ridiculous the question sounded as soon as it came out of my mouth. "I'm sorry—that was a dumb question."

He laughed and looked at me. "No, it's not. I have a mother. She lives in Portugal. My father died earlier this year." He turned onto the main highway heading in the direction of Portsmouth's main square.

"I'm sorry." I'd heard the sad tone of his voice at the mention of his father and my heart went out to him. "How did it happen?" I was almost afraid to ask but I wanted to know.

"Heart attack. He was forty-eight in case you were wondering." He kept his eyes on the road and I stared down at the cake in my hands. I'd made him uncomfortable now and I wondered how I could turn things around.

"I'm sorry. I shouldn't have asked—it was rude of me." I tried another, happier topic. "How do you feel about vanilla cake?" I smiled at him and he glanced my way, grinning his devastating, white smile. My heart skipped multiple beats.

"My favorite—and it wasn't rude," he said. "Here's where I live." We turned into the hidden drive that I had wondered about and drove down the gravel driveway. It was longer than I'd thought and there was nothing but towering trees on either side. The drive curved to the left and we drove on. *How far back is this house?* I wondered. Just when I thought it was a big joke and he lived in the trees, a large, single-story white house came into view. The view behind it was even more spectacular. The house was situated on the Sakonnet River. There were no other buildings on the property except for a detached garage off to the left. It was serene—bucolic even. He parked the car in front of the garage and turned off the engine.

"Oh, I better text my mom and let her know I'm gone. She wasn't home when I left and I forgot to leave a note," I said as I pulled my phone from my jacket pocket.

Miguel laughed. "Don't worry, Laura. I wasn't planning to harm you…but we could go back and leave a trail of cake crumbs if it would make you feel better." He opened the car door and hopped out.

Oh, boy. Clearly I'd given him the wrong impression. I got out of the car and walked up to him. "Hey, I wasn't thinking that! If I were afraid then I wouldn't even be here, would I?" Now that I thought about it, his words had actually stung a bit. I was surprised that my necklace hadn't attacked me, too.

"I'm kidding—really," he smiled. I followed him to the front door and he opened it with his key and allowed me to enter first. I stepped over the threshold and stared in amazement around the open-floor-plan rooms. It was beautiful—all dark woods, rich carpets and old paintings on the walls, a style reminiscent of a European palace from another era. "Wow," I breathed. There was a gorgeous clock on the wall and an ornate, gilt-framed mirror over the fireplace. It was like a museum, only with a homey, lived-in feel. And I noticed the acute absence of a woman's touch. It was overwhelmingly masculine.

"It's my uncle's—he likes to decorate," said Miguel, as if he'd read my mind. "Can I get you something to drink? I think we have some Coke or Pepsi and maybe some lemonade."

"Pepsi is good but anything is OK," I answered. He walked toward the kitchen and beckoned to me to follow him.

"Come with me—there's a couch in the kitchen." The kitchen was painted pale blue and the cabinets were a dark oak, and an island stood in the middle surrounded by stainless steel appliances. And sure enough there was a couch in the room—over by sliding doors that led to a deck that overlooked the back yard and the river. I walked to the sliding doors and took in the view. The fact that the sky was overcast and the wind brisk added to the mysterious atmosphere of Miguel's home. *Miguel's home—what am I doing here? How did I get here? This is so surreal.* My mind became a tangle of thoughts.

Suddenly he was behind me. I felt him before I saw him. I jumped and nearly dropped the plastic container of his cake that I completely forgot I was holding. He caught it before it could hit the floor and grinned at me, that devastating grin that would be my undoing—if I let it.

"Sorry—didn't mean to scare you. Maybe I should eat this cake now. Have a seat." I slipped off my jacket and sat down on the couch— it was actually a loveseat. He'd placed two glasses of Pepsi on a coffee table in front of the loveseat. He sat next to me and pushed one of the drinks closer to me. Then he removed the lid from the container and brought it up to his face. "Hmm. Smells good. And I see you even included a fork. Nice touch." He took the fork from the container and cut into the cake. "Would you like some? I'm happy to share."

"No thanks—it's all yours. There's plenty more of that at home." I watched him take a bite of the cake and I had to turn away. There was no way I could watch him eat something. It was too…intimate. I reached over and picked up my glass and took a sip, then set it back down, noticing that my hand was shaking. *Please don't let me spill anything*, I silently pleaded to whoever was listening.

Miguel put the cake down on the table next to the drinks and took my hand. I turned to him expectantly, completely unable to function and I prayed he couldn't tell. I tried to make my face a mask but inside I was Mount Etna in all her glory. "Laura, you're trembling. Why?" His hand was warm on mine. I was so close to him–it was hard to breathe. I tried to speak but no words would come. I couldn't actually remember how to speak, come to think of it.

"Do I make you nervous? I'm sorry if I do. I don't mean to." His voice was hypnotic. I was falling under his spell and I couldn't help myself. "Laura?"

"Oh," I attempted to take a breath as goose-bumps formed all over my body. "I…think…I'm…just…cold," I said, my words coming out almost staccato-style. I tried to concentrate on not hyperventilating.

"I can fix that," he said, a husky tone to his voice. He pulled me gently into his arms and I just folded myself into them as if it were the most natural thing in the world to do. But then the alarm bells went off in my head. I had to stop this. I couldn't let this happen. I forced myself to think of Andrew—to see his face in my mind. I tried to conjure the taste and feel of Andrew's mouth on mine but my brain no longer worked. And then Miguel was tilting my face to his and he touched his lips to mine. His lips were warm and soft and magnetic. I felt his hand slip under my hair, his thumb rubbing the base of my neck rhythmically. The kiss deepened and I felt a surge of passion not unlike the descent on a roller coaster ride. He moved his lips from mine and snaked a trail along my jaw-line to my ear. He pushed my hair away from my ear and pressed his mouth to it. I could hear his breathing and feel the sweetness of his breath as he kissed my earlobe. He whispered something foreign to me. I knew it was Portuguese but it could have been Mandarin Chinese for all I could comprehend. My arms finally moved on their own command and I wrapped them around Miguel and I felt him shift further into me. And then I felt the unmistakable heat radiate from my chest into his, and he made a slight moan in the back of his throat. He looked down at my chest where the talisman lay under my sweater. I followed his eyes downward. And I saw it—the faintest glow emitting through the cotton threads of my sweater. I gasped and stiffened and Miguel suddenly crushed me to him and whispered, "It's OK, Laura. It's just a chemical reaction to your passion—don't be afraid of it."

But it did scare me, even as it gave me a sense of security. I didn't understand this strange, alchemic phenomenon. "Miguel," I whispered against his chest. "What is this thing? I've never heard of jewelry that burns…and…and…glows…it isn't normal."

He stroked my hair and continued to hold me close against his body. I could hear his heartbeat and feel the rise and fall of his lungs under my cheeks. I smelled the faintest hit of cologne—a fresh scent like a summer day, and I had the distinct feeling that I was being drugged by his very essence.

"Ever heard of mood rings, from way back in the '70's? I know it was a long time ago—way before our time—but sometimes people still wear them today—they change color based on your mood. Your talisman adapts itself to your emotional state. Always trust it, Laura. It won't ever steer you wrong."

He touched his fingertips to my chin and tilted my face up to his, kissing me again. I whispered against his lips, "How do you know so much about this talisman?"

He leaned his forehead against mine and said, "Remember, I told you we had one like this in my family a long time ago—I've heard the legends. Promise me you'll protect it and wear it always."

Before I could answer, a noise came from the direction of the front door. Miguel kissed me once more and then reluctantly pulled away. Three imposing men walked into the kitchen and stopped dead still in their tracks, staring at us. Miguel got up from the loveseat and turned to the men—two of whom I could see were technically not men but rather his younger brothers who were quite possibly bigger than Miguel. The other man was older—maybe late thirties—and he had a goatee and black hair and dark eyes like Miguel and his brothers. I could see the strong family resemblance.

"Hey, guys," said Miguel. "This is Laura Calder—she's a friend of mine from school. Laura, these are my brothers Tomas and Mateo, and my Uncle Antonio."

I swallowed my nerves and smiled, extending my hand in greeting. They each shook it and said hello. I felt awkward—not sure if I should be here—or if I was even allowed to be here. But Antonio smiled warmly as did the two boys and I allowed myself to relax.

"We were down in Newport checking out Uncle Antonio's boat. It's already half-way finished," said Mateo—at least I thought he was Mateo. Their resemblance to one another was freaky, but then again they were twins.

"Yes, we are right on schedule. I'll be installing the navigation system soon," said Antonio.

Miguel turned to me with an explanation. "My uncle is a boat-builder. He's working on a commission right now for a Newport man who ordered a boat to be used in the America's Cup."

"Wow, that's amazing," I said, impressed. "My father is an avid sailor. Actually, he's kind of obsessed with it."

The mention of sailing was all it took to start a conversation about all things nautical. I'd finished my drink finally and I realized I needed to heed the call of nature. I leaned toward Miguel to ask about the whereabouts of the bathroom.

"I'll take you," he said. "Excuse us, please." He got up and I followed him down a long hallway. He pointed toward the door and I went inside. I took a moment to catch my breath and look at myself in the mirror. My face looked flushed as if I had a fever. I pulled out the talisman and studied it in wonder, baffled but also convinced of its magic. I dropped it back inside my sweater and when I finished, I washed my hands and opened the door. I could hear their voices in the kitchen as I walked slowly down the hall. The walls were adorned with pictures of landscapes and ancient family portraits.

And then I noticed one in particular. I stopped still in my tracks, my hand going automatically to my throat. Before me was an antique picture of a beautiful, exotic young woman. She had long black hair and piercing dark eyes. A beautiful tiara of diamonds and sapphires adorned her head. I saw the necklace hanging down into the V of her ornate navy gown. It was, without a doubt, identical to my own. I shook my head in disbelief as I stared at the crossed swords on the talisman that hung from her delicate neck. There was no way the one around my neck could possibly be the same as the one on the woman in the portrait—was there? It was impossible.

Miguel appeared at the end of the hall. "Hey, I thought maybe you got lost." He smiled as he spoke but when he saw me turned toward the portrait he stiffened ever so slightly. I started to speak but then his uncle appeared behind him. He saw where I stood next to the portrait and I'm sure the look on my face must have registered something amiss, judging by his suddenly rigid stance. A prickle of fear snaked its way through me. Something was clearly not right. I felt that dizzy feeling and wondered if I was going to faint. And then Miguel was beside me, taking me by the hand. We walked back into the kitchen where Mateo and Tomas were laughing about something funny one of them had said. I turned to Miguel then.

"I think I should get home. My mom's probably wondering where I am." I turned to his family. "It was nice to meet you all."

Antonio smiled warmly at me. "Nice to meet you, too, Laura. Come any time. Don't be a stranger." They said good-bye as Miguel and I walked toward the front door—I grabbed my jacket from the arm of the loveseat on my way by. We walked in silence to the Suburban and Miguel opened my door for me. I climbed inside, buckled my seatbelt and let out a deep breath—I didn't even realize I had been holding it so long.

As soon as Miguel was behind the wheel and we were heading down the long driveway, he looked over at me, his face serious. "I know you have questions, Laura. I can see them in your eyes. But I'm asking you for patience and trust. The world works in mysterious ways—I'm sure you've heard that before. Everything has a way of working out and puzzles will be solved in their own natural time. Now I'm sure I'm not making sense to you, but I'm asking you anyway—do you trust me?"

I nodded but remained silent and looked out my window at the endless trees. And then we were at the highway and Miguel was waiting for traffic to clear before making his turn. I thought about his words—words that made no sense—and I somehow knew not to question him—except about one thing—the one thing that I had to know. I turned to face his profile—admiring its perfection—and asked my one question. "Does this have anything to do with Andrew and his family?"

Miguel stared straight ahead at the road. He didn't answer right away. I watched as he worked his jaw. I resisted the urge to reach over and touch it—to calm it.

"Yes. But, Laura…I'm begging you…please don't ask any more than that. And whatever you do, don't mention to Andrew about anything that's on your mind—just trust time and your talisman—and me. Promise you'll do as I say. I need you to promise me this." We arrived at my house and he put the car in park, letting it idle in the drive. He looked over at me and took his right hand off the wheel, extending it toward me, palm up. I glanced at him and at his hand, and I placed my left hand in his. He grasped mine tightly and brought it up to his face, pressing my palm into his cheek for just a moment.

"I promise," I said quietly as he turned his mouth into my palm and kissed it tenderly.

"I had a nice time with you today. The cake was delicious. Thank you." His voice had a hint of sadness—it sounded like a bittersweet good-bye.

"You're welcome…and happy early birthday." I brought my hand down to his arm and gave it a gentle squeeze then got out of the car.

He drove off and I stood there for a moment before realizing that the on-again, off-again rain was coming down again.

C h a p t e r   T h i r t e e n

THE MAZE

I forced myself to spend the morning of Columbus Day with Lily and Gretchen at Lily's house—not that being with them was such a sacrifice, but my mind was checked out. We'd listened to music in Lily's bedroom and let her monopolize the conversation about her new guy, Brent. I surreptitiously watched the clock on her nightstand, waiting for a suitable time to leave. Gretchen must have been paying more attention to me than I'd thought because she called me out on my clock watching.

"You must be excited about seeing Prince Charming tonight, huh?" she said. "You keep looking at that clock as if you're willing time to speed up or something."

"Sorry," I said sheepishly. "Yeah, I didn't see him yesterday so… well…you know how it is…" I grinned. If they only knew—knew the real reason for my distracted state. The truth was I was worried about seeing Andrew. And I was confused about my feelings for Miguel. I didn't mention this to them, though, because I knew they would never understand about Miguel. I steered the subject back to Brent and Lily became glassy-eyed all over again. Finally it was time to go. We all walked downstairs together and said good-bye at the front door. Gretchen stopped me just as I was getting into the Jeep.

"Hey, Laura…you gonna do the maze this year? I remember how much you enjoyed it last year. I'm sure you wouldn't want to miss it!" She gave me a devilish laugh and watched as I cringed at the memory.

"I'd rather not…but…we'll see." I waved at them and headed back home to get ready for my date with Andrew. On the drive home I thought back to my experience last Halloween in the maze at Escobar's Highland Farm and shuddered.

Every fall Escobar's Highland Farm created an eight-acre maze carved out of a cornfield in Portsmouth that drew crowds from all over the region to revel in its confusion. Each year the maze took on a different shape—last year it had been a Rhode Island Red Rooster. I had spent an hour lost in the rooster's body and had to be rescued, an awful and embarrassing experience, and I vowed I would never subject myself to that kind of humiliation again. I had just read recently in the newspaper that this year's shape was a giant lobster—and I could just see myself trying to fight my way out of one of its huge claws—no thanks.

Once back in my room I got ready to meet Andrew. I'd been consumed with guilt all day about yesterday and Miguel. I had to admit to myself, as awful as it was, that I was cheating on Andrew. And I had to do something about it, but what? I had convinced myself that I was falling for Andrew—sometimes I still felt that way—but just the thought of Miguel…of his eyes, his hands, his lips, his scent…made me scream inside my head so loudly that I brought back the stupid headaches that I thought had gone for good once I'd gotten my new glasses. Which reminded me, I hadn't worn them lately—I couldn't even remember where they were at the moment.

My mom called up the stairs to tell me Andrew had arrived. I put on a pair of black, low-heeled ankle boots and grabbed my wool coat. It was unseasonably cold tonight—the weatherman had gone so far as to predict snow before Halloween much to my horror. Andrew was already waiting in the front hall—I hadn't even heard him come in.

"Hey," he said, grinning widely. "I missed you yesterday." He held his arms out to me and I embraced him though I was keenly aware of my mother's presence. I felt my face blush crimson and couldn't wait to get out the door. I didn't necessarily have a problem with public displays of affection—but not in front of my mother. We told her goodbye and headed out. The blast of cold air on my face helped to temper the heat rush on my cheeks.

In the car, with Peter ensconced at the wheel as usual, Andrew pulled me into his arms and kissed me. I made a conscious effort to remain relaxed and attentive and, as he told me about his family's engagement of the previous day, it was actually easier than I'd thought to keep thoughts of Miguel at bay. Andrew was too happy and animated in conversation to *not* pay attention to him. I commented on his state of excitement.

"I'm just happy to be with you—I missed you terribly. I'm thinking that going for twenty-four hours without you shouldn't even be a consideration." He took my chin in his hands and tilted my face to his, kissing me tenderly. I caught sight of Peter in the rearview mirror, watching us, but he turned away when our eyes met.

We drove to the movie theater in Newport where we watched the new James Bond film. During the movie, Andrew kept his arm tightly around me. He was soon engrossed in the movie but my mind wandered with confusing thoughts. As much as I loved a good Bond flick, James wasn't enough to distract me from my dilemma. With Andrew, everything was light and fun and carefree. He was handsome and kind and I did not doubt my attraction to him in any way. But in the darkness of the movie theater, thoughts of Miguel seeped into my mind. As much as I was attracted to him—of that there could be no doubt—I couldn't help but feel a sense of foreboding when he was near—as if something bad might happen. I had never thought it possible that you could love two people at the same time—and maybe love was too strong a word—but I was definitely torn. It was like I was being pulled between darkness and light. Well, there was safety in light, so I'd always heard, so maybe that was all I needed to know. I tried to convince myself that I should distance myself from Miguel and concentrate on my relationship with Andrew. I only hoped that it wouldn't be easier said than done.

After the movie, Peter drove us to the Harbor Inn for dinner, a place on the marina I had not been to in years. It was a favorite restaurant of my father's—he and his sailing buddies often ate here after a day on the water. We sat at a window table which afforded an amazing view of all of the boats dockside, bobbing in Newport Harbor, as the sun set in the distance. I wondered if my dad's friend's boat was one of them. Andrew ordered lobster and I ordered North Atlantic cod and while we waited to be served, Andrew asked me what I'd been up to the day before. I grabbed my glass and took a long pull on my ice water while I tried to formulate an answer.

"I helped my mom around the house. Cleaning and laundry and stuff. And I baked a cake."

"Oh, yum. What kind of cake?" he asked.

I kept my voice light as I answered. "Vanilla with vanilla cream cheese frosting."

"Sounds divine. Is there any left? Perhaps when I take you home, you'll offer me a piece. I would love to sample your culinary talents." He held my hand in his across the table as he spoke.

"Of course. There's plenty." *Thank goodness for the cake*, I thought. Our meal was served and I was content to let Andrew monopolize the conversation. He talked about his life in England and told me about what it was like to grow up in a royal family. It was a fascinating life and I had to pinch myself at the thought that I was, in fact, dining with a real prince, albeit one far removed from the top of the royal family tree. Andrew likened his position in the pecking order as one who gets to enjoy all the perks without having to do too many actual royal duties of great importance.

After dinner Peter dropped us off at my house and we went inside. I led Andrew to the kitchen and we sat at the dining room table where I sliced generous servings of cake for both of us. He told me that he had never baked a cake in his life. Nor had he ever washed a dish or operated a washing machine. He'd never shopped in a grocery store or, until this year, attended a regular school. He'd never pumped his own gas at a gas station or for the most part, ever been denied anything he'd ever wanted. He had not said these things to me in a boastful way either. Rather his words were tinged with sadness and even regret.

"Even Prince William and his wife cook for themselves. Am I a shallow person?" He had a half-smile on his lips as he asked, but I sensed it was a serious question. I weighed my words before I answered.

"Shallow? No. Deprived? Yes." And then I laughed and grabbed his hand. "OK, Mr. Easton. It's time to wash the dishes. Come on!" I pulled him up from the table and pushed him gently toward the sink, bringing our dishes with us. I set them in the sink with the few other items that were waiting to be washed and I opened the dishwasher. It was already mostly full of dirty dishes so this would be a good lesson for him in the kitchen cleaning department.

"Oh, boy. Here we go!" He laughed good-naturedly and carefully rinsed the dishes and filled the dishwasher under my tutelage. When it was filled, I showed him where to find the detergent and watched as he poured some into the soap compartment. I showed him how to turn it on and then gave him the dishcloth to wash off the table. He was completely game for these cleaning tasks and when the kitchen was spotless he beamed with pride. "Do you have any dirty laundry?"

I burst into loud laughter and impulsively threw my arms around him. "See? This domestic stuff isn't so bad, is it? Wait till we graduate to cleaning the bathroom. You're gonna love that!"

He grimaced. "Ooh, I don't think I'm ready for that yet," he said. "You know what would be amazing though?" His voice had softened to a whisper. He tightened his arms around me, pulling me closer. He nestled his face into my hair and I felt his lips graze my temple. "Being domestic with you would be amazing," he whispered.

I felt myself stiffen the slightest bit. My thoughts muddled again and my breathing went all funny. His words were beautiful but loaded with uncertainties. Was he implying a more permanent relationship? It sounded that way. I searched for something to say that would appease him and buy me time to assess the meaning behind his words. "Aren't we a little young for that?" I teased.

He pulled back from me and looked down into my eyes. "Age is only a number, as they say. I could wait till I'm thirty to tell you how I feel about you, but think of all those wasted years. I love you, Laura." He pulled me into his chest then and pressed his body against mine. And then I felt it—my constant companion—the talisman reacting. But it offered none of its earlier heat, instead exuding only coldness. I had the sensation that someone had just dropped ice down the front of my shirt. I was sure he could feel it, too, but if he did, he said nothing. I had to bite my tongue to keep from verbally reacting to the icy chill. Andrew continued to kiss me and while the kiss deepened I waged a war of words in my head as to how to respond to his declaration of love when we finished this sweetest of kisses. But the problem took care of itself. My brother chose that moment to walk into the kitchen. He cleared his throat as he entered and Andrew released me, looking down shyly. I felt my face burn even as my chest froze. Nick stared at us with a loopy grin on his face.

"Hey, Andrew." He proffered his hand and Andrew shook it. I noticed that Andrew's face had a hint of pink on his cheeks and I felt better about my own embarrassment. "What's Tristan up to?"

"Oh, the usual…hanging out at the stables mostly." Andrew replied.

"Of course. He sure loves his horses, doesn't he?" As Nick spoke, he helped himself to the cake and filled a glass with chocolate milk from the fridge.

"Yes, he's obsessed with them," said Andrew. "Always has been. He was riding horses before he could walk so we've been told by our parents."

Nick laughed. "He's a nice guy, that Tristan."

"Yes, my brother's a good guy—thanks," Andrew grinned.

They launched into a discussion about sports so I excused myself to go to the bathroom.

Once I was alone I put the seat down on the toilet and sank down on top of it. Nick had saved me—but from what? Emotions swirled inside me. When I was with Andrew I couldn't imagine being with anyone else. He was everything a girl could ever want. For crying out loud—he was a prince! It didn't get any better than that. And to top it all off, he loved me. And I knew beyond a shadow of a doubt that I had feelings for him—feelings I could not dismiss. I resolved in that instant that I would explore my feelings for Andrew and see where our relationship was headed. I would not allow myself to think about Miguel. One thing at a time—and right now I was Andrew's—and apparently, he was mine.

When I returned to the kitchen the topic of conversation had changed to Escobar's corn maze. Nick was telling Andrew about it and it seemed to have him quite jazzed up.

"Laura, Nick's been telling me about the maze. He says you go every year. And I hear you always get lost in it. It sounds like fun. We should go." Andrew was definitely excited, I could see.

"I have a love-hate relationship with that maze," I said. "Everyone seems to go into it and come out the other side within an hour or so and then there's me. If someone hadn't rescued me last year, I'd probably still be in there now rotting away." I shuddered at the thought.

Nick laughed. "Aw, come on, Laura. You know you wanna go back in. You'll conquer it one of these years. This year it's going to be in the shape of a lobster—sounds awesome if you ask me." Nick was clearly no help. He turned to Andrew. "The best night to go is Halloween. It's on a Monday this year so that's actually perfect for Laura." He looked over at me and grinned evilly. "You should be able to find your way out in time for the weekend."

"Ha, ha, very funny." I scowled at him. "I know the maze is supposed to be fun but I find it scary." I looked at Andrew and saw the twinkle in his eyes. I had a feeling that I would be going into that maze whether I liked it or not.

Andrew looked at his watch and took my hand. "We will talk more about this maze later. I want to do it. But I'd better go. Peter will be here any minute." He turned to Nick. "It was very nice chatting with you."

"You, too," Nick replied. He waved us off and Andrew and I walked out onto the front porch. I could see the lights of the car as it turned into the driveway. Andrew took me into his arms and kissed me—his lips were soft and tender as they caressed mine.

"Good night, Laura. I'll see you tomorrow. I'm picking you up as usual, yes?"

I nodded. He kissed me again and cupped my face in his hands. "I love you. I hope you love me, too, but you don't have to answer me now. But just know that I'm not going anywhere. I think I loved you before I met you, if that's even possible."

I smiled against his palms. "Isn't that a song?" I whispered.

"I think it is and it's true. Good night, Laura. Until tomorrow." He dashed down the steps, got into the car and was gone. And I was left with my talisman still unusually cold against my heart.

The next couple of weeks flew by in a rush. We were in mid-terms already and there were lots of reports due and tests to study for. We finally put *The Prince and the Pauper* to rest. It was a relief to finally have the characters of Tom and Edward in their rightful places. I made an effort to keep myself busy with Lily and Gretchen, too, as well as all the time I spent with Andrew. But Miguel was there, too, in and out of my subconscious as well as my line of sight. I saw his car in the mornings—sometimes we arrived about the same time. His brothers always waved and said hello to me if we had occasion to pass in the halls or in the cafeteria. Miguel was aloof and kept his distance from me and he didn't try to contact me. He was polite and quiet and he always, without fail, kept his distance from Andrew. I wondered what he thought of my relationship with Andrew. Did he wonder if I loved Andrew? Why didn't he make a move toward me—dare I say—*fight* for me? Did I even want that? I truly did not understand the way his mind worked. And I certainly didn't understand the way my own mind worked when I thought of him.

I was informed the Friday before Halloween that the trip to the maze was on. Gretchen and her boyfriend, Colin, were going, as well as Lily and her new boyfriend, Brent. A lot of seniors were planning to get there just before dusk, which was usually closing time for the maze, but sometimes on Halloween the owners relaxed the closing time a bit just for the fright of it. I heard lots of kids talking about it at lunch—including Miguel's brothers, who were sitting at the table behind me. It made me wonder if Miguel would be there, but for some reason I highly doubted it—mazes didn't seem like they'd be his thing. Of course, Andrew was excited about it. And he made me a promise which I intended to make him keep.

"Don't worry, Laura. I won't let you get lost. We'll stick together and everything will come out alright." He looked so earnest that I had to laugh at his worry of my fear of this thing.

"OK, if we must…," I sighed in resignation. Oh, how I really did not like this maze.

On Monday evening, Andrew and I and several of our classmates went out for pizza before going to the maze. I was surprised that he was willing to go out with other kids rather than just the two of us, which was his usual preference. About a dozen of us met at Captain Pete's Pizza Parlor in Middletown, which was extremely crowded, and I was secretly glad there were so many people eating here tonight because if we delayed things long enough, there was a good chance the maze would be closed by the time we got there. We had a long wait for a table although Andrew offered to pull some royal strings to jump the line. I flat-out refused, again citing fairness. I could see that in addition to learning about domesticity, he needed to learn about the natural order of life in a non-royal world.

We were finally seated and then it was almost another two hours by the time our pizza was served and we'd eaten. I ordered the salad bar and even though I'd eaten my fill, I kept going back for more just to cause a further delay in our departure. By the time the check came I was so full of lettuce and pineapple I thought I would blow.

It was quite late when we left Captain Pete's. I stole a glance at my watch and I was almost convinced we would be too late for the damned maze. But, alas, though most people had already cleared out, we were the last group allowed to go in. I was surprised to see Mateo and Tomas there and I wondered if Andrew had noticed them. I wasn't even sure if he knew Miguel had brothers. They were already heading into the maze as we paid our entrance fee and hadn't noticed me. I looked around for Miguel and felt a rush of nerves at the thought that he could possibly be here somewhere but he was nowhere to be seen. I sighed in relief…but also felt the sting of disappointment. I shoved the feeling aside as we approached the entrance.

The corn stalks stood tall against the dark menacing night, but a three-quarter moon sat directly overhead. I felt a tiny bit of comfort at that. I wished I had thought to bring a flashlight—*damn*. Then I noticed that there were people in costume and I heard Lily shriek. She was holding on to Brent for dear life and looking off to the edge of the maze. The grim reaper had just pushed his way through some stalks and waved what I hoped was a fake scythe in their direction. Oh, great, now we had to deal with costumed freaks inside the maze, too? I so didn't need the aggravation. Andrew was quite excited and squeezed my hand in anticipation.

"Are you ready for this?" he asked, grinning wickedly.

"Not particularly," I tried to muster a grin of my own but it came off as more of a scowl. I felt my stomach clench as we approached the opening of the maze.

Andrew stepped in first and turned back to me with his hand outstretched. "Here we go," he said. I took his hand and he tugged me inside the maze and we were off. He turned this way and that and finally he had to release my hand so he could feel his way along the cornstalks. I kept up with him, practically on his heels, and was thankful I could see the outline of his body in the pale moonlight. We talked to each other at first, more to allay my fears than to actually make conversation, and then finally we got quiet. I could hear his breathing and I was sure he could hear mine. It was cold enough that I could see my breath puffing out in front of me. From time to time we could hear other voices and footsteps and every once in a while the sound of a scream shattered the darkness. Lily's voice rang out a couple of times, screeching and laughing hysterically. We rounded a corner and

Andrew suddenly yelled and jumped back into me, knocking me head-long into the stalks. A skeleton loomed over me, glowing in the dark. I shrank back in fear into the damp ground and fought at the cornstalks tickling my face. "Andrew! Where are you?" I cried. I heard his muffled laughter as he reached down and helped me to my feet.

"That was bloody cool!" he said with excitement. "This is amazing! Come on!"

"Oh, it's amazing alright," I said, my voice dripping with sarcasm. We continued on deeper into the maze. I wondered what part of the lobster's body we were in now—maybe its belly or a claw. Around corners we turned, left and right, right and left. I started to relax knowing that Andrew was just ahead of me. And then around another blind corner we encountered the next fright—Dracula, with bloody fangs illuminated from below his chin with a small light attached to his coat collar. He lurched toward me and threatened to drink my blood. Instinctively I jumped back and turned away from him. I screamed as he chased me the opposite way I'd just come. *Where was Andrew now?* I gasped as I realized we were separated.

"Andrew!" I called his name. Dracula lunged at me one more time and I swiped at him. "Very funny, vampire!" I tried to act brave, like running into a vampire on a Monday night in the middle of a corn maze was something I did all the time. He laughed diabolically and ran around a corner in search of another victim. I ran on ahead a few feet and then stopped. I heard voices and footsteps and laughter and the occasional scream but nothing familiar. "Andrew!" I called out again, my breathing rapid and shallow. I thought I heard Gretchen scream somewhere off to my left. "Gretchen!" I called out but no answer came.

I decided I needed to retrace my steps. I looked up at the moon and tried to calm myself before taking another step. Which way had I just come? I heard a rustling sound to my right coming from inside the cornstalks. "Andrew? Is that you?" There was no answer. I felt panic setting in as I realized that once again I was lost in the damned maze and I would have to find my own way out. I walked a few steps back the way I thought I'd just come. The darkness was beginning to disorient me and I had the feeling I might hyperventilate. *Laura, stay calm. You can figure this out.* I tried to reason with myself—this silly game would be over soon.

I walked slowly forward and continued on, taking a series of right turns, pushing at errant stalks that tickled my face. I kept my hands out in front of me, feeling along in the darkness. Unfamiliar voices and laughter echoed all around me and I took comfort in the fact that some people were actually having fun out here, though, if I lived to be a hundred I would never understand the appeal. I walked for nearly thirty minutes, managing to keep my nerves under control, full of fear of another demon jumping out at me, but so far I had managed to elude them. Finally, I decided to make a left turn since the right turns weren't getting me anywhere and I walked right smack into the dark stalks and fell to my knees. The sharp grasses scratched my face on the way down—I'd hit an apparent dead end. I turned and felt the pointy end of a stalk poke my eye and I cried out in pain. I was on my hands and knees now in near total darkness and I knew then that I could not withhold my panic any longer. "Andrew! Where are you?" I yelled at the top of my lungs. Way off in the distance I heard a female voice giggle and an unfamiliar male voice responded. I had no idea what part of the damned lobster's body I was in. I could be in a claw which I surmised was probably a dead end or even in the tail fins, which wouldn't be much better.

Suddenly, I heard footsteps running to my left. I struggled to my feet, my eye watering and stinging. I was just about to step into the aisle out of the stalks when the runner slowed near me. Thank goodness! Someone would finally lead me out of this damned maze. "Hey!" I yelled just as the figure turned the corner. "Can you help me out of…?" My voice cut off in a strangled cry of terror as Frankenstein jumped at me and stared glassy-eyed down at me. He was huge and his green face was also illuminated by a collar light. I screamed and fell back again and cowered in fear. But he just laughed and ran off, leaving me there on the damp ground, cornstalks covering me. And then I lost it. I began to cry like a baby, pulling myself up into a sitting position, clamping my arms around my legs and burying my face in my knees. It was useless. I would never be able to find my way out of here. Where was Andrew? Where were Lily and Gretchen? How long would it take before someone found my lifeless body—because I was sure I would die of a heart attack before someone rescued me. I continued to sob, eventually annoying myself with my cowardice. I sniffed and wiped my nose on my jacket sleeve and contemplated my next move, even as dry sobs continued to escape my lungs.

And then I heard it again—footsteps. I shrank back in fear. It could be another monster and he'd probably been trained not to offer aid to a lost soul. God forbid someone's fun should be spoiled—wasn't getting lost in the maze part of the draw anyway? Well I could certainly do without it. If this was fun I'd rather have a root canal. The footsteps stopped just around the corner from where I sat off the main trail. I held my breath and waited. The footsteps slowly passed me and I wanted so desperately to reach out and grab the leg of whoever was passing by but I was too afraid of whose or what leg I might grab. I couldn't handle another beast. An uncontrollable sob burst from my lungs as I drew myself up tighter. And then a familiar voice in the darkness.

"Laura? Is that you? Where are you?"

I hiccupped and rolled forward onto my hands and knees and poked my head out of the stalks. "Miguel?"

And suddenly he was down on the ground in front of me, pulling me into his arms. I could see half of his face in the moonlight, his eyes shining. "Laura! What the hell happened? Are you hurt? Let me look at you." He pushed me back slightly and his gaze raked over my face and body. I didn't know how he could see much of me in the half-light. With his fingertips he wiped away the tears from my cheeks and he saw that one eye was slightly more closed in comparison to the other. "What happened to your eye, sweetheart?" he whispered.

I collapsed into him, knocking us both backward. We lay half in and half out of the stalks now and I pressed myself into his body and cried. My shoulders shook and he kept his arms wrapped tightly around me and whispered soothing Portuguese words to me until I collected myself and started to relax. His face was beside mine—we were only inches apart.

"I got lost...and no one came to help me...only to scare me," I gulped. "My eye is fine—just a poke from a cornstalk." I rubbed it with the back of my fist. My hands were dirty and I was sure I must have just smeared mud all over my face, but I didn't care.

"You're safe now, *minha querida*," he whispered. "Shh." He rubbed my arm and, finally, when my breathing returned to some semblance of normalcy, he stood up and helped me to my feet. Once upright, his arms were around me again. I embraced him and held on for dear life.

"Where the hell is everyone?" I asked, suddenly noticing that it had gone awfully quiet. "Is the maze closed? Were they just going to leave me in here all night?" I was getting agitated now—and angry.

"Shh, shh," he whispered against my hair. "Yes, the maze closed a little while ago. They were just about to send in the owner to get you. Your boyfr—the *prince*—is freaking out at the gate. He wanted to come back in here to find you but they wouldn't let him. Good thing, since it's his fault you're lost."

I ignored that comment and turned my face up to his. "But how did you get back in here? How did you know how to find me?"

He tightened his arms around me. "I sneaked in one of the sides when no one was looking. And if I told you how I found you, you wouldn't believe me, so maybe we could just chalk it up to luck."

"No, no, no." I shook my head back and forth vigorously. "Tell me, please, how did you find me?"

He dropped his arms from around me and put his hands up to the top of my jacket. He picked up the zipper and unzipped my jacket half-way down. He reached up to my neck and I felt his fingers graze my collarbone. He lifted the chain of the talisman out from under my shirt and dropped it down in front of me. We looked down at it together. It appeared to be glowing—it had a red tint as if heat were coming off of it. I picked it up in my hand and sure enough, it was warm. Yet I had not felt its warmth during all the time I was lost and alone. He took it out of my hand and closed his fist over it for a moment. He looked into my eyes and then leaned down and kissed me—a slow, tender, sweet kiss—before stepping back and dropping the talisman back down my shirt. "It's like a homing device. It led me to you. You probably didn't feel it because you were panicking and sweaty and hot under your coat. But *I felt it*. You were never lost, Laura. I was always close."

"Oh, Miguel," I let out a sob and fell against him. This was absurd. Things like this didn't happen in real life. He had to be making this up. "This isn't possible."

"Anything's possible, Laura." He held me in his arms and I sagged against him, feeling tired and cold. "Let's get you back to the gate now."

He took me by the hand and we set off into the maze. We walked silently, the only sound coming from my quick breaths as I quick-ened my pace to keep up with Miguel's longer strides. He never questioned the turns, instinctively knowing where to go. After about fifteen minutes I was able to hear voices, including Andrew's agitated one. I could finally see the glow of lights from the parking area. We walked out of the maze and just as we stepped into the lighted area of the gate, Miguel dropped my hand and stepped to the side. Lily and Gretchen and their boyfriends let out a cheer and the owner smiled in relief. But Andrew was not smiling. He let out a growl from the back of his throat and was in Miguel's face before anyone had even seen him move.

"You!" he shouted. "What the hell are you doing here?" He lunged at Miguel who immediately put his hands and body in a defensive stance.

"Don't do this, Easton. Not here, not now…" The words came out of Miguel's mouth through clenched teeth.

I started to run toward them, but Lily grabbed my arm and stopped me from moving. "No, Laura. You could get hurt. Let them work this out." I stopped, debating whether to listen to her or go toward them. Someone needed to stop this madness before they could hurt each other.

"You stay away from her, do you hear me?" Andrew hissed. He circled Miguel in slow motion, like a lion stalking its prey.

"Maybe you should do a better job of protecting her," Miguel hissed back, standing his ground.

"Don't worry about Laura, Dos Santos…I can take care of her just fine," Andrew exclaimed.

"Well, you couldn't prove it by me," Miguel responded, his anger barely contained.

"You just wait, gypsy. You're turn's coming." Andrew's menacing tone was crackling with rage.

"Oh, yeah? I can't wait," Miguel spat the words out through gritted teeth as he clenched and unclenched his fists at his sides.

"Hey, hey, you two!" Someone shouted and rushed up to them. The man inserted himself between Miguel and Andrew. I recognized the owner of the maze and felt a wave of relief as he pushed them both backward, away from each other. "She's safe now, so let's everyone go on home. There'll be no fighting here tonight."

Andrew and Miguel glared at one another and then Miguel walked away. He gave me a look as he passed me but his face was stone-like—

I could not read him. He joined his brothers who were standing near the parking lot. I had not even seen them there.

Andrew rushed over to me and hugged me tightly. "Are you alright? Are you hurt? Did he hurt you?"

I gasped in shock. "Why on earth would Miguel ever hurt me?" I couldn't believe Andrew could even think such a thing.

"He has his reasons, trust me." He brushed my hair away from my face then and kissed my forehead. "You're a mess."

"I bet," I said, suddenly embarrassed. Then Lily and Gretchen came over to me and Gretchen gave me that look.

"Oops, you did it again—got lost in the maze." She sang the words to the Britney Spears song, putting her own spin on the lyrics. I was sure she had to be wondering about the exchange between Andrew and Miguel but she kept a poker face about it—Lily did, too.

"Ha, ha. What did you expect? I will never, never, never, set foot in a maze again!" I declared defiantly.

Back in the car, Andrew held me against him. But he was quiet and I could feel his jaw working against the side of my head in a grinding motion. I wanted to ask him what was wrong but I had a feeling I knew. I decided it was better if we remained silent on the ride home. He kissed me good night at the door and held both of my hands in his.

"I'm sorry about tonight, Laura. I don't know how we got separated in the maze. It shouldn't have happened. Can you forgive me?" He looked sad and contrite.

"Andrew, don't be silly. There's nothing to forgive. It's just the nature of the maze. I knew something like this would happen. Mazes and I don't make a good match." I forced a smile to make him feel better. He cupped my face in his hands and kissed me tenderly.

"Your nose is cold. Get inside and warm up. I'll talk to you tomorrow. I love you, you know."

I looked down at my dirty boots. "I know," I whispered into the darkness. But he was already gone.

Chapter Fourteen

INTERROGATION

Andrew wanted us to go out Tuesday night for dinner but I begged off. I told him I had a headache and needed to rest—I'd even stayed home from school to try to shake the headache. I was afraid he would insist on coming over to take care of me, but I was able to persuade him that I just needed sleep. And Nick had heard about my maze experience and proceeded to tease me mercilessly. My dad came down from Providence to talk to my mom. I could hear their voices in the living room. I assumed they were talking about their impending divorce but I didn't want to know or hear any details so I stayed in my room thinking about last night. I took off the talisman and laid it on my nightstand. I needed a break from the damned thing. I was getting tired of being in the dark about it and I realized there was an underlying question that I needed answered concerning it. I needed to know why it was in my possession. And even though Miguel seemed to be the expert on it, I knew my answer would have to come from Andrew. I vowed to myself that when the right moment came, I would ask Andrew to explain his connection. One way or another I would get to the bottom of the mystery of this damned necklace. Truth be told, there was an awful lot I needed to get to the bottom of.

I had vowed to myself that I would not contact Miguel, but I felt like I had not properly thanked him for rescuing me from the maze, realizing that this was the second time now that he'd saved me. It was becoming a habit and not a pleasant one at that. What if I got myself into something he couldn't save me from? I shuddered at the thought. I knew I couldn't relax until I'd reached out to him so I opened my phone and sent him a text: *Hi. Don't know if I thanked you for last night but consider yourself thanked for saving me—again.* I pressed send and lay back down on my bed and waited. Time passed and I got sleepy. I closed my eyes and could feel myself slipping into unconsciousness when suddenly the phone buzzed. It scared me and I snapped to attention, my heart pounding. I opened the text and read: *You're welcome. How are you feeling?*

I sighed as I considered his question. How *was* I today? I typed the following answer: *Tired...confused...wanting answers...can't you tell me what's going on? I know there's something...it seems bad...maybe I can help...a little trust would be nice.*

A minute later came his response: *Trusting you isn't the problem. It's others we have to worry about. I have a question for you now...but it's personal...*

I felt my nerves twitch as I wondered what his question could be. With trembling fingers I texted back: *I don't know if I can answer but you can ask.*

Mere seconds passed before his reply came: *Are you in love with Andrew Easton?*

I sucked in a deep breath and dropped the phone. Could I answer that question? *Was* there an answer? I waited five full minutes before I responded. *I don't know. I thought I was, but recently I've had doubts.*

His response: *What's causing the doubts?*

Again I dropped the phone. I could feel my whole body shaking. My teeth began to chatter and my stomach seemed to have relocated elsewhere in my body. I felt dizzy and weird all over. I knew why I had doubts. I knew the answer to his question but I was afraid to type the one tiny word that I knew to be the truth. But I took a deep breath and swallowed my fear and typed my answer: *You.*

And then nothing. I waited and waited and waited but there was no response. Nothing but complete silence. More time passed. And after more than two hours of this incessant waiting I realized that he was not going to respond. I'd scared him off. *Stupid, stupid, stupid.* I'd imagined the whole thing between us...it was obviously one-sided. *Damn it!* I paced around my room and tried to fight back angry tears. I felt humiliated. What was I thinking? Miguel was just playing a twisted game. He was toying with me. At least I knew how Andrew felt. Andrew I could count on. I shoved my phone under my pillow and went to take a shower. That was it. I was done with Miguel Dos Santos.

I was quite the butt of jokes at school the rest of the week. Apparently my reputation with the maze was more well-known than I'd thought. It seemed that every other person who passed me in the halls told me how *a-maze-ing* I was. I finally decided that the next person who said it would get a punch in the face. And my feelings still stung over Miguel's ignoring my sort-of declaration, even though I knew it was for the best. He was absent from English class two days in a row and I felt his absence acutely, but I forced myself to think about anything other than him. When he returned to school he was— Miguel—maddening, stupefying Miguel. Of course, Andrew was as sweet and attentive as always. His birthday was coming up in a couple of days and I puzzled over what to get him.

As he and the goon of the day drove me home after school the Thursday before his birthday which was on Saturday, he invited me to dinner at his house to celebrate.

"My mother is making a big deal because it's my eighteenth birthday. I would love it if you came. You could be my birthday gift." He squeezed my hand and gave me his crooked grin.

I laughed at his joke. "Right. Should I wrap myself up in ribbons and a bow?" I teased.

"Ooh, I like the sound of that—actually it's the unwrapping part I'd like the most." He kissed me then and I made a point to kiss him back with more passion than I'd shown of late. I'd been aware that I'd probably come across a little distant since the maze and I wanted to make it up to him.

"Well, we'll see about that. So what *do* you want for your birthday—really?" I asked. I had no idea what a prince would want or need. He could undoubtedly buy himself anything the world had to offer.

"Only you, my love," he said sweetly and nuzzled his nose into my hair. "You don't have to get me anything. There isn't anything I need anyway. Just please come for dinner, OK?"

"Of course I will."

At my house I told him good-bye and said I'd see him Saturday. There was no school tomorrow because of Veteran's Day and I had promised to spend the day with Lily and Gretchen at the Warwick mall, shopping and seeing a movie.

"I'll send a car for you Saturday…six o'clock?" Andrew called out the window.

"See you then!" I waved and dashed inside the house.

The next day we had our girls' day out, which was fun and provided a much-needed distraction. I asked them for advice on a birthday gift for Andrew.

"Why not get him something commemorative of his time in Rhode Island?" suggested Lily. "I mean, he isn't going to be here forever, so why not get something like a sweatshirt that says Rhode Island on it? Or a key chain or something along those lines?"

I nodded—it didn't seem personal enough but it would make for a good memory for him anyway. I felt a twinge of sadness at the thought that he might actually leave one day. I couldn't imagine never seeing him again. I left Lily and Gretchen in a shoe store and I went across the way to a sweatshirt/t-shirt shop. I looked over the racks and bought one I liked–navy blue, with "Rhode Island" printed across the front in white block letters. I still didn't feel satisfied though so I walked further on looking into stores hoping inspiration would strike. I stopped at the Things Remembered kiosk near where Lily and Gretchen were still shoe shopping and checked out the trinkets. And then I had a brilliant idea. I purchased a five-by-seven silver picture frame and asked the clerk to engrave it for me. When she finished, I looked at it in satisfaction. *To Andrew with love from Laura. Happy 18th Birthday, 2011.* Yes—this would be perfect. We'd had senior pictures taken just a few weeks before school started. I would put my smiling mug in the frame and hope that Andrew would like it.

I looked at the clock–it was getting close to six and I still had to wrap Andrew's presents. I'd stopped in the Hallmark store at the mall yesterday and purchased a funny card and some gift wrap. Just as I'd finished affixing the bows on top of the presents, my phone alerted me to an incoming text. I assumed it would be Andrew letting me know one of the goons was on the way. I dug it out of my purse and took a look. It was from Miguel. Instantly I felt the physical reaction to the sight of his name on my phone. My heart went into overdrive, my lungs threatened to shut down and I felt light-headed. Just when I thought he was never speaking to me again—contact. I clicked on the text and closed my eyes for a split second before reading his words: *I'm sorry about the delayed response. It wasn't intentional, I promise.*

I felt myself shake with a mixture of frustration and anxiety. He was making me crazy. I decided to play the ignorance card. I texted back: *Response to what?*

A few seconds later came the reply: *To your text about your doubts about Andrew. I understand. Follow your heart.*

I cried out quietly in my silent room and typed my reply: *Well, my heart is confused, but at least Andrew makes sense. He doesn't play games.*

And then: *I'm not playing a game. I care about you—more than you could ever know. I'd hoped you could see that by now. I only want you to be safe...and happy.*

My turn: *How can I be happy when I'm always in the dark? Why can't you tell me what's going on? If you don't, then I'm going to ask Andrew to explain.*

His reply: *No! Just let time unfold naturally. Don't push him. I promise things will make sense soon. But don't tip him off. It isn't safe...for anyone.*

Oh, my god. This was beyond melodramatic. Was Miguel auditioning for a part in a movie? *Tip him off? It isn't safe?* What the hell was with him and all this mysterious jibber jabber? I'd had enough: *I have to go. It's Andrew's birthday and I'm having dinner at his house. Text me or call me when you can speak in plain English and not this mysterious nonsense.*

I snapped my phone shut roughly and put it into my jacket pocket, then jumped up to finish getting ready. My hands shook as I brushed my hair and applied a light layer of pink gloss to my lips. I grabbed my purse and jacket and Andrew's gifts and ran downstairs just as my mother opened the door to Peter.

"Bye, Mom. See you later!" I yelled as I dashed out to the car. Peter opened the door for me and I crawled into the backseat. It felt strange to be back here all alone. As we pulled into the drive at Andrew's house, I felt my nerves beginning to stir. I hadn't seen his parents and brother since the polo match. As I got out of the car, I glanced back toward the ocean, dark gray and rolling with huge waves. It seemed like it was going to snow soon. It never had snowed before Halloween as the weather forecaster had predicted, but it felt like it could tonight. I shivered and followed Peter into the house.

Andrew was waiting for me in the foyer. He crushed me into his arms, smashing his gifts between us in the process. "Oops, sorry," he grinned sheepishly. "Hope I didn't break anything there. I've missed you." He took the gifts from my hands and set them down on one of the hall tables and then wrapped his arms around me again. He kissed me and then realizing I was still in my coat, he helped me take it off and a maid suddenly materialized out of thin air and took it away. I shook my head in disbelief but didn't say anything. Andrew smiled.

"You'll get used to that, I promise."

My heart thudded at the implication.

Andrew glanced over at the gifts. "So, when do I get to open my presents?" He looked like a big kid on Christmas morning.

"For someone who didn't want anything, you're certainly eager," I laughed.

"Well, since you've gone to the trouble…I may as well…" His voice trailed off. He picked them up. "Come up to my room. I'll open them there. Dinner isn't until 7:30." He tucked the gifts under his arm and took my hand, leading me up the stairs. His room was the last room on the right. When I walked in, I was taken aback. It was stunning, decorated in a nautical theme with model sailboats on bookshelves, seashells placed strategically about the room, an anchor mounted on the wall and a mirrored ship's wheel over his dresser. The walls were painted pale blue above the navy wainscoting. He had a huge desk of dark cherry and a fairly elaborate sound system set up in one corner. And then there was the bed—king-sized and situated in the middle of the room. It was beautifully made up with shams and a thick comforter of navy blue and gold stripes. The room could've been featured in an issue of *Coastal Living* magazine.

"Wow," I breathed. "It's beautiful. My dad would love this."

"Thanks. It's nice, I suppose. Come over here, Laura." He beckoned to me to come toward the bed. I hesitated, my nerves getting the better of me as usual. He saw my hesitation and held out his hand to me. "Please."

We sat down on the edge of his bed and he turned his attention to the two presents. As he unwrapped the bigger one, he gave me a devilish glance. "Weren't you supposed to be wearing this?' He held up the bow. I just smiled nervously and watched him unwrap the sweatshirt. He held it up against his body. "I love it. My first official piece of clothing with Rhode Island on it. I'll wear it to school on Monday." He then unwrapped the smaller one. He held the picture frame in his hand, the back side facing him first. He read the inscription and looked at me as he turned the frame over in his hands. He saw my photo and sighed. "So beautiful. Thank you so much, Laura. I love my presents."

"Thanks. You're kinda hard to buy for so I was hoping you'd like these." He laid the sweatshirt and picture frame down on the other side of the bed and pulled me into his arms and kissed me tenderly. Then he dropped his arms and pushed himself back farther onto the bed up by the pillows. "Come here," he whispered.

I swallowed…my nerves were on fire. I felt that breathless feeling and wondered if a line was about to be crossed. I had to be careful here. As usual, when I was with Andrew, my attraction to him was not to be denied. And right now, alone with him in his bedroom on this huge bed, I felt powerless. I closed my eyes for only a second and then scooted closer to him. We lay back against the pillows, my head in the crook of his shoulder. We were silent for a moment—it seemed like so much longer. He shifted his body so that he was leaning over me. I looked into his blue eyes and felt my nerves completely liquefy. He leaned down and kissed me, softly at first, but then his passion grew. I felt his tongue against my mouth and I returned his kiss. But when his hand started to slide slowly up my shirt I grabbed it and held it tightly. He stopped kissing me and looked into my eyes. "It's OK, Laura. There's no rush. I'm happy just to hold you."

We lay still and quiet for a few minutes–a comfortable silence. I thought about my necklace which I'd left at home on my nightstand. I wanted to bring it up—now seemed like a good time—but my emotions were swirling to the point that I wasn't sure I would sound coherent. And I worried that mentioning it would affect the mood so I decided to wait. Andrew kissed me again and ran his fingers through my hair. Finally he broke the silence. "Shall we go down and see the parents before dinner?"

"Sure," I said a little breathlessly.

We went downstairs into the family room—salon—where the view of the ocean was exquisite. His parents were there—his father was standing at the window and his mother was seated on the sofa reading a book. Andrew re-introduced me and we sat down on a love-seat across from the duchess. I said hello and looked down at her book. "What are you reading?" I asked, a little nervously.

She held up the book. "*The Help*. It's really good. Have you read it?"

I nodded. "Yes, I have. It's great." She asked me about a few other books she'd read recently and I was amazed to find that we had similar tastes in literature. Andrew left us to talk and went over to join his father at the window. They talked quietly though not loudly enough for me to hear. His father had said hello to me initially but then had proceeded to ignore me. I decided this was OK because I didn't think my nerves could handle a chat with him.

At 7:30 a maid announced that dinner was being served in the dining room. Tristan was already there waiting. He greeted me warmly and we took our seats. It felt incredibly awkward being waited on. I thought about Mrs. Easton's book and the irony nearly made me choke on my water.

The meal was divine. The first course was roasted butternut squash soup and a mixed green salad. The main course was roasted chicken, mashed potatoes with chives and sweet, tender carrots. Bread was served along with butter and an assortment of jams and preserves. The duchess picked at her food but the duke ate heartily, as did Tristan and Andrew. I was enjoying the food immensely and knew that if I were eating this same meal at my own house I would be scarfing it down and probably going back for seconds. But in the dining room of the Easton house I sensed that this wouldn't be proper decorum. I'm sure if Gretchen or Lily were here they would tell me that cleaning my plate wouldn't be proper etiquette among the female royal set—that I would have to start starving myself if I hoped to fit in.

The duke and Tristan talked about sports and horses and sailing. Every so often, Andrew would chime in. He asked me questions about Rhode Island, trying to make me feel a part of the conversation though

I was quite happy to remain mute. A servant brought in dessert—a beautiful, elaborately decorated cake for Andrew's birthday. It actually looked like a wedding cake—three tiers of chocolate, light-as-air cake with a fudgy, creamy filling. It was so delicious that I committed what I was sure was a major faux pas—I actually moaned in ecstasy upon taking my first bite. I immediately glanced up and saw the duke's stony face. The duchess was studying her cake intently as if it were imparting an important message that only she could hear, but I saw a tiny smile play at the corner of her lips. Tristan looked up at me, grinned, put a large piece in his mouth and moaned in solidarity. Andrew burst out laughing and finally the duchess laughed, too. I was mortified and my cheeks flamed red hot.

"Are you a chocolate lover, Laura?" Tristan asked, giving me a wink.

"Uh, yes, sorry. I do have a weakness for it. This is a beautiful cake and very delicious." I stopped myself right there before I got a case of motor mouth. That would really get the duke's ire up, I'd bet.

We finished dinner and Tristan disappeared to another part of the house. The duchess excused herself and Andrew departed to go to the bathroom, leaving me alone with the duke. My stomach began to churn. I prayed I'd be able to keep my dinner down, especially dessert—that would be a tragic waste of chocolate. We were still seated at the table—the duke was having coffee. A maid had just refilled my ice water so I picked up the glass and sipped slowly hoping Andrew would be quick.

"So, Laura, what are your parents' names?" asked the duke.

I set my water glass down on the table and cleared my throat. "Linda and David...Calder."

"How do they make their living?"

"My father is an architect and my mother works in a bank," I replied. *So far so good*, I thought. That was an easy one.

"Does he have his own firm or is he part of a group?"

"He's part of a group."

"What is the name of the group?"

"Hansen-Lafayette Partners—in Providence."

"And the name of your mother's bank?"

"First Federal Bank of Rhode Island."

"What does she do there?"

"She's a loan officer."

"Do you have siblings?"

"Yes—an older brother."

"What is his name?"

"Nick—Nicholas." My stomach heaved. I grabbed my water again and took a long drink. I concentrated on breathing—slowly—in through my nose and out through my mouth. I felt like I was on trial—like I was the defendant on the witness stand and the evidence was stacked against me—what crime I had been accused of remained to be seen. I prepared myself for the next question but Andrew arrived and saved me from further interrogation.

"Come with me, Laura. Let's go relax. I don't know about you but I'm full enough to explode."

I practically jumped to my feet, nearly knocking the chair over in the process. Andrew grabbed it and steadied it, grinning at me. He raised an eyebrow at me in question.

"Sorry! It must be the sugar—it gave me an energy boost," I said, a nervous laugh escaping my lips.

We stepped back from the table and Andrew turned to the duke. "We'll see you later, Father."

The duke nodded at him and turned his eyes on me. His glare was menacing and it made the blood in my veins turn to ice. I turned quickly and followed Andrew down the hall. He led me to another room off the kitchen that looked out over the back of the property. Though it was dark outside, there were floodlights illuminating the vast expanse of lawn. We sat down on a couch that backed up to the window and he immediately put his arms around me and kissed the top of my head.

"My mother likes you. I can tell," he said.

"Hmph," I said rather abruptly. "Wish I could say the same about your father. He is definitely not my biggest fan."

"Don't let him get to you. He acts intimidating to cover up his insecurities—it's purely a defense mechanism."

"Why do you suppose that is?" I asked. I truly wanted to know the psychology behind the duke's personality.

"Well, between you and me and that lamp over there…," he pointed to a beautiful antique standing lamp in the corner, "I think he has a lot of resentment about his place in our family history—about his position in the chain of hierarchy. He is many, many times removed from the throne and that fact makes him bitter. For the life of me, I cannot fathom why anyone in their right mind would want to be in a position of that level. I'm quite sure I would hate it."

I leaned into his shoulder and rested my head there. We were quiet for a while. I felt myself getting sleepy and I stole a glance at Andrew. His head was against the back of the couch, his eyes closed. I could tell by his even breathing that he was asleep or damned close. I snuggled into him and he tightened his hold around me but didn't fully wake up. We must have dozed like that for quite some time because we were both awakened by the sound of someone entering the room. It was one of the goons—one I had never seen before. At least I assumed he was a member of the security based on his all black attire.

"Excuse me…Prince Andrew…?" the man said quietly.

"Oh…yes, Keith?" Andrew sat up and rubbed his hands over his face. He looked down at me. "Did we fall asleep? I'm sorry, Laura."

"It's OK—I got sleepy, too." I looked at my watch—it was after eleven. "Wow. It's late. I should go."

"Sir, your father had Peter bring the car around for you. It's ready out front."

"Alright, thanks." Keith disappeared. We walked out to the foyer and the maid who had disappeared with my coat a few hours earlier had magically reappeared with it—and Andrew's, too. Andrew helped me into mine and then donned his. We went out to the already warm car and set off for my house. It occurred to me that my mother might have texted me, wondering why I wasn't home yet—not that I'd ever given her the need to enforce a curfew—so I reached into my jacket pocket for my phone. I dug all around in my pocket but my phone wasn't there. I distinctly remembered putting it in my pocket after I'd texted with Miguel. I knew I'd had it with me. It must have fallen out somewhere. I started to mention it to Andrew when I decided to check the left pocket. My phone was there. But how? I never put anything— keys, sunglasses, phone, anything—in the left pocket. I pushed the button on my phone to wake it up and the dial showed that I had no messages. Well, good. At least I hadn't ignored anybody. But when I checked closer, I was stunned to see that my text messages were gone. All my recent texts with Lily and Gretchen and Andrew and my parents and brother—and Miguel—had been deleted. I felt blood rush to my face. A wave of fear flowed through me. Someone had been in my phone—reading my texts, probably listening to any voicemails I might have had. I looked over at Andrew and started to tell him, but I stopped myself. He might think a member of the staff had done it and I couldn't let an innocent person get blamed. I couldn't make an accusation unless I had a suspect in mind. Who would want to read my texts? Why on earth would anybody care? I was stunned and suddenly anxious to get home. I tried to remain calm as Andrew held my hand while we drove along in the darkness.

At my house I said good night and told Andrew to stay put. "You need to get home to sleep—you're exhausted." I teased.

"I am...it must be my old age." We both laughed at his joke. I kissed him good night and stopped him with my hand when he tried to get out of the car.

"No—go home and go to bed...and happy birthday." I hopped out, waved good-bye and went inside. My mom was awake in her room. I stuck my head in to say good night. "Night, Mom."

"Good night, honey. Did you have fun?"

"Yes, it was...interesting," I said as I closed my bedroom door. I quietly paced the floor—something I realized I'd been doing a lot of lately. I looked at my phone again. I needed to confirm that it was indeed wiped clean of all messages. It was. A few hours ago I'd had hundreds of old texts and now I had zero.

I went into the bathroom to brush my teeth. When I was finished I crawled into bed and stared at the phone. It didn't make sense. Who had done this and more important...why? I turned off the lamp on my nightstand and proceeded to have a fitful, sleepless night.

Chapter Fifteen

·DECLARATIONS

"Laura, would you like to invite Andrew over for Thanksgiving dinner?" my mother asked me. We were in the kitchen eating dinner. Nick was at his girlfriend's and I hadn't seen my dad in several days so it was just the two of us. "You could invite his whole family if you want but I can't imagine that the royals would come to a commoner's house for dinner." She laughed as if she'd just said the funniest thing in the world. Actually, come to think of it, it was rather hilarious in an ironic sort of way.

"You know, Mom, British people don't celebrate Thanksgiving," I reminded her.

"Well, when in Rome, I always say," she shrugged. "But at least invite Andrew, OK?"

"Yes, I will ask Andrew definitely, but I'd rather leave his parents out of it. His mother and brother are very nice but his father…," I hesitated, searching for the right words. "Well, let's just say the Duke of Easton won't win any personality contests any time soon."

Thankfully Mom didn't ask me to elaborate. We finished dinner and cleaned the kitchen together and I went to my room. I sat down at my desk and looked over my homework. I attempted to concentrate on math but it was useless. Ever since the birthday dinner at Andrew's house I'd been uneasy and nervous. I had debated over and over whether to mention the cell phone incident to him but I was too worried about one of the servants being wrongfully accused. The more I thought about it, the more I decided that, assuming it wasn't some major, massive malfunction of my phone, it had to have been one of the goons. And then another thought popped into my head and made my stomach quake—could Andrew have asked one of the goons to check my phone out of jealousy? To see if I was in contact with other guys? No. That was impossible. Besides, if that were the case, I would surely know by now. The goon would have told him I had been texting with Miguel and he would have absolutely called me on it. But we had been together many times since his birthday dinner and he had been his usual easy-going self. No. Andrew wasn't behind this. But who was…and…why?

And something else was bothering me. Miguel's behavior toward me had changed. Generally, he was cordial at best, aloof at worst, but lately, he'd been acting as if I had the plague. He wouldn't smile or say hello in class or even look me in the eye. The one time I'd managed to catch his eye—for one brief moment as he'd made to brush past me after English class in his haste to get out of the room—I thought I saw something sad—haunted almost—on his face. It was eerie and I felt a tug on my heart. That one quick glance had made me feel guilty—as if I had somehow hurt him. It must be because of Andrew—that's the only thing I could figure—it must be jealousy. But if Miguel were interested in me, why didn't he do something about it? And so the mystery that was Miguel Dos Santos continued.

Andrew seemed to enjoy his first Thanksgiving. My dad came down from Providence and Nick invited his crazy girlfriend Abigail. Mom made all the traditional delights—turkey, stuffing, deviled eggs, sweet potatoes, mashed potatoes and gravy, cranberry sauce and pumpkin pie. Andrew was amazed at how much food kept coming out of the kitchen into the dining room—a room we rarely used anymore except for special occasions. He was especially impressed that my mom did it all herself. I had offered to help, but aside from setting the table, she wouldn't even let me in the kitchen.

"It's amazing you do all this yourself without...assistance, Mrs. Calder," Andrew remarked to my mother, glancing at me as he spoke. I heard his hesitation before saying the word 'assistance.'

I rolled my eyes. Andrew knew how I felt about 'assistance.' But my mom seemed on board with the idea.

"Assistance...I like the sound of that–although my children are very good about helping around the house." She smiled at me and Nick when she said this. "But, boy, a chauffeur? Now that would be fantastic." Mom beamed at the thought.

"Oh, I can arrange that, if you like," said Andrew eagerly. "I'm sure my father can spare..."

"*NO!* I mean, no, thank you, Andrew." I cut him off before my mother had a chance to get her hopes up—not that she would have agreed to it anyway. "We will do our own driving. It's fun to drive anyway."

After dinner we moved into the family room to watch football. Andrew and my dad seemed to bond over it, so I just sat back and relaxed. It was a fun day and I was happy at how well Andrew was fitting into my family. Even Crabigail had been pleasant. All in all it was really fun and it took my mind off of troubling thoughts for a while.

Later when Andrew was getting ready to leave, he mentioned my upcoming birthday.

"So, it's your turn to be in the birthday spotlight next. What would you like?" We were in the front hall where he was putting on his coat and waiting for one of the goons to come for him.

"I don't want anything. Seriously, there isn't a single thing I can think of. My mom will make my favorite meal—she does it every year—and it'll be just another day."

"First of all, it isn't just another day. It's your eighteenth and that is a very big deal, my love. Second of all, I hope you will allow me to spend part of that night with you. I understand you'll be with your family, but after dinner, will you come out with me?"

"You can have dinner with us. It's spaghetti and meatballs and spinach salad and garlic bread and for dessert...you'll never guess!" I grinned at the thought of it.

"Let me think…could it be…cake?" he laughed.

"Yes…but not just any cake. It's my favorite and my mom only makes it once a year—especially for my birthday—Italian cream cake." My mouth watered at the thought.

"Yummy…sounds divine. I would love to join you for dinner. And I will think about what to get you, but I already have an idea…" He had a sly look on his face. I hoped it wouldn't be anything too extravagant—something that cost more than my parents' monthly mortgage payment.

Andrew left then and I went into the kitchen and helped myself to another slice of pumpkin pie with whipped cream, then took my stuffed self to bed.

My birthday was on a Monday this year and while I usually wasn't all that thrilled with being the center of attention, I was kind of excited for this one—eighteen. Wow. Legal age—I could vote in the presidential election next year. That was actually something to get excited about. The school day flew by and Lily and Gretchen met me after school to give me birthday gifts. Andrew had had to leave early to do something official with his parents but he assured me he would be at my house later this evening for my special dinner. I had also noticed Miguel's absence from school today and was hurt that he had not acknowledged my birthday. He probably didn't even remember anyway.

Lily, Gretchen and I sat in my Jeep with the heater running while I opened my presents. Lily got me a beautiful green sweater and a silver bracelet with green stones to match and Gretchen got me a gift card to my favorite store—Barnes and Noble—and a box of Godiva chocolates. I was touched and thrilled with my gifts. We chatted for a bit and then they went to their cars and we all headed off in separate directions.

My mom was home from work early and in the kitchen putting the finishing touches on my cake. I stuck my finger in the frosting on my way to the fridge and she swatted at my hand.

"Hey, now. No cheating. You're not supposed to taste it until after dinner," she admonished me.

I just grinned and showed her my gifts from the girls. My dad arrived then and soon Nick was home and it was almost time for dinner. It was getting close to six o'clock and I was starting to wonder about Andrew. He was generally the king of punctuality so I was surprised he was late and even more surprised that he hadn't contacted me about his delay.

I checked my phone but had no messages from him. I decided to send him a quick text and see how close he was to arriving. As I was typing my message, an incoming text beeped. It was from Miguel. My heart skipped about five beats and my breath caught in my throat. My hands shook as I saved Andrew's message and read Miguel's: *Happy 18th, Laura. Sorry I missed you at school today but I didn't want you to think I'd forgotten. I have something for you.*

I was a mess of nerves. I was in the front hall and I sank down onto the bottom step and typed my response: *Thanks. I wondered if I would hear from you today. Glad you didn't forget. What did you get me?*

A couple of minutes passed as I tried not to stare at the phone, willing it to work faster. I felt my appetite shutting down thanks to my nerves and jumpy stomach and grimaced. Up until five minutes ago I had been so looking forward to my special dinner. Finally a response: *You'll have to wait and see. I'm sorry about my last text to you...you didn't respond so I just want you to know that it's OK. I understand... or I'm trying to anyway.*

His last text? I didn't remember it. I went to check our last texting conversation to see what he was referring to and remembered that all my texts had been erased since the last time he and I had communicated. What exactly had he said in our last texting conversation? I couldn't remember. I typed: *I'm sorry—what are you trying to understand? I'm missing something here.*

I puzzled over this while I awaited his response. Damn whoever had erased my messages! Then a ping from the phone: *You forgot already? Wow. That hurts.*

My heart raced. I didn't understand his words. What had we been texting about that day? What was I missing? And then a horrible realization washed over me. Miguel said I had not responded to his text but I was sure I had responded to every text he'd ever sent me. Had he sent me a text that was erased before I'd had a chance to read it? Erased on the night of Andrew's birthday dinner? I felt dread seep into my bones. I responded: *I'm sorry, Miguel. Something happened to my phone recently and all my messages disappeared. Do you have a copy of the last text you sent me? If you do, could you resend?*

A minute later a text came: *Fwd: I don't mean to be mysterious. But if it's plain English you want then that's what you'll get: I'm in love with you but there's nothing I can do about it.*

I gasped and fell backward against the steps behind me. The edge of the stair jammed into my lower back but I didn't even feel the pain. The phone slipped out of my hands and landed with a thud at my feet. I couldn't breathe. I couldn't see. I couldn't move. It was as if I had been turned to stone. The only sensations I felt were the pounding of my heart and a rushing sound in my ears. My eyes filled with tears and dropped onto my cheeks as I leaned over and felt around on the floor for my phone. Just as I picked it up, the doorbell rang.

"Ooh, damn it!" I jumped to my feet and ran to the mirror. I wiped my eyes and cheeks as best I could and tried to control my breathing. Andrew must be here. I slipped my phone into my pocket and walked on shaky legs to the front door and prayed he wouldn't notice my splotchy face and agitated state. I took a deep breath and opened the door.

"Happy birthday!" All I could see was a gigantic bouquet of gorgeous roses—red, white, pink, yellow, orange—every color imaginable. Andrew dropped his hand down to waist level and smiled hugely at me. And then he saw my face and gasped.

"Laura!" He stepped inside. He immediately set the flowers down on the hall table and pulled me tightly into his arms. "What is it, love? What's happened?"

I returned his hug as my mind raced. I needed a believable answer and I needed it now. What reason could I give him for my sorry state? And then, as usual, Andrew took care of it for me.

"Oh, no, love." He pulled away from me and kissed my lips sweetly. "I'm so sorry. I know I'm late. I should've called or texted—please forgive me. We got delayed at that dumb ribbon cutting for the new pediatric wing at Newport Hospital. I wanted to call but I never got the chance. You thought I wasn't coming?"

I pulled him close to me and buried my face in his neck and nodded. What else could I do but go along with this charade?

He squeezed me hard and kissed the top of my head, then turned my face up to his and kissed my lips. "I would never do that to you, Laura Calder. You can always count on me, do you understand?" He held me against him and I allowed myself to relax. I had just dodged a bullet and I was very grateful.

"I'm sorry. I don't know why I'm blubbering. Maybe it's my advanced age—can't control my emotions. You'd better watch out, I might start drooling next." We laughed at my poor attempt at humor and then Mom called us in to dinner. I grabbed the flowers from the hall table and put them in a vase and set them on the sideboard in the dining room. I managed to relax enough to eat dinner, although my stomach protested with each bite. My mom noticed me playing around with my food and not eating much.

"My spaghetti not up to par this year, darling?" she asked, pointing with her fork toward my plate.

"Oh no, no. It's awesome as usual, Mom. I think I'm just excited that it's my birthday—eighteen—woohoo," I tried really hard to act excited and hoped I was convincing everyone.

After dinner we cut the divine Italian cream cake, which Andrew thought was mind-blowing. I'd already opened presents from my parents and Nick earlier this evening and now Mom and Nick were cleaning up the dinner detritus and my dad was getting ready to go back to Providence. And Andrew was suddenly antsy.

"Laura, would you come for a drive with me?" he asked. He looked like the cat who'd swallowed the proverbial canary.

"Sure. I just need to use the ladies' room. Give me a couple of minutes?" I asked.

"Of course. I'll just pop back into the kitchen and see if your mother needs any help taking care of that cake." He grinned and winked then headed into the kitchen.

I hurried upstairs to my bathroom and shut the door. I pulled out my phone and sat down on the side of the bathtub. I had been anxious all through dinner because I had not responded to Miguel's text. I needed to respond now. I opened my phone and saw that I had a new text—I hadn't even heard it beep. It had probably come when everyone was singing happy birthday to me. It was from Miguel. My heart sank as I read it: *Your silence tells me everything I need to know. I guess I read you wrong. I'm sorry. But even though you don't feel the same, it doesn't change anything.*

I was stunned. I needed to respond immediately. My hands were shaking so hard that I fumbled over the letters on the tiny keyboard. I cursed and had to start over: *No! I'm sorry. Andrew is here. I can't talk. You didn't read me wrong. But I'm confused. Please be patient with me. This isn't easy.* I hit send and hoped I wasn't too late.

I hurried through my bathroom ritual and looked at my face in the mirror. It was equal parts pale and flushed. I noticed I had hives on my neck and the top of my chest. *My necklace!* I wasn't wearing it! But I needed it now. I needed its comfort and security. I ran to my room and found it on my nightstand. I dropped it over my head and tucked it down inside my sweater. As soon as it hit the skin beneath my bra line I felt myself begin to relax. I felt its warmth instantly and I knew everything was going to be OK. I would figure this out. Nothing bad was going to happen. I took several deep breaths and went downstairs.

Andrew was waiting for me by the front door. He already had his coat on. I slipped mine on and called out to Mom that we were going for a ride and I would be back later.

"OK, you two. Have fun. Be safe," she called back.

Peter was at the wheel tonight. We climbed into the car and I turned to Andrew and asked where we were going.

"To my house," he replied. Then he gave me a wink and reached for my hand. "Your hands are freezing. Do you have gloves?"

"Yes, in my pocket." I answered. He rubbed my hands inside of his to warm them up. I forced myself to stay in the moment and not let my mind drift to Miguel.

When we arrived at Andrew's house, we went inside the front door and Andrew immediately pulled me into the library. He shut the door and we were in darkness. I could hear him breathing and then I felt his breath against my cheek. "Laura, we are going to be a little sneaky tonight. Are you game?"

I hesitated, my breath stopping short in my lungs. Every nerve came alive and I had that dizzy feeling again. I couldn't imagine what he meant and I wasn't even sure I wanted to know.

He whispered against my ear. "I stole a set of keys from one of the drivers who's off tonight. It's for one of the cars that doesn't get used much. You and I are going for a ride. In case you hadn't noticed I haven't given you your birthday present yet. We're going to leave this room and walk to the kitchen. There's a door there that opens onto a short hallway which leads to the garage. My parents are out to dinner tonight so they won't be a problem, but there are a few security people around. They play poker at this time every Monday night in a room at the opposite side of the house from the garage. If we act normally, no one should pay any attention to us, OK?"

"OK," I whispered, even as every fiber of my being told me this wasn't the best idea. Even the chain of my necklace seemed to agree. It sent the faintest wave of heat snaking down my chest and around and up the other side. I bit my tongue to keep from crying out at the shock of it even though it was painless.

We stepped out into the hall and Andrew and I walked slowly and quietly to the kitchen. The room was empty and the only light on was one above the stove. We continued on down the hall and slipped quietly into the garage.

"Won't they hear the garage door open or the engine when you start the car?" I whispered, as I glanced around the interior of the cavernous garage.

"I hope not, but in any case, when we pull out of the garage we're going left away from the house out the back of the drive. Even if they hear something they won't know which way we've gone. They know my cell phone number and they might try to call me but I can either ignore it or tell them I'll be back soon and not to bother looking. We won't be gone so long that it'll be a problem anyway. They were teenagers once—they know I like a little privacy once in a while."

He opened the door of a black Mercedes parked at the far end of the garage. We got in and he pushed the remote and the garage door opened. He started the engine and we were out of there so fast no one could have caught us.

"Where are we going?" I asked breathlessly.

"I'm taking you to Brenton Point. You've been there before, I presume?" He looked over at me and then made some adjustments to the heat and the radio.

"Yes, many times. But I don't think I've ever gone there on a cold winter night." Brenton Point was a beautiful state park on Ocean Drive and I'd been there probably hundreds of times over the years. I wondered what he had in mind that required a trip there.

We crossed over Goose Neck Cove and passed the Newport Country Club, entering into the park. The sky was black but the moon was full and it shined over the ocean, causing the waves to sparkle. It was a little windy and I could make out tiny bits of snow fluttering in the air. Andrew pulled the car into the parking lot and turned off the engine. He turned to me and held out his right arm. "Come closer, love," he said, his voice husky. I swallowed an invisible lump and unbuckled my seatbelt and moved closer to him.

"Laura?" he said my name on a whisper in my hair. I felt his lips graze my temple and move along my jaw to my lips. He kissed me as I answered him.

"Yes?" I thought my voice would crack on that one tiny word. To say my nerves and stomach were in turmoil was an understatement. I was a quaking volcano inside, not knowing his intentions.

"Have you ever heard of a grand gesture?" He continued to kiss my lips and my jaw and he weaved his hand into my hair and rubbed his fingers lightly against my scalp.

"Um, I mean…I know what a grand gesture is, yes, but I can't say that I've ever experienced one." I was really afraid now. I looked out the window briefly and noticed we were the only ones here. It was inky dark but the moon was bright and the stars were out in full force. Across Ocean Drive the Atlantic roared. Waves crashed onto the rocks dramatically. The moonlight lit up the rocky walkway that jutted out into the ocean. Tiny snowflakes danced on the wind, looking like tiny ghosts shimmering out on the water.

"Well, you're about to have one. Come on!" And with that, he opened his door and walked around to my side of the car. I was frozen to my seat—from both cold and nerves—but he opened my door and pulled me out. "We should do this fast because it's cold out here!" He laughed and I could see the excitement on his face. Whatever he was planning he was certainly jazzed about it. He took me by the hand and we ran over the grassy knoll that bordered the parking lot and crossed over Ocean Drive. As we crossed the street one lone car came around the curve and drove past us. I didn't pay any attention to it—my mind was too caught up in Andrew's goofy behavior.

We stopped at the top of the rocks and looked down. Waves were washing over them, back and forth in rhythm. Andrew pointed down to the rocky causeway and said, "Over there, Laura!"

He started down the rocks and I stopped short. "No, Andrew! This is dangerous. It's too windy and it's slippery. You don't want to break your neck, do you, just for a grand gesture?" I held back, not feeling good about this.

"Come on, love! It's not that far." He pulled something out of his pocket and held it up above his head. It was a small box. "I have your birthday present right here. Come with me so I can do this right!" He took another step onto the rocks and then reached back for my hand.

Every ounce of me wanted to stay put—to stand my ground. But he seemed determined. And I couldn't let him go out there alone. A gust of wind blew my hair across my face and I pushed it back. "Andrew! Wait!"

I took a tentative step down onto the first rock. The stones made a natural stepping pattern if you knew where to look—in daylight and with no wind this walk would be a piece of cake, but tonight, with only the full moon for light and the brisk wind and the snow, it was treacherous and slow going. I caught up to him and took his hand and we slowly made our way down to the promontory. It took a while but we made it and Andrew turned to me and grinned.

"See there? Nothing to worry about." He pulled me in close to his body and my teeth chattered against his chest. "I'm sorry, darling. I know you're cold. I'll get to the point." The wind blew my hair around both of our faces and tiny snowflakes swirled all around us. Sea water rushed back and forth over the rocks and it came dangerously close to our feet. I could feel the sea-spray spitting on my face and hands in little bursts. And all I could think about was how insane we both were to be standing out here on these rocks in this weather at night. I watched as he pulled out the box again and handed it to me.

I took it and tried to open it but my hands were shaking so badly I couldn't get the clasp to release the lid. The wind howled and the waves crashed angrily over the promontory. We were getting wetter and I was freezing. Luckily we had not walked all the way to the end of it. I would have drawn the line at that. The farther out into the ocean the causeway jutted, the smaller the rocks were, and walking that far would have been suicidal. He took the box from my trembling, frozen hands and opened the lid, turning the small box toward me. By the light of the moon, I saw the gorgeous ring nestled there. It was a large diamond with smaller ones surrounding it, set in a silver band. I heard a strange strangulated sound in the night air and realized instantly that it had come from my own throat. And then Andrew was down on one knee and I felt light-headed. *This would* so *not be a good place to faint*, I told myself. Andrew must have seen the panic on my face because he took my hand and squeezed it tightly. My hands were so cold I could barely feel his fingers on mine.

"Now don't freak out, Miss Calder. I know what this looks like. You think this is a proposal of marriage, don't you?" He grinned a little wickedly at me. A burst of wind suddenly hit us and he wobbled on the rock and nearly lost his balance. I screamed and clutched his hand. "Andrew!"

"I'm OK," he said, not even frightened. "As I was saying, I bet you think this is my way of proposing, yes?"

I nodded. My head seemed to be the only thing capable of movement at the moment. I noticed that Andrew had to raise his voice now to be heard above the wind and the crashing waves. I suddenly had that weird sense that I was going to fall—the way I sometimes felt when I was on the top floor of a tall building looking down.

"I know we're too young for marriage even though I told you before that age is just a number so who really cares, but I want you to wear this ring as a token of my intent to propose to you one day—when we're older—because I could date every girl in the world but there could never be anyone I will ever love as much as I love you. So, Laura, will you do me the honor of..."

His words were cut off instantly as a massive wave broke over the rocks. I was knocked down on both knees as I clutched at Andrew's hand. He fell sideways and let out a loud yell of pain as his body slammed down onto the rocks, his hand slipping out of mine. I felt massive agony in both knees as I grabbed for something to hold onto. Andrew had fallen into the water and was clinging to a rock. His body was in the water but he was hanging on, his head above the waves.

"Andrew!" I screamed. "Hold on!" I lay down on my stomach to try to gain more leverage as I held out my hand to him. "Take my hand!" He was close enough that I knew if I could pull him just a little way, he would be able to pull himself up out of the water.

"The ring!" he shouted. "It's gone! *Damn it!*" He looked around at the dark swirling water and cursed again. The waves were rushing all around him, threatening to pull him under.

I couldn't believe he was worried about a piece of jewelry when one more rogue wave could sweep him out to sea and there wouldn't be a damned thing I could do to save him. "Forget the damned ring!" I shouted. "Take my hand!" And then another wave hit and his left hand came loose from the rock. I heard him scream in pain as his body struck hard against the rocks. The waves were coming in droves now and Andrew's body continued to beat against the sharp rocks as he struggled to hang on.

"*Andrew!*" I screamed. I was crying now and panic was setting in. He couldn't possibly hang on much longer. I pushed myself a little further out toward him, extending my right arm as far as it would reach as I held onto the rocks with my left hand. "Andrew, please…stretch… take my hand!" I lurched forward toward him—too far—and suddenly I felt myself falling off the rock, slipping into the ocean. A scream jammed in my throat as I slid downward head first.

And then strong arms were around me, lifting me up to my feet. I was unsteady—my knees throbbing, buckling. I started to fall forward but the arms held me steady. And I heard the familiar voice of my life saver, coming to my rescue again. "Laura, you're OK. Sit right here and hang on to this rock—this rock right here!" Miguel was being very specific. I turned around and saw where he was pointing. It was a larger rock higher above the waves. I tried to move to it but my legs wouldn't work. In one swift move, Miguel lifted me up and sat me down on the rock. And then I screamed. "Andrew! *No!* Miguel—*save him, please!*"

Miguel turned away from me, his attention on Andrew, just as a gust of wind knocked Andrew sideways, once again slamming his body into the rocks. He yelled in agony as his other hand slipped from the rock and he went under. I screamed and tried to keep from fainting. Miguel slipped into the water and grabbed blindly toward the spot where Andrew had gone under. "*Andrew!*" he screamed.

I couldn't look. I could not witness the death of this beautiful boy who had just declared his love for me. I would not survive this. I started to turn away just as Andrew's head broke the surface. He had drifted about fifteen feet out from the rocks—any further and there was the risk of the undertow taking him. Miguel pushed away from the rock toward Andrew. When he was within striking distance I saw him hold out his arm to Andrew. "Take my hand, Easton. *Now!*" he commanded. In the moonlight I could see the wildness in Andrew's eyes. I yelled as loud as I could.

"*Andrew! Take his hand! Please!*" I was near hysterics now.

"Easton, come on! Take my hand!" Miguel pushed closer to Andrew. The water swirled and the snow seemed to thicken. Finally Andrew snapped out of his panicky trance and put his hand in Miguel's.

"Don't fight this or you'll pull us both under, Andrew!" Miguel yelled above the roar of the wind and the waves. He turned and fought his way back to the rocks, pulling Andrew with him. Once back to the rocks, Miguel placed Andrew's hand on one of them. "Can you hang on until I get up there?" Andrew nodded. He was in shock, I could tell. So was I, or getting close.

Miguel pulled himself up in one smooth motion and turned to Andrew. He braced his feet to gain leverage and reached down and pulled Andrew up and out of the water. Andrew lay slumped on the rocks and moaned in pain. He curled his body and clutched at his stomach and ribs.

I snapped out of my shock, struggled to my feet and started to make my way toward Andrew but Miguel stopped me.

"No, Laura. Stay where you are. I'm going to get Andrew up and then we're going to walk straight up this rock path to the road. Look where I'm pointing, Laura. *Laura!*" He yelled at me and I shook my head, trying to focus on his words. I looked in the direction he was pointing. I nodded that I understood.

Miguel bent down to Andrew. "You're going to have to walk out of here, Easton. Can you get up?"

Andrew groaned and rocked back and forth. I could hear his muffled cries as he tried to contain his agony. He looked up at Miguel and whispered, "I'll try."

Miguel held out his hand and Andrew took it, grimacing with every movement. Miguel pulled him hard once and Andrew was up on his feet and howling in pain again. He doubled over and clutched at his sides, wincing with each gasping breath he took.

"You probably broke a rib or two. Come on. We've got to get you out of here." He put an arm around Andrew and they started toward me.

"Laura. You lead the way—carefully and walk in a straight line toward the road," Miguel ordered. I began the slow walk toward safety, Miguel and Andrew following carefully behind me. After a few minutes we were clear of the rocks and up on the grassy area that ran along Ocean Drive.

Miguel dropped his arm from Andrew's shoulders and let him walk off whatever he was feeling—physical pain, embarrassment, shock. I walked over to Andrew and put my hand on his arm.

"Andrew. I know you're hurt. We need to get you to the hospital. You may have broken a rib." I was sobbing and limping, trying to stop his pacing and calm him down. He was breathing hard and shivering fiercely. I was sure he was going into shock.

"No! I don't need a damned hospital. I'm fine. Just give me a minute." He shook off my hand and walked slowly in a circle, finally coming to a stop in front of Miguel.

My heart pounded. I felt sick. I wanted to faint. I prayed that Andrew would be grateful. If he was in any way mean to Miguel I swore to myself that I would never speak to him again.

Andrew and Miguel stared at one another. I could see their faces in the moonlight. I saw pain and weariness on Andrew's face and a stone mask on Miguel's.

"Thank you, Dos Santos. I guess I owe you one." Andrew looked over at me for a moment and then back to Miguel. "Make that two."

Miguel nodded but didn't respond right away. The he said something that made absolutely no sense whatsoever. I wasn't even sure I'd heard him right.

"Remember that when the flowers bloom in the spring, Easton." Then he walked over to me and took my arm. "Are you OK? Are you hurt?"

I sniffed and wiped my frozen hands across my face. "I'm OK. Thank you. Again."

Miguel squeezed my arm tightly for just a moment and then let it go. He walked away. I saw his Suburban parked on the side of the road. As he neared it, he turned around and looked back at us. "Get those ribs checked, Easton." And then he got in his car and drove off.

Andrew walked slowly toward me. His face was angry and he cursed several times.

"Shh," I tried to comfort him. I couldn't be sure what was hurt more—his body or his pride. "We need to get you to the hospital. Come on." I took his arm and tried to lead him back to the parking lot. But he shook off my arm and cursed again.

"Son of a bitch!" he yelled. He started walking toward the car, seeming to forget I was still here. I held my ground. Whatever his problem was, I deserved better than this. I felt like I'd played some small part in his rescue.

"What the hell is your damned problem, Andrew?" I screamed and then burst into tears as I sank down to the wet ground. My shoulders shook and I sobbed. I could feel the shock taking over again and I wanted so badly to be warm and dry and away from here. And then Andrew was there, pulling me up even as he winced with every movement.

"I'm sorry, baby," he whispered. He wrapped one arm around me and the other around his own body. "I'm sorry. Come on. We need to get warm. I'm sorry, sweetheart. It's OK."

We walked to the car and got inside. He started the engine and cranked up the heater. I even felt the seats begin to warm. I shook uncontrollably and my teeth threatened to shatter into a million pieces. I didn't know how Andrew could even function after having been submerged in the frigid Atlantic. He shook, too, as he put the car in gear and slowly drove out onto Ocean Drive.

"The hospital is that way," I pointed to the right.

"I'm not going to hospital. I'll be fine. There's nothing that can be done for broken ribs anyway—and they might only be bruised." I heard his teeth chatter as he talked. His hands were shaking on the steering wheel. Every so often his body would convulse. He was scaring me.

"Andrew, please. You need medical attention," I pleaded with him.

"No!" he shouted angrily. Then his voice softened. "I didn't even ask—are you hurt? Should I take you to the urgent care?"

"No, no. You're the one who needs urgent care. I just want out of these wet clothes. I feel like I'll never be warm again."

He pulled his frozen hand off the wheel and took hold of mine. It was hard to tell whose was the coldest. We both felt like huge blocks of ice.

"I lost the ring." He was dejected and I could tell he was heartsick over it.

"I'm so sorry." I didn't know what else to say. I hoped he'd had the sense to have it insured. And I fervently hoped it wasn't a priceless family heirloom. That would not sit well with the duke.

"I'll get you a new one. I promise." He sounded contrite—like that was the worst thing that had happened today—worse than nearly drowning in the Atlantic Ocean.

We drove in silence for a while, the heater blasting, until finally arriving at my house. He leaned over and kissed me lightly with icy lips.

"I am so sorry about everything. I ruined your birthday. How can I ever make this up to you?" He looked so sad that I started to cry again.

"You *made* my birthday—by not dying!" I swiped at my tears as he kissed me once more. "Now, go home, get warm, and pray the goons don't know you've been gone." I got out of the car, waved and went inside. I went straight to the shower where I finally started to feel warm again. Every part of my body cried out in relief as the blood started to flow normally again. I felt my tears mix with the water as the shock of the evening started to dissipate. I dried off, slipped into flannel pajamas, and curled up in my bed, my wet hair still wrapped in a towel. I clasped my hand tightly around the talisman—it glowed and warmed me into a deep sleep–a sleep filled with dreams about flowers and springtime.

Chapter Sixteen

TRUE LOVE

When I awoke late the next morning I felt like I'd been drugged. My hair was a mess inside the towel, knotted and still damp in places. I took another shower and when I was dressed and feeling more human I called Andrew. I needed to know how he was feeling and if he was still in pain. Maybe I could convince him to go for x-rays at Newport Hospital. When I got his voicemail, I didn't bother to leave a message deciding texting would be faster: *Good morning. How are you feeling today? How are your ribs?*

I never got a response and the day dragged on. I stayed home from school and since the goons hadn't come this morning I assumed Andrew was staying home, too. It was now several hours after my initial text and I'd heard nothing from him though I'd sent a few more texts throughout the afternoon. And it scared me. I decided I couldn't wait forever to hear from him so I took the Jeep and drove to his house. I didn't even stop to think that doing so could be a mistake, though I was a little wary at the thought of showing up at his house without an invitation. But there didn't seem to be any other way to get an answer and I needed to know if he was OK.

I parked in the driveway and took a moment in the warmth of the Jeep to gather my courage. Then I walked up to the front door and rang the bell. Within a few seconds the door was opened by a maid in a black and white uniform.

"Yes?" she said. "May I help you?" She stood in the doorway and didn't seem inclined to invite me in. As a matter of fact, she acted as if she had never seen me before. I was astonished.

"Hello, Jane? I'm Laura Calder—Andrew's friend. Is he here? I really need to see him."

She took a step back and looked over her shoulder, then turned to me. "I'm sorry, Miss Calder. Andrew is sick and not taking any visitors today. I will be happy to tell him you called for him." She made to shut the door but, in an unusual burst of boldness, I put my foot on the threshold to prevent the door from being closed in my face.

"If you would please tell him I'm here I'm quite certain he would want to see me," I said with feigned authority.

I heard footsteps in the background. And suddenly the duke was there in the doorway glaring at me. He looked at Jane and said, "That will be all, Jane. I will handle our unexpected visitor." Jane disappeared instantly like a ghost fading into the woodwork. I looked up at the duke who was staring down at my foot. I slowly moved it back and clenched my fingers into fists at my sides. "What can I do for you, Miss Calder?" His voice was deep and menacing and I felt every hair on my head crackle with electricity.

"I came to see Andrew. Is he home?" I knew I sounded breathless and intimidated and I hated myself for letting this ogre see my nerves.

"Andrew isn't feeling well today. He'll be staying in bed for the next few days recovering." He glared at me and I swore his eyes were glowing fiery embers.

"Wh…wh…what's wrong with him?" I stuttered like a fool. My power of rational thought was shutting down under the duke's intense stare.

He emitted a low, ominous chuckle. "Now, Laura…I'm surprised you even have to ask, considering you were there when he was injured. Something about a little tumble into the ocean, cracking a few ribs against rocks…something like that. Very dangerous of you two to be out on the rocks in the dark and cold. What were you thinking?"

I didn't answer. I truly couldn't have if I'd wanted to. *What was I thinking*? What indeed. I just stared at him, not breathing, waiting for him to unleash his wrath on me, for I was sure he was blaming me for the incident.

"I'll let Andrew know you stopped by. And in the future, please be more careful. There is already enough danger in this world without inviting it in. Good day, Miss Calder."

He stepped back, closing the door in my face. I turned and ran fast to my car. I couldn't wait to get out of there. I headed toward home, my hands gripping the steering wheel so hard my knuckles turned white. Tremors coursed through me, causing me to shiver and my breaths came rapidly—I couldn't seem to shake the duke's penetrating eyes from my memory. As I got closer to the turn-off for my neighborhood I realized that I didn't want to go home. I was so keyed up about Andrew that I couldn't concentrate. I needed to talk to someone and I knew there was only one person I could turn to. I headed in the direction of Miguel's house to pay my second unscheduled visit of the day. I only hoped I wouldn't be turned away from this house, too. As I drove slowly along the long, curving drive, heading into the tunnel of trees, it began to snow again—fat fluffy flakes—the pretty kind that made me not hate winter completely. I rounded the last corner and saw two Suburbans in the drive—one white and one black. I parked behind them and sat idling a moment as I tried to gather my courage. I was a shattered mess between worrying about Andrew, fearing his father and completely unsure what reception I would receive now at Miguel's door. I turned off the engine, took a deep breath and opened the door. As I approached the house I saw movement in the window. When I cleared the porch steps, the door opened and Miguel was there. I had one split second to drink him in, not even realizing the powerful hunger I had just for the sight of him.

"Laura? Hi." Miguel tilted his head questioningly at me. "This is unexpected. Everything OK?" I opened my mouth to answer him but only a pent-up breath escaped. I was so damned happy to see him that I couldn't function. I couldn't make anything work. He reached for my hand and gently pulled me inside and closed the door. Without saying a word, he helped me out of my coat and led me into the kitchen. If there was anyone else in the house, and judging by the presence of the white Suburban in the driveway I assumed there was, I didn't see or hear them.

Miguel took me to the loveseat and indicated that I should sit. Then he walked over to the stove and turned the burner on under a tea kettle. I watched in silence as he took two mugs from a cupboard and dropped teabags into them. He set a sugar bowl and two spoons on the counter and then came back to sit beside me. I listened to the sound of the hum coming from the kettle as the water slowly heated. I wished that I could heat up like that. I still had the feeling that I would never be warm again. Miguel took my cold hands in his and smiled at me.

"How is Andrew today?" he asked quietly. The concern in his voice sounded genuine.

As much as I tried to fight it, I felt a tear slip from the corner of my eye and begin a slow descent down the side of my face. I wiped it away and sniffed. I didn't want to cry.

"I don't know. I tried to contact him today but he never answered so I went over there to see him and the maid who answered the door pretended like she'd never seen me before in her life and then the duke came to the door and…" My voice broke off in a pathetic sob.

"What did the duke do to you?" I heard the instantaneous change in his voice. I watched as he worked his jaw back and forth and I saw the darkness in his eyes. He reached up and stroked my cheek and then wiped the tear that was falling from my other eye.

"He didn't *do* anything. I don't get him. He wouldn't let me see Andrew. He said he was sick or something. He knew what happened last night and I had the distinct feeling that he was blaming me for it. I truly do not know why he hates me so much." I cut off another sob that threatened to escape from my throat.

Miguel rubbed his hands over mine to warm them. Then he brought each of my palms to his lips and kissed them. I felt myself melting. I wanted to throw myself into his arms and stay there forever.

"The duke has no reason not to like you, Laura, but he doesn't need a reason. It's just the way he is. He's not a nice man. He bullies and threatens people and I think it's because he's dissatisfied with his lot in life—ironic as that may seem."

"How do you know so much about him?" I so desperately wanted an answer to this question.

The tea kettle whistled and Miguel got up. He poured water over the teabags and brought them over to the table in front of the loveseat. He got the spoons and sugar and helped himself to three generous teaspoons. I did the same and then leaned back savoring the heat of the mug in my cold hands. I waited for an answer.

Finally he sighed. "Listen to me, Laura. There is so much I want to tell you. But I'm afraid to. I feel like you're safer if you're in the dark about…some things. But I can promise you this, in a few short months, this will be over. And then we…"

I cut him off there. "*What* will be over? *Damn it*! Andrew said nearly the same thing! What the hell will be over? Tell me, please. I'm begging you." I felt agitation stirring in my gut and my teeth chattered. A new wave of coldness was settling into my bones and I shivered.

"Let me explain something to you, Laura. I'm going to tell you why you're so much better off not knowing. *Because you would go straight to Andrew*. You would tell him you talked to me. And he would tell his father and then…" He hesitated a moment and looked down at the floor. Then he looked into my eyes with a mixture of anger and fear. "Then…I have no doubt that the duke would…harm you."

I shook my head in disbelief. He was doing it again. Going all theatrical all over the place. It was enough to snap me out of my despair. "Puhleeze, Miguel. Not this again. I do not want to hear any more nonsense about danger and secrets and sh…"

Miguel cut *me* off this time. He snatched the mug of tea from my hands so roughly that hot liquid sloshed over the side onto my leg and the floor. I flinched from the heat and jumped as he slammed it on the coffee table next to his, causing more to spill over. And then in one lightning fast movement he grabbed me and crushed me to his chest so hard I cried out as I felt the wind get knocked out of me. He was trembling…with rage? With fear? I couldn't tell. But I was frightened as he whispered in my ear. His voice was harsh and menacing and I knew in this moment that he was not playing a game.

"This is no joke, Laura. This is life or death. Now you listen to me. You will remain in the dark for your own safety. But I will tell you this much so you won't feel so blind and deaf. I believe that Andrew is good. He probably does love you. But you need to avoid the duke as much as possible. He is an evil man. I hold him responsible for the death of my father."

I started to speak but Miguel clamped his hand over my mouth and held it there firmly. I sagged against his chest and he relaxed his grip on my body slightly but kept a hand over my mouth. "I know what you're going to say. I told you my father died of a heart attack. And that is the truth. He was a healthy man who, by all rights, should've lived to a ripe old age, but the duke killed him. Not by his own hand but with his words. Now, before you go thinking that I'm here to kill the Duke of Easton and get revenge and you feel a loyalty to Andrew that requires you to tell him so, know this: If I wanted the duke dead badly enough, he would already be six feet under. I have no intention of killing anyone. But the duke doesn't have any such compunction about the sanctity of life. I have told you so much more than I'd intended and I am asking you to keep my words between us—between you and me. I'm begging you, Laura, for your own safety, to remain quiet, do not question Andrew, and avoid the duke at all costs. Please nod if you understand and promise to honor my wishes."

My tears were pouring now. I nodded as I twisted my mouth against his hand. I didn't know if I should fear him or trust him. Should I make a run for it or stay and believe that he had nothing but my best interest at heart? A sob broke through as he relaxed his hand over my mouth. Again I tried to speak but he placed his fingers over my lips and shushed me.

"I'm not finished talking yet. Listen to me." He pulled the talisman out from under my shirt and forced it into my hand. "Do you feel that?" I nodded and began to tremble uncontrollably again. He wrapped his other arm around me and stroked my back. "The talisman knows. You can feel its heat. It's protecting you. Never let the duke get his hands on it."

"Can I talk now?" I asked on a whisper. He nodded. "It was Andrew who gave it to me. Why did he give it to me?" I struggled to control my ragged breathing.

Miguel dropped his arms from me and got up. He walked over to the sliding glass doors that led out onto the back deck and stared out toward the river. "He gave it to you? I thought you told me you found it."

"Well, I did…sort of…but I believe Andrew arranged for me to find it. But I don't know why. I've wanted to ask him so many times but I know he will deny it." Talking about my necklace made me feel better—less afraid—less shaky. I sipped my tea which had cooled off considerably.

"Now why would he do that?" Miguel muttered under his breath— talking to himself now. "He wouldn't have done that if he had known the significance of his actions. He made it so easy…"

He stopped and shook his head as if he were trying to make sense of something. His change in mood made me uneasy. I got up and joined him at the glass door. I put my hand on his arm and turned him slightly toward me. "Miguel? What are you talking about? Andrew made what easy? "

He sighed. "It seems there are things that even I don't understand, Laura. We're both in the dark, I guess. Just forget it." He turned to me then and his arms went immediately around me pulling me close into his body. "The important thing is that the right person is wearing the talisman. It was meant for you—to protect you—to lead you to me."

Oh, how I hoped his words were true. I buried my face in his neck and breathed in the scent of his skin. "I don't want to be afraid anymore—of the duke or Andrew or…you…" My voice trailed off in a ragged sigh.

Miguel tilted my chin upward and held my gaze. "I told you that you can trust me. I would never, ever hurt you." He grinned then and laid his forehead against mine. I could feel his sweet breath against my lips. "How many times do I have to save your life before you believe me?"

I snuggled into him then and sighed. "There is so much I don't understand. But I will do as you say. I do trust you. Where's your family? Your house is so quiet."

"They're in other rooms giving us privacy. They saw you drive up." He kissed my nose and flinched at its coldness. Everything about me was cold, it seemed.

"Oh, I've run them out of their own kitchen then, have I?" I felt badly for that.

"It's OK. Are you feeling any better now…about things?" He put his fingertips to my chin again, tilting my face to look into his eyes.

"Definitely not. I am more in the dark now than I was before I came here. I am more confused than ever. I have so much to think through and I don't know what to do about Andrew. I love him but…"

Miguel winced at my words. I felt him stiffen and knew he'd misunderstood. "I don't want to hear that," he said.

I tried to explain myself. "I mean I care about him and he seems to love me. But I have doubts…about…everything."

"What were you two doing at Brenton Point? When I looked down and saw you there I thought he was proposing to you. Tell me I'm wrong about that." He held me close against him again, his arms enveloping me into his warmth.

I hesitated and then told him about Andrew's unusual proposal. "But before he got the words out, he fell into the water. He dropped the ring. I'm sure it's half-way across the ocean by now."

"Wow. He really must love you then." I felt his heart beating against my cheek and I realized how much I loved the feel of it. His next question caught me by surprise. "What would your answer have been?" It seemed like he was holding his breath as he awaited my response.

"I don't know. I'm too young to get married—we both are. And Andrew knows that—he said as much. But turning him down when he'd gone to so much trouble would have been awkward." I shuddered at the thought.

"Avoiding an awkward situation is not a good enough reason to accept someone's proposal of marriage." Miguel dropped his arms from me then and led me back to the loveseat. We sat down and I leaned back and rested my head on the cushion.

"I know that. I would have figured a way out of it. Even if it meant accepting the ring but returning it later…" My voice trailed off. Then I remembered about my cell phone and the missing messages. "Miguel—something did happen when I had dinner at Andrew's house on his birthday. Someone took my cell phone and erased all of my messages—including the one you sent me…you know…the one I never responded to that you had to forward to me. Could it have been the duke? And if so, why?"

Darkness washed over Miguel's face. I felt his body tense beside me. "I wouldn't be surprised. But why? I don't know. But you can understand even more now why I tell you to stay away from him. You can never trust the Duke of Easton." He got up again and took our cups to the kitchen sink. He didn't speak for a few moments. He seemed to be working something out in his head. Then he returned and sat back down next to me. I saw emotions pass over his face and he seemed to relax the slightest bit. He leaned over to me then and cupped my face in his hands and redirected the subject elsewhere. "By the way, happy birthday—a day late. Remember I told you I had something for you?"

I felt a surge of excitement. "You did mention that, didn't you?" I grinned.

He got up. "I'll be right back." He left the room and disappeared down the hall.

While I was alone I took a moment to think. My questions had not been answered to my satisfaction. If anything, I had even more now. But I had to trust Miguel. He was absolutely right about one thing: how many times did he have to save me to prove he cared? I owed him my trust and my silence about what he'd told me today. And I knew that any information he was withholding was because he wanted to protect me. I would just have to live with that.

Miguel returned and sat back down next to me. He handed me a small gift-wrapped box. My hands trembled slightly as I took it. I looked at him questioningly and he grinned. "Don't worry. It's not an engagement ring," he chuckled. I smiled back as I opened the box, suppressing the pang in my heart at those words. I refused to even consider why my heart had negatively reacted to that offhand comment. Inside the box was a small, purple, velvet pouch. I opened the pouch and turned it upside down, pouring the contents into my hand—a delicate pair of expensive-looking sapphire earrings in a silver setting. They were stunning. I sucked in a breath of astonishment and let it out slowly.

"Wow…Miguel…are these…real?" As soon as I asked the question I felt a stab of guilt at how rude that must have sounded.

He smiled, not offended by my words. "They are…I've always liked sapphires." He picked one up out of my hand and held it against my cheek. "It looks beautiful next to your pale skin, against all that blonde hair and your…blue eyes…" I noticed the deepening of his voice as he spoke, his voice becoming husky and soft. He dropped the earring back into my hand and wrapped his hand into my hair, pulling my face toward him—his lips grazing mine feather-softly. I felt a swooning sensation wash over me as he kissed me—his lips were so soft, tender and warm. I put my arms around him then and let myself go—into the kiss—deeply—tasting his sweetness. His tongue tangled with mine and I felt that roller coaster freefall sensation again. If I died in this very moment it would be the sweetest of deaths. Finally he released his hand from my hair and cupped my cheek in his hand. "Laura…I…"

"Ahem." The sound came from the doorway. I jumped back instantly, my face turning crimson. Miguel's Uncle Antonio entered the kitchen and glanced over at us—a telltale grin playing at the corners of his mouth. "Sorry to bother you two, but I've got a couple of hungry teenagers wanting me to fix some food…" His voice trailed off into a chuckle.

I got to my feet then and put the earrings back into the pouch and put the pouch into the box. Miguel stood, too, as I tried to compose myself.

"Laura, good to see you again," said Antonio. "Please stay for a meal. I have no idea what I'm making but I'm sure it will involve meat and potatoes. Those two brothers of yours…" He looked at Miguel with a shake of his head. "They're eating me out of house and home." He grinned and began taking items out of the fridge and assembling kitchen utensils on the counter.

"Thank you. I'll take a rain check if that's OK." I turned to Miguel. "I'd better go—my mom will be needing her car soon."

We walked to the front door and Miguel helped me into my coat. As soon as my arms were through the sleeves I threw them around his neck and squeezed tightly. "Thank you so much for the beautiful earrings, Miguel. I love them."

"You're welcome." He kissed me then, again so tenderly that it was all I could do to restrain myself. I wanted so much more. "Let me know how Andrew is as soon as you know. And try not to worry about things that don't make sense to you now. Just remember what I told you about the duke. Your safety is the only thing that matters. Call or text me if you need me." He kissed my forehead…then my temple, the hollow behind my jaw and finally my lips, causing me to emit a tiny groan. It was all I could do to keep from melting into the floor—his effect was so powerful.

We said good-bye and I got in my car and drove off. Miguel was still standing on the porch as I rounded the bend in the driveway—I saw him wave in the rearview mirror as I drove out of sight. As I headed home my thoughts raced. I had more questions than ever. I wondered what words the duke had said to Miguel's father that had caused him so much stress that he'd had a fatal heart attack as a result. So much swirled in my mind as I drove. I had a dreadful feeling in my stomach—a sense of impending doom. And I had a huge problem that I had to face—that I had to deal with. I knew I could not let this go on any longer with Andrew. Every moment with Miguel—and even moments away from him when he was on my mind—made me know with absolute certainty that I had to break up with Andrew. I had to end it because I was cheating on him and I didn't want to be a cheat. My heart ached at the thought of hurting him. His declaration of love last night was just as sweet as it was foolish, but I couldn't let guilt or fear of hurting his feelings prevent me from doing what I knew to be right. Because there was one thing I knew for sure, beyond any shadow of a doubt: I was deeply, endlessly, hopelessly in love with Miguel Dos Santos.

Chapter Seventeen

GOOD-BYE FOR NOW

It seemed like forever before Andrew finally contacted me. He called me just as I had finished having a bite to eat with my mother. I mouthed Andrew's name to her as I pushed away from the table and went upstairs to my room so I could talk to him in private.

"Laura! I'm so sorry about what happened. I want you to know when I found out you'd come by and they wouldn't allow you in, I was livid. I think for once in my life, I actually put my father in his place. I thought I saw your car driving down the driveway and Jane confirmed you'd been here and she told me Father had spoken to you. I really am sorry." He spoke in a rush of words and my heart went out to him.

"It's OK, but I've been worried sick about you. How are your ribs? Your father knows about what happened—did you tell him?"

"Unfortunately, yes. In retrospect, I should have lied, but one of the goons, as you call them—and I have to agree with that assessment—mentioned the wet mess in the car and one of the servants found my wet clothes and then I sort of vomited blood and, well, it was all downhill from there."

"Wait! What the hell do you mean you vomited blood? Andrew! Please tell me you went to the hospital!" I was shocked and horrified.

"Yes, I know I probably should have gone to hospital immediately but I really thought my ribs were just bruised. Actually two are broken. The blood? I didn't know what that was about but it scared me enough that I got Tristan and he called Father and the next thing you know we were off to hospital. I actually spent the night there. I wanted so badly to call you but all telephone access was cut off from me. Father didn't want me to have any distractions, or so he said."

"Oh, my god, Andrew! I am so sorry. You must be in awful pain. I wish I had known. All sorts of things were going through my head because I hadn't heard from you." I felt a sense of relief now that I had heard his voice and I knew he was going to be OK.

"Well, it certainly hurts to breathe. I thought I heard mention of a punctured lung but I was rather out of it. It's funny because I knew I'd hit the rocks hard but it didn't seem that hard at the time. Of course, I was so numb from the cold water that that may have anesthetized me. In any case, I'm home now and I so desperately want to see you." He sounded tired and so…earnest.

"Should I come over?" I had mixed emotions about that, but worry for Andrew's health and safety trumped any guilt I had at leading him on.

"Personally, that would be the best get well gift I could ever have, but Father is in a bit of a state so you'd better not. Just know that I miss you and I love you and I can't wait to see you. I don't think I'll be coming to school for a few days though. I have to wait for the all-clear from the doctor."

"Well, good. You should stay home—definitely. You could get jostled in the halls and you can't be carrying heavy books anyway. Just please stay in touch and promise me you'll get well soon."

"I will. I love you. I'll see you soon." And with those words he hung up before I had to agonize over how to respond to his declaration of love.

As soon I hung up with Andrew, I called Miguel. I could have sent him a quick text but I so badly wanted to hear his voice. He picked up on the third ring. "Hi. It's me. I have an Andrew update."

"Hey there. How is he?" Miguel sounded distracted. Maybe I had interrupted something. I told him about Andrew's situation and he was quiet. "Miguel, are you there?"

"Yes, I'm here. It's good he got medical help. He should've gone immediately. How are you doing today?"

"I'm good. You sound distracted. Did I call at a bad time?" I hated the thought of our conversation ending so soon but I didn't want to be a nuisance.

He laughed. "No. I was just helping my brothers with some home-work that's due tomorrow that they waited until the last minute to do."

I felt relief wash over me. "Of course they did," I laughed. "I wanted to thank you again for the gorgeous earrings. It was so thoughtful of you." I picked them up now and held them in my hand. They were quite delicate and I feared I would lose them.

"You're welcome. I'm happy you like them. Laura, I need to tell you something." He hesitated and I felt my nerves begin to tingle.

"Yes...is everything alright?" I asked quietly.

"I have to go to Portugal for the holidays to see my mother. It's our first holiday without my father and I don't want her to be alone. She's missing us. My sister is there but I know she wants to see her sons."

"Wait! You have a sister?" Yet another piece of the Miguel puzzle being unveiled.

"Well, technically she's my cousin but my parents raised her from childhood after her parents died in a plane crash. She's like a sister to me. Her name is Catarina."

I thought of two things I'd always wanted to know about Miguel and now seemed as good a time as any to ask: "Why did you move here to Portsmouth? I mean...I'm glad you did, but I've been wonder-ing what prompted the move. And also, how do you know English so well? Aside from a slight accent, you speak it like a native."

He didn't answer right away. After a few moments had passed and he still had not answered, I looked at my phone to make sure the call had not dropped. "Miguel?"

A deep sigh escaped his lungs before he answered. "We moved here to be with our uncle while he builds a boat for a client. My mother thought it would be good for us to experience life in another coun-try. And she worried about Uncle Antonio being lonely...so...we decided...why not? As for my English, my parents had us educated in the American School in Lisbon."

I heard something in his voice that didn't sound right...or maybe it was what I wasn't hearing that disturbed me...like maybe there was another reason he was in Rhode Island and he didn't want to tell me. But I didn't push it. "Well, I'm glad you did." I said quietly. "When will you return from Portugal?"

"We'll be back in time for the new year. We're leaving soon but I'll be in school for a few more days."

I could hear noise and voices in the background. It sounded like his brothers were rough-housing.

"I hate to cut this short but my brothers are pestering me so I've got to go. I'll see you later, OK?"

My heart seized. I didn't want to hang up. I wanted to know more. But I said, "OK, see you." I snapped my phone shut and collapsed onto my bed, hugging my pillow tightly to me. And then Miguel's words suddenly hit me like a proverbial ton of bricks—he was going away for the holidays. That was too long to be without him. I could not imagine how I would survive it.

The days flew by fast and I realized that Christmas was now nearly here and I had not given a single moment of thought to shopping. I just wanted the holidays to be over so that Miguel would be back. Of course, he hadn't even left yet so I tried not to fall into the misery of anti-climax. I saw him at school and when our paths crossed in the hall it was all I could do to keep from launching myself into his arms. I was sure if he knew my thoughts he would get a huge laugh out of it.

English became my favorite class of the day. But I never heard a word the teacher said because I was distracted by Miguel's presence behind me. Sometimes I could feel his fingertips graze my back or touch my hair. I knew that if Andrew had been in class, Miguel would not have touched me or probably even talked to me so I was thankful for these moments that were secrets between us. I was in contact with Andrew and I knew he was recovering well from his injured ribs. He was planning to return to school on Friday and Miguel would be leaving Thursday. And I felt torn in two.

After English class on Thursday Miguel and I walked together out to the parking lot. I saw Lily and Gretchen getting into Lily's car—I knew they'd seen me talking with him several times this week and I'd seen the questions in their eyes though we hadn't talked much lately. We were planning a Christmas shopping trip to Providence Place Mall on Saturday though, so I knew to prepare myself for the onslaught of questioning that was sure to come.

We walked to my Jeep and I asked Miguel if he would sit with me for a minute. We got inside and I started the engine to get the heater running. I turned to him as he reached across the middle console and took my hand in his. "So you're really leaving tonight?" I could barely get the words out.

"Yes. We have a late flight out of Boston. I should probably get going but…" He stopped talking and glanced out the window. Fluffy snowflakes were swirling about in the grayness of the afternoon. I looked out, too, and was surprised to see one of Andrew's cars driving slowly through the lot toward my car. My heart rate instantly tripled in speed and I felt my lungs threatening to shut down.

"Oh, my god. Andrew—what's he doing here? What should we do?" I could barely function, as if I'd been caught red-handed stealing the queen's jewels.

"It's OK. You're allowed to talk to me." He squeezed my hand as we watched the car approach and slow as it passed. I saw Peter at the wheel. He looked straight at me as he drove by. The back windows were so darkly tinted that I had no way of knowing if there was anyone in the backseat.

"This is bad," I gasped. "What if Andrew saw us?" I knew I had to end things with him but I wasn't prepared for it to be this soon. I'd thought I had more time. I watched as the car continued past my Jeep and exited the lot then turned out onto the main road.

Miguel's sudden intake of breath caught me by surprise and I jumped in fright. "*Damn it*! I can't believe I'm leaving town. You're too vulnerable, Laura. I shouldn't be leaving you like this." It seemed as if Miguel were talking as much to himself as he was to me.

"But what do I have to fear? Tell me! The duke? If so, why? I can handle Andrew. I have to break up with him. I can't let this go on any longer, Miguel, because, I'm…" My words tumbled out in a jumbled burst but I stopped myself—suddenly too afraid to say more—to say out loud the words that I was screaming inside my head.

"Laura…just remember this—avoid the duke. Keep yourself safe and out of trouble while I'm gone. I know you don't want to hurt Andrew but you have to follow your heart even if it's painful. When you do what's right, things have a way of working out."

I nodded as I stared at his face and memorized every inch of it— his endless dark eyes, his perfect nose, the jaw that looked as if it had been sculpted by an artist. I wanted to touch his black hair and kiss his lips. I felt light-headed and woozy. Under my shirt my necklace began to tingle. I brought my hand to my chest and grabbed my shirt and let out a surprised gasp. "Ooh, wow!"

Miguel reached over and placed his hand on mine. "Listen to it, Laura. It knows."

I started to ask what the necklace knew but Miguel put his fingers to my lips and stopped me from speaking. "I have to go. I'm going to miss you. I want to kiss you right now but…" He looked around the parking lot. Many students had already left and the lot was less than half full but there were still people coming out of the building. "I don't want to cause you any trouble."

I didn't hesitate. "I don't give a damn. Kiss me, *please*…" I begged, leaning toward him, my head spinning, my heart pounding, my lungs frozen in mid-breath.

He closed the distance over the center console and touched his lips to mine. I grabbed his arm and held on as the kiss deepened. His lips were killing me—they were so warm and tender. Never in my life had I experienced this kind of bliss. He touched his tongue to my lips and I groaned, pressing mine closer. He pulled back for a moment and whispered words to me in Portuguese. They sounded beautiful. I didn't understand what he was saying but I knew I could listen to this forever. His eyes were dark, filled with passion. We kissed with a fervor that left me beyond breathless…and then he put his hand on my cheek and pushed me back gently.

"What are you doing to me? How can I leave you now?" he whispered the words as his fingers caressed my jaw.

"Don't," I whispered, leaning into his hand. "Don't go."

He dropped his hand and took hold of mine. "I have to. We have a plane to catch. And I see my brothers over by my car. They're being patient but if I don't get over there and unlock the doors they're going to be inviting themselves into your Jeep to get warm."

I chuckled nervously. "Be safe…and…hurry home, OK?"

"I will." He straightened and reached for the door handle. As he opened the door and stepped out, he leaned back in and gave me a reassuring smile. "Laura?"

I gripped the steering wheel in an attempt to keep myself from grabbing him and pulling him back inside the car. I couldn't bear the thought of his leaving. "Yes?" I looked at him and fought back tears that suddenly threatened to fall.

"I love you. But you already knew that, right?" His voice was deep and soft and I was drowning in it.

I thought my heart would burst at that—it couldn't handle much more emotion. "I was hoping. You know I love you, too. I'll get things sorted with Andrew. I promise."

"Just be careful…and merry Christmas."

And then he was gone. And I was a mess. I could barely see to drive home because of the endless tears. As I left the parking lot, I caught a few stares from fellow students looking at me as if I had just sprouted horns but I didn't care. Let them think what they wanted. I knew I looked like the biggest cheater on the planet. A big cheat choosing the gypsy boy over the handsome prince, but I didn't care. I drove home and went up to my room to wait for Andrew's call. It was only a matter of time before he confronted me about being in the Jeep with Miguel. I lay on my bed and tried to think of what to say to extricate myself from this relationship and I knew it would be painful—for both of us.

Chapter Eighteen

With This Ring

Andrew texted me just before I went to bed and told me he would pick me up in the morning as usual. I wanted to tell him I preferred to drive myself but I couldn't think of a good excuse. Besides, it might be easier to keep things relatively normal since Miguel wouldn't be here distracting me. My own mind was my biggest distraction anyway, and I would have to try very hard to keep it in check. Mentally I was somewhere in Portugal. But I would figure this out—figure out how to pull myself as delicately as possible from Andrew's sweet clutches.

But Andrew was not going to make it easy. He picked me up on schedule the next morning with Peter at the wheel and another goon in the passenger seat. I slid into the car beside him and he immediately leaned over and kissed me—I didn't even have a second to prepare myself. But then he gasped and leaned back, moaning. "Ow! Damn! I have to remember—no fast moves for a while." He tried to grin through gritted teeth. He held my hand as we drove to school and asked me questions about what I'd been up to. I saw Peter's face in the rearview mirror, staring at me as if he were just as interested in my answer as Andrew was. My mind raced for a truthful answer.

"Just homework and, you know, not much really." Peter was still staring at me and I wanted to stick my tongue out at him or cross my eyes or something wicked. He was bugging the hell out of me with his judgmental expression. On the other hand, I might owe him a big fat thank you as Andrew apparently had no idea I had been with Miguel. If he had, I doubt he would be this sweet and attentive. "I have to go Christmas shopping this weekend though. Lily and Gretchen and I are going. I have never waited this long to shop for Christmas before. I'm way behind." I forced myself to ignore Peter. Andrew rubbed his thumb gently over the back of my hand.

"I feel like I haven't seen you in so long. What are your holiday plans? Does your family have a big meal? Does Father Christmas come?"

I laughed. "Yes, Father Christmas, aka Santa, comes and we have a huge meal—it's pretty much the Thanksgiving meal all over again."

We talked a bit more about holiday traditions as we pulled up in front of the school. The goon from the passenger side got out and opened my door and Peter opened Andrew's. Peter got back in and drove away leaving the other goon behind who was standing on the sidewalk holding Andrew's school bag.

"As you can see, I'll have company today," he smiled, and nodded in the goon's direction. "Laura, this is Nathan—Nathan, Laura Calder." Nathan looked just like all of the other sniper-types—tall, dark, all dressed in black and mysterious. *Does the duke roll these guys off of an assembly line in the palace basement?* I wondered yet again.

Nathan shook my hand in greeting and we all walked into the school. I said good-bye and hurried off to class. I had a hard time concentrating throughout the day—all I could think about was how to break up with Andrew and how much I missed Miguel. Thinking of Andrew now was bittersweet. I still felt some kind of love for him—he was impossible not to love and if Miguel didn't exist—I shuddered at the thought—Andrew might have been the one. I sighed and continued to drift from class to class.

After English class, as Andrew and I headed to his car with the lovely Nathan trailing along behind, I heard Lily call my name. She was standing by the front doors. "Are we on for shopping?" she yelled.

"Yes!" I gave her a thumbs-up. She smiled, waved and disappeared into the crowd of students heading to their cars and buses.

In the car, Andrew once again took my hand in his. "Hey," he said quietly. "All day long I've fantasized about kissing you. Come here."

I swallowed and felt my stomach tighten. I knew Peter was watching in the mirror as I leaned over and kissed Andrew. I wanted it to be quick but I couldn't suddenly stop without causing suspicion. As awkward as it felt, I knew Andrew was in the dark about the emotions swirling inside of me, so I kissed him as I normally did and it seemed to make him happy. If he sensed any stiffness or reluctance on my part, he didn't seem bothered.

When we arrived at my house we talked for a moment about the holidays again.

"We have a big dinner on Boxing Day, which is the day after Christmas. You'll have dinner with me and my family, yes?" he asked.

I hesitated. "Maybe you better check with your parents first and make sure I'm welcome," I said, hoping I wouldn't be, even though I felt guilty just thinking it.

"Oh, no. You're my girlfriend. They would be surprised if you didn't come. Besides, I seem to recall how a certain birthday gift disappeared and I need to rectify that. So you'll come?"

Oh, no. I was stuck. Another ring? I couldn't accept his ring. But with Peter watching my every move, I couldn't think what to say. I swallowed a lump and nodded yes.

"Good. Call me later if you want to get together. I'll just be home missing you." I smiled at his sweet words and started to get out of the car but he grabbed my arm. "Hey, you're forgetting something."

I mustered a smile and leaned over and kissed him. We said goodbye and I waved as they drove off.

I went inside to the kitchen for a drink. I turned the tea kettle on to heat water for hot chocolate and sat at the table, staring into space, considering my damned dilemma. No matter how much I tried, I couldn't stop thinking about Miguel. I even caught myself comparing him to Andrew—the differences in their kisses, their touch, their scents, their voices in my ear—one so carefree, sweet and charming, the other mysterious, dark and seductive. I questioned my judgment and my sanity and wondered not for the first time what I'd gotten myself into. But there were no answers in the bottom of my mug—only chunks of bitter chocolate powder.

Andrew texted me about our getting together but I was able to evade him thanks to my mother's work party. Every holiday season her bank had a party for the employees. The employees were allowed to bring their families and I hadn't been forced to go since I was little girl but I told Andrew my mother was making me go, crossing my fingers as I lied through my teeth. I horrified myself with the realization that not only was I a cheater but I was now a bald-faced liar as well. He was sad but understanding. I hated the deceit but until I found the courage to take the bull by the horns, it would have to continue.

I stayed holed up in my room Friday night with a grilled cheese sandwich, a book and my own misery for company. Though I couldn't stop thinking about Miguel, I forced myself to think about Andrew, too. Sweet Andrew, who truly seemed to love me. I thought about his father—a man who mystified me to no end. I wondered what had made him so bitter. Finally, to keep from going off the rails, I decided to make a Christmas shopping list. Eventually I grew tired and called it a night. A series of weird dreams interfered with my sleep, so it was a relief to see the light of morning seeping through the blinds.

My day with Lily and Gretchen at the mall flew by and I managed to find presents for everyone in spite of the fact that it was Christmas Eve and the mall was crowded with last-minute shoppers. Once again I was faced with the dilemma of what to get Andrew, finally deciding on a book called *Haunted Aquidneck Island* and a collection of sailor's knots mounted in a glass–fronted wooden case. It was quite unique and I thought it would look nice in his room with all of the other nautical decorations. I purposely didn't buy anything for Miguel because I promised myself I wouldn't think about him. When I did, I lost focus and I didn't want to have to answer any probing questions. As it was, Lily did ask about him just as we were approaching the Newport Bridge on our way home from the mall.

"So, Laura…I've been meaning to ask. What's with you and the gypsy? I've seen you talking to him a lot lately and you always look so intense, like you're discussing nuclear fission or something."

I looked out the side window for a second and hoped my face wouldn't give me away by turning every shade of red. "We were probably talking about homework or something. I don't even remember."

"*Right*," said Lily, clearly not buying it. "Miguel is strange, don't you guys think? He's so quiet and always keeps to himself. I wonder what his home-life is like."

"He may be a gypsy and he may be strange but he is totally hot—I'll give him that," added Gretchen.

"Anybody got a token for the toll?" I changed the subject as we headed onto the bridge. A good song came on the radio then and I cranked it up. We sang along as I thanked my lucky stars for having dodged yet another bullet. I was used to sharing everything with my two best friends but this felt different. There were too many unknowns in my complicated relationships to talk about them with anyone and I felt a strong desire to protect both Miguel and Andrew.

I helped my mom decorate the tree and even made a batch of sugar cookies. I had the sense that I was just marking time waiting…waiting for something to happen. Andrew and I talked several times on the phone and texted occasionally but I managed to avoid him until the day after Christmas—Boxing Day. He sent a car for me in the early evening and I was surprised that he wasn't in it—it was Peter who came to the door to get me. My mother forced me to take a gift for Andrew's parents though I was horrified at the thought. I knew there was nothing I could bring that would be good enough in the duke's eyes. But I acquiesced and took an assortment of the goodies we'd made together—some cookies, fudge and pecan tartlets. Peter helped me carry the boxes to the car along with the gifts I'd purchased for Andrew. I'd paid careful attention to my outfit, wearing a navy skirt, white blouse and a gray sweater. I kept my necklace tucked down inside my blouse and I wore the beautiful earrings Miguel had given me. I'd realized as I was getting ready that I was trying to prepare myself in such a way as to minimize any faults the duke could possibly find in me. But it would probably be a moot point—I was never going to make his list of favorite people.

Andrew was waiting for me at the door. He looked incredibly handsome in a dark gray suit, white shirt and a red tie. I felt a catch in my throat when I saw him and he pulled me into his arms and kissed me hello. I'd almost forgotten how devastatingly gorgeous he was in his own right. Peter came in behind me and placed my bags with the goodies and Andrew's gifts on the hall table.

"Finally! I thought you'd never get here," Andrew exclaimed, clearly happy to see me. "I'm sorry I didn't come to get you personally. I had intended to, but when I came downstairs Peter had already left without me—the idiot." He glared at Peter, who just smiled to himself and continued on down the hall.

"It's OK. You look handsome," I said a little breathlessly. "How are you feeling? Still in pain?"

"I'm great but just don't squeeze me too hard," he chuckled. "Although that would be so nice." He glanced at the table where my packages lay. "What's all this?"

I blushed, worried again about bringing the sweets. "Just some goodies to munch on—we always bake a lot during the holidays and then share it with everyone we know—it's my mom's thing. I hope it's OK. You don't actually have to eat any of it. And those other two boxes are gifts for you." I pointed to the gift-wrapped items next to the tins of treats.

"Yum. Of course we'll eat them. I'm going to try some now," Andrew smiled. He opened one of the tins and popped a Mexican wedding cake into his mouth, showering his chin and suit with crumbs and powdered sugar. I automatically reached to wipe his suit and rub the sugar from his chin. He grabbed my hand and pulled me close, his arms coming around me. He kissed me tenderly and I tasted sugar and almond on his lips. "Oh, I've missed you, Laura," he whispered against my jaw. I returned his kiss, making a concerted effort to keep my mind blank.

"Laura, welcome," said a voice from behind me. "We're so glad you could join us today." It was the duchess. She looked lovely in a dark green dress and beautiful pearls. She opened her arms to me and I pulled away from Andrew and embraced her warmly. Her tactile welcome was unexpected—not that she had ever been unwelcoming, but more reserved toward me.

"Thank you," I responded. I felt my nerves begin their internal assault on my confidence—I figured the duke could not be far behind and I had no idea what his demeanor would be today.

We went inside the salon where a tea service had been laid out. Andrew fixed tea for both of us and we sat side by side on a velvet settee and chatted with his mother about school, holiday traditions, the weather—inconsequential chatter that didn't do much to help my nerves. I kept expecting the duke to enter the room and I was unable to relax. I sat stiffly next to Andrew and he must have noticed my uncomfortable state because he took my teacup out of my hands and proceeded to hold both of my hands in his and rub his thumbs over them softly and soothingly.

When the door opened, I felt my heart seize. I prepared myself for the duke's entrance. But it was Tristan. He came in carrying one of my tins of goodies. He, too, had powdered sugar all over his suit front and cheeks. I fought to suppress a smile.

"Hey, Laura. How are you?" He smiled and nodded in my direction as he sat down across from us on a red velvet Louis XIV chair. He held up the tin. "Did you bring these? They're incredibly delicious." He brushed away the crumbs and smiled warmly at me. "Do you know that I know your brother, Nick? Very nice guy—and very funny, too." We talked about Nick then and the duchess asked me questions about my family. I finally felt myself relax as the conversation continued. A few minutes later a uniformed maid announced dinner. Andrew took my hand and as we walked to the dining room, I had the distinct feeling that I was being led to the gallows. I swallowed my nerves and tried to calm my quaking stomach.

The duke was standing at the window when we entered the dining room. He turned and smiled widely at me. "Laura! So lovely to see you." He walked straight to me and pulled me into his arms in a tight bear hug. For one lone second I thought he would squeeze the air right out of my lungs. He released me and I emitted a small gasp and nearly stumbled but Andrew was there beside me, pulling me to a seat next to his at the table. I felt a rush of fear so intense I shuddered and I prayed no one had noticed. I bit my teeth down hard to keep them from chattering. Under the table Andrew held my hand and I had the feeling that his hand was my only connection to normalcy. He seemed to sense my unease and seemed determined to calm me with his gentle touch and a look of concern in his eyes.

Lobster bisque was served and the duke began talking about their home in England. The conversation was pleasant and non-threatening and I felt myself begin to let down my guard just a little bit. Andrew and Tristan made comments and we all laughed at Tristan's goofy asides. I was enjoying the meal and even feeling brave enough to speak from time to time, to contribute to the conversation. And for one moment I felt like I was looking at a normal, loving family. But then something changed—a transition in the tone—and I felt my guard easing into place even as my necklace sent heat waves rolling against my chest.

Somehow the subject had taken on a serious tone—I hadn't even felt the shift occur—and the duke's demeanor had darkened. He was talking about loyalty and honor and…love. I blinked and wondered what I'd missed. I'd been trying to enjoy the beef tenderloin and cauliflower au gratin even though my nervous stomach was warning me not to eat too much. I swallowed the bite of buttered roll I'd just put in my mouth and looked at the duke who seemed to be mid-thought. I wondered what I'd missed—whatever he was talking about I had the feeling it was meant for me.

"Where I come from, love, honor and fidelity are the cornerstones of family. We must carry on the traditions and decrees of those who came before us, even if those decrees are unpleasant. It is how we, as royals, survive in this modern world." He looked at Tristan as he spoke. Tristan continued to eat and appeared to be ignoring his father. The duke continued. "Some European royal families have been rendered obsolete because they did not honor their traditions. They lost track of their priorities and their own governments turned against them, like the Greeks and the Italians and…the Portuguese."

My fork fell from my hand and clattered against my plate. I jumped and nearly knocked over my water glass but Andrew caught it before it could spill. "Sorry!" I whispered to Andrew. He gave me an encouraging smile and under the table I felt his hand gently rub my thigh. Then he patted me and removed his hand. The duke resumed his monologue.

"As I was saying, and you, my sons, know this to be true—when we make a promise it is kept. Our word is as good as gold. Sometimes I think our word is the only thing we have left—the only thing we can depend upon. We are still making good today, on the promises our past generations have made." He sighed and leaned back in his chair, raising his wine glass to his lips. As he sipped, he looked at me over the rim of the glass. "I'm not sure that you Americans have this same sense of honor and duty. Is that the case, Laura?"

I froze. The only thing able to move was my throat swallowing a lump of anxiety. I had the sense that the weight of America's integrity had fallen upon my weak shoulders. I opened my mouth to speak but no words came out. I glanced at Andrew as I felt my face redden in embarrassment.

"OK, Father! That's enough serious talk, don't you think?" Andrew came to my rescue. "Mother, what's for dessert?"

A maid came in then and cleared away the dishes while another one brought in dessert—crème brûlée—and coffee and tea. I tried to force tiny bites of the dessert into my mouth—normally I would have eaten double the portion I was served—but my stomach wanted no part of any more food. I was too nervous to eat any more. I laid down my spoon and sipped my water slowly. I could see the duke watching me and I knew he had been trying to tell me something. He was sending me a message as was the talisman under my blouse. I could feel its heat against my chest. Finally, the meal was finished and Tristan excused himself. He winked at me as he passed by me and I forced a small smile. Andrew stood and helped me to my feet. "Shall we?" he said.

"Thank you for dinner," I said to the duchess. "It was amazing, as usual." I purposely addressed Andrew's mother only. I couldn't bear to look at his father who I knew was still looking directly at me.

"You're welcome, my dear. I will pass on your compliment to the chef. I can't take the credit." She smiled and waved us off.

In the hall, Andrew pulled me to him. "That wasn't too bad, was it?" he said quietly. "I'd told Father to be on his best behavior."

I wanted to ask if that was really his 'best' but I was sure I knew the answer already. Andrew took my hand and led me upstairs to his room. My dinner started churning in my gut and I felt the rush of nerves again. I knew what was coming now and I didn't know what to do or how to handle it. Before this day was over I was bound to have an ulcer.

Once inside his room, Andrew closed the door and turned me so that my back was against it. He placed his arms on either side of my shoulders against the door and looked down into my eyes. Apprehension made goose-bumps break out over my skin. He leaned down and kissed me hard—the intensity was unexpected—and when he finished I was gasping for breath. "What was that?" I panted.

"That was me telling you how much I love you. I'm not sure what was happening down there"—he nodded over my shoulder toward the door—"but I know you were nervous and trembling. I don't want you to feel that way every time you come into my home. I want you to feel as if you belong here—as if you belong with me. I feel like you're pulling away from me a little bit and I can't stand that feeling. I've never been happier since you came into my life. I don't ever want to lose you. There's something you should know about me, Laura." He pulled me close against his body and hugged me to him. I could feel his breath on my hair and his lips grazed my jaw and moved up to my ear. "I always get what I want." He snaked a line of kisses along my jaw and settled on my mouth. I felt his tongue pushing its way into my mouth and I needed to stop it. I needed space to breathe. My head felt swimmy and once again I had that feeling of free-falling. I instinctively reached my arms around his body for leverage but he mistook my action for passion. I heard him moan as he pulled me to him hard—it must be hurting him to hold me like this when his ribs were still healing.

"Andrew, be careful…your ribs…," I whispered against his mouth. "Stop before you hurt yourself more."

"I'm OK." But he relaxed his grip a bit. Then he stepped back and walked over to his bed and pulled something from underneath the pillow. It was a small velvet box and I had a flashback to Brenton Point. I had to stop this from happening. I had to do something—now. But I was frozen.

"I want to try this again and I want to get it right this time—no more grand gestures—just you and me." He opened the box and turned it toward me. "Laura, I love you. And I want you to wear this ring. It's not an engagement ring—don't worry. It's just a promise that I will always love you." He sat down on the edge of the bed and held it out to me. "Look, it isn't even like the same ring I lost in the ocean. It's completely different. By coincidence it matches those pretty earrings you're wearing. Are those new?"

I nodded. "Birthday gift." I hoped he wouldn't ask me who gave them to me because I would have to lie. I looked at the ring inside the tiny box. It was lovely—a sapphire with small diamonds on either side. It didn't look like an engagement ring. I could already hear myself giving excuses for taking this ring so I wouldn't hurt his feelings. My mind swirled in confusion. I needed to buy time...and then I felt it again: my talisman, sending me a message—a signal. I could feel its heat snaking along the chain.

"Andrew, there's something I need to know." I walked toward him and took the box from his hand. I closed the lid and gave it back to him. I saw the hurt look on his face and I felt an intense stabbing sensation in my heart. "I'm sorry. But I need to know why I have this." I pulled the talisman out from under my blouse, the disk lying flat on my palm. I sat next to him on the bed and waited. So much depended on his answer.

"You found that," he said too quickly. He looked away.

"You wanted me to find it. Why?" I said the words firmly so he would know I wasn't pulling a bluff that he could talk his way out of.

He sighed and got up and walked toward the window. With his back to me he gave me an answer of sorts.

"I don't know how to explain this so I don't sound like a...a... stalker," he said. He turned toward me then and I could see a hint of pink in his cheeks. He passed his hand through his blond hair and rejoined me on the bed. "I wanted to meet you before I ever set foot in the United States. I knew of your existence from a website that had pictures of Portsmouth students."

I inhaled slowly and held my breath. I was familiar with the online yearbook. I waited as he continued.

"I saw your picture and I kind of fell in love with you—love at first sight and all that. And Tristan had given me this"—he picked up the disk from my hand and let it dangle from the chain around my neck—"and I just wanted you to have it. I put it on the ground just before you came out of the door that day and I told you you'd dropped something."

"It could've gone wrong, you know." I said. "Someone else could've found it or what if I'd just tossed it away or given it back to you. I knew I hadn't dropped anything."

"I knew no one else would find it. I wouldn't have let that happen. And I just hoped you would keep it. I sensed that you would. I love that you wear it a lot." His voice was tinged with melancholy.

"How did Tristan get it?" This talisman had to have come from somewhere and I wanted to solve its mystery. And I knew I could not mention Miguel's connection to it—I wasn't even sure what that connection was though I remembered the portrait in his hallway of the beautiful young woman wearing one just like it.

"From my father. But Laura, I have a feeling if my father knew you had it he might not be happy. He might want it back. So don't let him see it. Maybe you should stop wearing it around him."

I dropped the necklace back down my blouse and adjusted my collar. I did not mention the magic I felt in the talisman. If Andrew knew how it warmed and cooled and sometimes sparkled, he himself might want it back. But it was mine now and I would never give it up.

"I won't let him see it. And I suppose I owe you a thank you for it. It truly is beautiful."

"You're welcome." He took my hand. And then he asked me point-blank, "How do you feel about me?"

My mind raced. I wasn't prepared for this question. I wasn't prepared to hurt him. I wasn't even sure I was prepared to give him up. I suddenly doubted every feeling I'd ever had about Andrew…and Miguel. Why wasn't Miguel here to save me now? To save me from myself? I had the perfect opportunity right now this moment to end things, but I just couldn't do it—not now, not like this. There were too many unknowns. I didn't know Miguel at all. And I knew Andrew only marginally better. But I knew he loved me—I didn't doubt that. I could not hurt him because I wasn't strong enough to live with the guilt. There had to be another way to let him down but I didn't know what that way was. And I didn't want to be the bad guy. And I knew that my hesitation had gone on far too long.

"I'll be honest, Andrew. I truly am confused. I know I care about you—love you even—but I'm not sure that we are compatible. Our lives are so different. And in a few months you'll be going back to England and then what? And I know your father doesn't approve of me. I just don't think that…"

Andrew crushed me to him, moaning in pain as he did. He stopped my talk with his mouth against mine, kissing me roughly. I groaned, tried to speak, but he didn't stop. His arms were tight around me and I heard him whimper even as he continued to kiss me. He was hurting himself trying to prove something. Finally he stopped and panted, then leaned forward, moaning in agony.

"Andrew! Stop this. Let's not talk about this now. You're hurting. You need to recover."

"Damn it! I love you and I just want to make sure you don't have any...doubts...about *that*." He was breathing hard. He got up and paced around the room. I went after him and grabbed his arm—stopped the pacing so I could look at him.

"I don't doubt you. I think you're amazing. I just want to make sure we don't rush into anything and make a mistake. Can you understand?" I pleaded.

"What about the ring? I already lost one and I can't take this one back. It would mean the world to me if you would accept it—just as a gift—a token of my affection—whatever you want to call it. But I want...I *need*...you to have it. Can you do that for me?" He sounded weary.

I said the word before I could stop myself. "Yes." I bit my lip and knew I couldn't take it back.

Andrew smiled and took the ring from the box. He reached for my left hand but I pulled it back and gave him my right hand instead. He looked askance at me but didn't say anything as he slipped the ring on my third finger. It fit snugly—I suspected it would fit better on my left hand but that had too much significance so it would have to stay put on my right. I admired its sparkle—its loveliness. "Thank you. It's beautiful. Now, where are the presents I brought for you?"

He got up and went downstairs, then returned with his gifts. He opened them and exclaimed with satisfaction, "I love them. Thank you, my darling." He found a place to display the knot board and he put the book on his nightstand. "I'll start it tonight," he said. Then he suddenly became reticent.

I took his hand in mine. "What is it?" I touched my other hand to his face and turned him toward me. His eyes looked troubled and I felt my heart's pace quicken. "Andrew?"

"Can I hold you?" he asked quietly. "I want to feel you in my arms."

I slid closer to him, my pulse racing. I could not handle seeing sadness or fear or whatever this emotion was that was running through him. He put his arms around me. "What's wrong, Andrew?"

He kissed the top of my head. "I don't know. I just feel like this day isn't going the way I'd hoped. Are things OK between us?"

I swallowed and let out a pent-up sigh. "Things are fine—no worries. But I think you need rest. You've over-exerted yourself and you're acting like everything's normal but I don't think you've healed up all the way yet. Now, I would like you to get some rest. I can find someone to take me home."

He clamped his arm tighter around me. "I don't want you to go, but you might be right. It does rather hurt to breathe. I think I'll be back to normal in another day or two. I'll walk you down and find Peter."

We went downstairs and Andrew called for Peter on one of the house phones. He appeared instantly and within moments I was ensconced in the back of the car on my way home. I felt a sense of relief. And there was one thing I could most definitely agree with Andrew about—this day had not quite gone as planned. I looked down at my beautiful ring and sighed.

Chapter Nineteen

FALLIŊG

I made a concerted effort to stay busy for the rest of the holiday break, seeing a couple of movies with Lily and Gretchen and helping my mom around the house. Mom was never one much for keeping the decorations up too long after Christmas so I helped her take them down and we rearranged the living room. My dad had come down from Providence and spent the holiday with us. Nick was around off and on. He did make a startling announcement on New Year's Eve morning though that was cause for celebration. At long last he had broken up with Abigail. They'd actually started dating two years earlier after getting together at a New Year's Eve party so it seemed fitting, as he'd said, to end it on the exact same day. I was thrilled and I didn't even feel guilty about feeling that way—and my parents were in agreement.

The whole senior class had been invited to a New Year's Eve party at the Portsmouth Youth Center. Every year the town hosted a New Year's Eve party for the senior class hoping to curb drinking and drug use so that no one would do anything stupid and get into trouble—or worse. Most kids had planned to boycott it until word got out that a local Portsmouth kid who'd sort of made it semi-big in the music business was coming to the party to DJ and host it. I knew of the kid—Derek Houghton—though he was three years ahead of me in school. He came from a nice family and I seemed to remember all the girls used to be in love with him. The party would be catered by Joe's Clam Shack so we knew the food would be good. Lily and Gretchen were going and bringing their boyfriends—Colin wasn't a student at Portsmouth but seniors were allowed to bring a date. Andrew had asked me about the party and after discussing other options we decided to go to it together. I knew Miguel would be home soon but that didn't mean I would get to see him. Our relationship, such as it was, was a secret and I knew it had to stay that way for the time being. So Andrew picked me up at eight o'clock and we headed to the youth center. I'd left my necklace and special earrings at home for safekeeping but I wore Andrew's ring to avoid questions.

Peter dropped us off and Andrew told him he would call when we were ready to leave. At the door we paid our admission fee—the money was to be donated to a local charity—and stepped inside the noisy, carnival-like atmosphere. It seemed that the powers that be had actually gone to a lot of trouble to make the place festive. There were carnival-style attractions set up around the cavernous room—games of chance, food booths operated by Joe's Clam Shack and the Newport Creamery which had set up an ice cream sundae station, creepy clowns, jugglers, stilt walkers—all sorts of madness. At one side of the room were a large dance floor and the DJ booth and along the other wall were tables set for eating. In the front of the room was a giant screen which would display the ball dropping in Times Square and the midnight countdown. Streamers and balloons and confetti adorned every inch of space.

"Wow!" said Andrew, amazed at the spectacle. "Is this normal for a New Year's Eve celebration?"

"I guess so though I had no idea the city went to all this trouble. It's kind of cool though—except for the clowns. I could do without those." I grimaced and recoiled in horror as one walked past me and tried to tweak my nose.

We made our way through the crowd toward Lily and Gretchen. Derek Houghton had arrived and was spinning records and greeting old friends. He was even signing autographs for people, which seemed strange to me—I mean this kid was one of us just a few short years ago. I found the concept of fame odd and knew I would hate it.

"Would you like a drink?" Andrew asked. He pointed to the drinks station. "Shall I go see what they have?"

"Yes, surprise me. I'll drink whatever," I said. He, Colin and Brent disappeared to get us drinks. I looked around at the mass of people—

it looked like the entire senior class had turned out for this event. A bunch of people had gathered for a magic show up front near the big screen. I heard the magician call out for a volunteer to be cut in half. The only thing I hated as much as clowns was magicians—I hated the trickery—so I pushed Lily and Gretchen toward the stage for a closer look and then retreated as far away from the stage as I could get. I knew it wasn't real, but there was a part of me that feared something could go wrong and I didn't want the stress. I couldn't even handle watching acrobats at the circus. My parents had taken me once and I had cried the whole time—fearful of the clowns, certain the acrobats would fall to their deaths, suspicious of the magicians who made things appear and disappear at will and worried about the poor animals that I longed to set free. We'd never gone again.

I saw Andrew coming through the crowd, drinks in hand. "Hey! There you are. I seem to recall your preference for diet?" He smiled and handed me a red plastic cup.

"Thanks." I took the cup and drank thirstily from it. I'd been feeling the slightest hint of a headache coming on all day and I hoped the caffeine would keep it at bay.

"What are you doing over here? Do you want to go watch the magic show?" Andrew asked, looking over as Lily was about to be sawed in two.

I shook my head but caught myself watching in horror from a distance anyway. Eventually Lily returned to Brent all in one piece and we turned our attention to the DJ booth where Derek was spinning some techno-funk that caused people to gravitate to the dance floor. Andrew asked me to dance and though I wasn't much of a dancer I was willing to give it a try. Pretty soon the dance floor was so crowded that the dense mass of bodies rendered the need for dancing talent useless. It was fun and I worked up an appetite—maybe some food would help my headache, too, I thought.

"Let's get something to eat," I said loudly to Andrew, trying to be heard above the music. He nodded in agreement and took me by the hand and we worked our way around the food booths, filling our plates with crab cakes, French fries, hush puppies and brownies. We found a seat in the eating area with Lily and Brent. Gretchen and Colin were still dancing. I glanced up at the clock. It was only 10:30. I had an anxious feeling I couldn't seem to shake and no idea what was causing it. I kept thinking I was seeing Miguel's face in the crowd and as such my heart was in a constant state of attempted arrest.

"I'm going to win you a stuffed creature of some sort," said Andrew when we'd finished eating. "Come on!" He grabbed me by the hand and dragged me around to various booths, eventually winning me a stuffed pink teddy bear with lop-sided ears by knocking over stacks of bottles. Then more dancing and I was dying of thirst again. I looked at the clock. It was now 11:40. I turned to Andrew.

"I'm going to use the ladies' room and then get a fresh drink. I'll see you shortly," I said, breathlessly. It was warm in the hall with so many bodies moving and dancing. The music was loud, the bass pulsating in my chest. I felt a throbbing in my head and wished I had some Tylenol with me. I went out into the lobby and made my way down the long hallway and turned the corner in the direction of the restrooms. Once inside I caught sight of my flushed face and bright eyes in the mirror. I looked rather sickly and hoped I wasn't coming down with something. I would hate to start off the new year sick. I tried to tame my hair and reapplied my lip gloss. There were two other girls in the side-by-side stalls. I could hear their conversation as I ran my brush through my tangles. Suddenly their words stopped me cold and I felt all the air rush from my lungs.

"Did you see the gypsy? He is so freaking gorgeous. What's his name again?" said a voice from one of the stalls.

"Miguel Dos Santos. I know, right? They just don't make them like that in America. Wonder if he's here with someone?" said the voice from the next stall. I didn't recognize either one. My hands shook as I shoved my brush back in my purse and slipped into the stall at the far end of the row.

"I heard he was sneaking around with Laura Calder," said the first voice.

"No freaking way! Isn't she dating the prince? That's like so not fair!" shrieked the second voice.

"Yeah, she is, but seriously, wouldn't you rather have the gypsy? He is so gorgeous!" said voice number one.

"The prince is nothing to scoff at—he's just as hot. And anyway, I'd rather have the prince with the castles and all that royal stuff. Don't gypsies like live in caves or something?" said voice number two.

Both toilets flushed at the same time and I heard the girls at the sinks. My hands shook and my stomach was in knots as I waited for them to leave. I quickly used the bathroom and washed my hands and when the coast was clear I stepped into the doorway. Miguel was here somewhere. I needed to see him. Even if we didn't talk. Even if he didn't see me, I just needed a glimpse. I walked on shaky legs down the hall and was just about to turn the corner into the lobby when a hand grabbed my arm and pulled me into an alcove. I gasped and turned in fright, ready to scream.

"Sh, sh," whispered Miguel. "Hey, beautiful."

To say I swooned would be an understatement. My mind checked out for a second and I fell into his arms, unable to breathe or speak. He wrapped his arms around me and I buried my face in his neck. "You scared me," I breathed out the words in a raspy whisper against his jaw. I ran my hand through his hair and kissed his neck.

"I'm sorry. I wasn't sure if you'd be here but I couldn't wait till school. I missed you." He tilted my face to his and kissed me. His lips tasted of mint and sugar. It was all I could do to restrain myself from a full-on attack. What the hell was wrong with me? I kissed him back as if my life depended on it and then I remembered where I was and who I was with and I pulled away from him.

"I'm here with Andrew. He can't see me with you. This is wrong." My nerves were shot. I peeked down the corridor and saw someone heading our way, probably to the bathrooms. "I have to go back in. What are you going to do?" I asked him anxiously.

"I'm going to watch the ball drop. You go in first. I'll stay away from you, don't worry." His voice sounded gruff as if it hurt or angered him to say the words.

I nodded, kissed him quickly, and went back into the hall. I opened the door to the main room and walked right smack into Andrew. "Oh! Sorry!" I yelped as we crashed into one another.

He steadied me and took in my flushed face. "You OK? I was getting worried. Let's get you a drink refill for the toast. It's almost time for the countdown. Let's go!" We stopped for Cokes at the beverage stand and then he pulled me into the crowd. We made our way to the front of the hall where the ball was in ready mode to drop and welcome in 2012. I looked anxiously over my shoulder scanning the room. I didn't see Miguel. My heart raced and my hands shook. I nearly spilled pop all over myself. I took a gulp of it to calm my nerves. All of a sudden, the lights went dark and I felt Andrew's arms around me. The countdown began:

"10...9...8...7...6...5...4...3...2...1! Happy New Year!" And suddenly it was pandemonium. Strobe lights flashed. Noisemakers screamed, confetti rained down from the ceiling, people were shouting and yelling out well wishes. Andrew kissed me hard on the mouth and whispered, "Happy New Year, Laura. I love you." I was dumbstruck— unable to move or respond. I think I kissed him back but I wasn't sure if my lips worked. Where was Miguel? Did he see me kiss Andrew? I felt the stabbing of a thousand knives in my heart. I was a statue. I felt a pain in my head and my mind went blank. What was wrong with me? I grabbed at my neck. Where was my necklace? At home? I think I left it home for safekeeping. Why was it so hot in this room? Why was it so hard to breathe? Why was it getting so hard to see? All the faces in the flashing lights started to recede. The music boomed in my chest. And then I felt a sinking sensation. I tried to speak but words wouldn't come. And then everything went black.

"Laura! Can you hear me? Laura?" I heard Lily's voice...then Gretchen's. People were calling my name. Where was Andrew? Where was Miguel? What year was it?

"Should we call an ambulance?" someone asked. Whose voice? I didn't recognize it.

"Is she breathing?" Was that Lily?

"Is she dead?" *Was* I?

Voices only, but no faces to match them. Why couldn't I see any-thing? My eyes were open but there was only darkness. Had I gone blind? My eyes adjusted to the dark. I felt hands on me, helping me into a sitting position.

"*Why are you here?*" An angry voice now—Andrew's voice.

"*Shut up, Easton!*" Miguel now.

"Hey!" My voice now. "Hey! Why is it dark?" Was that me speak-ing? I sounded strange—different.

"Sh...sh..., Laura. I'm here...you're OK. You fainted." Andrew was there, his arm around me. I could see him now—crouched beside me on the floor. I looked around—it was dark everywhere but I could see lights flashing, hear music playing. I was relieved to know I was not blind after all.

"What happened? Where's Miguel?" I asked. I saw him then standing behind Andrew. I looked into Andrew's eyes and saw anger mixed with concern.

"I'm here, Laura," Miguel answered me. "You fainted but Andrew caught you."

"You can go now, Dos Santos. She's with me…I can take care of her." Andrew looked at me as he spoke the words to Miguel.

"I'm not going anywhere until I know she's OK." Miguel stood his ground. I could sense commotion all around us. People were still dancing, celebrating.

"Gretchen?" Andrew turned toward her—I had not even noticed that she and Lily were standing nearby. "Please watch Laura for a minute. I need to have a talk with…Miguel."

Andrew leaned me back against Gretchen and touched my cheek as he stood up and turned to face Miguel. "Outside, Dos Santos. No need to wait for the damned flowers to bloom. Let's do this now, shall we?" His words came out in a venomous hiss.

"Forget it, Easton. *That* is between me and your brother. But this…," Miguel swept his hand in an arc. "This is a different battle and now is not the time. Laura needs to be taken care of now."

Andrew's fists clenched. He stepped menacingly toward Miguel. "Laura will be taken care of—she is not your concern. Now get the hell out of here or I'll…" He raised his arm as if to strike Miguel.

"You'll what?" Lightning fast, Miguel grabbed Andrew's arm, gripping it tightly. "You want to hit me? Fine. But not here…not now." He said the words quietly but there was no missing the menacing undertone.

"*Get your filthy gypsy hands off of me,*" Andrew growled through clenched teeth. He shook off Miguel's arm and swiped at his own, as if wiping off dirt.

This was crazy—pure madness. I had to do something. "Help me up, Gretchen!" I struggled to my feet. "Andrew! Please stop! What is with you two? Stop!" I took a couple of steps toward them. My head started to spin again. Somewhere in the back of my mind I heard a strange female voice—not mine—talking to me: "*Laura…there is a blackness around you. And yet, there is also light. Two opposing forces circling around you, confusing your aura. Have you experienced dizziness lately?*" Who was she? Where was this voice coming from? I felt another falling sensation and then strong arms catching me, holding me, saving me—saved by the darkness—again.

Chapter Twenty

THE GYPSY PRINCE

"Don't be ridiculous. My car's right outside. It'll take too long for your...*people*...to get here." I could hear Miguel's voice so close to me. I was being carried somewhere. I was in his arms and we were moving fast. The music was fading somewhere behind me. Then Andrew's voice was beside me.

"You'll pay for this, Dos Santos. Always interfering—why can't you leave her—*us*—alone?"

I heard doors opening and felt a rush of cold air hit me in the face. "Ooh," I cried out. "What's going on?" I looked up into Miguel's face and felt relief. If he was here then everything would be OK.

"Hey, Laura. We're taking you to the hospital to get checked out," said Miguel. I heard the sound of electric locks clicking. He barked an order to Andrew. "Open the back door, Easton. And sit in the back with her." To me he said more softly, "we'll be there soon. You're going to be fine, Laura, don't worry." Andrew climbed into the back of the Suburban and Miguel passed me like a sack of groceries into Andrew's arms. He climbed into the driver's seat and started the engine. Moonlight spilled into the back of the vehicle through the moon roof illuminating Andrew's pale face.

I turned my head toward Miguel. "Please, Miguel. I don't want to go to the hospital. Please. Then my parents will have to be called and I don't want to ruin their evening. *Please!*" I begged him. I was in Andrew's arms, shivering against the cold. I wondered where my purse and coat were—I even wondered about the whereabouts of the stupid teddy bear.

"Laura, you fainted—twice. Once is bad enough, but two times? You need to see a doctor," Andrew said as he brushed the hair away from my face and leaned down to kiss my forehead. I sighed and tried again.

"*Please*! I had a little headache earlier and the music was loud and I think I'm just overly tired. I have new glasses and I'm supposed to be wearing them. There's nothing *wrong* with me." I turned toward Miguel and caught his gaze in the rearview mirror—so strange to see his face there instead of Peter's. "If we could just go somewhere and talk. Just not the hospital, *please*."

Miguel drove south down Highway 114—I could see the lights of store signs and familiar landmarks as we passed in the darkness. He slowed his speed and he and Andrew exchanged a look in the mirror. "What do you think, Easton? The hospital or…somewhere else?" So he was leaving it up to Andrew to make the choice.

I turned to Andrew and put my hand against his cheek, turning his gaze down toward me. My cold hand seemed to sizzle against the heat of his jaw. "Andrew…I'm fine, really. Let's just stop somewhere for a minute. I know I'll feel better if I can talk to you both. I need…answers." My voice cracked on the last word and I felt hot tears slide down my face.

He wiped them away and kissed my forehead again. I saw Miguel's angry eyes in the mirror and felt the jerk of the car as he pulled it roughly off the road. The car stopped and Miguel put it in park and turned around to look at us both in the backseat. Andrew's arms were tight around me. I could feel the rise and fall of his chest as he breathed deeply. His arms were tense and his body under me felt like coiled wire about to come loose and unfold its sharpness around whatever it deemed threatening. I gently pulled his arms apart from me and sat up, shifting my body so I could sit beside him in the seat. I looked out the window and saw the familiar parking lot of Red Tide Beach, saw the waters of Narragansett Bay gently lapping the shore in the moonlight. The tension in the car was palpable—too thick for the strongest of knives.

"Why do you two hate each other?" I asked them both. I didn't care who answered. I just needed answers. But they were silent, each apparently unwilling to speak first. I turned to Andrew.

"Why, Andrew? Why do you hate him? What did Miguel do to you to make you treat him so cruelly?" My voice rose higher as I spoke. I was breathless and shaky and more tears threatened to fall.

Andrew looked at Miguel. I stared intently at the two of them as they stared each other down, mystified as to how two people I loved so much could harbor so much hatred for each other. But Andrew didn't speak. He just stared stony-faced at Miguel. I didn't even think he'd taken a breath in the last minute or so since I'd moved to sit beside him. Clearly I would have to take another tack. I looked at Miguel.

"OK, *you* answer then. What did Andrew do to you to make you hate him so much?" I said the words sharply and felt myself barely keeping control over my precarious emotional state. I pleaded for an answer from him with my eyes. "Tell me!" I shrieked. I leaned forward toward him.

"Hey, calm down, Laura," Andrew said, putting his hand on my arm and pulling me backward. But I shook his arm off roughly and snapped, "Don't touch me. Someone answer me!" And then like the big baby I was, I started to sob, covering my face with my hands. I felt Andrew's arm move against mine and then the car seemed to shift violently.

"Don't touch her!" Miguel's body was half-way over the seat now, preventing Andrew from putting his hands on me.

"Get your hands off me you damned gypsy!" Andrew shouted, grabbing at Miguel's arm. Miguel seemed to be coming over the back of his seat toward us. I flew into a rage and shoved myself between them, falling against Andrew's chest. Miguel fell back into his seat but remained twisted around facing us.

"Please don't do this. I'm begging you," I sobbed. Andrew embraced me protectively, shielding me from Miguel—Miguel, whose arms I longed for.

Andrew finally spoke—his voice calmer and more controlled. He held me tightly to him as he spoke, his eyes locked on Miguel's. "Here's the situation, Laura. Our families go back a long way—all the way back to George the First to be exact. We had a conflict that, unfortunately, wasn't able to be resolved back then. In a strange twist of fate, that conflict has managed to follow both of our families here to the present day. But we are working it out, according to the laws of the monarchy. The dispute will be settled soon and we can all get on with our lives...well, most of us anyway."

Miguel remained silent. He glared at Andrew, his eyes like daggers. I could hear them both breathing hard—I could feel Andrew's breath against my hair. I slowly unlocked his arms from around me and sat up—again situating myself so that I was seated next to him. I looked at Miguel. "Is this true, Miguel?"

Miguel shifted in his seat. I watched as he worked his jaw back and forth in that nervous way he had about him. His eyes were dark and he looked from me to Andrew and back to me again. "More or less. But I believe there are far better ways to solve a conflict than the barbaric way your *boyfriend's* father has planned." He turned back to Andrew. "And, for the record, you're not the only one with a family history crying out for revenge."

Andrew lurched forward suddenly toward Miguel. "You're nothing but a cowardly gypsy. My brother will make mince pie out of you!" he hissed.

Miguel glared at Andrew. "Your brother has no more interest in this vendetta than I do. Just ask him! But, oh, how I wish this were between you and me. Then I might change my mind."

I put my hands to my ears to shut them out. What in the name of hell was this can of worms I had just opened? I shook my head back and forth. "Stop! You're not making sense any more. Stop fighting!" I shouted.

Miguel turned in his seat to face the front of the car. "We're getting out of here. Laura, you need to go home and get some rest. And you… Easton…where can I drop you…besides the Atlantic Ocean—which is where I should have left you in the first place." He started the car and pulled out of the lot.

Andrew grimaced and clenched his teeth. "You can take us both back to the youth center and I will make sure Laura gets home safely. And don't argue with me about it. You'll lose." Andrew spat out the words and snapped his seatbelt into place. "Laura, buckle up. There's a maniac at the wheel."

I heard Miguel give a menacing laugh under his breath. I remained silent, unsure of what to say or do. Once again, I had asked for answers only to end up with more questions. But I could tell by the atmosphere in this vehicle that asking more questions would result in nothing but stormy silence—or worse. I watched as Andrew pulled his cell phone from his pocket, sent someone a text and snapped it closed, slipping it back into his pocket. He looked at me and I thought he was about to reach for my hand but he seemed to think better of it and just folded his hands in his lap instead. Miguel kept his eyes on the road as he drove, his only movement coming from his jaw as he ground his teeth silently.

At the youth center the goons were there waiting—Andrew's car idling, the back door already open. Miguel pulled up next to it and I saw the look of total and complete shock on Peter's face when he saw whose car we were getting out of. *Were the goons in on this madness, too?* I wondered. Andrew exited the car and leaned in to reach for me. I looked at Miguel in the mirror but he did not look up. His hands were gripping the steering wheel so tightly it looked as if he could tear it out with little effort. As Andrew pulled me from the car I reached my hand back and slid it along Miguel's shoulder, touching the warm skin of his neck. He quickly reached up and pressed his fingertips lightly to my hand as I stepped out of the car. I was fairly sure Andrew did not see this exchange. I only hoped that Miguel knew it was my way of telling him it would be OK and that I was still his—if he wanted me. I hoped he understood.

As soon as Andrew slammed the Suburban's door, Miguel was gone—out of the parking lot so fast I didn't even see which way he went. We climbed into Andrew's car and when he tried to pull me into his arms I resisted.

"Don't, Andrew." I said more harshly than I'd intended.

"Laura, listen to me. You need to let this go. Miguel is dangerous. You need to stay away from him. He and his whole family are nothing but bad news."

"Stop, Andrew. I don't want to hear anymore. I don't trust either one of you." I folded my arms across my chest and stared out the window. Then I remembered something. "Where is my purse? My house keys and phone are in it."

"Gretchen has it. She'll undoubtedly get it to you tomorrow."

We were silent the rest of the way to my house. Peter parked in the driveway and Andrew started to open his door to accompany me but I stopped him. "I don't need help. I can get in by myself. I'm going to sleep. Good night, Andrew." And with those words, I got out, slammed the door and let myself inside the house, using the spare key we kept on top of the doorframe. The car drove away and I ran upstairs. The house was quiet. My parents and brother must still be out ringing in the new year. *My* new year had gotten off to a rocky start and as I collapsed onto my bed in exhaustion, I couldn't help but think that the worst was probably yet to come.

"What's happening with Andrew these days, darling?" my mother asked me. We were two weeks into the new year and I had been in a morose state for most of it. My mom had given me her Jeep and had purchased herself a new Honda for a Christmas present. I refused to ride with Andrew any more but we were still speaking. Miguel had resumed his quiet demeanor but with a stealth-like quality, as if he were always on guard, always waiting for something. I had found my glasses and I realized that wearing them every day not only helped me to see clearly but my headaches seemed to dissipate—*but then that was the point, wasn't it?* I told myself.

"We're taking a break, I guess," I said. "It was getting too intense." I was folding laundry at the kitchen table and Mom was on her laptop paying some bills.

"Oh, I'm sorry, honey. Can you two work things out?" She looked over her shoulder at me and smiled that mom-like smile of reassurance.

"We'll be fine. I don't want to talk about it, if you don't mind." I folded my jeans and matched up some socks and gathered them together to take upstairs. Mom called me back before I got too far.

"Have you given any thought to college? It's getting late to send out applications, isn't it?" she asked.

"Oh, Mom. I don't want to think about it. I used to want to go away to school but that's too expensive. Besides, I'll probably major in English anyway so I may as well do what Nick is doing and go to CCRI first. I can always transfer somewhere after that and have the college experience later. I'll figure it out."

I dashed upstairs before she could press me further on the subject. I put away my laundry, sat down at my desk and opened my laptop. I'd done my homework earlier but now I wanted to surf the net. Something had been on my mind for a while and I wanted to check it out online. I opened up Internet Explorer and clicked on the Google icon in my favorites bar. I typed "King George the First" and checked to see if he was the one history referred to as the Mad King, but that turned out to be George the Third. Of course, that didn't mean George the First wasn't a little nuts himself. I'd about decided that all of royalty were a little off their rockers considering they were still playing kings and queens in their castles in 2012. Weren't we beyond all that fairy tale stuff at this point in time?

I perused the entry about George the First on Wikipedia. He didn't seem too awful—he'd married his cousin though—that was gross but I guessed back then there weren't too many choices when it came to picking a spouse. I read further and didn't find him particularly remarkable. He'd had some mistresses and some illegitimate children but that wasn't so shocking either. I thought back to what Andrew had said about a conflict that couldn't be resolved back then…one they were going to settle soon. What could that mean? There didn't seem to be any Portuguese connection to George the First. I went back to Google and typed 'George the First Portuguese Conflict.' Several hits popped up but they all seemed irrelevant. I was about to give up when something at the bottom of the screen caught my eye: *Portuguese Royal Family Has Ties to George the First?*

European royal historians have unearthed a connection between King George the First of the House of Hanover and the royal family of Portugal—the House of Braganza. It has been previously documented that George the First had three illegitimate daughters with a German mistress but historians have recently learned that the king also had a son with the Portuguese Princess Gabriela of the House of Braganza. The child's heritage was not known at the time of his birth in December 1700, but was discovered through old documents and diaries unearthed in the Portuguese palace's archives. Prince Felipe was believed to have been raised by gypsies before learning of his royal birthright and returning to his family's kingdom. It is believed that his mother, Princess Gabriela, was murdered shortly after the prince's birth by a member of King George the First's army. It is rumored that she placed a curse on King George and his descendants just before her death—a curse that, according to historians, is alleged to be fulfilled in the spring of 2012, the fulfillment of which, some say, would result in the end of the line of the House of Hanover. However, there are some who believe the curse was just the ramblings of a princess who, in the face of death, bellowed false bravado to mask fear of her child's unknown fate. The revolution of October 5, 1910, a republican coup d'etat, resulted in the deposing of King Manuel the Second, the last sitting king of Portugal, thereby establishing the Portuguese First Republic. King Manuel went into exile in England. He died childless in 1932 and descendants of Dom Miguel claimed the throne. In 1950 Portugal repealed the law of exile, allowing the Braganza family to return to their homeland.

I stopped reading and tried to breathe. Questions and thoughts tumbled in my head like raging tornadoes. What did this mean? Was Miguel a member of this House of Braganza? Andrew had said that Miguel was dangerous and his family was bad news. I shivered and my teeth began to chatter. I copied and pasted the article and sent it to myself in an email. Then I shut down my computer and huddled in my bed under my comforter. I couldn't shake the coldness that seeped into my bones. I ached all over, from exhaustion…and fear. Miguel was not who he appeared to be. This boy that I had fallen in love with *was* dangerous. I remembered his lips, so warm and tender on mine, his eyes so dark and endless, the line of his jaw and the silky black hair, the strength of his arms—arms that had saved me time and time again. He was a gypsy prince and I was in love with him. I was in love with darkness. I thought of Andrew, so kind and sweet and full of light. Perhaps I had misjudged him—misjudged them both. Perhaps I'd had it right the first time when I thought Andrew was the one I loved. I buried my face in my pillow and muffled a scream. I felt the tears flow, soaking my pillow. My head throbbed and after a very long while I fell into a fitful sleep filled with dark dreams…dreams that pulled me back and forth between darkness and the light.

Chapter Twenty One

Tristan Falls

I was beginning to feel like a recluse. I didn't want to go anywhere or talk to anyone. I felt as if the world I knew didn't exist anymore. I could have walked up to Miguel or Andrew at any time and demanded answers but I knew what that would get me—nothing. Andrew called but I found ways to avoid him. It was hard at school seeing them both but I had nothing and everything to say to them. I looked at Miguel differently now. I hated myself for being afraid of him and for believing what I'd read on the Internet. And I felt fear for Andrew and his family. All this fear and tension were wreaking havoc on me and I developed a head cold that lasted for a week. I'd just about decided that I needed to open the lines of communication with them, especially Andrew, when they both beat me to the punch.

I parked my Jeep in my usual spot in the school parking lot and was just about to get out when I heard a knock on the passenger side window. I'd been so distracted that I hadn't even seen anyone approach my car. I looked up and saw Andrew tapping on the window. Without hesitation I pressed the button to unlock the door and he climbed in beside me.

"Hey," he said. He sounded a little out of breath. "Hi."

"Hello," I said quietly. I looked down at the console, avoiding his eyes.

"Laura? I can't stand any more of this silence between us. It's killing me. I'm not even sure what I did wrong. But I've given you time and space and now I need us to work out whatever is wrong between us." He started to reach out to me but changed his mind, pulling his hand back.

"I don't know, Andrew. All I ever get from you—and Miguel—is…cryptic talk…and avoidance of issues that I don't understand. It's like we're all playing some stupid giant chess game and I never know who moved what piece where or if maybe I'm not even a player in the game but rather a piece in the game—a pawn…or something." I sighed and looked out my window.

"Look at me, please, Laura. Look here." He leaned toward me over the console. I turned toward him. "Let's start fresh—me and you—a clean slate. It's a new year and time for a new beginning. What do you say? I've missed you so much." He looked earnest and I felt the tiniest bit of my resolve give way.

"I need you to answer a question." I looked into his blue eyes. I really looked at him for a long moment—he had a beautiful face, with a straight nose and thick blond hair. His jaw was strong and his lips full. I felt my eyes narrow as I studied his face as if seeing him for the first time. I sensed that he really did radiate light in some way. "What's going to happen in the spring when the flowers bloom?"

He sat back abruptly against the passenger seat and stared straight ahead through the windshield. He let out a deep sigh and put his face in his hands. I remained silent, fighting the urge to put my hand on his arm to comfort him. Until I knew what he needed comfort for, I had to be strong and get some answers. "Tell me."

He dropped his hands and turned to me. His eyes were troubled and I could almost see the wheels turning in his head as he tried to find words to pacify me—to satisfy my curiosity—god forbid he should just tell me the truth. "That's when the…problem…between my family and the gyp…Miguel's…will be laid to rest per the decree issued by King George the First."

I clenched my hands into fists and pounded the steering wheel. "Andrew! Be specific! What decree? What problem? What has to be done to settle the…*problem*? Is it something…illegal? Damn it! Tell me!" I pounded the steering wheel again and hurt my hand in the process. "*Ow! Damn!*"

In one swift motion, Andrew turned to me and grabbed my wrists, pulling me over the console. I gasped in surprise as he leaned against me, as close as the console would allow. His lips were against my jaw and I felt his breath in my hair as he spoke urgently. "I need for you to trust me. To trust that I would never do anything illegal or hurt anyone...unless..." He hesitated and laid his forehead against my temple. "Unless it were a matter of life or death. And I need for you to know how much I love you and that I want you to come to England with me after graduation and to go to school there and one day I want you to marry me and be the mother of my children and grow old with me...and...be my...princess." His voice caught on a sob. I pulled my hand free and laid it on his cheek, then tried to lean back a bit so I could see his face. I saw a tear escape and begin a slow journey to his jaw. I gasped in shock as I stopped it in its tracks with my thumb.

"Andrew? What is it? Why are you crying? Surely there's nothing so bad that it can't be fixed. What can I do to help you?" I felt my own tears now starting to form. I rubbed my finger along his jaw. "Please... what can we do?"

He sniffed and leaned back, swiping at his face with his left hand. "I'm sorry. That wasn't very...macho of me. I guess I'm just frustrated. And I have hated every moment I've been apart from you." He looked around us at the parking lot. There were no people around—everyone had gone inside. A light snow was falling and the skies were a dull gray. "We're late for class. We should go."

"Andrew, wait." I grabbed his arm. "This conversation isn't over. Whatever it is, we can get through it together. Maybe you should start trusting *me* more."

He didn't respond. He opened the door and got out, shutting it behind him. I sat stone still wondering why he was acting this way all of a sudden—closing himself off from me. But then he walked around the front of the Jeep and opened my door. I saw a determined look on his face as he pulled me from the car into his arms and hugged me tightly to him. He kissed my lips and for the life of me I didn't understand my reaction—that swoony, woozy feeling again. The talisman reacted—I felt its heat—the damned thing sent me more mixed messages than ones that made sense. I returned his kiss even as I felt like I should be resisting his touch. His lips were warm and demanding and his tongue searched for mine. I suddenly felt myself returning his kiss with the same fervor. What was happening to me? I had truly lost my mind. And worse than that, I didn't care. Finally he stopped. He cupped my face in his hands and kissed me one more time and nodded toward the school. "We'd better get in there."

I nodded and closed my car door and we walked together, hand in hand, into the school. As we walked to our separate classes I saw a movement out of the corner of my eye near the entrance to the gymnasium. I glanced up as I was about to enter my first period class. Miguel was standing there, staring at me, a look of anger and fire on his face. I nearly stumbled over my feet at the sight of him. He disappeared into the gym as I walked into class, my insides turning to Jello. He'd looked mad...mad enough to kill.

After lunch I stopped in the front office to say hello to my guidance counselor, who had been asking me about post-graduation plans. He was busy with another student so I waited at the front of the office staring through the glass walls that looked out onto the parking lot. Off in the distance I saw two familiar black cars tearing up the drive toward the school at top speed. I felt my heart begin to race as I stepped out of the office and walked trance-like to the front doors. The cars slammed to a stop and Peter was out of the first one like a lightning bolt. He ran up the front steps and burst through the front doors, zooming past me without appearing to notice me. "Peter?" I called out but he kept running down the hall. He turned a corner and disappeared from sight. I felt a sense of dread and tasted the bitterness of fear on my tongue. Something was wrong. My heart pounded as I stood there waiting. Moments later I could hear footsteps running toward me. Peter and Andrew raced around the corner toward the front doors. "Andrew? What's happening? Where are you going?"

Andrew stopped for a second in front of me. "Laura, I have to go. Something's happened to Tristan—an accident. I don't know the details but...it's...bad. I have to go." He touched my face feather-lightly then followed Peter out the door. They were in the car and gone before I'd even had a chance to register what had just happened.

I felt heartsick. Poor sweet Tristan. What could have happened to him? I felt numb. I couldn't move. I saw the secretary beckon me into the office with a wave but I couldn't go in there now. I shook my head and pointed to my watch. Then I forced my legs to carry me to the rest-room. I stood in the stall and tried to compose myself. My imagination was running away to scary places I didn't want to go. After a couple of minutes I walked to class and tried to concentrate. I just wanted the day to be over. Finally it was time for English class. Miguel would be there. What would he think if he knew something had happened to Tristan? Would he care? I sat down in my seat and turned to look out the window. I wanted to go home…to be with Andrew…to know if Tristan was OK.

I felt his presence before I saw him. Miguel moved past me and took his seat behind me. We made eye contact for a moment but I felt myself tense up and I turned back to the front of the classroom. My lungs stopped working. I had the sudden strong desire to open my mouth and scream at the top of my lungs to get them to work again. I needed to look at Miguel and to study his face. I needed to know if he already knew about Tristan. The teacher was writing on the black-board and the other students were oblivious to my agitation. I slowly shifted my body sideways and turned to face Miguel. He looked at me. A tear slipped from my eye and fell to my cheek. He saw the tear and tilted his head questioningly. His hand moved as if to touch me but he gripped the side of the desk instead. I let out a pent-up breath quietly, releasing some of the pressure on my lungs. He raised an eyebrow and worked his jaw. His eyes narrowed and he mouthed my name silently in question. I gave a slight shake of my head and turned back around to face the chalkboard. A second later I felt his fingertips brush through my hair and slide down my back. I shivered and feared I would black out. His fingertips blazed into the knitted wool of my sweater and I felt their heat against my skin. My talisman burned at my chest, the chain sending a wave of heat around my neck. I bit my lip to keep from cry-ing out and fought back tears, nearly choking on a sob. Mrs. Clanton glanced at me and stopped her lecture.

"Laura, is there a problem?" she asked with concern.

I gulped and grabbed my bag. "I don't feel well," I said. "I need to use the restroom." I got up and dashed across the room as fast as my wobbly legs would allow. I heard her say something as I passed her desk but I couldn't make out the words. I stumbled out into the hall and took deep breaths of the cool air. I leaned against the lockers and closed my eyes, letting my book-bag slide to the floor. A second later

I heard the classroom door open and close and Miguel was in front of me.

"Come on, Laura, before she follows me out here. I didn't exactly ask permission to leave the room." He grabbed my bag from the floor and slung it over his arm with his own bag and took my hand with his free hand. We walked fast down the back hall, not speaking as we moved. Once we were far enough away from our English class, Miguel stopped and turned to me. "Go to your locker, get your coat and meet me at the side of the school by the band room. I'll see you there in a couple of minutes." And then he was gone, running silently through the corridor. I didn't stop to think about what I was doing. I ran to my locker, put on my coat and dashed to the band wing. When I opened the door that led to a side parking lot where the teachers parked, I was amazed to see that Miguel was already there in his Suburban waiting for me. I jumped in and slammed the door and we were off. We didn't speak until we were off the school grounds and heading south toward Newport. Snow swirled all around us and I trembled violently. Miguel turned up the heat and drove on.

"Where are we going?" I finally asked, my voice barely a whisper.

"Some place where we can talk," he replied. We drove on through the snow, through Middletown and into Newport. He turned onto Ocean Drive and we drove alongside the water. The waves swirled and crashed as the snow disappeared into its depths. We passed Brenton Point where Andrew had made his disastrous grand gesture on my birthday. Finally Miguel pulled into the parking lot of Old Barnacle Lighthouse and parked the Suburban facing the ocean. He made an adjustment to the heater and then unbuckled his seatbelt. He turned to me finally. "It has been too long since we've spoken. I have no idea what's been going through your head, but I'd like to know. What happened back there...in class just now? Why the tears?" His voice dropped and he leaned toward me slightly.

"You mean, you don't know?" I asked in shock. I stared at him in disbelief.

"Know what? What the hell are you talking about?" He sounded agitated.

"Something happened to Andrew's brother...Tristan," I answered, watching his face closely for any sign that he already knew.

"What?" His surprise seemed genuine. "What happened to him?"

"I don't know yet. Andrew's security came to the school earlier to get him. I saw him in the hall. He said something bad had happened to Tristan and then he left. I haven't heard from him so I don't know what's going on."

"And yet you somehow assumed *I* would know what had happened to him? Why, Laura? Why would you think I already knew?" His voice was rough and I heard the pain in it.

"I don't know. I'm not sure what I thought. I guess I…" I stopped as a wave of guilt washed over me.

"I know *exactly* what you thought. *Damn it*, Laura! You *thought* I did something to him. *Didn't you?*" He yelled and slammed his fist into the steering wheel just as I had done earlier this morning in my own car.

"I'm sorry. What did you expect?" A sob escaped from my mouth and my eyes welled with tears.

Miguel twisted in his seat and reached across the space between us but stopped short of touching me. "I did not harm Tristan. I don't know what happened to him. But just so you know, the day is fast approaching when he intends to harm me. And I won't go down without a fight." He leaned back in his seat and swore. "Damn it. I should not have said that." His hand slammed down again on the dash this time. The car shook with the force of it.

"Does this have something to do with Princess Gabriela and the gypsy curse?" I asked quietly, sniffling and wiping my eyes.

"How the hell do you know about her? Did Easton say something? *Damn it*," he cursed again.

"No! Andrew doesn't even know I know. I found out on my own. It's amazing what a person can learn on her own when no one is willing to give her the answers she has a right to know." I was angry now, my voice rising. "I know you're supposed to put a stop to the House of Hanover somehow. Does that mean kill someone…like Tristan?"

"*I'm* supposed to kill someone? Are you serious? It sounds like you don't have all the information. It's more like the other way around." I heard frustration in his voice.

"Someone's supposed to kill *you*? Why would someone allow this to happen? What is the point of all this…insanity?" I unbuckled my seatbelt and slumped forward onto the dash, burying my face in my arms. I felt the warmth from the heater rush against my face and I pressed closer—anything to ward off the incessant cold that always seemed to find me.

"Laura, please, listen. We're going to get this worked out…without violence. I told you before that you could trust me. Did you think I was lying? I will never lie to you. I think you've forgotten something important." He got quiet and when he didn't continue, I sat up straighter and pushed the hair out of my face which felt warm from its proximity to the heater. I wiped away more tears and sniffed. I turned to him and waited expectantly.

"What?" I asked on a shaky breath.

"You're forgetting the most important thing. That I'm in love with you. That has not changed. Maybe *you've* changed though…changed *your* mind…" His voice softened.

I looked at him then. And just as I had studied Andrew's face this morning, I studied Miguel's now. His dark eyes were locked on mine. I saw his beautiful cheekbones, the strong jaw, the lips I longed to taste again. I shook my head…tried to keep my thoughts pure…tried to keep my wits about me. This wasn't right. To want Andrew so much this morning and now wanting Miguel? *Who was I?* What had happened to Laura Calder? I had no idea. But I knew this—if Miguel did not kiss me now I would faint from longing. The talisman throbbed against my breasts. It ached for him, too. I didn't wait for him to make a move. I made the move. I turned my body toward him and reached for his arms, grasping them and tugging him toward me. I put away thoughts of Andrew and Tristan and the guilt that caused me. He met me half-way and pulled me hard into his body. I pressed my lips to his and kissed him as if the world were ending tomorrow. He groaned against my mouth and pushed his tongue into mine. I moaned against his lips and whispered, "I love you."

His kiss deepened as his hand found its way into my coat. He touched my breast and felt the outline of the talisman, hot and glowing. His mouth made a trail down my jaw to my chin and continued down my neck to my collarbone. I felt his hand slide under my sweater and I heard the alarm bells going off in my brain. I had to stop this. I had to keep my head. His fingers touched the disk and pressed it into the skin below my bra. I felt the heat branding me and I arched my back, groaning. His hand slipped under the edge of my bra and I had the feeling I was in a do or die situation. I never wanted this moment to end. I wanted his hands on me. I wanted Miguel. But fear crept into my mind. Andrew's face pushed its way in...and Tristan's. Just as Miguel's fingertips touched my breast I placed my hand over his and stopped him there. I leaned into his hair and breathed him in. "Miguel...we should stop...before..." My breaths were coming in ragged huffs now. Miguel slowly pulled his hand away and brought it up to my face. He kissed me tenderly and held me. We were silent for a time. And then I felt the vibration of my cell phone in my pocket. I dug it out and saw Andrew's name on the screen. I opened it and with a pounding heart, I read his text: *Can you come to me? I need you. I'm at Newport Hospital.*

"It's Andrew. He's at the hospital. He wants me to come there." I felt the pain in those twelve words and I swallowed the bile that threatened to rise up from my stomach.

"I'll take you." Miguel said. He turned and put the car in gear.

"No. I need my car. Please take me back to the school. I know I'm losing time but it'll save me trouble later."

He nodded and headed back to Portsmouth. I responded to Andrew's text: *I'll be there soon. How is Tristan? How are you? Love you.*

I don't know why I typed those last two words. But it was too late to take them back. Andrew needed my love and support now for whatever lay ahead. I would soon know.

Back at the school Miguel pulled up beside my Jeep. "Please text me or call when you know something, OK?" he asked.

"I will. I'll see you soon...?" It was more question than statement.

"Yes, of course," he said. I started to get out of the car but he stopped me. "Listen...I want you to know that even though Tristan may want me dead, I don't feel the same way about him. I'm not a monster." His evident sadness scared me. I had never seen Miguel show any hint of weakness. This vulnerability was hard to take.

"I know you're not. I cannot imagine why anyone would want either of you dead. I'll text you when I'm able." I started to leave again but he gripped my arm.

"I love you." His voice was quiet... resigned.

"I love you, too." I moved toward him and he kissed me. It was soft and tender and too short. He leaned back and gave my arm a gentle squeeze.

I smiled weakly and got out of the car. I jumped in the Jeep, waved, and headed to Newport Hospital. I shook all the way there out of cold and fear of what I would find waiting for me there.

I wasn't sure where to go once I got to the hospital so I pulled into the emergency room lot and parked. I pulled out my phone and texted Andrew: *I'm here. Outside the ER. Where can I find you?* I locked the Jeep and walked into the lobby. It seemed too quiet here—there was none of the frantic activity I expected to find. And then Andrew came through some automatic doors and ran to me. He was crying and he pulled me into his arms so fast and hard that it nearly knocked the wind out of me.

"What happened?" I pulled back and looked into his eyes—they were bright and teary. I felt my own tears start to burn. I didn't want to know—didn't want to hear what had happened to Tristan. I wasn't sure if I could be strong enough for Andrew. He led me to a corner of the waiting room and we sat side by side in green plastic chairs. He took my hands in his and for once his were colder than mine.

His shoulders shook as he tried to compose himself enough to speak. I let go of his hands and wrapped my arms around him. "Oh, Andrew…please…tell me…is Tristan…?"

"No!" he spat out the word, shaking his head. "He's alive…but… when he wakes up…he'll wish he weren't. I can't bear this…can't bear this for him."

I didn't speak. I had to let him tell me in his own time. I held him as he shook against me and finally his tears subsided and he let out a pent-up sigh. "He's paralyzed—from the waist down. He'll never walk again." He put his head in his hands and leaned forward, resting his elbows on his legs. I rubbed his back, my tears flowing now, too. I couldn't imagine Tristan never walking again. All I could think was that a terrible mistake had been made and we would soon learn the truth—that he was fine and he would walk out of here and ride his beloved horses again.

Andrew sat up and brushed his hands through his hair. "He was at the stables, grooming his horses. And one of them went nuts—no one knows why—and kicked out at him. I guess one of the stable hands showed up and tried to pull Daisy away. She knocked Tristan down and came down on his back…snapped his spine…and just like that…" His voice broke off in a sob.

"Oh, Andrew. I'm so sorry." My heart ached to the point of breaking. "How is your mother? And your father?"

"My mother wouldn't leave his side. They had to pry her off him so they could take him to surgery. My father…," his voice trailed off. Suddenly he jumped up and ran outside into the parking lot. He ran to a garbage can and kicked it hard, knocking it over. He screamed and I ran outside to him, my arms extended. "Andrew, I know you're hurting…and angry. Let me help you. Come here, darling."

He turned toward me and stared right through me. He looked fierce and I was frightened. I slowly approached him. I held out my hand and he looked at it as if it were a new invention. Finally he held out his hand and slipped it into mine. He pulled me into his arms—he was shaking—from cold and despair. "What are we going to do? Tristan won't survive this…mentally, I mean. Why did this happen?" He took me by the shoulders and shook me but not hard. "Do you know how good he is? A good person, I mean? Tristan is the perfect son. This… is…not…fair!"

"Come inside with me. You're freezing. You can't afford to get sick. He's going to need you and so will your parents. Let's get you warmed up. Please?" I pleaded with him.

We walked back inside the ER and I spotted a coffee machine. I gently pushed him into a chair and got us two cups of black coffee. We sat side by side and sipped the coffee and finally Andrew seemed to calm down. When he finished his drink, he got up and threw the cup away. "I need to get back up there. Will you come with me?"

I felt panic set in. I didn't think this would be a good idea. The duke was probably beside himself as it was and my presence would only agitate him more. I started to shake my head but his expression stopped me.

"Don't worry about my father," he said, as if he'd read my mind. "My parents probably won't even notice you're there. I need you, Laura." His spirit was so crushed that it was killing me.

"Of course." We walked through the ER and got on the elevator. When the doors opened on Tristan's floor I was shocked to see the duke standing in front of them as if he had been waiting for an elevator himself. His face was white, his mouth drawn. His hands were clenched at his sides and I felt the icy river of fear begin to flow through my veins. We stepped off the elevator and the duke let the doors glide shut.

"He's out of surgery now. He'll be sedated for a while. Your mother is with him but she's…" he turned away, his face stony.

I wanted to reach out to him but I knew it would be a mistake. I remained quiet at Andrew's side.

"What did the doctors say?" Andrew asked quietly. He reached for my hand and I squeezed his tightly.

The duke cleared his throat and looked out the window at the end of the hall. He seemed a million miles away. My heart went out to him. I knew he was hurting. But then his next words chilled me to the bone.

"It's the worst possible news—just as they'd said. Tristan will never walk again." The duke turned his gaze on me and then on Andrew. His stare was blank as if he were looking into empty air. "This changes everything." And with those ominous words, he walked to the exit door and disappeared into the stair well.

I looked up at Andrew. He was stoic—his face a mask. But he ground his teeth, his jaw moving back and forth. I could see the anger in his eyes as he struggled to control himself. I stayed silent as he worked through his inner turmoil. Behind him came members of the security detail down the hall. I saw Peter wipe away tears and Nathan also. They nodded at us and continued into an elevator that had just opened, their eyes downcast. The doors swished closed. A nurse walked past us carrying a vial of medication and disappeared into a patient's room. Finally Andrew spoke.

"I'm sorry, Laura. He isn't himself. And I'm sorry I dragged you here."

"No, no, no…," I whispered. "I don't want you to be alone. I know you have your mother but I'll always be here for you." I put my arms around him and hugged him tightly. "Your mother may need you now. I don't want to interfere…but I'll do whatever you want me to do… stay here or leave. Tristan may not want to see anyone but his family when he wakes. It's going to be hard for him but you have to be strong and give him whatever he needs to get through the days ahead—your love and patience and support."

He kissed the top of my head. "Thank you, Laura. I love you so much." He looked down at me and I knew I had to say the words he needed to hear.

"I love you, too." He kissed me then—hard—and let me go.

"You should get home. You're probably hungry and I'm going to be here all night. But I'll call you tomorrow. Be safe, my darling. I love you so much."

I reached up to kiss his cheek. He turned his face and my lips grazed his. We kissed again and I reached over and pushed the button for the elevator. I stepped inside. He held up his hand in a wave. I waved back as the doors closed. I pressed the lobby button and began to sob silently into my hands. I ran through the ER and drove home as fast as I thought I could get away with safely. This felt like the worst day of my life. That thought left a bitter taste in my mouth. This was the worst day for Tristan. I didn't really believe in God or any religion but I prayed now for him—for his spirit and his fortitude—he would need so much strength to survive this.

Chapter Twenty Two

THE DATE IS SET

When I got home Nick was there. *Nick!* Who liked Tristan and always spoke so highly of him. I walked into the kitchen and he took one look at my face and exclaimed, "Good god, Laura, who died?" I shook my head as the tears fell down my cheeks. He was up and at my side instantly. "Hey, I didn't mean it. I was kidding. What's wrong, sport?" He rubbed my shoulder awkwardly unsure of how to handle my emotions.

"Oh, Nick. It's horrible news. It's Tristan. He's…" But Nick put up his hand and backed away from me.

"No, don't say it. I just saw him yesterday. We had coffee after class. He was fine. Don't tell me anything bad."

"He had an accident," I sobbed. "At the stables. A horse kicked him and then stepped down on his back and…crushed his spine. He's… paralyzed." I could barely say the word.

Nick leaned up against the sink and shook his head back and forth. "No, no. This can't be. Not Tristan. I don't believe it."

My mother walked into the kitchen then and saw our stricken faces. "What's going on?" she asked.

I told her about Tristan. Though she didn't know him she sensed the palpability of our grief. She put her hand over her mouth and shook her head in disbelief. We sat together at the table while Nick tried to process it. Mom made us hot chocolate and asked about dinner but we didn't want food. My stomach was so erratic lately that it was all I could do to eat enough to sustain myself as it was. I thought of Miguel and excused myself. I needed to let him know about Tristan. I squeezed Nick's shoulder. His face was pale and drawn.

Upstairs in my room I lay down on my bed and tried to calm and center myself before calling Miguel but it was useless. I dialed his number with shaking fingers and he answered immediately.

"I've been waiting for you to call. How bad it is it?" I heard the concern in his voice and I knew he would never want harm to come to Tristan—or anyone.

My voice cracked as I tried to speak. "It's bad. He was kicked and trampled by one of his horses and his spine was…severed. He's never going to walk again."

I heard Miguel's sharp intake of breath. "Oh, my god. Not Tristan. He's good, Laura—one of the good ones in this messed up world. This is…heart-breaking."

Miguel's words shocked me. I figured he would be sympathetic but this…was unexpected. "You know Tristan? I mean I know you know *of* him, but you've spoken to him before?"

There was a long silence except for Miguel's quiet breathing. Finally he spoke. "Laura? Can you keep something between us—just me and you. You won't tell Andrew—or anyone?"

My heart skipped a beat. I didn't think I could cope with any more shocking news or revelations. But I promised anyway. "Yes, of course."

"Tristan and I knew—*know*—each other. I reached out to him a few months ago and we talk sometimes. We talk about his father and mine and this burden that our ancestors have placed on both our heads. We agreed that we would ignore the decree and the curse and every-thing else and let each other live in peace. We shook on it. You know he is—was—supposed to kill me, don't you?"

I jumped from my bed and paced the room. My hand shook so badly I could barely hold the phone to my ear. "I don't know the details but I gathered that someone was to be…killed. I thought *you* were the one who was going to…you know…" The sentence was too absurd and awful to finish.

"I'm going to spare you the details for now but Tristan was sup-posed to kill me. But this changes everything now."

I gasped. "The duke said those exact same words to Andrew today at the hospital! What's changed? This means no one has to hurt anybody, right? No more vendettas or decrees or ancient curses?" I felt hopeful and yet it was bittersweet if it came at the cost of Tristan's health.

Miguel was silent. I waited for him to reassure me that this craziness was over and we could all get along. I waited but his silence continued. "Miguel? Are you there? Answer me!"

"Laura." Just my name...nothing more. I waited.

"Tell me," I begged. "What else is there?"

I heard Miguel's long sigh. When he spoke his voice was deeper—and flat. "It's on Andrew now. If anything were to happen to the first-born son then it falls on the second son. Andrew will have the job of killing me now. And I'm quite sure he will relish every moment of trying."

No...no...no. I didn't want to hear this. I pulled the phone away from my ear. I could hear Miguel's voice calling my name. I didn't want to hear any more about killing and vendettas and family honor. This was 2012—we lived in a civilized world where life was sacred and respected. There wouldn't—couldn't—be any killing...2012...2012... it was 2012, after all.... It was 2012 and that was *exactly* why there would be violence. I tasted the bitter irony in my mouth as I remembered the numbers on the talisman. I heard Miguel calling my name. I put the phone back to my ear. "I'm here."

"Are you OK?" he asked. He sounded a million miles away.

"Yes...no...I don't know." I didn't know what I was. I thought of Andrew then and felt better. He wouldn't hurt Miguel. He couldn't kill anyone. Everything would be fine. "Andrew won't try to kill you. He's every bit as good as Tristan. He has a temper but he's not his father. He'll end the vendetta. I'm sure of it."

There was a long silence on Miguel's end. I felt a wave of exhaustion roll over me. I was hungry and tired and wanted to sleep. Finally Miguel answered. "We'll see, but I won't count on it. I'll see you tomorrow, Laura. Good night." He hung up abruptly. I stared at my phone...wondering...what was going through his mind? I closed my phone and slid under my blankets fully clothed. I was too tired to change or brush my teeth, and despite my hunger, I knew I couldn't eat. I closed my eyes and saw images of Tristan—riding his horses, playing polo, walking. I balled my hands into fists and punched at my pillow repeatedly. How could something so horrible have happened to someone so sweet? It wasn't fair. I soaked my pillow through with my tears and fell into a fitful sleep.

The next couple of weeks were awful. Andrew was never in school anymore. I would see Peter or one of the other security guards at the school from time to time picking up and dropping off homework. The teachers were being very understanding considering the situation. We talked every day, though, and he kept me informed as to Tristan's recovery and state of mind. Tristan was seeing a psychiatrist to help him cope with his new way of living and his mother was with him every moment. Andrew didn't say much about his father other than that he wasn't coping as well as the family would have hoped. And then Andrew called me one evening, sounding almost like himself again.

"Hey, there. How are you?" he said. "I'm missing you terribly."

"Hi—me, too. How are you...and Tristan?"

"I'm OK and Tristan...well, he seems to be coping fairly well. Did I tell you he laughed the other day?" Andrew sounded so excited about something that to most people would be a non-event. It made me feel a burst of happiness.

"Wow...that's something. What made him laugh?"

"It was something he saw on the telly—that damned groundhog in Pennsylvania...what's his name? Punxsutawney Phil? He didn't see his shadow and Tristan burst out laughing. Who would've thought a rodent could make him laugh?"

I felt my moment of happiness fade. An early spring—was the irony of the groundhog's prediction lost on Andrew? Because it wasn't lost on me and apparently it wasn't lost on Tristan either. I remembered Miguel's words about his secret truce with Tristan—their promise and handshake—that the vendetta would be ignored and they would live in peace. I still didn't know the details of this vendetta or decree or whatever they were calling it but as long as it was cancelled that was the most important thing.

"That's great. Tristan is strong. He just might surprise the hell out of everyone with his recovery and his spirit." I prayed I was right. We talked a few more minutes and made a promise to see each other soon. I hung up and tried to concentrate on homework but my mind kept drifting—as usual. It would be a miracle if I passed all of my classes and got to graduate with the rest of the class. I thought about calling or texting Miguel but I knew that would only further weaken my powers of concentration. I forced myself to buckle down and get my work done.

I noticed the change in the weather when I was leaving for school early one morning. It was cold as expected but the sun was bright and glorious and the air crisp and sharp. I studied the ground as I walked to my car. It was coated with a light dusting of snow. We were having the mildest of winters and normally I would have loved that—would have loved knowing that spring was imminent. But this year spring was a portent of something ominous and I couldn't make sense of the contradiction it had become.

The school day went by in its usual blur. After English class Miguel and I walked outside together—something we'd been doing lately since Andrew was studying at home or at the hospital so he could be at Tristan's side. We walked to my Jeep and Miguel saw his brothers waiting at the Suburban. He waved at them and pressed the key to unlock the doors for them then turned to me. "If I give them the keys, will you give me a ride home?" He had a strange smile on his face and I wondered what was up.

"Sure," I said, raising an eyebrow at him. I watched as he ran over to his brothers and handed Tomas the keys. The boys hopped into the Suburban and drove off and Miguel joined me in the Jeep.

"Mind if we take a short drive?" he asked mysteriously.

Again I raised an eyebrow at him. "OK…where to?" I smiled.

He directed me to go right out of the school lot. I drove toward Middletown and soon we were driving alongside the ocean. He had me pull into the lot at Easton's Beach and I parked facing the water. I kept the car running for warmth and waited expectantly.

"Happy Valentine's Day," he said quietly. He pulled out a small, red, heart-shaped box from inside his coat pocket. "I hope my body heat didn't melt them." He smiled as he handed me the box of chocolates.

"Wow—it *is* Valentine's Day, isn't it?" I took the box and shook it gently. "They don't sound too melty." I felt my face flush as I looked into Miguel's endless eyes. I wondered whose Valentine I was—whose I was supposed to be. Pangs of guilt stabbed at my heart for Andrew. This wasn't right—this playing both ends against the middle—how could I have let this go on for so long? But how could I hurt Andrew now when Tristan's accident was still so fresh? Would there ever be a right time to hurt him? The question was preposterous. I focused my attention back on Miguel. "Would you like one?" I started to open the box of candy.

"No. I'd rather have this…" Miguel unfastened his seatbelt and then mine and opened his arms to me, pulling me into him. He kissed me fiercely, taking my breath away—my heart went into overdrive and I felt myself melt into him. His lips and tongue were all I could taste and I knew they were sweeter than the chocolates inside the heart-shaped box. His hands wound into my hair, pulling out the band that held it in a ponytail. It fell around my shoulders and he ran his fingers through it. He kissed my jaw and my temple and whispered those mysterious and intoxicating Portuguese words in my ear. My heart felt like it would beat out of my chest and my body burned with a fire that could bring down a forest in the blink of an eye. And then the car shifted violently and Miguel jumped away from me as a tall, dark figure pounded on my Jeep.

"Get your hands off her! Get out of the car, you filthy bastard!"

"Stay in the car, Laura!" Miguel yelled as he opened the door and was out in a flash. I saw him hit the ground, the dark figure on top of him. I jumped out of the Jeep and ran around to see what was happening. That's when I saw Andrew's black car parked behind mine. I saw Peter at the wheel and another goon in the passenger seat watching the spectacle on the ground. Why weren't they stopping this?

"You son of a bitch!" Andrew cursed. He threw a punch that grazed Miguel's jaw. Miguel rolled away and jumped to his feet but Andrew attacked again—charging him, his fist flying.

"You don't want to do this now, Easton!" He blocked Andrew's incoming fist. "Don't make me hit you!" he yelled. He and Andrew circled each other now in a replay of the last time we were on this beach.

"Who do you think you are, *damned gypsy thief? Who?*" Andrew's anger was out of control. He went at Miguel again, this time with a left hook that connected with Miguel's stomach. Miguel doubled over and fell backward and Andrew was on top of him as Miguel struggled to catch his breath. Andrew's fist smashed into Miguel's face. I saw blood splatter on the ground.

"*No!*" I screamed. I was frantic. I ran toward them and grabbed at Andrew's jacket. I had to stop him from killing Miguel. Andrew's arm came around instinctively and pushed me back. I fell onto the parking lot pavement, using my hands to break my fall, and the pinging of pain in my wrists erupted as I hit the hard surface. Miguel staggered to his feet then and rushed at Andrew.

"You're the son of a bitch!" he yelled. He hit Andrew square in the jaw, sending him flying into the air and landing on the sand that edged the parking lot. That move finally got the attention of the goons. Peter was out of the car and charging at Miguel now, the other goon close behind.

I had to stop this. It would be three against one—or two—and we were out-numbered. "Peter! No! Please stop!" I ran toward him but the other goon grabbed me, preventing me from getting too close. "Let me go!" I screamed but he held on tighter.

Andrew stood up on wobbly legs and staggered in Miguel's direction. They were about to charge one another again but Peter grabbed Andrew by the arms and the other security man blocked Miguel as he continued to hold onto my arm.

"We're not done here, Dos Santos." Andrew spat out the words and struggled against Peter's arms. He rubbed his jaw. "It's between you and me now."

"Name the date, Easton! Name the place!" Miguel exclaimed through clenched teeth. He wiped the sleeve of his coat across his bloody face.

"No!" I screamed again. "I won't let you. I'll call the police!" The goon holding me suddenly pulled me into his chest and clamped a hand over my mouth.

"Hush, Laura. They have to work this out themselves. Calling the police will only make it worse—for everybody." The goon whispered the words quietly in my ear. I didn't think anyone else heard him. But Miguel was watching and he charged at the goon.

"You! Let her go!" Miguel yelled. The goon released me and grabbed Miguel in a tight lock.

"Stop, please! No more!" I couldn't stand this. I had to get help before someone went too far. I looked around frantically and started back toward my car.

"Laura! What are you doing?" It was Peter talking to me. Suddenly all the goons had voices. "Don't move." I stopped and turned toward him.

"Laura." Andrew this time—finally acknowledging me. I waited. He was silent, staring at me. Everyone stood motionless. Miguel and Andrew were breathing hard. I wasn't breathing at all. Peter released his hold on Andrew. He rubbed his jaw again and walked toward me. Fear coursed through me as I watched his approach.

"Easton!" Miguel yelled. He struggled against the goon's tight grip. "What are you doing, Easton?"

Andrew stopped in front of me. I looked into his eyes and saw the hurt there—and the pain—the pain of my betrayal. I couldn't stop the tears that rolled down my cheeks. I gasped for breath. "Andrew? I'm…sorry. I'm…" He shook his head and held up his hand to stop my words. He stood only an inch away from me. He positioned himself beside me and looked at Miguel, still struggling for release from the goon's tight hold.

"It's OK, Laura," said Andrew. "This isn't your fault." His voice was even–an eerie monotone. "He's just trying to get his clutches into you to get at me. I don't hold you responsible for this…betrayal. I know how his mind works. He's just using you." He looked at me and then at Miguel.

"Don't listen to him, Laura. He's lying. He'll say anything now." Miguel tried again to shrug off the goon.

Andrew touched his cold hand to my cheek. I flinched but didn't knock his hand away. "He's trying to poison you against me. You can't trust him, Laura. You cannot trust a gypsy." He pressed his hand into my cheek and then dropped it and turned to Miguel.

"Midnight. March 12. Brenton Point. Come alone and I'll do the same. No weapons. Just hand to hand. A fair fight. Flowers or no flowers. Do we have a deal?" He walked over to stand in front of Miguel.

The goon released Miguel and he straightened, shaking out his arms to get the circulation flowing again. They stood face to face. The same height. Probably the same weight—maybe Miguel a little heavier. One as dark as the other was light. Their eyes bored into one another's. No one moved. No one breathed. The goons were like statues. I was frozen in place.

"Deal." Miguel extended his hand and Andrew took it in his own. They shook hard once and dropped hands.

I forced myself to move. "*No!* You're not doing this. I'll stop you. I'll make sure this never happens."

Andrew turned to me. "Laura, this is the way it's supposed to be. You can no more alter the course of history or its path than any one of us."

I looked at Miguel. "Miguel? You don't want this. I know you don't."

"It'll be alright, Laura. This has been in the works for hundreds of years. It's time to end it."

"Brave words…for someone who's going to die," said Andrew menacingly.

"No!" I shook my head back and forth. I felt myself sink to the pavement in front of my Jeep. "No. Please. You can't do this."

"This is between him and me, Laura. You cannot interfere." Andrew said quietly. He looked at Miguel. "I'd offer you a ride home but I'd hate to dirty my car with gypsy stink."

"I'd rather walk." Miguel looked at me then and I saw pain in his eyes and worry. But I didn't see fear. "Good-bye, Laura." And he turned and walked away.

"Miguel! Wait! I'll take you home!" I shouted, pushing myself up from the ground. I started to run after him. But Peter grabbed me as I went by him. "Let go of me!" I shouted at him.

"It's OK, Peter. You can both go. I'll ride with Laura." Andrew started toward my car.

"No! I'm leaving—*alone!* Stay away from me, Andrew!" I ran to my car and climbed inside. I quickly locked the doors so he couldn't get in. I started the car and drove off. I had to fight through tears to see the road. I stopped a little way up from Easton's Beach and scanned the road and beach for Miguel but he was nowhere in sight. I dialed his number but he didn't answer. Where had he gone to so fast? How would he get home? I saw Andrew and the goons leave the lot and drive into Newport. I drove slowly along the road searching for Miguel but he was gone. I sent him a text but he didn't answer.

I sobbed all the way home. Everything had spiraled out of control. Someone would die if I didn't stop this showdown. I wouldn't let them hurt each other like this. *I don't even know what they're fighting for*! I screamed the words inside my head. I could not—would not—believe that these two boys—*men*—would go through with this. But if that was truly their intent, then I would be there, too. One of them would have to kill me first to get to the other. I was banking on their love now. Did one of them love me enough to stop the madness and call this nightmare off? Well, it was on Andrew. He seemed to be calling the shots. Time would tell who loved me more—or who I loved more. I would sacrifice myself for the greater good and hope they didn't call my bluff.

Chapter Twenty Three

SACRIFICES

Just when my life was spiraling out of control and I didn't think things could get worse, they did. It had been a week since the showdown on Easton's Beach and I had not seen either Andrew or Miguel. I'd walked through the school days like an automaton, barely registering the activity and conversations around me. And then I came home from school one day and sensed instantly that something was wrong in my house. Nick was standing in the kitchen, a dark look on his face, and my mother was sitting at the table. She was home early from work and she was crying. It must be bad if whatever it was could make my mother cry. Crying wasn't in her nature. On the table in front of her lay a piece of paper. And I suddenly feared whatever words were on that paper.

"Mom? What's going on?" My breath caught in my throat as I paused in the doorway.

"It's OK, honey. Everything's going to be fine. I've just had some bad news but I'm sure it's going to get worked out." She took the paper and crumpled it in her hands.

"What's on that paper?" I pointed to the paper and willed my hands not to shake.

Nick walked over and sat down next to Mom at the table. He pulled the paper from her hands, smoothed it open and looked at it. "She might lose her job. She got this letter today from her boss."

"Why?" I didn't want to see the letter. I just needed to know how bad this situation was. "Tell me what it says."

Mom wiped her eyes on the corner of a napkin and answered me. "Apparently we're being taken over by the Royal Bank of Scotland and some of the employees who've been there the longest are being let go. I've been there ten years which isn't that long in terms of retirement options but I'll be one of the first to go."

"Can't Mr. Aldean do something? I mean…aren't you dating him or something?" I asked.

"No! I'm not dating my boss. How could you think that? Just because he gave me a ride to work a few times? And besides, he got a letter, too."

"Can't they just reassign you somewhere else or let you stay in the new version of the bank?" asked Nick.

"You would think so. But the new people taking over are set on bringing in their own crew from England at least for the immediate future." She sighed and ran her hands through her hair. I noticed gray at her temples and the tiredness around her eyes.

"What about other banks? Can't they help you find a job somewhere else?" I asked. There had to be an easy fix to this problem.

"I'll look for a new job but it won't be easy in today's economy. I'm sure all the good jobs are taken."

"Does Dad know? He'll help, won't he?" I knew my parents were getting a divorce but my dad wouldn't let anything happen to my mom—financially or otherwise—I felt certain of that.

"I don't want to burden him with this. Speaking of your father, he's coming to see you kids tomorrow so make an effort to be here—maybe have dinner with him or something. Can you do that?" She sounded so forlorn. I walked over and gave her a hug.

"We'll work things out, Mom. We'll get jobs—won't we, Nick?" Nick had always worked in restaurants throughout high school and he would be working in one now if the latest restaurant he'd been working for hadn't suddenly closed due to mismanagement and bad food. He nodded and went to the refrigerator.

"How about I make us some dinner? I'll put my amazing cooking skills to work for you ladies." Mom smiled at that and Nick winked at me. I appreciated his trying to cheer Mom up. I gave Nick my input on dinner ideas and went upstairs to my room. I had a good feeling that everything would be OK and this was just a bump in the road.

But then Dad came the next day and brought some bad news of his own. I was stunned at his announcement. The architecture firm where he had worked for so many years was being sold to a foreign company and all of the employees were put on notice.

"Your mother and I discussed things and I'm going to move back in here with you guys. We need to economize until things get figured out. We're putting the divorce on hold for now." Dad was at the kitchen table now, seated across from Mom. Mom's face was pale and Nick stood stone-faced at the stove where he was heating water for instant coffee.

I was shocked at this turn of events. Both of my parents losing their jobs at the same time? Could the world really be that cruel? I suddenly felt a coldness invade my body to the point that my teeth threatened to shatter. "Are we going to be…alright?" I asked quietly.

My dad jumped up from the table, nearly tipping over his chair. "Yes, baby. We will be fine. We have some savings and if it comes down to it we can apply for unemployment. I'll find another job. We will absolutely be fine." He sounded so adamant that I had to wonder who he was trying to convince—us or himself?

Later, up in my room, I lay on my bed and stared at the ceiling. I was miserable. I was worried about Andrew and I missed Miguel so much that the ache it caused me was almost too much to bear. I stared at my phone and wondered if I should contact either one of them. I wanted to desperately but I didn't want to make the first move. I cried angry tears. My talisman was on my nightstand. I hadn't been wearing it much lately and I wondered if I'd been causing myself bad luck by not doing so. I put it on now and felt its weight and comfort against my skin. My room was getting dark with the setting sun, and now in the gathering darkness I saw a faint red glow coming through my blouse. The talisman was reacting to me—turning hot against my skin and emitting this crimson glow. I reached into my blouse and grabbed the disk in my hand and held it tightly in my fist. "What are you trying to tell me?" I asked it. "Please tell me. I don't know what to do!" It seemed to throb in my fist—sending me a message I didn't understand—or maybe it was a warning. I buried my face in my pillow and sobbed myself into a state of near hysteria. I couldn't stand this. But I had no idea what to do.

It was the last day of February—Leap Day—one extra day in the year to feel miserable. I'd just left English class and was walking to my car, watching Miguel walk to his. He'd sat behind me and kept his silence and his distance. I had not seen Andrew in quite some time and I'd just about decided he'd forgotten I even existed. I hadn't talked to Lily or Gretchen in so long they probably forgot I existed, too. I got in my Jeep and sat there unmoving. I was way past miserable. I laid my head on the steering wheel and cried—my shoulders shaking, my breath coming in staccato gasps. I didn't even care if anyone saw me. I was so tired of crying all the time—it's all I ever did anymore. I couldn't eat and I couldn't sleep without having such bad dreams that it didn't pay to close my eyes. I heard a light tapping on my window. I brushed the hair out of my eyes and looked up at Miguel. I pushed the button, lowering the window.

"What is it, Laura? Why are you crying?" he asked me. His voice was soft and deep and I wanted to pull him through the window into my arms and never let him go.

I sighed. "I'm tired, Miguel. Just tired. Of everything."

He reached inside and took my hand and leaned in close to me. His face was inches from mine. I wanted him to kiss me but I knew it would hurt too much. I couldn't take days and days of silence followed by moments of passion only to go back to silence again—it was too exhausting.

"I'm sorry. I wanted to call you—to reach out to you—but truthfully, Laura? I don't know where I stand with you. You say you love me but you haven't broken up with Easton. And there are some things I won't share—namely you. Are you still with him?" His thumbs caressed the sides of my hands and I looked down at them—his hands were so large that they dwarfed mine.

"I don't know what I am. He hasn't been in contact with me very much but I'm sure that's because he's with Tristan. But, Miguel..." I looked into his eyes. "I love Andrew...but...I'm *in love* with you... and there's a world of difference between those two kinds of love." I couldn't believe I'd had the courage to say those words out loud—I hadn't even known I was going to say them—but when you feel like you have nothing—and everything—to lose, you can say anything, I guessed.

Miguel was quiet. He seemed just about to speak when he glanced to his right and then back to me again. He pulled his hands away from mine and stepped back from the car. "I love you, too, Laura. Never forget that." And then he was gone—in his Suburban and out of the parking lot in a flash. I was stunned at his abrupt departure. And then I saw the black car behind me. Andrew was here. No wonder Miguel left in such a hurry. The school parking lot was not the best place for another knock-down, drag-out fight. I saw the door open and someone approaching me. But it wasn't Andrew. It was Peter. I stuck my head out the window. "Peter? Something wrong? Where's Andrew?"

"Hello, Miss Laura. Would you be able to come to the Easton house? Andrew would like to see you. He's sorry he couldn't come himself but he says it's urgent. We can take you now, if you're free."

I looked back at the car and saw another goon in the front passenger seat. I hesitated. I couldn't believe Andrew would send his goons for me. What was so damned important that he couldn't come get me himself? I thought it over and decided I would go and when I got there I would give Andrew a piece of my mind—what little there was left of it. "I don't want to leave my car here. Will you follow me home so I can drop it off?"

Peter nodded. "We'll be right behind you." He went back to the car and waited for me to leave.

Damn—these goons were weird. I'd never seen anything like them. I put my car in gear and a few minutes later I was in my driveway. My house looked dark and quiet. There must not be anyone home yet. As I walked to the black car I looked up at the sky. It was a cloudy day with a few flurries but the sun looked like it wanted to break through the cloud-cover just in time to set. There was an eerie, almost ominous glow to the sky. The goon from the passenger side already had the back door open for me and I climbed in and fastened my seatbelt. I felt my talisman heating up against my chest and I wondered why now? I didn't understand its patterns and signals. But my heart was suddenly racing, so maybe that was the cause of the sudden warmth.

We drove through Middletown and entered Ocean Drive. I stared at the ocean and remembered my ring. Some day someone would find that thing and make a lot of money from it. I kept my mind filled with incessant babble in an attempt to keep my nerves at bay. I had no idea what Andrew's mood would be or what he wanted to talk to me about but I guessed it had something to do with the state of us. Peter drove the car around to the back of the house and parked. Instead of entering the house as I usually had in the front we went in through the garage. Once inside the house, Peter took my coat and led me to the salon.

"Have a seat, miss. I'll have someone bring you some tea." I nodded and sat down to wait. There was a light on in one corner, but otherwise it was a bit gloomy in the room. Everything was neat and tidy—I bet there wasn't a speck of dust to be found anywhere. A few minutes passed and no one came. Where was Andrew? I was getting even more anxious than I'd felt in the car. Well, I would give him two more minutes and then I would go looking for him. I felt my talisman warming against me again and I remembered what Miguel had said about not letting the duke get his hands on it. I doubted the duke was even here but my instincts were telling me to take it off so I slipped it in my pocket anyway just to be safe. I pulled my hand from my pocket just as Peter walked back into the room.

"Come with me, please," he said. His voice sounded stern and I suddenly had the feeling I was being sent to the principal's office. I got up and followed him down the hall and we turned down a corridor I had not been down before. He stopped at the last door and tapped on it lightly. I heard a deep voice say to come in but it was definitely not Andrew's voice. Peter opened the door and stepped onto the threshold but I didn't follow him. All of a sudden my instincts were telling me to run—to get out—but I ignored them. I was being ridiculous.

"Please, miss," Peter beckoned. Against my better judgment I stepped into the doorway and Peter moved aside to let me pass. He immediately stepped back out into the hall and shut the door behind him and I heard the sickening sound of a lock clicking into place.

"Hello, Laura. Thank you for coming," said the Duke of Easton. He was seated behind a huge mahogany desk. I was in an office of some kind—there were bookshelves on two walls and a large window formed the wall behind the desk where he sat, his hands folded on top of a blotter.

My heart raced and I wasn't sure if I would be able to speak without stuttering. "Wh...where's Andrew?" I asked, my heart thudding hard in my chest. I felt a rushing sensation in my veins and my knees threatened to buckle.

"Andrew won't be joining us tonight. Please have a seat." He pointed to a hunter green wing chair with brass accents in front of his desk.

I couldn't move—my legs didn't work. I decided I would have to stand. "No, thank you. I prefer to stand." I clasped my hands behind my back so he couldn't seem them shaking.

"It wasn't a suggestion, Laura. Please have a seat." I heard the dark tone in his voice and I shivered. I forced my feet to move. I made it to the chair and sat down across from him.

"Why am I here? Where is Andrew?" I could hear the nerves in my voice and I was sure he could hear them, too. There was no denying my fear. I suspected he thrived on inducing fear in others and I told myself to fight it—to be strong—and get this over with—whatever he had to say, I would listen and get out of here. And I would not come back—not even for Andrew.

"You and I are going to have an important chat—a discussion of sorts, Laura. I like that name, Laura. What is your middle name?"

I failed to see the relevance but figured if I cooperated and answered his questions we could get this over with and I could go home. So I answered. "Michelle."

"Lovely. Laura Michelle Calder. A beautiful name indeed."

I swallowed hard and shifted slightly in my seat.

"I brought you here today because I need your help with a particular matter. And if you help me, I will offer you something as well." He was sitting up ramrod straight in his chair. He wore a navy blue sweater over a white dress shirt. I noticed other details now, too. My senses were on alert—tuning in to sounds, scents, sights. His thinning blond hair was shot through with gray and he had a pair of glasses tucked into the pocket of the sweater. There was a table lamp on the desk with a dark green shade, the same color as the chair I was sitting in. I could hear the low hum of the heating system and I smelled a hint of musk in the air. I waited, saying nothing.

"I have so much to say to you that I don't even know where to begin. But I suppose the past is a good place to start. I understand you have questions about our family history—about certain legacies waiting to be fulfilled. Am I correct in this?" He stared at me intently.

"I don't know what you're talking about." How could he possibly know what I knew or didn't know about the vendetta?

"Oh, I think you do. My security detail is very thorough. They keep me informed of everything they feel is relevant, especially when it concerns my sons. I know you think I'm not much of a father, but the fact is, I love my sons very much. This…accident…that has crippled my son is eating away at me, but Tristan has surprised me. His mental state is actually much better than mine would be if I were in his situation. We will get through this nightmare and Tristan can still have a life."

I let out a pent-up breath. "I'm happy to hear that. My heart aches for him and if he is coping well already then it should help speed up his recovery. Tristan is a lovely boy." I finally felt like the duke and I could have a conversation that wouldn't frighten the daylights out of me. Maybe this wouldn't be so bad after all.

"Getting back on track…I know that you are aware of a certain… decree…that has been issued in my family's history. I want you to know the details of it so we can clear up any confusion you may have. I will give you the short version." He leaned forward across the desk and stared at me, his eyes dark.

"I come from the House of Hanover and am descended from King George the First. Some three hundred years ago—give or take, King George had an affair with a Portuguese girl whom he thought to be a gypsy. He'd met her one day when he was out riding his horse. She was living in a gypsy camp not far from the palace. But it turned out that she was, in fact, a princess from the House of Braganza. She became pregnant with his son but, unfortunately, she hid the baby with gypsies and met an untimely end. Before she died she placed a curse on the King and his descendants—a gypsy curse. To counteract that curse, the King issued a decree. According to that decree the eldest son in the line of descendancy will take the life of the eldest son in the line of descendancy in the Portuguese royal house. The gypsy curse and the decree have coinciding dates—spring of 2012, when the first flowers of spring bloom. Before you protest the barbarism of this situation, you should know that this decree has been signed off on by every monarch since King George the First, including my current

Queen, Elizabeth the Second. She will be expecting the delivery of the Portuguese prince's left hand as proof that the decree was carried out."

A cracked sob escaped from my throat. I bit down on my lip and tried to keep my composure. He stopped talking for a moment to study me. He seemed to be assessing how I was taking the information so far. I tried to remain stoic and expressionless even as I wanted to cry out in a rage at the stupidity of his words and this completely insane decree. I fought to remain silent, suppressing the sobs tearing at the back of my throat and he continued.

"I have no idea what the gypsy curse is destined to be. As far as I am concerned, the curse arrived prematurely with the crippling of my son, Tristan. If there is another curse to come—the real curse—then naturally I want to prevent that from happening. And I am quite sure Miguel Dos Santos would like to keep his hand as well as his life."

I flinched at the mention of Miguel's name but I remained silent and kept my face a mask.

"I know of your flirtation with the Portuguese prince. Were you even aware of his royal ancestry?"

I refused to answer and stared straight ahead at the duke.

"In any case, the contents of your cell phone were enlightening— they still are. Although for a teenager you don't text as much as most. I've been monitoring your texts—did you know I receive a copy of every text you send and every one you receive? One of my *goons,* as you are so fond of calling them, installed a monitoring chip in your phone that connects to my email."

"That's illegal!" I cried. "How dare you!"

The duke stared over my head. "She reacts to the tapping of her phone but not to the threat against the life of the gypsy prince?" He returned his gaze to me. "My dear, your priorities are slightly out of whack."

I clenched my teeth and bit back a response. I gripped the arms of the chair and tried to control my breathing. How dare he judge me.

"With my queen's blessing I am prepared to vacate the order against your precious gypsy prince. And just so you know, I am aware of what happened at Brenton Point in December. I know that your gypsy saved my son's life. Obviously I cannot allow an act of that magnitude to go unrewarded. But you will have to do your part. And now we need to talk about Andrew."

I made a concerted effort to control my breathing. My heart was on the verge of pounding out of my chest and every hair on my head tingled. I was amazed that I had not broken down yet. I hoped I could survive this nightmare without falling apart.

"Are you aware of the fact that Andrew is in love with you?"

I let another pent up breath slowly escape from my lungs as I nodded.

"Andrew is a good boy. He has a good heart and he has never given me a moment of trouble over the years—for the most part. And his happiness is essential to me. He wants nothing more than to marry you and make a life with you. How do you feel about that?"

I was shocked to hear these words even though they weren't exactly news to me. But to hear the duke say it freaked me out. Had Andrew told him this? Or had the ever-present, eavesdropping goons told him? I was stunned. And now the duke wanted an answer. "I care very much for Andrew. And, yes, I agree that his happiness is important. But marriage? That's a bit…much, don't you think?"

"It's what he wants. I already have one son who is broken—physically, Laura. But I won't stand by and allow my other son to be broken, too. Not when the solution—*the key*—to his happiness is so easy to provide."

I sat up straighter in the chair. "What are you saying?" My stomach threatened to fail me—I forced myself to breathe in slowly through my nose and out through my mouth to keep what little food I'd eaten lately down. I was shaking inside to the point that I was amazed I had not toppled onto the floor.

"I'm saying that you will make a beautiful bride. You will make my son the happiest man on earth." He stood then and came around to the front of the desk and leaned back against it. He was now only about a foot away from me. I wanted to get up and run but there was nowhere to go. I knew that the door was locked. I wouldn't be surprised if this room were soundproof, too.

"I'm too young to get married. So is Andrew." It was all I could think to say.

"People tend to marry young in royal circles, Prince William notwithstanding."

"But I don't want to marry Andrew. I care for him, yes, but…" I stopped myself. I feared anything I said could be used against me somehow.

"You had better more than care for him, Laura. You had better care for him as much as you care for your gypsy. Do you understand what I'm telling you, Laura?" He leaned toward me and I sank back into the chair.

"I...don't...know...I'm...not sure...," I stammered. I was confused now—not sure what answers to give—what was the right thing to say or the wrong thing.

"Let me explain it so you understand. If you want that gypsy thief—thief fits him so much better than prince—to live, then you will marry Andrew. It's that simple." He folded his arms across his chest and looked at me smugly.

"Andrew will never go for this. He would...*ooh!*" In a flash the duke was in my face, his hands on the arms of my chair. I could smell his stale, hot breath on my face and I shrank back in fear. I felt the tears forming and I couldn't stop them from falling.

"Andrew will never know about this conversation. *No one will.* Is that clear?" When I didn't answer, he said it again—more menacingly this time. "*Is that clear?*"

I nodded and turned my face away from his awful breath and his dark, hate-filled eyes.

"How are you parents, Laura?" His voice was cold and calculating.

"Fine. Why?" I choked out the two words.

"Fine, you say? Are you sure about that? I heard a rumor your mother might be losing her job. A take-over of some sort? The Royal Bank of Scotland, isn't it? And speaking of take-overs...I've always loved architecture. I will enjoy revamping Hansen-Lafayette Partners."

"No!" I cried out and made to jump up from the seat but the duke pushed me back down hard into the chair.

"Stay seated, Laura. We're not finished yet."

"You're behind my parents' losing their jobs? What kind of monster are you?"

"Again with the priorities, Laura. You don't get this upset when I mention your gypsy prince's precarious hold on life. Marrying Andrew shouldn't be such a hardship for you then, should it?"

"You don't know anything about how I feel about Miguel. His life is the most important thing to me!" I spat out the words and hoped I showered his royal highness with my saliva.

"Let me get to the point, Laura Michelle Calder. It's as easy as one-two-three. You marry Andrew—whom I know you care for, so it won't exactly be a hardship for you—and your mother keeps her bank job, your father keeps his architecture job and your precious gypsy gets to live. It is absolutely that simple. Do you understand?"

The duke stepped away from me then and circled around me, stopping behind my chair. I felt his hands come down hard on my shoulders. I cried out in pain.

"Sh, sh…Laura. Listen carefully. You will tell no one about our chat of this evening. *No one.* You will not even talk about this to your own reflection in the mirror. That's how secret this is. Oh, don't worry. There are others involved. You will be followed twenty-four seven. Your every move monitored. Your parents keep their jobs, Miguel Dos Santos gets to live—even your brother Nicholas can have a nice, safe life, as long as you do this one simple thing for me. Marry my son and make him happy. It's that easy. As I said, it's not like it's going to be a hardship. You'll get to have a nice life, an education, fine clothes, fine foods and wines, the best of everything. Congratulations, Laura. You just won the lottery."

I shook under his hands. I tried to contain my sobs but I couldn't. I was going to be sick if I didn't get out of here. But he wasn't done with me yet.

"You'd better be a damned good actress, Laura. Because if anyone sees through your charade, Miguel Dos Santos will be the first to go. The plan is already in place. All it will take is one phone call from me and *poof*! He's gone. Just like that. So what do you say? Are you up for the challenge?" His hands were tight on my shoulders. I thanked my lucky stars I'd had sense enough to hide the talisman.

I stared straight ahead but saw nothing. My peripheral vision no longer worked and everything in front of me seemed to fade in and out. I struggled to breathe and remain still in the chair. The duke's hands on my shoulders were pushing me down into the chair rendering me immobile. I felt the weight of the world on my shoulders literally and figuratively. Hot tears continued to roll down my face and I wanted to scream for help but I knew it would be pointless. Finally the duke relaxed his hold on me and came back around in front of me. He leaned against the desk and folded his arms across his chest and stared down at me, waiting. I knew I had to say something, but what?

My mind swirled with thoughts and faces and voices. My parents who had worked so hard for their livelihood, our home and well-being. I saw their faces and I knew I had to protect them. And Nick—the thought of anything happening to my brother made my blood run cold. Miguel—whom I loved—his life meant more to me than anything in this equation and I knew I could never in a million years allow his life to be taken out of my own selfishness. I convinced myself that this was a small price to pay considering the alternative. If I agreed to the duke's demands, my parents and brother would be safe and Miguel could have a life without having to look over his shoulder every day wondering when or if the duke would send one of his goons to kill him. I could do this—make this one small sacrifice—and someday I would find a way out.

"I'll do it. I'll marry Andrew."

The duke grinned. "Excellent decision, Laura. I knew you would do the right thing. Of course, you're going to have your work cut out for you, you know. I expect you to be very convincing. Andrew must have no doubts of your love for him. It shouldn't be that hard—he's easy to love, don't you agree?"

I didn't answer. How easy it was to love Andrew was a moot point as far as I was concerned. I wished this monster would finish his ranting so I could leave.

"As for your gypsy boy…I want you to stay away from him. As far as I'm concerned you've seen the last of him. And don't even think about trying to get a message to him—you will get caught and he will die. It might even happen right in front of you. Remember, you are being watched around the clock. You will never be alone."

I closed my eyes and tried to focus on my beating heart. It was racing so fast I thought I might be having a heart attack—heart failure at eighteen. It could be worse, I guessed. He continued.

"Your parents aren't going to like this next bit…" He stopped and stared down at me, grinning as I gasped. *What next bit?* He put his hand on his chin as if in contemplation. "But when we have dinner and get to know each other they will understand. They will understand why I feel Tristan's recovery will progress at a faster and more optimal rate if we take him home to England, back to our estate where he can recover in the comfort of his own home with our personal physicians. Tristan's health and recovery are top priority. They will understand that as Andrew's future wife you will have many lessons in royal protocol to learn—hmm, maybe I can get the team that schools the Duchess of Cambridge—Kate has been such a quick study. She is such a lovely girl. You will like her. But I digress. They will understand that you can complete your high school education in England and attend college there. It's going to be your new home after all. You'll love England—it isn't all doom and gloom as people might have you believe. Are you with me so far, Laura?"

All I could do was nod…and shake.

"Excellent. I will have my secretary arrange a lovely dinner to meet your parents so we can get them on board with our plans. We will be returning to England in just a couple of weeks—mid-March. I want to make sure you have enough time to tell your friends good-bye. They are going to be so envious of you—marrying a prince. Please don't concern yourself with a lot of packing. You'll need a new wardrobe—something more suitable than your current attire." He looked down on me then, waving his hand over my clothes.

"When you leave here tonight, Laura, you will go home and think about all of the things we have discussed this evening. If you have questions you can call me anytime." He walked behind his desk and opened a drawer. He pulled something black out of it and came back around and handed it to me. It was a cell phone. "This is your new phone. Your old one is already gone."

My phone—in my coat pocket—my coat, which Peter took from me when I arrived earlier. It was gone forever I was quite sure. I took the phone with shaking hands. I had to resist the urge to throw it with all my force at the duke's fat head.

"I realize that things are happening quite fast. We'll be announcing the engagement very soon and releasing a statement to the press. Perhaps we should move you in here—for your own protection, of course, although I'm sure your parents would want to be with you as much as possible so maybe that won't be necessary. And soon we will be off to England. I am so anxious to get my family back home. Do you have any questions so far?"

Questions? I really only had one question…and it frightened me to ask it. "How am I supposed to do this?"

"Laura, Laura, Laura. It is simply miraculous what one can do when one's loved ones' lives and welfare are on the line. I recommend you just have fun with it. Go with the flow as they say. You'll get used to your new life and soon you'll realize you weren't really living before. Doesn't every girl want to be a princess? Don't answer that. It was rhetorical."

I was stunned…in shock. What had I agreed to? How had this situation spiraled so far out of control? Could I pull this off? I swallowed the bitterness on my tongue and told myself I could do whatever it took to keep Miguel alive. I could never assume that the duke was bluffing. I had to take him seriously. There would be no gambling with my family's future or Miguel's life. I could do this and I would be convincing. I wouldn't even allow myself to think about Andrew's' part in this—he would be in the dark about it all—oblivious to all the lies and deceit. He would be a pawn in this madness, not even realizing it was all a sick game. I almost felt sorry for him and his ignorance. He deserved better.

"Well, then, if there are no further questions, I can let you go now."

I wanted to get up but my legs were numb. I was chilled to the bone and every fiber of my being was like pudding. My face felt hot as fire but my hands were two blocks of ice. I felt sick and exhausted. I tried to regulate my breathing and compose myself. The duke pressed a button on the phone and a green light flashed on the dial for just a second.

"Peter will be here in a moment to take you home. Listen carefully, Laura. You will go home and act completely normally—whatever you have to do to make that happen, do it. Andrew is going to pick you up tomorrow and the two of you are going to rekindle your romance. Remember, Andrew is coming to you from a pure place—a place of love and devotion. He knows nothing about any of the things you and I have discussed tonight. You should take comfort in that. You can always know that he loves you truthfully and honestly and I urge you to return the same love to him. You must be convincing at all times. Do not hurt my son. Do not ever break my son's heart. I *will not* have two broken sons. Do you understand me?"

I nodded and forced myself out of the chair. I had to get out of here. I needed air. There was a knock on the door.

"One moment, Peter," the duke called out. I started to walk toward the door but the duke grabbed my arm. "Oh, Laura. I almost forgot. There is one more, tiny thing I need from you. Just a small thing.

But it's important. It's sort of like insurance, I guess you could say. It's something that will serve a dual purpose. It will prove that your love for Andrew is real and also guarantee the future of the House of Hanover. It's something that takes on a new sense of urgency in light of Tristan's…condition."

My heart stopped. I shook his hand off my arm and stepped back trying to put distance between us. I thought my knees were going to buckle but I willed them to hold me up so I could get out of here. *Please don't let me fall.* My lungs were threatening to quit again. I didn't move as the duke gave his last command.

"I would like a grandchild. A grandson preferably, but a granddaughter will be acceptable, realizing that some things are beyond one's control. And don't keep me waiting long. I'd like to be a young grandfather. Just to be clear…I'm not asking…I'm ordering. Good night, my dear."

I heard the lock click and the door swung open. Peter was there with my coat. He put it on me and half-carried me down the corridor and out the back of the house to the waiting car. He settled me into the back seat and I felt his hands fastening the seatbelt around me. For one quick moment I thought I saw a look of sympathy in his eyes. He shut the door and drove me home. I sat in the back seat unmoving, statue-like. I was dead inside. I felt nothing now—not the heat from my cheeks or the cold that surely must be floating around me like breaths on a cold winter morning.

When we pulled into my driveway I snapped out of my trance, unbuckled my seatbelt and was out the door before Peter had even come to a complete stop. I let myself in quietly and hesitated at the bottom of the steps. In the living room sat my parents, going over their checkbooks. My mom called out hello to me as I ran on silent footsteps up the stairs. I croaked out a response as I ducked into my bathroom and locked myself in. I turned on the shower as hot as I could stand it and stood under the hot spray until the cold melted away. I didn't know how I had survived this day. How would I survive the days to come? How would I survive Andrew tomorrow? Could I be convincing? Could I love him as I once had? Could I…have his baby? Oh my god. My mind went instantly to Miguel then. I would have to find a way to tell him good-bye. I would never see him again. And I knew that would be the one thing I would not survive. I sank down into the tub and sobbed myself into a numbed state, staying there until the water ran cold.

Chapter Twenty Four

End of the Beginning

When I awoke in the morning I realized that school was now completely irrelevant. I didn't have to worry about homework anymore or tests or essays or final exams. I would not be graduating with the class of 2012. I choked on a sob at the thought. As it was, I couldn't have gone to school today if someone had paid me. My head throbbed and my eyes were so swollen from endless crying that I was sure I must look as if I'd spent the night in a beehive. I thought about my cell phone and wondered if anyone had been trying to reach me—Miguel or Andrew or Lily or Gretchen. Thinking of my two best friends brought on a fresh wave of grief. I wished I had been a better friend to them. I hoped they would not forget me. I would have to tell my dad to cancel my phone. I'd say I lost it and he would believe me—it wouldn't be the first time that had happened anyway.

The house was quiet. My parents would already have left for work—to jobs they still feared they were about to lose. Nick would be at school. I knew I needed to eat something but there was no way I could trust my stomach to keep food down. In the kitchen, I poured a glass of orange juice and took it back up to my room. Then I took another shower and went about trying to make myself look human again. Once I had dressed and applied some make-up I felt a little better, although my eyes were still puffy and my complexion was ghastly. I was just about to go downstairs and make an attempt to put some toast in my stomach when I heard the doorbell ring. I froze at the top of the steps. I prayed that whoever was at the door was just someone collecting for charity or wanting to convert me to some religion. I walked down the steps and peered through the small window. It was Andrew.

I grabbed my stomach and suppressed a wave of nausea. I wasn't ready for this. I was not a Hollywood actress. I couldn't pull this off—but I knew I had to try. For Miguel and my parents and my brother, I would give it my all. I opened the door.

"Hey, Andrew," I smiled, trying to make the smile reach all the way to my eyes. "I was beginning to think you'd forgotten about me."

Without saying a word, he was over the threshold and pulling me into his arms. I knew my body was stiff and I tried to loosen my muscles. I reminded myself that Andrew was just as innocent as every other victim in this game and I knew I had to play my part well.

He tilted my face up to his. "I've missed you. When I didn't see you at school this morning I had Peter drive me here. I needed to make sure you were alright. Are you...alright?" He was studying my face and I was sure he was seeing the puffy eyes and pale skin. I must look frightful.

"I've been a little...sick. But I'm better now—now that you're here." Wow. I hadn't planned to say that. I was surprised at how easily the words had slipped out of my mouth.

"I've missed you." He cupped my face in his hands and pressed his lips gently to mine. His kiss was sweet and tender and I returned it in kind. He pulled me closer and I felt the heat of his skin against my face. I breathed in his scent—a light, citrusy aftershave—and I tucked my head into his neck and wrapped my arms around him. We stood like that, not speaking for a minute. I controlled my thoughts by remembering how I used to feel with Andrew. I resolved that I would feel that way again—for however long it would take to extricate myself from the duke's clutches. He pulled back from me and studied my face again. "Is your family here?" he asked, looking over my shoulder toward the living room.

"No, they're at work. Nick's at school. It's just me."

"Good. Let's sit. I want to talk to you, OK?" I nodded and we went into the living room and sat down on the couch. He shrugged out of his coat and I noticed his clothing—black dress shirt and dark jeans. I had never really paid much attention to the details of his wardrobe before but I did now. I felt as if I needed to be on guard and hyper-aware of my surroundings now—at all times—so I didn't slip up and make a mistake. I needed to see everything and hear everything and know everything so I could be prepared for whatever the future held. I needed to try to make myself feel something, but then again, this was Andrew in front of me—sweet, kind, loving Andrew. As the duke had said, how hard could it be?

"I can't go on like this anymore. The long stretches of time without seeing you, Laura. Now that Tristan is recovering, I want you to know I'm back and I'm here to stay—with you. That being said, I have to tell you something—something that just came up. Father feels it's best if we move Tristan home to England. He thinks Tristan will be happier in our home among familiar things. So we're going soon—in a couple of weeks. But I cannot be without you. So I'm asking you again…to come with me to England. I know we're too young to get married. I get that. But I don't want to live without you. I love you so much and I need to know if you love me, too. We can do it on your terms. You can call the shots. But I want you. I will fight…" he stopped for a moment, searching for a word, "*whoever* I have to, to make you mine—to prove how much I love you."

I felt my ever-present tears well up. They started their slow descent down my cheeks. I knew I had to give Andrew what he wanted but I had to make sure Miguel would be OK. Just thinking his name felt like a million stabs of a knife in my heart. "What about the vendetta? You're supposed to be fighting Mi…Miguel," I stumbled over his name, "on March 12. If you love me, then that cannot happen."

Andrew reached for my hands and brought them to his lips, kiss-ing each one. "I know. I will meet with him as planned at midnight at Brenton Point. But I promise I won't try to kill him. I truly never wanted that. I'm not an evil person, Laura. Tristan didn't want that either. We'll make a truce and go our separate ways and live in peace—just as you want. But Laura, I need to know something. Do you love Miguel?"

I closed my eyes and resisted the urge to pull my hands from his grasp. My heart thudded as I considered how to answer this loaded question. I didn't want to lie but I knew the truth would lead to Miguel's death so I had to find a way to answer Andrew's question that would protect Miguel and also assuage my conscience. I opened my eyes and squeezed Andrew's hands tightly—so tightly he moaned and raised his eyebrows at me in surprise. And then I gave him an answer that I knew I could live with. "Not in the same way I love you. Not even close."

He pulled his hands from my tight grasp and took me in his arms then and held me so tightly I couldn't breathe or move. His lips were on my cheek, my jaw, my mouth. He kissed me as if his life depended on it—with a raging surge of passion. He had interpreted my words exactly as I knew he would. I turned my head for a quick second to catch a breath of air and he kissed me again, his tongue finding mine. I went numb inside but forced myself to react—to his touch, his kiss, his desire. And little by little he wore me down until I felt passion begin to stir inside me. And that's when I broke off his kiss, pushing him back and taking deep gulps of air. "Wow," I said.

"I'm sorry, sweetheart. I got carried away. It's just so amazing to hear you say those words that I've waited so long to hear. I love you so much. Come here, darling." He leaned back against the couch and opened his arms to me. I settled myself into his body and lay my head against his chest. I felt the thumping of his heart under my cheek. I felt his warmth and for the first time, I felt a new kind of fear. The duke wanted a grandchild. As much as I knew I was willing to do anything to save my family and Miguel, I wasn't sure I could fulfill that com-mand. But that was a long way off—I had time to figure it out. Now I pushed the thought away as Andrew rubbed his hand up and down my arm. He cleared his throat then, took me by the arms, and pushed me up. "So, my love…what are your terms? I said you could call the shots. Will you come to England with me? We can go to school there—finish high school and then college—and when you're ready…" He stopped and changed tack. "Or maybe I can convince Father to let me finish school here and then we can go to England after graduation. What do you think? I know it's a lot to take in."

It *was* a lot to think about it—for most people. I would love to stay here and finish school with my friends whom I'd known my whole life—Lily and Gretchen especially—but I knew the price that would be paid if I didn't do this the duke's way. I was certain I knew the answer he would want me to give Andrew and so I gave it. "I'll go anywhere with you—any time. You decide."

I saw the shock of my words as they registered in his eyes—he lit up like the sun. "Really? You'll come to England with me? I mean…I was prepared to beg if it came down to it," he laughed.

"Yes, I will come to England with you but I should tell you…my parents are a little conservative about shacking up." I had no idea if this was true or not—my parents had been on the verge of one of the most amicable divorces I'd ever seen so I doubted *conservative* was the right word to describe them. "Do you understand what I'm saying, Andrew?"

He jumped up then and pulled me to my feet. He grabbed me and swung me around, nearly knocking over a lamp and some framed photos on an end table. "I'm sorry but you have no idea how happy you're making me right now! I don't know what I did to deserve this but I would do it again a million times! I love you." He kissed me then and tangled his hands in my hair. He kissed my cheeks and my chin and my nose and finally he rested his lips on my forehead in a feather-light kiss. "I understand what you're saying and I agree with your parents." He pushed me gently down onto the couch and dropped to the floor on one knee. I gasped and covered my mouth with my hand. I wasn't ready for this. He took my hand—suddenly an ice cube—and looked into my eyes. I was thankful I'd thought to put on his ring this morning, thinking I'd better get used to wearing it, along with my talisman which was back around my neck—and strangely silent. "Will you do me the honor of marrying me, Laura Calder? I promise to love you forever and we won't have to live in sin for long—just until after graduation. What do you say?"

I swallowed audibly and looked into his eyes. He was so damned earnest all the time. I leaned down and wrapped my arms around his shoulders. I swallowed my nerves. "Yes."

He laid his head in my lap and I looked down at his silky blond hair. I touched my hand to it, feeling its softness. I had a vision of black hair in my hands—of Miguel's head on my lap—and I bit back a sob. I cleared my throat to mask the sound and Andrew lifted his head and turned his face to me. He saw the tears sliding down my cheeks and he wiped them away.

"I promise I'll you get you a new ring to replace the one I lost. But I'm glad you're wearing this one. It can be a place holder for now." He rubbed his finger across the ring. "Will you come to my house with me? I want to tell my parents the news. Or…maybe you're not ready?"

"I'm ready. I'll just get my coat." I got up and went to the front hall closet and pulled out my coat. The cell phone the duke had given me was still in the pocket. I reminded myself not to take it out—Andrew couldn't know about that yet. As I buttoned my coat over my throat I felt it—finally—the talisman was talking to me. I reached inside my sweater and picked up the disk—I felt it turn to ice in my hand. A soft cry escaped my lips and I dropped it fast, shoving it back down inside my sweater—its iciness hitting my chest and making me jump. I looked at my hand and saw a round red spot on my palm. Andrew came to me then and grabbed my hand in his.

"Wow, Laura, you're freezing." He lifted my hand to his lips and kissed the cold spot on my palm. I looked away. There was no misunderstanding the talisman's message this time.

This past hour with Andrew had been a mere quiz compared to the test that awaited me now. I couldn't help but notice the look Peter had given me when he'd opened the door for me in my driveway—I hadn't even realized he had been out here waiting for Andrew. The expression on his face made one word come to my mind—guilt—as if he felt some sense of remorse for being a part of this deceit. We drove to Newport and though I was aware that Andrew was talking beside me my mind kept trying to drift away. I was preparing myself for the duke and not feeling confident. But Andrew would carry me through—without even realizing, he would help me get through this.

The Duke and Duchess of Easton were in the salon when we arrived. Mrs. Easton greeted me warmly and I could tell by her demeanor and body language that she was just as much in the dark as Andrew. The duke appeared normal but I sensed a tenseness in his being, a coiled snake prepared to strike if necessary.

"We've just come from seeing Tristan. He is so happy about returning to England. Of course, he's concerned about his horses, but you'll see to them, won't you, dear?"said the duchess.

"I'll see to them alright. The one that hurt Tristan should have been destroyed on sight," he declared. He was standing at his usual spot by the window, the duchess seated on the settee.

"Father! Stop! It wasn't like the horse meant to hurt him. If you destroy the horse, you'll destroy Tristan," Andrew exclaimed. He gave me a look as if to say things weren't off to the best of starts. "Anyway… Mother…Father. Laura and I have something we want to tell you."

The duke turned from the window and walked toward us. His eyes rested on mine and I saw his body tense, saw his fists clench and unclench at his sides. "Please tell us. I hope it's good news—Lord knows we could use some," he said.

Andrew put his arm around my shoulder and drew me close. "Laura had agreed to come with us to England and even better—she accepted my proposal. We're going to be married."

The duchess jumped from her seat and rushed to us both. She drew us into her arms and cried, "This is so wonderful, Andrew…and Laura. I'm so happy for you both. Don't let anyone judge you because of your youth. The duke and I weren't that much older than you when we married. This is the best possible news. We needed this—needed something to celebrate. Have you told your family yet, dear?"

"No. Andrew only just proposed a little while ago." The duchess hugged me again and then went over to the duke.

"Isn't this wonderful news, Ernst?" She embraced him.

"It is indeed. Come here, you two," he said. We walked toward him. I was thankful for Andrew's hand to hold. I felt myself turn to stone when the duke's arms circled around us. I squeezed Andrew's hand and prayed he would never let it go. The duke released us then and walked back to his spot at the window. "We have a lot of plans to make and execute. We will be leaving in two weeks. I've already made the arrangements for Tristan's transport and medical needs for the flight. You two should go see him. He'll be glad to hear some good news. It'll help perk up his spirits."

"Laura," said the duchess. "We will need to get together in the next day or two to discuss your needs and wishes for the trip. I don't know what you two have planned exactly but this is all happening so fast, especially for you. Part of me says we should stay here and let you finish out the school year—there's such a short amount of time left—and yet we need to get Tristan home and he won't want to be separated from his brother. And you will be the sister he's always wanted. I can see already how much joy you're going to bring to our family."

I blushed crimson and looked down. *Wow. Dig the knives in deeper, please, I haven't felt enough pain yet.* "Thank you. I'm quite… excited…about everything."

We talked a few minutes more about the move and school and then the duke brought up my parents.

"We'll have your family to dinner and get to know them. I want them to be reassured that they are placing you in good hands," he said, a tad smugly or so I thought.

"I'm not sure my father is going to be thrilled with this engagement. He may need some convincing," I couldn't resist a little dig. Of course, it backfired instantly.

"Oh, I have a feeling he'll get used to the idea pretty quickly," said the duke, a villainous grin on his face. "After all, it's not every day a man's daughter becomes a princess. And besides, he'll be so busy with his work he won't have to time to dwell. I've been reading in the papers that there's going to be a boon in new construction around Providence—I hear architectural firms are placing bids on the new hospital—perhaps your father's firm will be the designers."

I puffed out a breath and forced a smile. "I hope so," I said and looked away. I turned to Andrew then. "Maybe we should go. I'm actually starving. Would you like to go somewhere for a bite, Andrew?"

"Absolutely. I'm hungry, too." We said good-bye to his parents. They walked with us to the door and just as we were about to leave, the duke suddenly pulled me into his arms in a bear hug. "Welcome to our family, Laura," he said loudly enough for all to hear. But in my ear he whispered words meant only for me. "Well done." He let me go and I kept my eyes downcast as we left through the front doors.

The early days of March were a blur. I walked through them as if in a trance. My parents met the Eastons and though they were shocked at the news of our engagement, they seemed to take it in stride. They'd recently learned that their jobs were safe and so they had many reasons to celebrate. I was a little disappointed that they were so quick to allow me to drop out of Portsmouth and transfer to a school in London.

I had banked on their putting up a big fight about that, but it was not to be—it was like they'd lost their minds. And Mom mentioned that maybe marriage counseling was a better option than divorce and Dad had agreed. That had shocked the daylights out of me, but in a good way. Nick thought my pending nuptials were the coolest thing in the world and he was also ecstatic to have been given the go-ahead to visit Tristan at the hospital.

Tristan had taken our news in stride, too. It was my first time visiting him and I was nervous as hell. I had never known anyone who was paralyzed before and I was afraid of saying the wrong thing. But he was sweet and gracious and I felt like I was seeing the old Tristan. He was sitting in a wheelchair by the window, reading a book when Andrew and I arrived. Nick had visited earlier in the day and had brought him lots of reading material.

"So I hear congratulations are in order," he smiled.

I couldn't believe how nervous I was. My insides were churning and I felt dizzy. I didn't know what I had expected regarding Tristan but he seemed…normal. It was like he was just sitting in any old chair and any minute he would get up and walk across the room.

"Thanks," Andrew said. "You up for being my best man?"

"If you don't mind my rolling down the aisle instead of walking, then, yeah, I'm up for it." Tristan gave a little laugh. "Welcome to the family, Laura. I've always wanted a sister."

"Thank you. I'm…happy…to be your sister. I see Nick brought you plenty of reading material. He mentioned he was going to Barnes and Noble last night. Looks like you're pretty well stocked up there."

"Yes, he has good taste. I'm excited to read them all."

We talked a while longer and soon it was time to go. As we got up to leave, Tristan asked Andrew to give him a moment alone with me.

"You're not going to try to scare her off, are you?" Andrew laughed. Tristan just smirked and waved him out of the room.

I walked over to him and sat beside him in the chair Andrew had been sitting in earlier. To say I was scared was an understatement. I grasped my knees to keep them from knocking together and held my breath as I waited for him to speak.

"I just wanted to tell you that…I know my father can be hard to deal with. And I know he can be scary. But, Laura, always remember that you have an ally in me. I know so much more than anyone gives me credit for about the past and about the present. Only the future is a mystery. But there are always clues. I don't mean to be cryptic but just know you can come to me if you ever need someone to talk to. And, Laura, take care of Andrew. He really loves you and you two can have something I will never have now…now that I'm…this." He waved his hands over his still legs. "So take care of that, will you? Be good to my brother, yeah?"

Tears streamed down my face faster than I could wipe them away. He reached for my hand and it was hard to tell whose was the coldest. This dear sweet boy was giving me his blessing and something more. "I will." I could barely get the words out. "Thank you, Tristan."

"I'll see you soon. Now stop with the tears already. You're making me feel bad." He laughed then and the sound of it eased the pressure on my heart a little bit. I stood and leaned down and kissed his cheek.

"See you soon," I said, and walked out the door.

In the hall Andrew was waiting. He saw my tears but didn't say anything. He seemed to understand that what had occurred in Tristan's room was a private moment between us—either that or he had eaves-dropped. We left the hospital and he took me home. I had another troubled night of sleeping but I had a feeling that unless I invested in some heavy duty sleeping pills, then I'd better get used to insomnia.

I wanted desperately to talk to Miguel, but I had no way to con-tact him and I knew I couldn't drive to his house because the goons were never far away. I saw them everywhere. I had contemplated ways to evade them but fear of getting caught outweighed any bravery I thought I could muster. Besides, I wasn't sure what I could say to him without giving myself away. The temptation to go to him and beg him to run away with me was so strong it woke me up at night. But I knew the destruction I would leave behind. My parents would mysteriously lose their jobs, it would put Nick in danger and Miguel and I would be on the run, looking around every corner expecting the other shoe to drop. So I didn't try to see him.

I had Lily and Gretchen over and told them the news. They were in shock but happy for me. They chastised me for ignoring my texts and calls but forgave me when I told them I'd lost my phone some time ago and hadn't replaced it yet. They were sad I was leaving so soon and not graduating with our class but I assured them I wasn't a total drop-out—that I would finish in England.

The morning of March 12 I awoke from a fitful sleep. Today was the day of reckoning—the one that had been cancelled, but Miguel didn't know that. Andrew had told me he intended to meet Miguel as planned at midnight at Brenton Point and I'd told him I was going, too. He'd tried to talk me out of it, reminding me that they had agreed to come alone, but I was insistent.

"I have the right to tell him good-bye. If you try to stop me or have the goons stop me I'll find a way to get there. This is non-negotiable." Reluctantly he'd agreed.

I felt listless and out of sorts. I'd told Andrew that I needed to do some packing and cleaning so I could get my life in order before leaving for England. But there was something else I needed to do and it suddenly seemed to be the most vital part of my existence. I needed to find a way to get a message to Miguel. Somehow I had to let him know what was happening without giving away too much. I was afraid if news of my engagement was just sprung on him tonight he might snap and kill Andrew.

I sat at my desk with a piece of paper and a pen and I thought for a long time about what I wanted to say to him. I needed to let him know how much I loved him…that I always would…that I was sorry I was hurting him…and beg him to never forget me. Finally I wrote:

> Dear Miguel:
> I'm writing this note to you to tell you good-bye. I've decided to move to England and start a new life with Andrew. I know this probably doesn't make sense to you but I've thought it over carefully and I feel it's the right thing to do—the right direction to go with my life.
> I know you're really a prince and not a gypsy as everyone seems to think. I actually prefer gypsies to princes, but then I'm different that way. However, Andrew loves me very much and I know he needs

me so I'm going to marry him and try to make him happy. It seems fast, I know, but there's no good reason to wait—it's inevitable.

I need you to try very hard not to hate me. When I said I loved you, I meant it. I still do, but some things are just not written in the cards. I need for you to be happy and to know that no matter where you are in the world there is always someone who loves you. Now that the vendetta has been lifted you can live in peace and never have to worry or watch over your shoulder. Andrew never wanted to hurt you in the first place and you already know Tristan didn't either.

So, good-bye, Miguel. Please, please, please don't ever forget me. For all the times you saved me—over and over—I'm happy to return that favor now. I love you.

Laura

I could barely see to write the words. Right when I thought I couldn't possibly have another tear left to shed, a million more fell. I signed my name and folded the letter as small as I could make it and put it in my pocket. Now I just had to figure out how to get it to him. I would try to find a way tonight at Brenton Point. I thought of all of the times Miguel had saved me—from the convenience store robbery, to when I was lost in the maze and that night on the rocks at Brenton Point—and I was so happy to be able to do the same for him now—to know that by obeying the duke I was saving Miguel's life. For the first time since the duke pulled me into this web of deceit, I could finally see the rightness in this situation. For all Miguel had done for me, this was a sacrifice I could—I would—make for him.

I stood up from my chair and glanced out the window. The sun was shining—it was cool outside but a beautiful day just the same. Then a flash of white caught my eye on the lawn. My heartbeat quickened and

I turned from the window and raced down the stairs and out the front door. I hurried to the white patch on the ground and sank to my knees. It was a crocus—the first flower of spring. I pulled it from the ground and lifted it to my nose. I felt the soft cold petals brush against my lips. I looked at it in the palm of my hand and then I closed my eyes and made a fist, crushing it as tightly as my hand would allow. I opened my hand and dropped the mess of green and white onto the lawn, then stood and ground it hard into the earth with my foot. I would never look at springtime the same way again.

The duke had told Andrew about my new cell phone, citing a need for security. As I was about to become a member of a royal family I couldn't talk on an unsecured line, or so the duke had said. It sounded preposterous to me but Andrew seemed OK with it and happy to have another way to communicate with me when we were apart. I was not allowed to give out the number to anyone without clearing it with the duke first and that made my blood boil. I considered getting myself a cell phone on the sly but I knew the goons would find out and rat me out so I resisted the urge. Andrew and I had agreed not to use the cell phones today because he didn't want his father to find out about the midnight rendezvous with Miguel. I knew that the goons were following me so ditching them completely would be difficult. They were under the assumption that the midnight rendezvous had been cancelled. Andrew was planning to walk to Brenton Point, figuring he had a better chance of sneaking out on foot. He would leave sometime after eleven and I would meet him there. Now all I had to do was figure out how to escape undetected. I didn't know exactly where the goons were but from time to time I would see a black car drive slowly past my house so I knew they were out there somewhere watching.

My parents were home tonight watching a movie together and having popcorn. I popped into the living room and asked Mom if I could borrow her car to go meet Andrew for some ice cream.

"What's wrong with your Jeep?" my dad asked. "And where are you going to get ice cream this late?"

"The heater's a little dodgy and it's kinda cold." I crossed my fingers as I told the little white lie. "We're just getting cones at McDonald's—they're always open late."

"It's 'kinda cold' yet you're going out for ice cream, huh?" laughed my mother.

"Ha, ha...I know...crazy, right?" I faked a laugh.

"Sounds like the thermostat's on its way out. I'll check it tomorrow," said my dad.

Mom waved me away. "OK, honey. Drive safely. My keys are hanging by the door."

"Thanks, Mom." I grabbed them and ran upstairs to my room. I changed into jeans and a black t-shirt and slipped a black hooded sweatshirt over my head. I tucked the talisman inside my bra and put my hair up in a pony tail, then tucked it inside the hood. Downstairs I grabbed my coat and quietly walked out the side door to the garage. I got inside Mom's Honda and pressed the garage door opener. It opened noisily and I started the engine. I left the headlights off as I crept out of the garage. I hit the button again and watched the door close slowly in the rearview mirror, glad my parents preferred backing their cars in. I glanced at the clock on the dash. It was 11:40. I felt sick to my stomach as I drove in the darkness using the moonlight as my guide down the driveway. I hoped my parents weren't watching out the window and wondering why their crazy daughter was driving with the lights off. I sat at the bottom of the drive and waited two whole minutes before venturing out. There were no other cars on the road as I made my way to Brenton Point. Once there, I pulled into the parking lot and saw Andrew sitting in the darkness on a rock. The stars were out in full force and the moon was mostly full. I could hear the crashing of the ocean against the rocky shoreline. I was already a bundle of nerves and didn't know how I would make it through the next minutes. The thought of seeing Miguel again was messing with my head and my heart. I felt sick with worry and fear.

I got out and pulled my jacket tightly around me and felt the talisman burning against my chest. Before this night was over I was sure I would need skin grafting. I walked toward Andrew and he hugged me and kissed me, cupping my face in his hands.

"You OK?" he asked quietly.

"No." I decided to be honest. I took his hands away from my face and squeezed them before letting them go. I didn't want Miguel to see me with Andrew's hands on my face. It didn't seem like the best way to start things off. I slipped my hand in my pocket and felt my note there.

"It's going to be OK, sweetheart. There won't be any violence, don't worry."

I saw the headlights approach then. The Suburban pulled into the lot and parked across from my car. And I knew as soon as Miguel got out of his vehicle that things weren't going to go so well. He looked murderous as he walked toward us. I fought a wave of nausea and knew my tears were on the way.

"What the hell are you doing here, Laura? You shouldn't be here." Miguel spat out the words, his voice hostile.

"Miguel, it's OK…there's…" I started to speak, but Andrew stepped in front of me and stopped me from finishing my words.

"Laura—this is between him and me. Please stay out of it." I wrapped my arms around my body and stood to the side watching, fearing whatever was about to happen.

"Miguel…I'm not here to kill you or hurt you. The vendetta has been cancelled." Andrew stood five feet from Miguel. They eyed each other intensely. I held my breath as I waited for Miguel to react.

"Says who?" Miguel stood tensed, hands in fists at his sides, ready to spring at a moment's notice.

"Says me. It's barbaric. There's no need for violence. Let's just shake on it and go and live in peace." Andrew held out his hand to Miguel.

Miguel stared at Andrew's outstretched hand. Inside my mind I begged him to take Andrew's hand—to let this end without bloodshed.

"You're a coward, Easton. That's why the vendetta has been cancelled. Because you're afraid I just might win." He ignored Andrew's hand and took a menacing step forward.

Andrew stood his ground. I stepped forward ready to throw myself between them if I had to.

Miguel looked at me. In the moonlight I saw his face—so handsome and hurt. He must have already known. My absence had been noted at school and most everyone had probably heard through the rumor mill that I was moving to England.

"You can think whatever you like, Dos Santos, but I will not fight you." Andrew sounded calm and confident.

Miguel closed the distance between himself and Andrew, and in a move so fast I almost missed it, had Andrew by the collar of his coat, his face only a mere few inches from Andrew's. They were nose to nose but Andrew did not raise a hand to defend himself. His arms remained limp at his sides.

"You want to kill me, Miguel? In front of Laura?" Andrew's voice was a harsh whisper.

"You were supposed to come alone, remember?" Miguel tightened his grip on Andrew's collar and I saw Andrew's body shift against the pull but still he kept his arms hanging down at his sides.

I rushed forward then and grabbed at Miguel's arm. "He couldn't keep me away. I had to be here. Please don't fight. I'm begging you." Miguel shook my hand off his arm and released his grip on Andrew's collar. He looked at me. I wanted to take him in my arms so badly that I had to grip my jacket to stop myself. He seemed to be searching my face looking for something—answers, I guessed, to unspoken questions.

"Is it true? That you're moving to England and that you're going to…" He stopped, unable or unwilling to finish the question.

The word came out on a sob. "Yes."

He took a step back. "*Why?*" The hurt on his face was more than I could bear. I couldn't stop the tears that streamed down my face in torrents, blurring my vision.

To save you—and my family. Because I love you more than anyone else in this world. Because I would do anything for you. But I could not say those words. I had to lie. "Because I love Andrew…and he loves me." My tears poured, my nose was running and I felt lightheaded. "Miguel, I'm so, so sorry. Please forgive me."

"I don't believe you," he said, his voice deep, troubled.

"Well, it's true, Dos Santos. Laura has made her choice and you're just going to have to live with it," said Andrew. He stepped closer to me and I stared at them both. I wanted the ground to open up and swallow me so this nightmare would go away.

I had never felt an ache in my chest like the one I was experiencing now. It *hurt*…bad. I looked at Andrew's angry face—so handsome and strong—and Miguel's—so beautiful and pained. How could I be this kind of a monster? All I had to do was run toward Miguel and tell him it was all a lie and we could escape right now. We could outrun Andrew. He didn't even have a car. We could drive as far and as fast as the Suburban could go. I wanted to force my feet to move. I tried to make my arms reach out—willed my voice to call his name—but I couldn't. I couldn't take the risk.

"Well, this is…unexpected," said Miguel quietly. "I hope you two have a nice life then."

Oh, no. He was giving up. So fast…too soon. He was going to walk away and I would never see him again. I couldn't survive this. "Miguel! Please wait." I turned to Andrew then. "Andrew, can I speak to Miguel alone for just one minute?"

"I don't think that's a good idea, Laura. I think we're done here. Unless you want to shake on it, Dos Santos, and call a truce?"

"Please?" I begged them both. Andrew extended his hand again toward Miguel. Miguel looked down at it and I didn't think he would do it. I didn't believe he would touch Andrew. But he surprised me. He placed his hand in Andrew's and they shook once. Miguel wiped his hand down the front of his jacket and looked away toward the ocean.

"Andrew? Just one minute, please?" I reached my hands into both pockets. I handed him my car keys. "I'll be right there. Please. I just want to say good-bye."

Andrew frowned but he took the keys and with one more look at Miguel, he walked over to the car. As soon as I heard the door slam shut, I turned my back on the car and reached my hand out to Miguel. He was not inclined to touch me so I grabbed his hand and opened it, pressing my note inside it and then closing his fingers tightly over it. I hoped Andrew couldn't tell in the dim light what I had done. And then Miguel pulled something from his pocket—a folded piece of paper— and did the same to me—pressed it into my hand. I slipped it into my pocket and faced him.

"I'm so sorry, Miguel. I wanted to talk to you so many times but it's been hard. I lost my phone and I…"

He cut me off—his voice gruff, his face dark and hurt. "I knew you'd show up here tonight. And you don't have to explain anything to me, Laura. I don't understand why you're doing this, but it's your life. But you should know that no matter who you marry, it will never change the way I feel about you."

I looked down at the ground and fought back tears. "I know the story now—the whole story. I know about Princess Gabriela and the curse and…and…everything. I know you're a prince and not a gypsy. I know you're a good person and you have a good heart and I didn't lie to you…before…when…"

He touched a finger to my lips to shush me and tilted my face to meet his eyes. "Yet you're lying to me now, aren't you?" His voice was quiet and I heard the pain in his words. "Are you wearing your necklace?"

"Yes, it's here—around my neck."

"Keep it safe, Laura. Princess Gabriela once said that 'she who wears the golden talisman is the future of the House of Braganza.' From the moment I saw it around your neck, I wanted her words to be true. But fate has other things in store, I guess."

"I'm so sorry. I love you. I do. But I…," my voice broke.

"Don't say anymore, please. I can't stand it. You'd better not keep your fiancé waiting. He leaned toward me then and kissed my forehead feather-lightly—it was over so fast I barely had time to register his lips on my skin—and then he turned and walked away. I watched him get into his car and drive off. He was gone just like that. I wasn't ready to spend forever without him. I would never be ready for that. I stood statue-like until I could no longer see the lights of his car. I felt sick…dead inside…as if someone had wrenched out my heart and left a gaping hole in my chest.

I knew I had to get to the car before Andrew wondered what was wrong. My legs felt as if they were filled with wet sand as I made my way to the vehicle. My talisman was quiet—no more messages tonight, I guessed. I slipped my hand in my pocket and felt Miguel's note. Later when I was alone I would read it and I knew that each word on the page would widen the fissure on my heart that much further. Andrew had started the car and it was warm inside.

"Everything OK?" he asked.

Not only was everything not OK, it would never be OK again but I nodded anyway.

He reached for my face and caressed my cheek. "I know that was hard for you. I know you care about him. But he'll be alright. We all will be." He reached inside his coat pocket and pulled out a small box.

"I realize this isn't the best time to give you this, but I need you to have it now."

He opened the box and there nestled inside the velvet was a ring identical to the one that had fallen into the ocean. He removed it from the box and took my hand and slipped it on my finger. I stared at it in disbelief. I didn't want this ring. I wanted Miguel's ring. I wanted Miguel. I choked back a sob and fell into Andrew's arms. I didn't have the strength to even hold myself up anymore. He held me and stroked my hair and turned my tear-stained face to his and kissed me. "I love you so much and I will do everything in my power to make you happy and feel safe and cherished. Do you trust me?"

I remembered a time when someone else had asked me that question and I wished now that I had trusted him more. There were so few people I *could* trust, especially myself. But I could trust Andrew. "Yes, of course I do." He kissed me again but my heart wasn't in it. I was too exhausted. "I'm so tired."

"I know, baby. I'll have you home soon. I can call Peter to pick me up."

I sat up then, remembering he'd walked here. "Oh, no. I can take you home. I'm not so tired that I can't drive myself home."

He started to protest but I cut him off. "No, really. I'm fine." We drove the short distance to his house and he kissed me good-night.

"I love you. I'll see you tomorrow." He waved and I waited until he was inside before I drove off. As I headed home I considered driving to Miguel's house. We could still get away. We could be long gone before anyone noticed. I had a passport. We could go to Portugal. We could go live with gypsies somewhere. We had options. But I knew I was too afraid to make that leap. Suddenly I just wanted to be home so I could read Miguel's note. I parked in the garage and let myself in quietly and went to my room. I sat at my desk and unfolded the paper. I was struck by the beauty of his handwriting. And I had been right. Every word on the page caused the crack in my heart to widen.

Dear Laura,

If you're reading this letter, it means I'm not dead, otherwise I wouldn't have been able to give it to you. But if Andrew is, then I'm on the run. That being said, I truly don't believe anyone is going to die tonight. Andrew is not a killer and neither am I.

    I know you've agreed to move to England and marry him. Word gets around. I don't understand your choice but I trust that you have your reasons. But I couldn't live with myself if I didn't say this. I need to make sure you know without any doubt that I love you. You once told me you loved him but you were in love with me. I may never know what made you change your mind, but I will never hold it against you. I don't have it in me to do anything but love you.

    So always remember that no matter where you are in the world, there is someone who loves you more than anyone else does. I will think of you every day and I'll be looking for your face in the crowds. I will never forget the taste of your kiss or the feel of your hand against my face. And I will never ever forget what might have been.

    Be safe, Laura, and don't forget me. Remember your necklace. Protect it with everything you have. Because, some day, if the world ever decides to make sense again, your left hand will wear the ring that matches the talisman. I'm saving it for you. I love you.

    Miguel

I moved like a robot as I folded the note and put it away in a safe place. I would cherish it forever. I fell onto my bed and cried myself to sleep. Before I slipped into complete unconsciousness, I sent a silent request to the ruler of the universe that I wouldn't wake up in the morning.

EPILOGUE

Saying good-bye to my parents at the airport was one of the hardest things I'd ever done. But they promised to come for graduation in June. I was going to finish my high school education at the American School in London in their semester abroad program. Andrew was going to finish at the Royal Exeter Academy, the school he'd been attending before his family had moved to Rhode Island. Tristan was going to begin intensive physical therapy at the Queen Elizabeth Royal Hospital. He would never walk again but he planned to be strong in every other way.

Though I would be living in Andrew's home, I had been told that I would have my own private apartment there so that my parents would feel better about the living arrangements. I suspected they didn't really mind one way or another but I liked the idea of having my own private place.

We had set a tentative wedding date for September 12, but nothing had been officially decided. If Andrew had his way we would be married already. He was pushing for a summer wedding.

The duke assigned a security detail to me and they were just like the goons—and one was a female. I knew it would be hard to have servants around me and I'd already decided that I wouldn't give them much to do—no one was going to clean up after me.

I settled into the seat next to Andrew and watched as the plane began its journey over the Atlantic Ocean. I realized I was still clutching my passport. I pulled out my carry-on bag and as I slipped it into the side pocket a memory washed over me. A memory from that carnival I went to with Lily and Gretchen in Watch Hill last August—a summer day that seemed like a lifetime ago now. That psychic—what was her name? Madame Jeanette? She'd asked me if I had a passport and I'd said yes. She'd told me I was going to the land of the gypsies. *Did they have gypsies in London*? I wondered.

I'd decided I had to be my own advocate for good mental health. I knew if I dwelled on Miguel I would never be able to function in society. I also knew that there was no one on earth I could confide in so I determined that I would overcome my sadness on my own and be the best fiancée I could be to Andrew. There was no reason for him to suffer just because I was miserable and I couldn't let him see my misery anyway. The duke and his goons watched me like a hawk and I knew that neither the duke nor I could ever let our guards down around each other. He would always be watching…waiting for me to make a mistake. And then there was Tristan. Without even realizing it, he was helping me more than anyone else ever could. If he could find a way to triumph over his tragedy which was so much worse than mine, then who was I to complain about my lot in life? I remembered his telling me he was my ally and I decided that if the burden to please the duke and keep the secret was ever more than I could bear, I would go to him and confess everything—and let the chips fall where they may. But I knew I would have to think long and hard before I chose that path. I always had to remember that my family and Miguel were dependent on me for their lives, even though they didn't know it.

And so I closed my eyes and let my mind drift. I only allowed myself to think happy thoughts. It was my strictest of rules. When I closed my eyes for sleep, only happy thoughts were allowed in. The flight attendant came by and offered us blankets. I took mine and covered myself. Andrew was reading next to me. Under the blanket I pulled out my necklace and held the disk in my hand. I rubbed my fingers over the surface to feel the grooves in it where the emblem was on one side and the swords were on the other. I rubbed harder and furrowed my brow. The disk felt smooth—I couldn't feel the grooves anymore. I felt a weird sense of panic and dropped it back inside my shirt. I excused myself to go to the bathroom. Once inside I pulled the talisman out and stared at it in shock. Every etching that had ever been on it was gone. It was as if it had been rubbed clean and was now completely smooth on both sides. I gasped in shock and let it fall to my chest. I gripped the edge of the sink and tried to avoid looking at my reflection. And then in the mirror I saw it…talking to me again… glowing…sending me a message…trying to help me…or warn me…I didn't know which. But it was definitely making its presence known. I picked it up in my hand and felt its heat radiate across my palm and into my wrist and snake its way up my arm. It was blank on the side facing up but in my palm I felt new lines engraving themselves into the coin. My hand shook and my knees knocked together. My lungs felt on the verge of collapse as I waited for the engraving to stop. And then it did. It glowed red for one moment and then went gold again. With trembling fingers and my heart in my mouth I turned the coin over in my hand and stared at the one word newly engraved upon it: *Miguel.*

To be continued in…
The Dark Prince

Check out this sneak preview of Book Two in the Talisman Trilogy: *The Dark Prince*

The Dark Prince

PROLOGUE

LAURA

They say that the universe is unfolding exactly as it should, even though it may not seem like it at the time. My universe was tangled and confused. I kept seeing a series of befores and afters: *before* I sat rather reluctantly inside a psychic's tent and *after* her ominous words unfolded in dark truths around me; *before* I met a prince and fell in love with his sweetness and innocence and *after* I met a gypsy and fell in love with *him*—mind, body and soul; *before* I knew what real pain and sorrow were and *after* when all I knew were pain and sorrow day in and day out. If my universe were truly unfolding exactly as it should, then why did it have to hurt? Why didn't I get a say in my own journey? How could my life have changed so drastically in such a short time through no obvious fault of my own? But perhaps it *was* my fault that I had ended up here, on this journey of despair. The psychic had said the words and I should have paid more attention: *"Your fate is sealed. Already I can see that it cannot be undone. It is what it shall be. That being said, you do have the power of choice. Always choose wisely but still knowing that your destiny has already been determined. The outcome will be the same but you have the power to make the pathway to your providence easy or difficult...short or long...happy or sad. Choose wisely."* I had to admit to myself that I had not chosen wisely. I had made a mistake. And now I had to find a way to fix it or choke to death on the tangled mess that was my universe.

Chapter One

Bonds

I never would have thought that my first time overseas would be under such strange circumstances. If someone had told me six months ago that I would move to London before graduating from high school I would have laughed myself into a state of hysteria. Everything about my life had taken on a sense of the absurd. I was in a state of uncertainty and fear twenty-four hours a day. But thank goodness for Andrew and Tristan. They had become my unwitting lifelines in this new world I was navigating. As long as one of them was near, I felt like I could survive another day. And I had school to keep me busy. For the first time ever, I actually liked school. I liked being in the classroom and forced to concentrate on something other than the dilemma that dominated my life.

Andrew and I and his family were living in the Easton mansion in London while we finished our senior year of high school. I was attending the American School and Andrew was at the Royal Exeter Academy. The schools were on opposite sides of London so we each had our own driver taking us to and from school each day. And somewhere in the heart of London was the Queen Elizabeth Royal Hospital where Tristan went daily for physical therapy. Already his upper body had grown so strong that he could beat every one of the goons that made up the Easton security detail in arm wrestling. He was quite proud of that feat. I loved watching him arm wrestle—it made me happy in the strangest way. I had taken to doing my homework in whatever room Tristan was in. There was something about him that made me feel safe. The fact that he was paralyzed from the waist down and in a wheelchair for the rest of his life made no difference to the security I felt when I was near him. Andrew had noticed the friendship developing between me and Tristan and one day he commented on it when we were alone in the lavish gardens behind the mansion.

"I can't help but notice that you and Tristan seem to be getting along quite well. That's nice," he said as we walked along a row of pink and white tulips. The brilliant spring sunshine shone down on us—a change from the rainy, dreary weather that had dominated my first weeks in England.

"Tristan's amazing. I admire everything about him." I said the words rather gushingly, knowing them to be the truth.

"Should I be jealous?" Andrew asked with a laugh. Even though he was making light of it, I sensed his insecurity.

"Yes, you should be," I said with a grin, playing into his fears. Andrew had no idea why I was so close to Tristan. No one did. No one knew just how much I needed Tristan—more than I needed anyone else, except for the one person I couldn't have. Tristan himself didn't even know how he saved me every day from sinking into a depression that I knew I would never get out of if I allowed it to consume me.

"Oh? Well, in that case, I think you'd better stay away from him for a while," Andrew said, plucking a tulip from the row and handing it to me. I couldn't tell if he was being serious but I sensed he was. I glanced up at him and tried to gauge his demeanor. He looked serious enough.

"Hey, don't be jealous. I just feel a kindred spirit in Tristan is all. You have my heart, Andrew. You know that." Every time I heard words like that coming out of my mouth I questioned my own sanity. I did love Andrew—truly I did. But it was a quiet love that I would have preferred to keep to myself. I was not in love with him as I once thought I had been—as I may have been if I had not met a certain gypsy prince who had my heart and always would until the end of time. But I was not allowed to think about Miguel. Just saying his name in my head was enough to knock the air out of my lungs and bring me to my knees. And that was exactly why I needed Tristan. Because fate had dealt him a blow much worse than mine—a blow he handled with such grace and dignity that I knew my problems were nothing compared to his. I told myself every day that I had no right to feel sorry for myself when Tristan was not letting his disability stop him from living a full life. So my heart was disabled. So it had been broken into a million pieces. But it still beat inside my chest, just as Tristan's did. I was alive and mobile. I knew that Tristan had gone through his dark time when he'd wanted death more than one more breath. And he still had to fight those demons every day. I admired his spirit and spending time with him helped heal my heart little by little, enough to live another day.

"I'm sorry, love. I was feeling insecure. Sometimes you seem to be somewhere else in your head and I worry that you're not happy here— that you're missing your family and your home in America." He took my hand and pulled me to him, wrapping his arms around me. I felt his heartbeat beneath my ear and I listened to its rhythm and felt the rise and fall of his lungs under my cheek.

"I do get homesick sometimes but it isn't anything I can't handle," I whispered against his chest. "Why don't we pick some more of these tulips and take them inside and find a vase?" I suggested. "I could use some pretty colorful flowers in my room to cheer me up and help me fight the homesick blues."

"OK, but just so we're clear…you're not having a torrid affair with my brother, are you?" He said it so damned seriously that it was all I could do to keep from bursting out laughing. He pulled me away from him so he could look into my eyes.

"You're silly. There's only you," I said, trying to mean it with every beat of my heart. "Now let's get a few more of these flowers and then it'll be time for dinner soon. I need to freshen up."

"The gardener will kill us when he sees how we're desecrating his masterpiece," laughed Andrew, as he plucked more tulips from the earth. We took a half dozen inside and Andrew asked Sarah, one of the maids, to find a vase for them and put them in my room. I would have preferred to do it myself but, as Andrew had told me repeatedly, I needed to get used to being waited on. I didn't like it one bit and I tried my best to minimize their duties where I was concerned. Being waited on and 'served' went against everything I believed in. This was just one aspect of royal life I was trying to become accustomed to, along with formal dinners and the occasional public service commitment. I had only been here in England for a month but already I felt like I had lost whatever autonomy I'd thought I had.

Alone in my room, I changed for dinner. It was expected that everyone 'dressed' for dinner. For me, that meant a skirt—never pants—and a blouse and nice shoes. Every time I changed for the evening meal I longed for my mother's simple, homemade dinners around our kitchen table with my dad and brother. Sometimes we'd have breakfast for dinner and wear our pajamas at the table. I missed that. I swallowed a lump in my throat as I fastened my beautiful sapphire earrings into my earlobes. These earrings were precious to me for they had been given to me for my eighteenth birthday—a gift from Miguel. No one knew they were from him, so I could wear them freely, unlike my gold talisman, which I had to keep hidden. I went to the massive closet and pulled out my carry-on bag where I kept my passport and other personal items and reached inside to the secret compartment at the bottom where I kept the necklace—my most prized possession, along with the note Miguel had given me the last time I'd seen him at Brenton Point. I purposely avoided looking at the note, even touching it, because it caused me too much pain. I removed the talisman from the small velvet pouch I kept it in and held it up to my cheek. I thought back to that moment in the airplane's bathroom when I had felt the talisman engraving a message into itself…just one word…*Miguel*. But his name had faded now and the original designs had slowly returned—the crossed swords and the coat of arms. The numbers were gone now though, as if they had been rubbed off, but the foreign words were still there:

Royal Birth—Gypsy Death—In Darkness, Light

I pressed the disk to my lips and kissed it lightly, letting it linger. Sure enough, as I knew it would, it responded to my kiss. It warmed and glowed and gave me comfort. Even though I could no longer risk wearing it for fear of the duke seeing it, I still touched it every day and felt the assurance it gave me that all would somehow work out for me. It gave me hope that somewhere out in the world Miguel was waiting for me, trusting that we would be together soon. I had to believe it or else I couldn't make it through the days. I placed the disk back in its pouch and hid it away in the closet, then finished dressing for dinner. My heart was heavy and I didn't want to face yet another meal with the Duke of Easton but at least Tristan would be there, my secret reminder that I could persevere through anything.

But even the talisman and Tristan's presence could not prepare me for the announcement the duke made at the evening meal. My vision blurred and I had to hold onto the edge of my seat under the table to keep from falling to the floor. My stomach heaved and I tried hard to compose myself and not draw attention even as the duke watched my every move and reaction to his words as he spoke.

"We've cleared the date for your wedding, Andrew and Laura. I know you had talked about September 12, but that seems so far away—five months—much too long to wait. I think a summer wedding is much more ideal. Besides, doesn't every girl dream of being a June bride? Your parents will already be here for your graduation ceremony anyway, so having the wedding the following week will be perfect timing. I already have the invitations at the printer. It will be a beautiful affair. Doesn't that sound perfect, Andrew?" The duke turned his gaze from me onto Andrew.

Before Andrew could respond the duchess spoke up. "Ernst… shouldn't you have talked with the children first before making such an important decision? It is, after all, *their* wedding, you know." She clucked her tongue at the duke and smiled sheepishly in my direction.

"Beatrice…everyone knows that a wedding is a family affair. Andrew and Laura may be the stars of the show, but we have no time to waste. There's no need to wait. Don't you agree, son?" The duke looked at Andrew expectantly.

Andrew reached under the table and pried my hand away from the edge of my chair where I had a death grip on it. He squeezed it gently and glanced at me and then answered his father. "I do think you should have discussed this with us first, Father. Laura has already had a lot of changes in her life what with moving to a new country and adjusting to a new school and a new home. A wedding may be a fun event but it does come with a level of stress. She—*we*—thought we had more time to adjust before planning a wedding."

"You don't have to plan anything," said the duke. "The staff will take care of everything. All you two have to do is show up. And that reminds me, Laura? If there is someone special you would like to invite, I will need their names and addresses by tomorrow morning for the printer."

I opened my mouth to answer but the words wouldn't come. I reminded myself to breathe and I felt Andrew again squeeze my hand gently. He knew I was frightened of his father and as such, he'd tried many times to reassure me that the duke's bark was worse than his bite, but I knew better. I finally managed to croak out a response. "My friends Lily and Gretchen. I would like to invite them and then just my parents and brother is really all..." My voice tapered off. The fewer words I spoke in front of the duke the better. I always had the sense that anything I said would come back to haunt me later.

Tristan spoke up then. "Are you at least going to let her pick out her own wedding dress, Father, or do you have that already decided as well?" I heard the warning tone in his voice as he stared the duke down, almost daring him to give the wrong answer.

The duke picked up his wine glass and downed half the contents in one swallow. He wiped his mouth with a cloth napkin and looked at Tristan. "Of course, Tristan. Don't be ridiculous. Your mother and Laura will take care of the aesthetics—flowers, cake, music, all the girly stuff. I will handle the logistics. Everything will run like clockwork. It will be a lovely event and, you, Laura, will be a beautiful bride."

"Thank you," I said, barely recognizing my own voice. I looked down at my plate and knew I couldn't possibly eat another bite. It wasn't that I was full but rather my stomach couldn't handle much food these days. I had lost so much weight over the last few months that just before I'd left for England my mother had taken me aside and asked me if I had an eating disorder. I was horrified that she would think such a thing and I'd promised her I was fine. I knew I should eat more, but I just couldn't risk that it might come up later. I placed my silverware across my plate as the signal that I was finished eating and looked up, catching Tristan's eye. He gave me a reassuring wink and a smile and I instantly felt a slight lifting of the burden I felt I was always under. Oh, how I wished I could tell him everything. If only I dared.

The duchess pushed back her chair and stood up from the table. "Laura, I think we should go into the shops and see about a wedding dress. How about after school Monday? There's a lovely dressmaker about twenty minutes from your school who did the dress for Zara, Anne's daughter. It was lovely and I'm sure we'll find something perfect for you there that can be made to order. Why don't we plan that for Monday?"

"That sounds lovely," I replied. It truly didn't matter what I wore to this wedding. But I knew it mattered to Andrew and his family so I would try to muster some enthusiasm for this shopping expedition.

The duke and duchess left the dining room then and Tristan pushed himself back from the table and rolled around to my seat. "Hey, Laura…you ready for another chess lesson tonight?" He smiled his disarming smile at me and I knew I couldn't resist him anything. I looked at Andrew, though, in case he had something else in mind.

"You two go ahead. I need to go have a chat with Father about the wedding. I want to make sure he isn't planning some outrageous affair that will be more ostentatious than Prince William's wedding. I don't trust him." He turned to me. "Laura? Are you OK with my discussing wedding stuff without you? You can join me if you like but I'm guessing you'd rather play chess with Tristan."

"You're right. I would rather play chess. Even though I'm never going to figure out the difference between a knight and a pawn and all the other pieces." I grinned at Tristan and he shook his head at me. He knew my skills were pretty lacking but he was a patient teacher.

We left the dining room together and in the hall, Andrew pulled me into his arms and held me tightly. Tristan continued on to the library and I told him I would be there shortly. I nestled into the crook of Andrew's neck and breathed in his scent. I wrapped my arms around him firmly and willed myself to fall in love with him again. In two short months he would be my husband—a concept my mind was not able to process yet.

"Don't worry about anything, love. I know my father is domineering and demanding, but if at any time something is happening that doesn't meet with your approval, just tell me. This is *our* wedding and we should have some say in how it's run. At least he can't control the honeymoon." He rubbed his hands up and down my back gently and tangled his fingers in my hair.

The word honeymoon was enough to give me a heart attack. So far, Andrew had been the model of decorum where romantic activity had been concerned. He seemed to sense my nerves when he would start to push too far and he always controlled himself. He had no idea how much I appreciated his respect. The irony of it was, that if it were

Miguel, there would have been nothing to stop me from being his in every way. I shuddered the moment I thought his name and Andrew's arms tightened around me.

"I won't worry. I trust you. Now I better get to my chess lesson. I don't want to keep my teacher waiting." I smiled a little wickedly at Andrew, knowing my words would get under his skin a little bit. He shook his head at me and kissed me sweetly and headed to his father's office. I went into the library where Tristan already had the game set up and was waiting for me. I sat down across from him and already felt the comfort his presence always brought me.

"Hey, Laura," said Tristan as I settled in and looked over the board. "You doing OK?"

The minute he said the words I felt the tears pricking behind my eyes. I willed them not to fall but it was useless. They slid down both cheeks anyway and I immediately felt incredibly foolish. Tristan reached across the table and wiped first one tear and then the other. "Why the tears, honey? What's wrong?"

I stifled a sob and shook my head as I tried to regain my composure. "I'm sorry," I whispered. "I'm being a big baby. I should be happy, I know." I wiped my cheeks and forced a weak smile but I couldn't fool Tristan.

"Listen to me, Laura. I can see how unhappy you are. I see it every day. You don't have to go through with this wedding. You're only eighteen. What's the rush?" He took my suddenly cold hands in his warm ones and held them tightly. I wanted to crawl into his lap and hold onto him with all my might but I knew that wouldn't be a wise move. I suppressed a sob and tried to formulate an answer.

"We are too young, you're right. But this means so much to Andrew. I don't want to hurt him. And it would happen eventually anyway, so why wait? It's really OK. I think I'm just homesick, that's all. I feel a little...overwhelmed sometimes."

"You have more control than you realize. Don't let my father bully you. I seriously wanted to run this damned wheelchair over his toes tonight at dinner. He really pisses me off most of the time. I want you to know that you can always come to me if you need anything–or if you're scared or unsure. I know you have Andrew, but maybe there will be times when you don't feel comfortable talking to him about something. But you can *always* come to me. You hear me?"

I pulled my hands away from his and sobbed into them. I got up from my seat and came around to him and sank down onto the floor at his feet and leaned into his lap. He opened his arms to me and held me tightly. It was the first time in a long time that I had felt a sense of safety. I felt it with Andrew but it didn't compare to the way it felt with Tristan. In many ways I felt closer to him than I did to my own brother, Nicholas. "I'm sorry, Tristan. I don't know what's wrong with me. Sometimes I think I'm losing my mind."

He stroked my hair and my back and waited for me to compose myself. "Well, I don't know about your mind, but one thing you are losing is too much weight. You need to eat more. You didn't even touch your dessert and you barely ate any dinner. If I call for one of the servants to bring us some ice cream, will you eat it? It would make me very happy." I heard him chuckle and I looked up into his blue eyes.

"Actually, ice cream does sound kind of good right now. Sure. I'd love some." I pushed myself up and went back to my seat. Tristan pushed a button under the arm of his wheelchair and within ten seconds a uniformed maid appeared as if out of nowhere.

"Maggie? Laura and I would love big hot fudge sundaes with all the works. Can you take care of that for us?" He winked at me and smiled at the maid who curtsied and promised two sundaes coming right up.

"I truly don't know what I would do without you, Tristan Easton," I sighed, letting out all of the pent up air that had been stuck in my lungs for hours. I smiled weakly at him and he pointed at the board.

"OK, girl. It's time for a chess lesson. Put your thinking cap on. I can't wait to see what you remember from our last session." And with that, we played chess, ate ice cream and I experienced two blissful, stress-free hours. As I watched him trounce all over me, I thanked my lucky stars that I had Tristan in my life.

To be continued…

CPSIA information can be obtained
at www.ICGtesting.com
Printed in the USA
LVHW011510200920
666587LV00009B/738

9 780615 667744